HE HAD NEVER LOST A GAME . . .

Joseph removed the automatic and leveled it squarely at James's balls. "Very little prevents me from finishing you now. If you weren't an integral part of our operation, I surely would."

James saw the mad spark in the stranger's eyes and believed him. He shut up. Joseph holstered the gun.

"What I want is nothing short of what I've demanded. You play your normal game and do what you can. This will please me. However, when you meet Chekow — whether at Wimbledon or any other tournament — you lose. Understand?"

"Or?" James asked dryly.

"Or my home movies find their way onto the desk of every major newspaper in the world, plus a copy for Benjamen Smythe at Whiplin." He watched James devour the drink. "Think about it," Joseph said. "You have a whole minute."

UNTIL NOW!

"Rider McDowell's *Wimbledon* has it all — taut suspense, kinky sex and, more important, a real page-turning quality."

William A. Caunitz
author of
One Police Plaza and *Suspects*

WIMBLEDON

Rider McDowell

PaperJacks LTD.

TORONTO   NEW YORK

AN ORIGINAL

PaperJacks

WIMBLEDON

PaperJacks LTD.

330 STEELCASE RD. E., MARKHAM, ONT. L3R 2M1
210 FIFTH AVE., NEW YORK, N.Y. 10010

PaperJacks edition published July 1987

This is a work of fiction in its entirety. Any resemblance to actual people, places or events is purely coincidental.

US ISBN 0-7701-0633-1
Can ISBN 0-7701-0675-7

For Phillida
with love and squalor

WIMBLEDON

Chapter One

London, England

He stood just under six feet. Yet with all the publicity he'd been receiving, the endless talk shows his agent had persuaded him to do, the posters, the victories on court, the public had expected him to be bigger. If not taller, then perhaps a little huskier. Anything but skinny. But he was skinny and always had been. Even as a kid, a status he'd escaped since his twenty-first birthday two years ago, he had been small and thin. The bullied, never the bully. Though within his slight frame there harbored, also from an early age, the ability to excel at sports the likes of which his peers and instructors had never seen. It was this God-given genius that his father had first recognized in his only son. And it was the same genius that had prompted him to drive the kid every single morning for eight years to the public courts on the other side of town. The right side of town. There he would labor for an hour with James McLaren, Jr., in the hope that one day his son's ability to hit a ball over a net might deliver him and his wife from the dead-end life of a municipal clerk. How right he was.

He began as all youngsters do with the local, county tournaments, which, in actual fact, were more of a forum for social intercourse at the parent level than an allegiance to sport. From there he progressed to the state circuit, a move he found overwhelming at first, though within a month he was wiping up anything that came his way. Next came the all-Eastern circuit, a big step on paper, as this encompassed three states, but nothing really. As far as he was concerned, only the players' accents varied. The competition was just as good. Or bad. By the time he was thirteen he was the under-sixteen New York State champion, had offers from eleven different sponsors, had two coaches, and was getting laid five times a week by Beverly, the woman who worked in the pro shop.

"Is that him?" the voices asked outside Heathrow's Concorde arrival hall. "No, he's taller. Christ! I'm as tall as that bloke. I wonder if his girl friend's here. Look at that shirt. You'd think he was poor."

James McLaren strode calmly through the crowd, carrying in one hand a copy of *The Wall Street Journal*, in the other an ice-cream cone. Long behind him were the days of carrying suitcases of clothes he would never wear through airports he had seen before but couldn't place. As the number-one tennis player in the world, all he had to worry about was sustaining that status. Almost.

He hesitated before a cluster of photographers who had been waiting since eight that morning among the crowd. "Hello, boys. Nice to see you again," he said with uncharacteristic courtesy.

"Is it nice to be back in England, Mr. McLaren? Are you ready to defend your title?" inquired a tall fellow in glasses with half a dozen different cameras around his neck.

"Yeah, sure it is, and sure I'm ready. I'm always ready." He grinned and swallowed the last of the ice cream.

"What about your girl friend? Where's Janie? Is it true what they say about you two splitting up?" a short fat guy asked, obviously provoking him for a reaction.

James pondered the question. He breathed deeply and thought of what Brice Evans, his agent, had told him. *Patience off the court puts money in the bank. Nobody loves a twenty-four-hour rogue.* He smiled again. "Janie's fine. She'll be over. I need some time to practice alone, boost my concentration." He looked around for the Heathrow Airport representative, the man responsible for guiding him through the crowds of fans and newsmen upon arrival.

"What about your rivalry with Chekow? Do you think you can beat him?"

Another sore point: Chekow, the six-foot-two Russian who had beaten him twice in the last six months. Shit! They were determined for a reaction. For three and a half hours on the Concorde he had thought of little else but "play to the media, use them, don't be used. It buys things in the end like the newly acquired retreat on Nantucket, and the Chagall. Look at Borg." He repeated this to himself. "I've beaten Chekow before. I'll beat him again," he said tonelessly. Then, on a more jovial note, he added, "If I win every time, there's no excitement. And that's what the promoters pay for."

The short fat guy moved in. "So, McLaren, you say you're only in this for the money. Don't you enjoy the sport of it?"

"Yes, of course I do. Sport alone doesn't pay the rent."

"Or lawyers." The fat guy grinned. "Isn't that how you beat that coke rap on Long Island? Daddy bailed you out and called in reinforcements in the form of Epstein and Epstein?"

"That's none of your business. Let's talk tennis," James said. He controlled an urge to stick the camera down fat guy's throat.

"Okay," fat guy said, smelling blood. "Are you going to last the whole tournament without one public warning like you stated in *Playboy*, or are you going to blow it?"

It wasn't his question as much as his tone. James bristled. *Fuck Brice Evans!* he thought. If he was going to go, he'd take fat guy with him. "Blow on this," James said and unleashed a quick left cross that flattened fat guy's nose. James waited — poised in case fat guy wanted to retaliate, then turned and headed down the hallway pursued by the delirious crowd.

"But you broke his nose," a smiling newsman said, aiming a video camera a foot from James's face.

James turned and spouted the line that by appearing on the front page of every paper in Britain, would herald his ignoble arrival to the most prestigious tennis tournament in the world. "Put it on my fucking bill. I can afford it."

He hurried the length of the hall and ducked into the Concorde V.I.P. lounge at the end of the Arrivals Terminal. At the bar he asked for a double vodka-and-orange. He drank all his drinks with fruit juice; it gave the illusion of clean living to the public. Finding an unoccupied table, he sat down with his back to the crowd that had formed beyond the curtain and tinted-glass enclosure.

He was dying for a joint and flushed the wad of tissue from his back pants pocket and poked curiously at the half-used reefers. He had smoked them in the bathroom on the flight over. Looking at them, his thoughts returned to the altercation with fat guy and his stomach flipflopped. *Shit!* he thought, cursing the quality of the weed; if it had been any good, he wouldn't have minded what that fat fuck had said. He cursed Janie for scoring it, swigged down the drink, and left the lounge via the emergency exit. Fuck the airport representative! Let him lose his job. He circumnavigated the outside hallway, breezed through Arrivals, and left unnoticed, wearing sunglasses. An obliging and unobservant cab driver gave him a cigarette and dropped him off at the Royal Garden Hotel, Knightsbridge.

It was all there, as the Whiplin people had said it would be: his luggage, his suits, and, most importantly, his Whiplin racquets. He went over and acquiesced to the almost magnetic spell the grip of a tennis racquet still held for him. He took one, handled it gingerly. Grabbing a sock from the open suitcase, he formed it into a ball and lobbed it. The smash put a six-inch dent in the leather lampshade, as was intended. He retrieved the sock and repeated the gesture, this time knocking the porcelain lamp clear off the table. It hit the rug with a thud and a pop as the bulb blew. He went over and examined it. The porcelain was still intact. "Amazing," he said seriously. As an afterthought he went back and turned the lamp over to check the manufacturer's name. "Asprey's," he mused aloud. "Not bad."

He set the dozen racquets in a stack beside the double bed, then put away his clothes, laying out a suit for the evening. For dinner he had arranged to meet the president of a top tennis clothing manufacturer — an American who was in London for Wimbledon. Contrary to the image painted by the world press, not everything he touched was accorded the same irreverent attention. He was well aware he had contributed to his iconoclastic image by parading through the streets in T-shirts and old sneakers. Of course, his antics on the court didn't help matters. But inasmuch as that life-style accurately represented him, so, too, did his clandestine, often nocturnal meetings with a bevy of sponsors and accountants — in particular, the fat cats from Whiplin, his major sponsor. Whiplin, the once-tiny sporting goods firm from Lake Forest, Illinois, had become *the* name in tennis. And all thanks to the boys on the top floor in charge of promotion. Whiplin was the first tennis manufacturing firm to go in for big-time sponsorship, and it paid off bigger — say to the tune of five hundred million dollars for last year alone.

James McLaren was their number-one commodity now. His controversial victories on the professional circuit and number-one ranking had upped profits by twenty percent in the last year alone. Of course, McLaren knew this and delighted in letting Whiplin know he knew this. But for two million dollars to swing a particular brand of racquet and bare his teeth to an advertising photographer once every two months, he didn't have much to complain about.

He moved the empty suitcase off the bed and walked around to extinguish the last vestige of the reefer still smoking in the ashtray. In the sitting room, as always, a video set and a private bar had been set up, compliments of the Royal Garden management for gracing their hotel. The bar was well stocked with American Miller beer in the fridge, his favorite, and Gordon's gin. He checked the freezer and smiled at the bottle of Stolichnaya vodka. He removed it and, after almost dropping it, poured half a glass into one of the monogrammed glasses on the shelf (his monogram, not the Royal Garden's). He drank it quickly in one motion and reveled in the icy trail it traced down his chest. Then he opened a beer and drank most of it. On his way to the bathroom, he paused long enough to slap a cassette into the stereo built into the wall. It was an old Rolling Stones tape, one of fifty Whiplin had been instructed to have on hand wherever he stayed. He went in to shower.

The pulsating jets of hot water beat down on him, invigorating the hard lean muscles of his upper body. He had worked a double session in Los Angeles yesterday, and had practiced for nearly eight hours, a move that would allow him to compensate for the few days missed due to jet lag. Normally, he practiced three hours a day, six days a week, two of those days with Hal Jimson, his coach. He never missed a practice. Part of the drive that kept him going through all the airports, all the strain, all the lonely hotel rooms, and all the bullshit, was the insuppressible urge to dominate his sport, to be absolutely the best there was; at age twenty-three, he was.

He stepped out of the shower in midstream and examined his penis in the light. It was red and scaly on the underside from screwing Mrs. Timmerman all last week. Her daughter Betsy was on the tour, and for the last six days of the Simonson Tournament in Los Angeles he had practiced the *Kama Sutra* with Mrs. Timmerman, née Janis, in his hotel room.

James recalled what an animal she had been, taking it everywhere as often as he could get it hard. It was his first experience with what he assumed must be a nymphomaniac. Even his own insatiable appetite had ceded defeat to the viselike thighs and willing mouth of the fifty-one-year-old woman. Christ! He felt the germ of an erection and stepped back into the shower, smiling. His free hand grabbed the soap.

Dressed in a pair of boxer shorts, he emerged from the bathroom toweling his hair vigorously. He poured a gin and was in the process of switching tapes when the phone rang.

"What?"

"James, what the fuck happened? The N.U.J. is threatening to boycott Wimbledon, and there's talk of a million-pound lawsuit. Look, I know the guy was a shit, but did you have to hit him in the nose? Broken noses influence court cases." Brice Evans's manner was wrought with an uncharacteristic nerviness.

James assessed the situation. "Give 'em five grand and two center-court tickets, for Christ's sake. It's only some dum photographer. It's not like I bopped the Queen."

"Not quite," Brice said. His tone was less agitated. "There's still this business of the boycott. I know it's bullshit, but it reads bad. Whiplin won't like it."

"Whiplin can shove it. There wasn't even an escort at Heathrow. They know how those places get to me," James said through a mouthful of ice-cube bits. "I didn't even hit the guy hard."

"It was hard enough. He's over at Charing Cross

Hospital right now with his lawyers. What's more, the whole incident's on tape."

James set his drink down. Lifting the phone, he moved out of the sitting room and shut the separating doors to quiet the blare of music. He dropped onto the bed and rolled over onto his stomach. "You're a lawyer. What should we do?"

"You should have thought about that before you hit him," Brice replied, a bit too tersely.

"Evans, I don't pay you two hundred thousand a year for answers like that. You figure it out or *you're* out." The line grew silent. James knew Brice Evans, knew about his five children, three in private schools and two in Ivy League colleges. He knew of the new place on Barbados and the housing development under construction in the south of France. He also knew what the loss of two hundred thousand dollars a year would do to these people and projects. In spite of all this, he knew Brice Evans to be the best personal manager in the world and that he liked the guy. "Come on, Brice, this isn't half of what the coke case was. I'll leave it to you to figure out. Go to ten thousand if you have to," James said, assuaging the hurt. "Okay, Bricey?"

"Sure, James, it's nothing really, I guess." Brice paused. "By the way, Whiplin called. Sidney Hughes is in town, so they've appointed him chargé for the tournament. He's at the Dorchester."

"Sidney Hughes — that douche bag. Why is it that shithead always rears his little head at the biggies? Forest Hills, Monte Carlo, and now Wimbledon. They know I can't stand him," James said.

"The board can stand him. His old man presides over it. Besides, he's not that bad. Just a bit of a jackass."

"That's what they said about Hitler in '33," James said. He wished he'd brought his drink in here. "I suppose if he gets around as much as you say he does, he can't be a bad guy to know. Who knows, I might even score some coke off him."

"Now listen, will you knock off that coke business? You're on probation for the year. They find any of that shit on you and you're in the can for two years."

"Bricey, this is jolly old England, home of the sovereign, land of the Ripper. They're not going to give three fucks if I happen to get caught with one measly gram. Now, if it was 'H,' well, that's one thing. . . ." He grinned as he pictured the expression on Brice's face.

"It may be jolly old England, but your popularity is waning after last year's tournament, and now Heathrow. And you'd still do eighteen months on a first-time conviction. Come on, James."

James's laughter reached across the line to New York where it dumped on Brice Evans. "Just kidding, pal. You know I've got more sense than that."

"I often wonder," Brice said. "I spoke to Smythe about renegotiating the contract for next year. He's offered you an option on Aristocrat stock. They'll give you a hundred thousand shares with an option for another hundred thousand within the next six months. That's a clean million plus the chance to clear at least another two if the stock rises, which it's bound to."

"Jesus! Four hours and four thousand miles in an airplane to be confronted with this." James dragged on the reefer and spat it out. "What's the stock now?"

"Ten dollars. Once it goes public on Monday, it'll hit fifteen. That's one million alone you'll make if you take up the option."

"I don't get it. It's not like Whiplin to throw their money at me. What's the catch?" he asked.

"Well, the stock option is in lieu of the percentage scheme. You get your standard cut, of course, but any profits over that are the company's. Then there's the possibility the stock might sink. Larger-headed racquets are still a bit of a novelty," Brice explained. His nasaly tone echoed across the transatlantic line.

For the past three years speculation had been mounting over the appeal of a tennis racquet with a twenty percent larger face. Theoretically, the advantages were obvious: more power, greater target area, and accuracy. In spite of this, all the market research teams and Gallup polls in the world had yet to determine the public's true reaction. Sales of a smaller company specializing in the racquet were steady, but insignificant. The same company had even succeeded in signing up a dozen ranked players to use and promote the large-faced racquet. With the exception of one woman, the players had enjoyed the same insipid level of achievement as the racquet sales. James thought back to the article on oil refineries in Florida he had read during the flight. If they could sell oil back to the Arabs, they could sell a tennis racquet with a larger head.

"Have you spoken to my dad about this, Brice?" he asked cautiously.

"No, not yet," Brice replied.

"Good, then don't. Buy the stock and take up the option. Get in touch with some wire photographers and have them photograph a practice session at Hurlingham tomorrow morning. Nine-thirty British time. I'll see those racquets get the publicity they need."

He could hear Brice thinking over the phone. "But James, Whiplin won't go for that. Your contract states that all matches, either exhibitions or tournaments —"

He cut him off. "Listen, I know what the contract states. But there's no law about practicing with the goddamned thing. Besides, even if I'm not signed by Aristocrat, the exposure'll benefit Whiplin in the end since they own both companies."

"Yes, it might, but honestly —"

James cut him off again. "Honestly, you think too much. Have two UPI photographers at the hotel court in the morning, and pick up that stock."

"I already have," Brice intoned from his office on Park Avenue. "I already have."

James hung up. A strong sense of satisfaction swept through him and remained after the receiver was replaced. He knew Smythe, the president of Whiplin. His penny-pinching was legend. Ninety-eight percent of the players on the circuit with Whiplin sponsorship received a meager paycheck once every three months according to their W.C.T. ranking. If the player had done well, his check would reflect his added earning power — say, an extra few thousand dollars. If for some reason the player's ranking had slipped, the information would be relayed up the line to the top banana, Smythe, then back down to the bottom: the certified public accountant who issued the checks. The accountant would add or delete as necessary.

Dissatisfaction with the capricious nature of the system had caused many a player to jump sponsors, but since Whiplin essentially cornered the tennis market, the chances of finding a remotely competitive deal were nil. Everyone knew this. Benjamen Smythe, for one. James McLaren, for another. James had never been able to forget his days in the bottom one hundred. For three years, from the ages of fifteen to eighteen, he had been subjected to the humiliating — indeed, demoralizing — nature of the sponsorship. Those days when he needed it most, for his family's sake if not his own, the money had been slow and less sure. Until he had adapted to the pace and competition of the circuit, his ranking had stayed in the low sixties. And for three years he had been prey to the "hunter-gatherer" mentality of the Whiplin people. Things had changed.

He rolled over and sat on the edge of the bed. The exposure he would give the Aristocrat racquet tomorrow morning, a week before the start of Wimbledon, would ensure that the stock would double — if not triple. For every point it raised, he would receive two hundred thousand dollars. It was almost too much to comprehend. He was the big fish in the biggest of ponds now, and he loved it.

Chapter Two

Pamela Donaldson adjusted the tail of her silk shirt and tucked it deeper into the skintight jeans so that it showed off her high martini-glass breasts to better advantage. She examined herself in the mirror and with her thumb and forefinger tweaked the tiny sleeping nipples, puckering them. She stood sideways to the glass and, satisfied with the profile her erect nipples cut, turned off the vanity light.

She was a tall, slim girl, five feet, nine inches, with coltlike legs and straight auburn hair that settled in a crook between her shoulder blades. The hair was a disadvantage of sorts, for she was forced to secure it behind her back as a precaution against it getting in her way when she played. On top of this she was conscious of how her hair looked tied back there, and she didn't like it. She had contemplated cutting it short like the other girls, but had decided to put up with the inconvenience. Compensation came in the way it looked as it caressed her breasts when she went shirtless.

She went to the portable bar her roommate had set up near the stereo and poured a whiskey. What was left of the ice had been transformed to water long ago, so she was forced to make do with whiskey-and-water, a combination which, in her opinion, ruined the whiskey *and* the water.

Sheila, her roommate, had rented the four-room Wimbledon flat a month earlier. That way she could be on relatively familiar turf for the Stella Artois tournament and then Wimbledon. Familiar turf to Sheila was the family's sprawling twenty-eight-room Palladian-style mansion on Brook Road in Brentwood, California. Porsche sunglasses, movie stars, and maids straight out of a Lausanne charm school. It was due partly to her family wealth that Sheila footed most of the two hundred eighty pounds, or roughly five hundred sixty dollars a month rent, and Pam paid a token fifty dollars plus ten for the woman who cleaned the place. It was also partly due to Sheila's basic generosity and her devotion to Pam. With her performance at the Stella Artois tourney, Pam's ranking had leaped nine places to put her at twenty-nine in the world against Sheila's eighty-third. Fifty odd places in the top one hundred constituted the distinction between being somewhere and being nowhere. Pam was somewhere, and through her close association with Sheila, Sheila was partway there at least. Pam was also twenty-one, and Sheila was pressing thirty.

Pam breezed through the kitchen and picked nervously at the leftovers from a late lunch. They had all been there, all the girls, primarily Sheila's friends, and mostly older; still, Pam always enjoyed their company. Whether it was in the dressing room or at some post-match restaurant, Pam found herself consistently amused by the antics and often childish games of the "Super Six," as Sheila had christened them, six of the best women tennis players in the world.

Pam laughed at the way they always had a one-liner response to the teasing of the men on the tour, and at their cynical impersonations of the umpires on the circuit. One girl, Stacey Parker, who ranked number nine, never failed to solicit gales of laughter as she mimicked the more notable male players on the tour. Pam's attraction exceeded mere amusement. She looked up to these players, watched and studied them. She emulated their performance on and off the court with the sole aspiration of achieving the greatness they, without exception, had achieved in the game. To her they represented an oasis of stability in the precarious world of professional tennis. In many ways they had reciprocated and taken

Pam under their guiding wing to protect and comfort her: one big happy family with only the husbands missing.

Pam picked at the side of a turkey breast on a casserole dish. Idly, she began washing up, arranging things. She covered the turkey with aluminum foil and placed it in the fridge so it wouldn't spoil. Five years on the tour, never earning less than forty thousand dollars a year in prize money alone, and she still couldn't stand the slightest waste. Hers had been a difficult childhood. The third of seven daughters of an alcoholic shop foreman in a little town in southern Utah, she knew what it meant to go hungry, and the trauma of poverty was branded indelibly across her brain.

Except for the ladies at the tennis courts, she had never known a mother. It was there she went each day after school seeking refuge from a house full of squealing sisters and a father with an eye for liquor and a maturing bosom. Her story read like so many on the tour: first the counties, then the states, with a little luck a sponsor, an interested coach, then maybe a ranking, and finally, if it all worked, a chance to join the tour full-time. It had worked in her case. She had made it work, and never for a moment had she forgotten to appreciate that it had.

She returned to the mirror with another whiskey in her hand. Nervously, she sipped at it while she reexamined her clothes. Her nipples had gone soft, so she brushed them with the cool surface of the glass. They puckered obediently. If nothing else, she could have been a model. She had always been told that from the start. Why work for it when you could get paid to smile? But modeling was too easy and she had long grown a slave to the sudden ephemeral rushes of adrenaline that followed the final rally of a winning match. Still, she often consoled herself that if it all went tomorrow — the arm, the eye, the concentration — she could always turn to modeling. Sheila never stopped telling her how lovely she was. And, after all, she was only twenty-one.

She crossed the room, finishing her second whiskey, and picked up the phone. It was silly for her to be on edge because of a stupid little party. She'd call James, she resolved. If James was going, she'd be fine.

She managed to dial the first four digits of the Royal Garden Hotel when the metallic-blue BMW cruised up before the short drive to the complex of flats. The sound of the car horn destroyed any notion she had of talking to James. "Okay, keep your hair on," she said aloud, groping for her purse and sweater. She flicked off the light, slammed the door, and double-locked it. "I'm coming, for Christ's sake! Stop honking."

She jogged down the flight of red brick stairs with the purse against her chest to keep her breasts from bouncing. Being rather plump and ski-sloped, they had a tendency to bounce. Sheila got out of the car wearing a denim pantsuit and clasping a bottle of beer. "My, aren't we looking smart," Sheila said. "It's only a tennis party."

"I know," Pam said as she crossed the last patch of lawn to the car. "But you never know who you might meet. Maybe Prince Charles will be there to carry me away from all this."

The grin receded somewhat from Sheila's face. "He's married."

"Well, maybe he has a friend," Pam replied.

"Okay," Sheila said sardonically. "Get in, Cinderella."

It wasn't until she stooped to get in that she noticed the car was packed. Including Sheila, Pam counted five of the Super Six. "Hello," she said, leaning in the doorway. "Can we fit?"

Fifth-ranked Toni Lovett reached an arm out and took Pam's hand. "Of course we can," she said in her own husky way.

Pam withdrew her hand. "Wonderful." She squeezed in and sat on Toni's lap. "Are you sure this isn't killing you, Toni? I can always take a cab," she said. She arched her head down to speak.

Stacey Parker, the girl famous for her impressions, patted Pam's knee affectionately. "Don't worry, honey. It'd take a lot more than you to put a dent in that lap," she said, referring to Toni's thick muscular legs.

"Anything you say, Twiggy," Toni responded.

Pam laughed. The petty surface tension was inherent in the way the Super Six behaved. Pam said hello to the three other Super Sixes. These included Marge Snyder, the seventh-ranked platinum-blond

Australian; Lynne Heiv, the tenth-ranked with a caustic dry humor that never failed to get a laugh; and Julia Collins, the twelfth-ranked six-foot-tall youngster. At twenty, Julia was the closest to Pam's age.

The sweet aroma of marijuana filled the interior as the car drove away. "Let's share the wealth. Pass it back," Lynne called. Julia extended two fingers over the headrest to the backseat. Lynne plucked the four-inch joint from her grasp.

"It's excellent stuff!" Julia exclaimed, exhaling a lungful. "Colombian. So take it easy."

Lynne was already upon it, sucking deeply, with all the strength her thirty-year-old lungs could muster, before passing it to Pam.

"I'm going to need this," Pam said, taking it. "Nerves."

"What's to be nervous about, Pammy?" Sheila asked. "It's only us, and a few others."

Pam waited until the hit took effect, then released it. "It's the few others who worry me. Tennis groupies, especially in England, are hard to take. They make a point of trying to make you look small." She was suddenly aware of the strength of the drug. Her head grew light and lazy and her thoughts began to wander. She passed a tongue over her lips, and was amazed at how numb they felt.

Toni drew a leg up toward her chest, lifting Pam momentarily. She polished the toe of her cowboy boot where some ash had spilled. As though reading her mind, she leaned toward Pam and confided, "We got some PCP from Lynne's trainer. It's on the joint. Can you feel it?"

She could feel it, but she didn't like it. It seemed the girls were always searching for a new high, which they would inflict unwittingly upon newcomers to the group. In this case it had been PCP, Angel Dust, a crude pain-killer comparable to uncut chloroform. Only a few drops painted on the paper of the reefer were capable of rendering the smoker numb all over. Nice, if that's what one wanted and chose. But Pam's innate sense of the puritanical caused her to draw the line with grass. And even then only occasionally. She was hooked on a far more deadly narcotic, a legacy from the father she despised. Alcohol.

She regretted taking the second hit the moment the smoke filled her lungs. Her thoughts fogged and began to race within her head. She fought to maintain her balance on Toni's knee, but it was pointless. Her buttocks slipped and she found herself sinking into Toni's strong dark arms. Warm hands grazed roughly over her bosoms as Toni moved to support her under the arms. Toni was talking but the words eluded her. Pam looked at her chest as the twin points of her breasts jutted sharply against the silk shirt. The car stopped as they arrived at their destination.

Sheila escorted her inside. Pam recalled a brief argument with Toni over who was going to assist her, but Sheila must have won, for Sheila was helping her. They were in an elevator and the lights above were indicating the speedy succession from floor to floor. Even in the elevator the fumes from the opiated cigarette hung in the air like a miasma and choked her. Lynne was leaning over her, offering it to her. It was all Pam could do to shake her head.

The flat was spacious and, in a modern way, elegant, and very dark. Music was seeping from louvered panels in the wall. She recognized Anne Marie, the sixth Super Six, and gathered from the exchange of comments that this must be Anne Marie's flat. She managed to resurrect enough strength to extend her hand in greeting, but she was pulled in and embraced firmly. Her own firm chest crumpled against the loose flesh of Anne Marie's bosoms. Pam drew away and was led to a chair in the living room near a table stocked with food and wine. Beyond it, she noted an aggressive-looking black woman in a French maid's uniform dispensing drinks. She recalled the woman as the ex-collegiate tennis champion of a few years back and wondered what the hell she was doing here. Had she turned pro?

"Is honey girl feeling better?" Sheila cooed, bending over Pam. Her breath smelled of mint. Sheila combed back Pam's long hair with her fingers and wiped the perspiration from her forehead. Instantly, Pam felt better. Then Sheila leaned forward and kissed her softly on the lips. Pam recoiled instinctively. Sheila went away, leaving Pam to regard the night's proceedings from her perch on the copious leather chair. The music stopped, momentarily ceding to the raucous conversation of a dozen women, then started again, this time with a low soul beat. The walls seemed to throb in reaction. Women strode languorously to and fro. Some of them, some Pam had never seen before, hesitated as they passed by her. Some stopped to chat congenially, but always it seemed Sheila was there to intervene and speak to them and they retreated.

It occurred to Pam as an afterthought, having sat there for an hour, that only two men had joined the festivities. Two men, neither one of which she found remotely attractive. She observed one waiting for a drink and noted his narrow boyish waist and baby-faced complexion. Despite his having attained middle age, she suspected he had never shaved before. Nor had he ever needed to.

Then suddenly there was no one there. Nothing but the stereo churning out its track after track of discordant soul. She stood up and watched the whole room spinning. A moment later it was still again and she wondered where they had all gone. Had it ended so soon? Had James never shown up? She remembered then she hadn't called him. But what of Sheila and the Super Six? Or even the black barmaid? What if she had wanted another drink?

Step by laborious step, she crept up the passageway toward the kitchen and the front door. She was unsure of what she would do once she got there, but at least it was progress of sorts. The vacant room was quickly beginning to depress her. She missed the fraternity of her friends; she missed James.

Not voices exactly, more like sounds, began to emanate from behind a door to her left as she approached it. Was someone being sick in the bathroom? Maybe they were in trouble and needed help? She recalled an article she read in a dentist's office in Los Angeles about cardio-pulmonary resuscitation. "Head back, count to three, inhale, exhale." Automatically, she began repeating the procedure. "Head back, count to three, inhale, exhale." She was fully prepared to administer CPR to the person beyond the door when, seemingly of its own accord, the door opened. "Head back, count to —" Pam's jaw literally fell open, and she felt her knees weaken. "Oh, Christ!" she whispered. Her fingers froze to the doorknob.

Her first thoughts were that the I.R.A. had struck, devastating the building with a ton of explosives, and what lay before her reflected the carnage of their campaign. But they were still alive. Some were smiling. Through the blue haze of the smoke that filled the room, she watched them. They were all here. Sheila, the Super Six, even the black woman and the two slightly built men. They were on the bed, the carpet, the chairs, sprawled out in some great carnal circus.

She tried to swallow but couldn't. She watched Sheila, hypnotized as her slender fingers rose and fell about the glistening entrance to Toni's vagina. Sheila withdrew her fingers and waved them drunkenly at Pam. On the bed the black lay gasping audibly, her fat lips gnarling, ivory teeth snapping lustily. The source of her apparent discomfort was Lynne's ponytailed head pumping fiercely between the long brown legs.

Even the men had forsaken the opposite sex and were busy on the floor, each fondling the hot ready genitals of the other. Pam watched their massaging hands and opened mouths as they took hold of each other, their narrow boyish hips bucking rhythmically to the piped-in music.

Pam's arms wrapped instinctively about her shivering body in a feeble attempt to protect herself from the menagerie at her feet. She felt all at once cold and so very alone. If only James were here, he'd know what to do. Then something — some force — drew her in; she took a hesitant step forward. The door swung shut behind her.

Her haunted eyes searched the distant corners of the room for a place to hide in until the nightmare subsided. But did she really want it to subside? Standing there watching them, she found her body being drawn closer to the source of their obvious delight. It was, after all, a new experience, and didn't she welcome any new experience? Would it not enhance her attraction as a woman, her savoir faire? So long as it remained purely physical, she told herself, then it was not so bad. Purely physical.

She came close enough to touch the dark patch of hair between Anne Marie's open legs. Her outstretched fingers felt the heat of Anne Marie's body as it escaped from her womb. Her thin nose expanded to usurp the distinct scent of sex in the room. No! Her hand pulled back as her eyes flooded with tears. Oh, God, no!

She retraced her steps slowly, afraid to signal an alarm that might cause the others to restrain her. Suddenly, she stopped and turned, crouching slightly to shield herself from her pursuer. Thank God! she breathed. It was only Marge. Lovely, considerate, platinum-blond Marge. Relief spread through her in waves from her gut. "Oh, Marge," she said aloud. "I'm so glad it's only you." She listened as her words reverberated in the heavy atmosphere of the room.

Marge only smiled. She recognized Pam's plight for what it was: the twisted conscience of the neophyte. Marge let the towel drop from her waist. She spread her arms and beckoned Pam to advance. Pam's stare moved to the large breasts she had noticed so often on court when Marge played. She moved closer. The milky whiteness of the perfect breasts astounded Pam. She had never seen nipples so large, even in the men's magazines that mysteriously found their way into the ladies' locker rooms from time to time. Marge directed Pam's shaking hands to the hotness down there. Pam's fingers relaxed and worked the folded skin — and Marge cried out as she forced Pam's head down to the fount of her forbidden pleasure.

It took James twenty seconds to determine the cause of the ringing noise. He crawled on his elbows to the edge of the bed and grabbed the phone. "Yes," he said. He surveyed the room quickly and remembered where he was.

"Mr. McLaren, this is your alarm call. It's six-thirty." He thanked her and hung up and wondered if she meant A.M. or P.M. Then he saw the suit hanging from the closet and remembered dinner and the guy from Top Wear. He cursed softly. In his dream he had succeeded in removing the garter belt from the blue-eyed stewardess. He looked down at himself, huge and hot against his belly, and laughed.

He took a cold shower, then stepped out to dry himself, allowing the water to drip all over the floor. He looked in the mirror. "Jesus! crow's-feet at twenty-three." He ran the tap to the sink, plugged it, and submerged his face in the cold water. With a towel he patted his face dry. Normally, he cared very little about his appearance, but tonight he had a meeting with the guy from Top Wear clothes. James knew he'd get the Top Wear contract, and on his terms, but it helped to look presentable. His frantic style of living had taken its toll on his classically handsome face. If the Top Wear honcho thought he was aging prematurely, that just might reduce his bargaining position. After all he reasoned, they didn't want some withered old fart with a face like a dried apple modeling their clothes.

He fixed himself a large vodka-and-tonic and switched on a tape.

The charcoal-gray suit fit him all right, but the cut of the cloth made him look a touch on the corny side. He stood before the full-length mirror examining the way the jacket sloped on his shoulders. His main criticism was the length of the jacket and the double-vented back. Since he bought the thing, he had grown to like single vents. Anger bubbled in his stomach as he remembered buying six ready-made suits. The buxom salesgirl had kept telling him how "suave and sophisticated" he looked, and like an idiot he had fallen for the spiel to the tune of six suits, two overcoats, and sixty-two hundred dollars. But that was two years ago. He'd aged a lot in two years.

"Fuck 'em." He stripped down to his boxer shorts and deposited the suit in a wad at his feet. From inside the closet he removed the three suits hanging on the bar. He took the whole funereal pile and stuffed it in the trashcan in the sitting room. "So ends my membership in the bourgeoisie," he said.

He dressed instead in a khaki safari shirt and conservative light flannel trousers he had bought at Brooks Brothers six months ago but never worn. He ran a brush over his mat of curly blondish hair. Before departing for dinner, he grabbed the telephone and dialed a number from a card in his wallet. The phone rang twice, echoing the funny unfamiliar cadence of the British telephone system.

"Hello?" a full-blooded American voice inquired.

"Who's this?" James asked.

"Sidney Hughes," the voice said. "Why?"

"Never mind why. This is James McLaren. I understand you're the man from Whiplin's who's elected to take care of me. Get my measurements from the tailor at Top Wear clothes in Chicago. Then bring them around to Kirk's Tailors on Beauchamp Place, first floor. Tell Ron Kirk I'll be in before lunch tomorrow to pick out some cloth and answer any questions."

"Okay, James," Sidney said with enthusiasm. "But can't I just call them in?"

"No, you might fuck up. More to the point, Ron might fuck up. Get them from Top Wear and bring them around to Kirk's on paper. I've got to go."

He hung up and entered the words "Kirk's before lunch" in his address book under Tuesday. He'd make old Sidney work for his money.

Before leaving, he returned to the sitting room, poured another vodka, and flicked on the television. A news commentator wearing a toupee warned the viewers to stay tuned to the program to see the film of the "McLaren fisticuffs incident." James grinned. "McLaren fisticuffs incident," he repeated bemusedly. Then he added, "To hell with that, I *am* the McLaren fisticuffs incident." He flicked on the video recorder and walked out of the suite without bothering to turn off any of the machines or lock the door. Then he returned, quickly, to retrieve the vodka and the suits. He finished the vodka and threw the suits on the floor in the hall. *Maybe some poor son-of-a-bitch will fit them*, he thought as he entered the elevator.

Typically, the faggot maître d' in the Royal Roof restaurant refused to admit James without a jacket and tie. James thought *Fuck the appearance!* and put on the first thing offered him, a black dinner jacket with silk lapels. Surprisingly, it fit him better than any of the ones he had discarded. The tie had the hint of a gravy stain in the center, so he wore it only as far as the table, then pulled it off. He stuck it in the jacket pocket.

The stocky bald guy who greeted him at his table looked more like an aging busboy than someone who'd be offering him a million-dollar contract over dinner. In fact, James thought, he could have been related to the same guy whose nose he'd broken at Heathrow. It would not have been impossible. James shook hands, eyeing him obliquely.

"Mr. McLaren, Norm Feldman. It's nice of you to take the time to meet with me. I know how demanding your schedule must be." Feldman cupped a hand and leaned closer. "What with all the poontang comes your way."

Poontang? James tried not to smile. It was the first time he'd heard the word outside of a Mickey Spillane novel. He ordered a round of drinks and laughed inwardly. He sensed already he would like the guy.

"What part of Brooklyn are you from?" James asked him between sips of a gin gimlet.

Feldman scrunched up his face and bared his perfect teeth. He smiled. "It shows, does it?" His teeth were capped, James thought. "Funny, because you know I've been away from there for more than thirty years. It just goes to show what an impression your birthplace has on you, don't you think?" he asked.

"Oh, I don't know. I was born in Germany when my old man was over there in the service. I don't go around shouting 'Heil Hilter!' everywhere."

"I see your point." James perceived a feeling of embarrassment on Feldman's part when dealing with his Brooklyn roots. He let the topic die. "How do you like London so far? You like it much?" Feldman asked.

"It's all right. The people are a bit uptight and the women pompous, but it's all right. I like the nightclubs." He noticed Feldman had finished his drink and was waving his hand about imperiously to order another.

"I bet you like the nightclubs. I read about your exploits after hours." They both laughed. Feldman struck a serious pose, the first and last of the entire evening. "You know, of course, Mr. McLaren — James — that we can't have any similar incidents like the one on Long Island. It wouldn't help our image. But of course your private life has nothing whatsoever to do with me or the company or anybody else for that matter." He spoke the last sentence quickly, as though cutting off any rebuttal from James on this sensitive subject. None came. James knew on which side his bread was buttered. He knew sponsors had to answer to their public and that too many "incidents" could seriously damage sales.

"Don't worry, Feldman. That won't happen again," he said. He still regretted leaving the stuff in the car that fateful night. It was Janie's anyway, the silly bitch.

Feldman issued another conciliatory statement in case one was necessary. "What you do with your life is your business. So long as you keep your prick off the front page, we'll be A-okay." The imagery was classic. James fell back laughing, feeling the afternoon's drinks.

"Feldman, if that happens, I could always switch to promoting jockstraps."

Now it was Feldman who was laughing. Heads craned about the room and focused on the curly-haired young man and the fat bald guy. They had all seen the six o'clock news and here were McLaren and the wounded journalist. It did their hearts good to see the two had resolved their earlier differences and made up. Or so they thought.

James had the waiter pour another glass of port. About halfway through the meal, he'd been aware of a sudden halt in Feldman's alcoholic intake. He knew why. Underneath that unsophisticated veneer lay the heart and soul of a businessman about to make a deal. James had stopped drinking at exactly the same moment. The two glasses of port came on a full stomach at the end of the meal. He filled his lungs with the cool fumes of a French cigarette and sat back, crossing his legs. The floor show starring Norm Feldman was about to begin.

"So, James, do we have a deal or what, my friend?" Feldman asked.

"I don't know, Norm," James said, not having heard the question. His eyes lingered on the brunette dining alone three tables over. Her inviting eyes and warm smile amused him. He turned back to Norm. True to any successful business dinner, it was Norm and James now.

"What do you mean, James, you don't know? Let's talk figures then. What don't you like? Me? The designs? The money?" Norm asked. He waved his cigar around like some deranged orchestra leader flailing a baton.

"You," James said, smiling. He turned and gestured toward the brunette. "Now, if you were her, we'd have a deal already, but as you're not, well, those figures have got to improve." James realized he was mildly drunk.

"Okay, so let's improve them. I offer two hundred seventy-five thousand. You want more. How much more?" Feldman asked.

"I can get that kind of money for walking through a sit-com on TV. No, really, Norm, let's be serious," he said.

"He says be serious." Norm threw his head back for effect. "Okay, but how much more? We are not bloody Du Pont, you know. We've got a limited amount of funds to put behind this thing."

James eyed him closely. He flicked his cigarette casually on the tablecloth. "You also have fifteen million bucks' worth of stockpiled clothes with my signature scribbled across them just waiting to hit the stores, and probably another fifteen in standing orders. When I sign, that figure should triple. Don't shit me, Norm, I do my homework."

The color was returning to Norm's bulldog face. He straightened up and signaled for the waiter to bring some whiskey. When it arrived, he kept the bottle. He finished the first drink and was pouring another. "You're right about the clothes, but not the orders," he said, his voice soliciting sympathy. "We should sell twice what's stockpiled. I say *should*. Half of that goes into production costs, another quarter into labor. That leaves five, maybe seven, million after tax and insurance — and most of that's got to be deployed in dividends so we don't show a fucking loss." He finished his second drink.

James turned back from mouthing words to the brunette. "My heart bleeds for you, Norm, but, my friend, I couldn't touch the deal for less than two million. Even then I'd only be doing it out of my love for you."

Norm finished coughing. He dismissed an attentive waiter and finished what was left of his glass of water. "McLaren, you're absolutely fucking nuts. Two million? Do you know what two million would do to us? I'd be in the kitchen there washing dishes."

He had not been far off with his busboy analogy, James thought. "Norm, that's my final offer. Take it or leave it. I won't bargain." He waved to the brunette.

"One million two hundred fifty thou," Norm said quickly.

"No, Norm, I'm sorry. Two million or I'm out. Find yourself another man. Try Chekow."

"Okay, James, I'll go to one and a half million plus two hundred thou in shares in the company," Norm said. His tone voiced the finality in his words.

James pondered the proposal. One and a half million to be renegotiated in twelve months, plus another two hundred thousand in stock in the firm. Not a bad offer. That Norm was offering so much indicated his company was thriving. Once James had signed with him and the clothes were in the shops, the stock price would rise. He nodded; it was a sound agreement. Damned sound considering that Brice's investigations estimated he could get a maximum of one million three hundred thousand. He would have to have a talk with his agent.

"Norman, you're one hell of a businessman. I accept." He crushed the cigarette dead and extended his hand. They shook.

"I'm one hell of a businessman?" Norm said sarcastically. "I think you're in the wrong business, James. You should be running General Motors." He placed his hands palms down on the immaculate linen tablecloth. The twinkle returned to his eyes. Leaning toward James, he said, "Now go ball the ham off that brunette before your knob knocks the table over."

James just smiled.

She was fondling him the minute they hit the taxi. Her hungry fingers manipulated his stiffening cock beneath the lightweight flannel while her open mouth and battling tongue sucked and caressed his lips. A tiny dark stain appeared through the crotch of his trousers. James was ready to take her there in the car, but he knew what a sensation that would cause should they be discovered. He remembered what Norm had said about keeping his cock off the front page and laughed.

"What's so funny, darling?" the brunette asked as she unzipped his pants. She thrust her hand deep into the opening and found him. His erect penis sprang out of the tightness of the flannel.

He watched as her head sank down to his lap and felt the warmth of her breath. "Driver," he said, pushing her away. James tapped on the Plexiglas separation. "Take us through Hyde Park and then to Soho." The driver nodded indifferently. He flicked his indicator and swung the cab around, avoiding a twenty-ton truck by inches. He was preoccupied with getting the Wimbledon men's finals tickets from the ticket scalper who had called in at the station the day before. One hundred fifty pounds was a lot of money for a ticket with a face value of three pounds, but the driver figured it was worth it for the hottest ticket in town. How many people got to see a player like McLaren in action in person? Not many. He glanced at the running meter and headed the cab into the park as James McLaren repositioned the brunette's willing mouth.

Over two bottles of third-rate red at first-rate prices and a Cantonese-style duckling, they talked. The staff at the Chinese restaurant was thrilled with having McLaren seated at one of their tables. They had tried to stick him at the front table overlooking the street, but James had refused. He recognized their ploy and figured he did enough advertising in the "on" hours, to contemplate doing it in the "off." He tipped the owner five pounds and got him to switch the dreadful Cantonese folk music to a Beatles tape they had lying around.

"How is it, darling?" she asked.

He swallowed another mouthful of duck and washed it down with a glass of wine. "I've had worse," he said. Instinctively, he was wary of anyone who dispensed their "darlings" so liberally.

She looked at the skeleton of the Canton duckling shipped up from Wiltshire. "You can't possibly be hungry after that big supper you had at the hotel."

she told him. It was the fifth time she'd called him "darling."

"So you're staying at the Royal Garden?" he asked, flushing a cigarette. She stole it from him. He leaned forward to light hers and then withdrew another.

"Oh, no, I was only eating there. I swim twice a week in their pool. Sometimes I stay and eat afterward, but not often 'cause the food's so terribly expensive. Terribly good, though."

"It's lousy. Pity you didn't join us. My meals are on the house. They think by putting me on show stuffing my face with the crap they serve, it'll attract customers. There's no limit either. I can bring as many guests as I want, so long as I don't exceed the bounds of propriety, whatever the fuck that means."

"Please, darling, your language." She began to giggle, then said, "It works, though. That's why I ate there tonight."

"I thought you swim there."

"I do, but I don't eat there much. Frightfully expensive. I met someone you know at a drinks party. Sidney Hughes? He said you'd be staying there."

Somehow he knew before she said it that it was Hughes. *That horse's ass. I wonder what the hell else he told her*, he thought. "You know him, do you?" He finished the bottle of wine. A waiter bounded over and opened another.

"Best if you let it breathe, Mr. McLaren," the waiter said from behind a phalanx of extended teeth.

James nodded toward the wine. "Let it breathe? I'm afraid that piss suffocated years ago." The waiter disappeared bowing adulation, not understanding the remark. James practiced blowing smoke rings at the brunette. "Where were we?" he asked, already bored with her.

"You were asking me about your friend Sidney Hughes," she reminded him. He noticed she punctuated each sentence with the kind of dopey little smile they put on animal characters in cartoons.

His thoughts returned to Sidney Hughes. Although they had met only a dozen times, always before or during tournaments, he disliked Hughes intensely. His feelings stemmed from the time after the Flushing Meadow tournament that he'd lost to Chekow in the finals. Instead of hanging around to see if he needed anything — a ride to the hotel, consoling — Hughes had ditched him to attend a party at the Chekow camp in a nearby club. It may have been rumor, as nobody James knew would substantiate at precisely what time Hughes attended the party. But behind every rumor there stood at least one grain of truth, he reasoned, and he had held it against Hughes ever since.

"You like Hughes, do you?" he asked her.

"He's marvelous. He's got the most amazing eyes . . . and his car — his car is one of those little . . ." He pulled a joint from his wallet and lit up at the table. He waited until the resiny fumes bit into his lungs, then exhaled. She continued talking for five minutes.

By the time they arrived at Annabel's, he had heard a blow-by-blow account of her entire life story, including the bits about her mother's hysterectomy and her father's insurance business. Apparently, she collected Pekingese dogs and had twelve of the things in her flat in Kensington. He told her the only place Pekingese belonged was between two halves of a roll, a remark that fundamentally terminated the conversation.

He left her talking shop with a half dozen girls of her genre, all still smarting over the fact that they'd let Prince Charles slip away. They were seated at tables near the dance floor with their dates. At the bar he ordered a double gin, signed two autographs for two unattractive and drunk females, then turned to signal to the brunette. She was too busy basking in the ephemeral glory he had brought to her to take any notice. He told the barman she was "on the wagon" and lit a cigarette.

"All dressed up with nowhere to go," a husky voice said. He looked around and saw a tall girl in a sailor's blouse and shorts. She crossed carefully holding her cigarette out in extended fingers as she appraised him. "Very nice — two points for fashion and her arms, another eight for having your fly undone."

His frown vanished as he turned away. He fixed his fly and leaned against the bar. He still had on the dinner jacket he'd been forced to borrow.

She leaned over next to him.

"Thanks," he said. "It's a good thing you're as horny as you are; otherwise, I'd be walking around with one draft I don't need."

"Sure." She smiled. She was dark-haired with a round handsome face and an eagerness in her eyes he'd seen before in every port he frequented.

"What would you like? To drink?"

"Anything. What's that?" She pulled his glass down to her lips and tasted the gin. "My, that's nice. What is it?"

He stared at her, a little surprised at the question. "Rum," he said.

"Is that what rum tastes like? Umm, I like rum." She licked her lips. "Get me a rum, a large rum." She was of the same extraction as the Royal Garden brunette, he thought: a Harrods shopper of another vein whose faint Cockney accent was meant to belie her privileged ancestry. Inverted snobbism. He'd seen it all before.

He handed her the gin he had ordered for her. She took it and drank most of it in one gulp. He held her arm. "Whoa! Slow down, cowgirl. There's enough for everybody. You finish that, I'll get you another."

She smiled at him as a drop of gin rolled from her mouth. "That's right, you can afford it." She giggled. "I saw the news, too. Boy, that punch was a real destroyer."

"Who brought you here?" he asked, studying her widely spaced hazel eyes, the mascara a bit too thickly applied.

"Nobody. My uncle had a party and I went along. They came here."

"Where are they now?" he asked.

"I don't know. Why should I? It's a free country." Her defensive tone amused him. He was finally beginning to see her for what she was.

"How old —" He stopped himself and finished the drink. He hadn't had a virgin in over a year.

"Do you think you'll beat them again this year?" she asked. "They say it's always the most difficult the second year running."

He was about to answer when she leaned next to him as she waved to the barman. James's heartbeat increased momentarily as he felt the warmth of her body through the shirt. She smiled at him and turned toward the barman. "Two large rums, please, with tonic."

His eyes pulled away from the imprint her nipples made against the thin cotton blouse. He leaned past her. "No, change that — two gin-and-tonics."

"Hey! What's the idea? I like rum," she argued.

"And I'd like to go to bed with you, sailorgirl, because you're just about the nicest thing I've seen since I arrived in this God-awful country."

She blushed slightly and nuzzled closer to him. "I think you're nice, too. I saw you with my father when you won Wimbledon last year," she said. Her voice lapsed out of the affected Cockney accent. She rubbed her head against his chest. "I used to dream that I would meet you one day and we'd have an affair. Isn't that silly?" He felt himself growing hard and swigged deeply from the fresh glass of gin.

"Where did you pick this up? In the schoolyard?" He turned around and looked at the brunette standing behind sailorgirl. Her derisive tone angered him.

"Say hello to sailorgirl." He pointed to sailorgirl.

"Sailorgirl, this is brunette." They regarded each other like two cats on a windowsill meant for one. Sailorgirl relaxed and smiled. Brunette relinquished nothing. She continued staring contemptuously at her younger rival.

"James, stop that. You know my name is Stephanie. Come on, stop it. Not tonight," she scolded. It crossed his mind that she may have been talking to someone else. He looked around but saw no one.

"I'm new in London," sailorgirl said to her. "Are you a regular here?"

Stephanie, the brunette, ignored the question. Moving to James, she said, "James, get me a drink, will you, darling? What are you having?" She sniffed at his glass.

"That's rum," sailor girl said proudly. "We're both drinking it."

Stephanie arched her fine back and waved her hand dramatically, as though it were the funniest joke of the evening. "Christ! You are young, aren't you? Why don't you go home and go to bed before you're missed?"

James took sailorgirl around her slender waist and pulled her flush against his hard-on. "That's almost exactly what I told her." He smiled. Her sad expression transformed back into a smile. She rubbed her face thoughtfully against his chest like a rewarded puppy.

Stephanie must have been even stupider than he'd guessed because she smiled at James as though they were enjoying some private joke. "James, my drink," she said imperiously.

He thought about giving her his drink — over

her head. *Christ! One blow job and she thinks she runs the fucking show.* "Coming, ma'am." Two couples entered the room behind them and noticed James. Stephanie saw them and went into her choreographed song and dance. She waited until they got near enough to see, then leaped forward laughing at some nonexistent joke. She kissed James hard on the neck and too loudly intoned, "I'll be back, James, darling." She waltzed over to act important with the new arrivals.

"Christ! I hope I never get that bad," sailorgirl said as she wrapped an arm about James's waist.

"You won't." He almost dropped the drinks as he felt her little hand grab his cock through his pants pocket.

"God! Is that what they feel like?" she asked him. It was all he could do to keep from coming on the spot.

They escaped through the club's dining room via the kitchen exit. James estimated they had a good five minutes before Stephanie would notice he had gone; she had been checking back to acknowledge him or watch sailorgirl at five-minute intervals all night. Her predictability had facilitated their escape by allowing them to wait for the downbeat, then skip out on the up.

They strolled hand in hand through Berkeley Square and on to Piccadilly Street, then took a taxi back to Knightsbridge. He asked her about school.

"Oh, it's not too bad. I've got a lot of friends. I think if I can swing it in a year I might try for Oxford. I've got a brother at Balliol and two at —"

He interrupted her by swinging an arm around her shoulders and bringing her closer. She had wonderfully strong and wide shoulders, which tapered down to a slim twenty-five-inch waist. He deftly undid the buttons on her blouse and snaked a hand inside. He kissed her while he massaged the swollen bud of her right breast.

"It feels good," she whispered. "Promise to make love to me all night." He did. Being a man of his word, he would try to oblige.

He gave the smiling cab driver a ten-pound tip as a precaution against his selling his story to the *Daily Mirror* for two hundred. "You didn't see anything. Got that, pal?"

"Nothing, Jimmy, nothing at all," the cabbie replied, already folding the bill into his wallet.

"What are you drinking?" he asked as he closed the door quietly and slid the lock. He realized then that the lights were out. "That's odd."

"What?"

"Nothing. I left the lights on when I went out. At least I think I did. Never mind. How 'bout that drink?" he asked again from the sitting room.

"Sure, a rum or gin, or whatever we had at Annabel's." He poked his head around the wall and grinned at her. "You tricked me," she said, feigning embarrassment.

He filled two glasses with gin and threw in some chipped ice. Over hers he added an inch of tonic. She joined him in the room and strolled over to admire the stereo system. "This is the life," she said.

She read the names of the artists on the cassettes to herself.

"Go ahead, put one on if you want," he said. He brought over the drinks.

"But the neighbors — don't you think they'll mind? It must be past midnight."

It was ten to two. "I could care less what they think. What I do in here's my business. Let them get fucked." His anger subsided as he gazed upon her. "Put it on, they won't hear it."

Sailorgirl looked at the tape deck quizzically. She looked around coyly and handed the tape to James. "I don't know how." He traded the tape for a gin and smacked it in. The quadrophonic speakers throbbed with the sound of the music. "Nice," she said.

She began a tour of the room, opening cupboards, looking at pictures, furniture. He stood there and watched her with his tongue in the gin. She interrupted her tour to smile at him. "I'm so nosy." She giggled. He confronted her and stuck his face into the pile of curly dark hair on her head. She smelled clean and sweet, almost childlike. His free hand moved up from between her knees, bisecting her. She jumped as it moved over the space between her legs. Finally, it nestled on her left breast and encircled it. He kissed it through the blouse, leaving a faint water mark where his tongue was. She backed away. The look in her eyes was no longer the look of a nightclub tart, but that of a little girl. Her fear had destroyed the well-constructed façade plastered together with rouge and raw nerve. "I'm scared," she said slowly. "I want to, but I'm scared."

He combed down her pile of hair and smiled. "Sailorgirl, don't be scared. Drink that and you'll feel better."

"I don't want it to hurt me." She spoke into her glass.

"It won't hurt."

She gulped down the rest of the drink. The miniature mascara suns that were her eyes peered up at him trustingly as she drank. "There!" She gasped. "All gone." She handed him the glass. "Can I have another?"

He answered her with a kiss full on the lips. She pushed forward with her tongue working in a frenzy. Her eyes closed. He pulled back and kissed her forehead. "Slowly, lover, we've got all night." She nodded eagerly and returned to him.

He hadn't felt such unadulterated passion in years. This was not pure sex, as so many of his encounters were; his heart reached out to embrace her and comfort her and win her affection. He broke the bond of their mouths and started kissing her lightly about the face. His hands removed the sailor blouse and drew it back over her shoulders to expose her breasts. They were lovely and uptilted and soft. He experimented with their malleability, using his thumbs to rotate and brush the hardened nipples. He would move them first clockwise, then reverse the direction, each time engendering a faint whining sound from her as she responded to the magic feeling.

He sketched a trail of kisses across her neck to the cleft in her chest where the neck stopped and the chest began. His tongue lapped about her chest, alternating from breast to breast, then down to the tight girlish stomach. He retreated to his knees, kissing her belly while he undid the button to her shorts and slid them off. She wore nothing underneath. His probing tongue found her and she answered instantly with a high, stifled squeal. Her breathing became irregular and her thighs tightened about his head. He could feel the first faint shuddering as she neared a climax. A moment of utter stillness followed. Then she gasped, "Oh, God Almighty!" And she rocked violently against his mouth, eventually collapsing wetly against him.

He took her gingerly with a patience he had long forgotten. Every caress upon her magnificent body was firm but gentle — inadvertently expressing his affection for her. As he sat her on the towel, his fingers were already rekindling her previous fire so that when he mounted her, she was arching her flat tummy with legs taut, arms opened invitingly. He slid in easily while she drove against him, ridding herself of the last vestige of her childlike body. He came at once in hot ferocious thrusts that quenched the fire inside her. She was just sixteen.

His head pounded from the effect of the night's drinking and he cursed himself for not taking any aspirin. He crawled over sailorgirl on the bed and kissed her beautiful dimpled cheek. She smiled in her sleep and shifted farther into the pillow in her arms. He picked up the ringing telephone. "Uh-huh?" he said gruffly, not yet awake. He realized the stereo was still on.

"James. Is that you, James?" Before he could

answer, the voice continued. "It's Pam, James, and I'm so sad and frightened and alone. Help me, please."

He heard her start to cry. The sounds of a nightclub came through the receiver. "Where are you?"

"I don't really know. Oh, Christ, James, I need you tonight more than ever," she said over the flamenco music in the club.

He was in great demand tonight. First the brunette, Stephanie, then sailorgirl, now Pam. "Find out from somebody, Pammy. Ask somebody. Christ!" he said.

"Oh, please don't be angry with me, James. You're my only friend in the world, don't hurt me," she slurred. The gravity of her words worried him. She was either drunk or stoned.

"I'm sorry. Look, turn to the closest person and ask the name of the place. That's all I need to know. Then I'll come around to pick you up. You can do that much for me, Pammy." Sailorgirl was up on her elbows wearing a puzzled look. James's gaze moved automatically to the tiny sleeping breasts hanging pendulumlike as she watched him. He rose a finger to his lips, then scratched her head lovingly. She curled up around him and stroked his back.

"I'll try, but I don't like it here, James. There's a man here who scares me. I'll try, though. Don't hang up on me."

"Of course not. Go ask, Pammy." He cupped the receiver and bent down to Sailorgirl. They kissed hot and wet. "An old friend; she's in trouble. I'm going to bring her back here." He read her expression and added, "You'll like her "

After a minute Pam's voice returned. "James?"

"Yes."

"It's the Riviera Club and it's on Draycott Avenue, but hurry. He's here again and he really scares me. Please . . ." The rapid succession of pips signaled the expiration of the ten-pence coin. James hung up. The Riviera Club — he knew it, a seedy cocktail lounge for the swinging singles of Chelsea. Not Pam's scene at all, he thought.

He sat up and yawned. "Shit! James McLaren. Big brother to the world. Available on easy terms any time of the day or night," he said aloud. He turned to her. "I've got to go. Do you want to stay, or do you want me to take you home?"

She looked startled and a little hurt. "Why?" she asked.

"Okay, then stay. If you need anything when I'm gone, call up and charge it. I'll be back in an hour."

"Are you going to sleep with her, too?" sailorgirl inquired.

He cuffed her jaw playfully. "Give me more credit than that, for Christ's sake." He stood stiffly and stretched his arms. "You think I'd take the chance of losing you?" he asked. She beamed. He headed for the chair in the room where his clothes were folded. "Besides, we wouldn't all fit." He ducked the pillow she threw at him and began dressing.

What Pam had neglected to tell him were the circumstances of her predicament and how the Argentinian dock worker came to bother her. It was one-thirty A.M. and the tears of her earlier shame had all but subsided. A surfeit of makeup, especially about the eyes, had disguised any trace of her earlier sorrow and its effect on her. She descended the length of the terra cotta stairs and depressed the tiny doorbell to the restaurant-cocktail lounge. Seconds later, a latticed wooden cube appeared within the cheap pine door. Narrow eyes appraised her. Then the door opened and a burly gentleman of obvious Latin extraction bade her to enter. She rolled her eyes coquettishly at his lecherous smile and sauntered past him.

"A coconut cooler," she told the man at the bar. "If I told you you had masculine eyes, would you make it a strong one?" Her provocative tone caused the Polynesian barman to stare curiously at her.

"Sure, missy. And if I told you you had a nice body, would you hold it against me?" he asked. She waved playfully at him. He paused while concocting the drink and jerked his head to his Argentinian friend sitting alone. The man read his signal and rose from his table in the crowded lounge. He lit a cigarette the way he had seen Steve McQueen do it in a film and strode over to her. He accosted her and stood inches from her chair. A knowingly playful look crossed his lightly bearded face. He intercepted the drink from his barman comrade and slapped down some pound notes on the bar.

She noticed his large hands. Each finger was encased in a thin gold ring with an inscription on it, so that the combined effect reminded her of a pair of brass knuckles. A scar protruded in a hump on the back of one of his hands. She could see the bumpy remains of the suture marks where it had been sewn crudely together. He was not good-looking. His face was long and flat, with high cheek-bones and slits for eyes. He was going thin on top with a hairline in the advanced stages of recession. His nose was flat and bumpy, with the skin stretched tightly across it, and his teeth were bad. But he was a man, and she had attracted him.

"My pleasure, miss," he said. His accent was cloying.

She took the drink from him and felt his fingers brush her hand. "To what do I owe this pleasure?" She smiled an exaggerated smile and held it.

"With a lady as beautiful as you, it is my pleasure to serve you. I know a woman of distinction when I see her." He moved in until she could smell his breath. It was stale and vaguely reminiscent of rotten eggs.

"Stop it." She smiled. Her hand tapped his chest playfully through the V in his shirt. She sought refuge in the drink and swigged deeply from it. Her painted eyes clamped shut. The strong concoction moved down her throat with the callous inertness of cool sand. She felt better at once.

He handed her empty glass over the bar. "Get the lady what she was drinking," he told the barman. "So you're from America. Why would someone as lovely as you leave such a country as America to travel alone? And in England? Answer me that."

"Because I heard so much about the men in London. Especially the foreigners," the voice said. She heard the words distantly, as if listening underwater, and wondered who had put them in her mouth. "They're very obliging to a lonely girl, isn't that true?"

True to some base Darwinian game, he threw his chest forward and assumed a pose. His hips extended until she could feel him hot against her bare leg. "You must have a very good source. All of your information is accurate. But you can't just take my word for it. That would not be right."

She glanced down at the bulge in his skintight jeans as it pressed against her. "Oh, no, I couldn't just take your word. You'd have to show me." He pressed closer as he moved to hand her the drink. His friend, the barman, in an unusually generous move, had given her two extra shots of rum at no additional charge.

"Here, my lovely American bitch. Drink to your health." Cigarette exhaust left his copious nostrils in tandem fumes that curled around her and sickened her. Again sanctuary came in the creamy mixture of rum and coconut. He watched her devour it. She raised her head drunkenly and looked at him. She could smell his breath as he drew closer to remove the white moustache from her upper lip. Her throat burned from the large dosage of rum.

She sat there feeling the heat of his burgeoning erection, wondering if tonight had really happened. Why had it happened? Why had she allowed it to happen? A tear clouded her eye and she removed it. Couldn't a psychiatrist do something for her, or was she destined to live life undercover as a lesbian? She would find a specialist, and a husband; she had loved men before, she simply hadn't met the right one . . . that's all it was. Her heart rose from the depths of its depression; her spirits rallied. Sure, she hadn't always enjoyed sex with men as much as she might have. Nor had she met many men who really and truly moved her. But she simply hadn't found the right man. "Plain bad luck," she said aloud. "Plain rotten luck."

"What is it, baby? Whose luck?" She almost jumped off the barstool. Her eyes leaped up and gazed upon his horrid yellow smile. She had forgotten all about him, for he was now dispensable. There was no need to rectify her problem through such drastic means so alien to her character. She could afford it; she would hire a shrink. The best in the world. After all, she rationalized, she was not that serious a case. She had only done it once, against her will, and surely that did not constitute being one of them. A shrink would probably prescribe some straightforward therapy and dismiss the condition with a consoling word and a smile. That's it, she would get help. For a moment her eyes sparkled.

Across the room a three-piece band erupted into a cacophony of irregular sounds. The Argentinian stood directly in front of her. His eyes groped for hers in order that she read his intention. Her head was tilted downward. "Come, we dance." He escorted her numbly through the capacity-filled tables. They joined another couple on the compact dance floor located immediately in front of the small band. He embraced her and took the initiative with the roaring flamenco number, whisking her about while observing the same tick-tock of the hips inherent in the dance. She relented to his crushing hold and allowed herself to be shuffled about like a child along the floor. The activity of dancing had a cleansing effect on her mind. She grew aware of the cheering audience and the way they rejoiced in the actions of her unsavory partner. Their vacant smiles, so anonymous and foreign, instilled her heart and soul with a dimension of despair she had never known before. She began crying on his shoulder. With all the strength in her arms, she pushed away from him. He spun away, totally off guard. "James!" she cried, as she searched for a telephone.

He smacked the telephone from her hands for the fourth time.

"James," she said, weeping. "I must call James. You don't understand."

"I understand you, you whore. You're a fucking cock teaser. You ain't going nowhere or calling nobody until you deliver what you promised. Fucking cunt." His words bit into her and cut her up inside. She had never been so scared. He slapped her flush against the face. Her head went numb from the shock. His ringed hand left an imprint on her cheek. She could taste the blood.

Back in the lounge the band had succeeded in luring most of the audience to its feet. They clapped and screamed as they bobbed around in erratic time to the tune. Pam's cries for help went unheard over the noise.

Three minutes later the Argentinian appeared in the threshold of the doorway with his jaw cocked in a derisive, satisfied sort of way. He adjusted his belt and confronted the bar. The barman lifted his thumb and forefinger, indicating his thoughts on the encounter. "She was a whore," he said, elaborating.

It was then that she called James, and he had promised to rescue her. But where was he? She returned to the acrid-smelling cubicle that doubled as a ladies' room. For the sixth time she positioned herself against the filthy sink and held her khaki shirt in her trembling teeth. She splashed the area about her vagina with warm water. With the decimated sliver of soap she did her best to cleanse herself from the poison he had injected unwillingly into her. Stretching fingers brought the thin lather up inside her as high as she could reach. She rinsed herself with warm water and placed toilet paper to act as a blotter in the crotch of her panties.

Her eyes were swollen and bloodshot. Her makeup had run with the inevitable flow of tears, leaving dark tracks across her cheeks. The starkness of black against her ivory skin had an almost hypnotic effect on her. That's how life was, she thought. *Black or white — you're either one way or another*. With little difficulty she could have crawled into the sink and slept soundly, content that it would be all over tomorrow. Where was James? She wiped away the tracks of her tears with toilet paper. Despite her recent desecration, she looked reasonably normal beneath the strings of displaced eye liner. This rallied her spirits. She combed her long thick hair with her fingers. It still smelled faintly of the chamomile shampoo she'd used that afternoon. She thought, *It's all going to be fine*.

In the eleven minutes it took James to find a cab

and arrive at the club, the glow had resurrected in the loins of the Argentinian. As with a prize bull, the lust had risen again inside him and he wanted her for another bout. She was his tonight and he would have her again, and again, until he was satisfied. He rose determinedly from the bar. The sound of the front doorbell went unheard over the blaring of the band.

A sudden burst of music penetrated the relative tranquility of the ladies' room. Pam could feel his presence. She jumped as she recognized the lust in his eyes. She watched him stroke his extended penis in the doorway. "Oh, God! Oh, James!" she cried inaudibly. Her spirits were collapsing. She tried screaming but the sounds caught within the dryness of her larynx. She realized then she was cornered and had brought this upon herself and that there was nothing she could do but submit to him . . . .

James saw the movement of a door closing from his position near the entrance. He had sneaked inside when a drunken Arab burst out the front door to be sick in the street. James walked around to the lounge, his eyes sweeping the orgy of drunken singers and dancers for some sign of her. No Pammy. He remembered seeing the door close and returned to it. He saw it was the ladies' room. In the moment he took to consider his next move, he heard the whimpering sound that convinced him. He kicked the door open.

Instantly, he surveyed the small room and sized up the situation. Pam was crushed against the wall, while the Argentinian fumbled with her panties. She turned toward James, her face without expression. In the two seconds it took the sex-crazed man to distinguish the presence of a third party, the fight was essentially decided. James moved reflexively like a cat. He sprang and seized the man by the curly hair at the back of his head. With two hands and the full weight of his one hundred sixty pounds, James smashed the head forward against the tiled wall. The Argentinian bounced off with a sticky sound. James's superb reflexes caught him on the rebound and repeated the action — slamming the head savagely forward. What James lacked in bulk was compensated for by the genius of coordination. Each terrible blow distributed his full weight with optimum efficiency, using every ounce of strength explosively like a boxer. He lost track of blows soon after the head in his hands stopped resisting. The fury in him subsided and he let the limp figure slide face forward off the wall to the floor. The battered Latin countenance mapped its descent with a crimson streak. Blood beaded on the tiles.

James fell to his knees exhausted. Automatically, his arms wrapped around Pam's upright figure. He breathed in hard through her khaki shirt and sucked in great gulps of air, which assuaged the burning in his lungs. He craned his neck. "Pammy." She said nothing. Her hands pulled him closer against her, shielding his trembling body.

Kneeling there, James began examining the ramifications of the attack. He looked at the figure on the floor and tensed. Pam gripped him at the shoulders to restrain him from delivering a final unwarranted blow. Another strike against the prostrate figure might have killed him. "Let go of me," he said. James crouched over the Argentinian. He rolled him over and without looking at him lifted a wrist and gripped it. The vital signs were there; he had a fast, though regular, heartbeat. He was breathing through the remains of the busted nose. The lacerations across his brow indicated that that part of the head and not his skull absorbed most of the impact of the blows. "Thank Christ for that," James said aloud. He slid his fingers into the gums on either side and forced the jaw open. The added precaution would provide a breathing space should the nose hemmorrage or clot or some such bullshit, James told himself.

He turned his attentions to Pam. "You okay?"

"Yes." She blinked her tears back. "Is he still . . . ?"

"He'll live. Whether he deserves to or not, he will." James was thinking clearly again; the fight was history. What mattered now was not jeopardizing his future. "We've got to get out of here. Just walk out calmly like fuck all's happened. If anyone recognizes you or me, just ignore them and keep moving and don't worry about it. You're okay, that's what matters." He went to the door and opened it a crack. The music was going strong. He felt for the light in the ladies' room and switched if off. "Walk calmly. Don't acknowledge anybody." He took her hand. "Okay?"

"Okay, James."

They slipped out of the room past the pine door to the stairwell. Once on the avenue they proceeded north on to Fulham Road and stopped a cab coming from the opposite direction. James put his collar up and kept his head down.

"Where to, mate?" the elderly cabbie chimed.

"The Dorchester." James had the driver stop a block from the hotel. Purposely he tipped him twenty pence and walked away.

The old cabbie dropped the change into a plastic box on the floor of the cab. "Cheap fucking tourists," he mumbled and pulled away.

They walked a block down Park Lane and caught a mini-cab near the circular drive to the Dorchester, where Sidney Hughes, the Whiplin chargé, was staying. The move was a precautionary one in case the Argentinian on the bathroom floor did not recover — James wanted no link, no matter how obscure, to the fight in the nightclub. "The Royal Garden Hotel," he told the West Indian driver. "In Knightsbridge." They held hands all the way.

Chapter Three

St. Tropez, France

Aysop Chekow rolled out of bed, pulled off his cotton pyjamas, and walked to the window. He ripped the curtain back and squinted at the sudden brightness of the summer morning. Returning to the bed, he lay on it and fired off a series of loosening calisthenics that got the circulation going through his lanky six-foot-two frame. "Merde!" he said aloud for no particular reason. He lay that way for half an hour, then sprang up and stood under the shower in the adjoining bathroom.

It was eight-thirty by the time he'd shaved and

dressed and it occurred to him that Viktor hadn't called. This was unusual. He combed his straight black hair close against his head; his ears seemed to leap out like tiny airplane wings on either side of his face. With a towel he disheveled his hair, then patted it down lightly, careful to keep the fullness. He was very self-conscious about the size of his ears. Often he thought of defying Viktor and ducking into one of the more fashionable hair salons in any city of the free world. They would cut it properly in layers and his ears wouldn't stand out. But Viktor Godon, his coach-manager, dismissed these urges as pure vanity, and vanity was one of the exponents of capitalism and for that reason should be denied.

Chekow peered at the row of grass courts outside the modest stucco apartment building. The sight of two young players batting the ball evenly over the net filled him with the anxiety of an athlete waiting to perform. But where was Viktor? Five days before the start of Wimbledon and Viktor was late by more than an hour. The superiors would not like this.

While he waited, he opened the tiny refrigerator that stood near the sink in the one-room flat. He removed an apple and a half-full quart of milk. He had decided the previous night that he would ask Viktor for some of the tour money. That way he could replenish the refrigerator with all the good things they sold in the giant food stores in town. He disliked going out to eat his meals every night. For the past four days they had eaten twice daily at the same Italian trattoria near the fish market. Here Viktor would recommend the various menus, always making sure Chekow chose the one Viktor preferred. It was no coincidence that Viktor had consistently chosen the cheapest fare available, and Chekow had begun to wonder where the generous funds from the Soviet Sporting Federation went. As the number-two tennis player in the world, he felt he was entitled to some luxuries.

But he did not complain. For one, it would be pointless. Viktor's indomitable personality and booming tone of voice would dismiss the inquiry with merely a wave of his massive hand. He might even consider it an affront to his noble character. Viktor was a very honorable sort of man. He spent too much time expounding on the iniquities of capitalism to do anything with the excess money other than return it to the state, Chekow resolved. But still, they didn't have to live this cheaply. He had a fair idea of what his Western contemporaries were earning, and this had influenced his thinking. He had no intention of emulating their capitalist ways, but still a little more money would make it easier.

Besides, he could be a lot worse off. He was grateful to the Politburo for having recognized his abilities as a tennis player. Similarly, he was grateful for the countless hours of first-class instruction he had received and the cornucopia of new equipment they offered him. Did he not own his own cottage in Georgia, with a flat in Moscow and one in Leningrad where his family resided? Were not the car he drove and the fine tailored clothes both he and his family wore rewards from the leaders of his nation for his unprecedented achievement? Never before had a

Soviet player gained the status of number two in the tennis world. Indeed, prior to his emergence on to the professional scene, a Russian player in the top twenty would have been viewed as a major step forward in Russian tennis. True, the brother countries were known to do this lately, particularly with their women. The "Satellite stars," as they were named by the Western press, were a force to be reckoned with on the professional circuit. Look at Navratilova. But never had there been a star of quite his magnitude to emerge from the amateur ranks of the mother country. He was unique.

Yet, as was so often the case in a country where politics were debased and ridiculed on the surface and manipulated brilliantly beneath it, he had received one further privilege. His talents had won his exemption from the National Service, which meant exemption from the conflict in Afghanistan. This bitter conflict had claimed the lives of three of his friends and two cousins and he was most grateful he did not have to fight in that war.

He finished the apple, core and all, and drank some of the milk. From the canvas gym bag on the floor he removed four different unmarked bottles of vitamins and minerals and poured two tablets from each into his hand. The amalgam of phosphates, brewers' yeast, calcium, and assorted vitamins tasted awful, especially with the milk chaser. When his Moscow trainer had first prescribed them, Chekow had welcomed any opportunity to accidentally on purpose forget to take them. Slowly, he'd grown accustomed to them. What's more, since initd all, and drank some of the milk. From the canvas gym bag on the floor he removed four different unmarked bottles of vitamins and minerals and poured two tablets from each into his hand. The amalgam of phosphates, brewers' yeast, calcium, and assorted vitamins tasted awful, especially with the milk chaser. When his Moscow trainer had first prescribed them, Chekow had welcomed any opportunity to accidentally on purpose forget to take them. Slowly, he'd grown accustomed to them. What's more, since initially taking them three years ago, his game had improved immeasurably. He had also grown four inches and gotten a lot stronger and now he observed the ritual of the pills as a Westerner might a religion.

He did not particularly smoke or drink or womanize, although recently he had gotten into the pants of a tennis groupie who for the last year had appeared at every single tournament in which he played. He also loved his mother, respected his father, wrote home twice monthly, and swore allegiance to the land of his birth. He liked children and little dogs and they liked him. He was, in a phrase, what every self-respecting girl would like to bring home to Mother. He was all of these things and one more. At twenty-two he was a murderer.

Some were born to notoriety; others had notoriety thrust upon them; others achieve it. Chekow had a small bladder. It was this aberration that had, in a roundabout way, plucked him from his relative anonymity four years ago. It happened after an exhibition match in Leningrad in the autumn of that year. The matches had been arranged as an after-lunch entertainment for visiting dignitaries from the Soviet bloc countries and others from the not yet aligned African states. As the eighteen-year-old number-seven-ranked player in Russia, he had been one of the star attractions of the day. The gangly youth was a favorite of the sports columns in the local journals, as well as in the party paper *Pravda*. Although ranked seventh, the beautiful natural form of the blue-eyed boy had already prophesied his eventual domination of the sport. It was simply a question of time and confidence before he dethroned the more seasoned players. He had the shots, a whole repertoire of winning hits, and the temperament. All he lacked was the psychological edge over the others, and three nights a week with a Jewish psychiatrist was changing that. Increasingly, he found that the subversive antics of his opponents no longer bothered him: the way they overemphasized their follow-through or called out the score too loudly to distract him. He learned to focus only on the ballistics of the approaching ball and the general position of his opponent.

This particular afternoon he had for the first time in his career succeeded in beating Onegin, the number-one player. Chekow took him in straight sets, and to add insult to injury, had prevented him from winning a single point in the last six games. It was a truly remarkable victory for the eighteen-year-old native-born Georgian. The crowd had cheered him and the dignitaries had praised him. Even Gromyko, the former Foreign Secretary, who was in attendance, stood and cheered. Chekow had finally done it, dethroned number one. He had the ability and now the confidence; the rest was easy.

He excused himself from Viktor, his coach even then, and ducked into the locker room to relieve himself. Normally, he could play out the full five sets and his small bladder wasn't a problem. The liquid that circulated through his system would find escape through his pores as he sweated about the court. But this day was different; the tournament hall was encased in a thick shell of concrete that contained the coolness of the air. Consequently, he perspired less. Secondly, there was the ease of the victory in only three sets, for a total of twenty-seven games. Even less sweat. Thirdly, the eminence of those spectating had unnerved him. These three factors resulted in his having more liquid in his bladder than usual and a more pressing desire to rid himself of it. He took off for the locker room in a slow jog.

The punch caught him squarely on the chin, knocking out two teeth and opening a gash the length of his lip. Then he saw it, a silver band of steel that jutted from the thick-fingered hand of his attacker. The overhead light winked off the blade as the man twisted it. Chekow recognised the smiling face of the squat, bristly-haired man as Igor, the trainer of Onegin; the dethroned number one. But Onegin was such a regular fellow, Chekow thought; cynical maybe, but nice. Surely he wouldn't send Igor after him. What possible good would it accomplish? They would all suspect.

He stood up and wiped the salty taste of blood

from his mouth. Something cut him from the inside of his lip. He spat out two scarlet pebbles, the remains of his two upper teeth. Instinctively, he circled Igor and mirrored the squat man's deliberately slow movements. The blade refracted the overhead light like a mirror, following him in his unchoreographed waltz about the locker room floor.

"You should not have caused shame to Onegin," Igor said resolutely. His words echoed off the walls and disrupted the stony silence. "This is not good. You have made light of him in front of half the Politburo. He will never recover from that."

Chekow wanted to explain to Igor his own pressures for winning the tournament. Onegin would have fallen one day, he would say. He was thirty-one. Didn't Igor understand that he had only been doing his job? Certainly Onegin would bear him no malice. Chekow wanted to say all these things to the deranged trainer, but the words wouldn't come to him. He shook his head. Blood rained upon his chest. He looked at it as it blotted onto the white shirt and felt weak.

"Now you have no place here anymore. I'm going to cut off your balls and make you choke on them. Prepare to die." Igor charged at him with the hunting knife. Chekow leaped back in time to feel the rush of air as the knife sliced the area before him. "Stand still!" Igor screamed.

Chekow darted across to a massage table at the trainer's end of the room. Igor sprinted after him, amazing Chekow with his bulletlike reflexes. Was there no escape? Cautiously, he paused, shaking, only the elevated massage table between them. "Die!" Igor yelled. He lunged again over the tabletop. Chekow recoiled, terrified, as the blade missed his throat by inches.

Igor was laughing now. His fat face contorted into a macabre grin, the brazen confidence in that face demoralizing the young Chekow. It was just a matter of time; then he'd be finished. He was sure of it. A warm sensation began in his shorts and trickled its way down his inner leg. The urine that so often followed the expiration of life had preceded his demise.

Abruptly, Chekow leaped to the tape basket riveted into the table beside him. He sorted furiously through it praying for time, and froze as he spied the plastic handle of the long kitchen dagger used by the trainers to cut athletic tape. Chekow prayed silently to whatever arbiter of his safety had seen fit to provide the dagger. "Give up or prepare to die savagely as I hunt you down and slice you into lots of little bits!" Igor cried. A queer satisfied glint appeared in the little man's eyes. His thick brow creased and he smiled. Igor's thin-lipped mouth opened wider. He thrust his bristly head back and began to laugh.

Chekow detected the sound of more laughter coming from behind Igor near the toilets. Miraculously, the stocky trainer dropped his guard and looked in the direction of the showers. It was now or never.

Within seconds Chekow had withdrawn the dagger from the tape basket and made his move. His own slender weight brought down the cumbersome trainer as he stuck the dagger under Igor's huge arm, surprised at how easily it went in, like carving jelly. Blood spurted; he forced the knife deeper, rolling with Igor on the tile floor. There was no resistance now in the once fierce figure of bone and muscle. Chekow stared into the face of the man he had just stabbed. It was tame, devoid of the earlier animation, and ghostly white. He had never seen such a whiteness even on paper or in paintings, he thought. The puddle of black blood gathering about the body contributed to the starkness of the colors. "Please!" Igor gasped. The life passed out of him in one final convulsion. Then it was over.

"You fool!" the voice cried. "It was only a game." Chekow jerked his stare away from the corpse in time to see Onegin running at him. Onegin, the same man over whose honor the surreal duel had been fought. "It was a game, you murdering bastard!" The words hung in the air beside the smell of death, meaning little to him. Chekow had heard the words, but somehow their meaning didn't register. "Only a game."

Onegin's face tightened. He dove for the knife in Igor's hand, unfurling the stiff chubby fingers and clasping it about the bloodied leather handle. "But this is no game. It's your turn to join Igor," Onegin said furiously.

With the invaluable power of experience behind him, Chekow knew how to react. Onegin, alternatively, had never killed a man before. The pause preceding Onegin's strike, a pause precipitated by his own misgivings about murder, was all the time Chekow needed. The young man stood up, then backed away from the wavering former champion. The angle of the hilt of the blade lodged in Onegin's ribs made Chekow wonder if he had killed him. He pulled the knife out. "Can you help me?" Onegin pleaded. He staggered a few steps before collapsing in a pool of blood beside Igor.

Chekow dropped the knife and fell down beside the carnage he had caused. Bloodied hands rose to shield his face. He tasted the salt of his tears as they poured down into his damaged mouth and stung the wound. Viktor's powerful hand grasped his shoulder. Chekow felt the strength in the hand as it shook him. Finally, he looked up.

"Did you do this?" Viktor asked. "Tell me, Aysop, did you do this?" Chekow nodded a confession. "Why?" He waited. "Was it self-defense?"

"Thelf-defenth," Chekow lisped through his broken mouth.

Viktor's steel-gray eyes rested on him, then flicked up to another man who had entered the room. "Fuck!" He scratched his broad chin while he thought. "Thank God he won today. Otherwise, fuck knows what would happen."

"You're right," the other man, a stranger, replied.

Chekow noticed the stranger for the first time. He observed him closely. The fine dark suit and the polished leather shoes told him he was not just any man. Probably from the Politburo, he surmised. He licked his lips and felt the cut. His tongue moved inside and probed the jagged edges where his teeth had broken off. He looked up at Viktor.

"Back the car around to the exit. Open the trunk and bring me the tarpaulin folded inside it," Viktor said to the stranger. His cracking tone asked for no reply and got none. The well-dressed stranger disappeared out the door of the locker room.

"Take off those clothes." Chekow stepped out of the bloodstained clothes and handed them to Viktor. His coach threw them down on to the pool of blood around Igor. Chekow was studying the blotting effect the cotton material had on the blood when Viktor said, "Go wash yourself. Put on the clothes in your locker. Hurry up."

He did as ordered. Before the square of mirror above the basin, he saw the true extent of his injuries. His bottom lip, probably the sole reason for his having any bottom teeth left at all, had cushioned half the blow. The two-inch gash went clean through it and created an impression of the teeth behind it. The other half of the blow had claimed the top two teeth. He experimented with a finger and wiggled the two teeth to either side of the jagged remains. He wondered if they could be saved.

"Finithed," he said. His fingers worked the last button of his sports sweater. "Now what?"

Viktor had arranged the bodies on the tarp side by side. He had rolled them out of the blood and had soaked much of it up with towels from a hamper. He was in the process of throwing down more towels. Viktor looked up at the younger man. His rugged face relented some. "Good. Get out to the car and lay down in the backseat." Chekow started for the exit. "And Aysop," he called after him, "don't worry."

His mother ladled the last of the chicken stew into his bowl. "Aysop." She smiled. "It's nice to see you eating again, my son. You need your strength to begin the tour next month. There are many players from many countries, and they will all be strong and healthy."

His father, a lean man with glasses and a kind face, wiped his bowl with the last of the rye bread. "Mama, let's not worry Aysop. He knows what he's up against. He played those boys from the Czechoslovakian and Rumanian teams. He knows what he has to do to win."

"I know, but it's still good to see him with an appetite again," she said. She patted her son on the head and returned to the kitchen.

"I just hope I beat them," Chekow said between spoonfuls of stew. "Viktor tells me I won't at first, but within a year or less, I will be one of the best."

"Nonsense! You'll win from the beginning. If it wasn't for the standard of tennis in this country, you'd be number one in the world already. Or very close," his father added proudly as he lit his cigar and smiled. His expression grew thoughtful. "Don't worry, son, you will."

His mother scolded the children as they sat behind the blanket separation in the next room watching television. They had yet to get over the novelty of the colored talking box, a gift from the state for their brother's having attained the number-one tennis spot in the country. Since the arrival of the television, Chekow's teeth had been filed and capped and his stitched lip had mended. All that remained was the tiny scar on either side of the lip, and a larger scar in his heart, where the trauma of that afternoon had affected him.

As Viktor had assured him while he knelt there mopping up the blood, there had been nothing to worry about. Nothing but his conscience. The drama that might have unfurled never did. A two-column article with as many photos in the sporting journal and a smaller space in *Pravda* had reported the men's deaths. Only the facts were wrong. They might indeed have died of internal injuries caused by sharp blows, but those blows were not from a car crash, as was written. Chekow wondered what had caused the fire that burned them "beyond recognition." On a more practical note, he wondered which car had been used in the spurious accident.

But life must go on, and it did. For six weeks he had been plagued with the mental reenactment of the fight: the sight of the knife piercing the chest of first Igor, then Onegin. And the blood. So much blood. Especially in his sleep, where his dreams were riddled with wild, exaggerated visions of the encounter, did he suffer. But gradually the dreams diminished in frequency as well as intensity. The long talks with Viktor, one of the few who knew the truth, had eventually brought him a kind of peace. He had done what he believed right at the time. It had been a straightforward case of self-defense. A metaphor for life and, even more so, a metaphor for competition and the life of the athlete.

He drank from the ornate goblet and enjoyed the bittersweet flavor of the wine. Since he was eighteen, his parents considered him an adult. He was now permitted to eat with them in the evenings, complete with wine from the goblets his grandmother had left them, and candlelight. Granted, having to wait an extra hour until his four brothers and sisters had eaten their supper was not easy. He was still a growing boy and had a huge appetite. The status enjoyed through participation in these late-evening meals, however, more than offset his hunger pangs.

Often, when he was alone after practice or when driving in Viktor's car to the courts, he wondered if his newfound rank as adult had something to do with being the silent breadwinner in the family. His father's job at the mill still provided a weekly paycheck and book of ration coupons. In fact, that check had mysteriously increased ever since his top ranking on the court. But it was Chekow's rapport with the leaders of the state that had gained the family such perks as the television set, the new clothes for everyone and the promise of a larger flat. Even their old car had profited from his notoriety. One afternoon a man had delivered a crate of spare parts needed to get it running again. Summarily, he and his father and Yuri, his next elder brother, had put it in working order over a month of weekends and summer evenings. Now they had a car.

"You think you'll enjoy playing away from home

for so long?" his mother asked as she returned to the table.

He ran his fingers idly over the lip of the goblet. "I don't know. It sounds exciting and I've always enjoyed the trips to Prague in the summer."

His father fired the embers of the cigar as he inhaled. "But this is not just Prague or Warsaw for three weeks. This is the West for six months. The capitalistic West, where the Americans run the show," he said from behind the screen of smoke.

Chekow wondered if he would miss the familiar scent of the cigar. He had always hated it as a kid. In a strange way he found that with the realization of losing it, he could only now begin to appreciate it and what it represented. "I liked America okay before." Chekow was referring to the dozen exhibition matches he had played at some of the larger colleges and universities nearly two years earlier. "Besides, that's where the competition lies. Until I win there, I am nothing."

"What do you mean, nothing? You are the number-one player in all Russia. The number-one player in the finest country in the history of the world," his father said defiantly.

In view of all the truths and half truths he'd heard about America and judging from what he'd seen of it, he wondered if this wasn't an overstatement. "I know, Papa. But the Russians are not tennis players."

"You mean they are not professional tennis players who exploit their natural gifts for material reward," his mother intoned calmly.

"Yes, but to be the best there is to be number one. Number one of tennis. Professional or not." He hoped he hadn't spoken too harshly. He turned to his father for support. "Isn't that right, Papa?"

"What . . . er . . . yes. It is. You must realize, though, your disadvantages. These men have been playing maybe not as much as you, but against better players and from as early an age."

"Yes, but Viktor said that all my extra hours of play will prepare me for that. He says I have the shots. All I need is to get used to their faster pace." He finished the last half of the wine.

As always, the topic of conversation had focused too much on tennis. Mama was the first to recognize that it had. "How long exactly will you be gone? Natashe will be heartbroken if she thinks you'll be away too long."

His father spoke up. "Let Natashe be thankful he is not in the infantry like the rest of those at his age."

Chekow thought briefly about Natashe. Would she really be heartbroken?

"I don't think it will be as long as six months. Viktor says we'll need four or five to acclimate ourselves to the pace of the circuit. Then we come back for a month to practice new shots. Then I don't know, it depends on my performance and what Viktor thinks."

"Viktor this, Viktor that. Son, watch Viktor does not begin to do your thinking for you. You are a fine, fine player, and Viktor, like so many others, recognizes this. You don't think he is taking liberties now that he has your confidence?"

"No, Papa. He has my best intentions at heart and keeps me out of trouble." He raised the goblet and simulated drinking, although it was empty. That last sentence had almost revealed too much and he wondered if they saw he was blushing.

They walked on past the housing estate out of earshot of the music from the dance. They had walked silently for nearly a mile in the dark. It was his last evening with her before the six-month tour, and this fact had saddened them. Words, though unnecessary, came as the inevitable consequence of their stroll. "How do I know you'll be all right? I worry about you all alone in that faraway place. You know what they say about Westerners," Natashe said. "What if they start a war and you're over there?"

Chekow used this line as an entrée to hold her hand. It felt clammy and warm despite the chill in the air. "Natashe, they won't start a war. I know it. But please don't worry about me. I couldn't enjoy it if I knew you were worrying."

"Then don't go. You know how much I care for you. I've never felt this way about anybody else." Her tone was laced with a possessiveness he'd never noticed before.

They sat down on a wooden bench just off the road. Already at this early hour dew clung to the grainy surface of the split log. Light from the tapestry of stars above reflected upon the individual droplets of the dew. He nervously wrapped an arm around her. "You know I have to go. It's everything I've worked for. If I don't go now, I'll never get anywhere."

"What about here? Is this nowhere, then? What would be so bad about staying here?" she asked coldly. "I intend to."

"Yes, I know, and someday I'll come back and settle down and do all that, but I've got to prove I'm the best player in the world. At least try. Then maybe I could settle here. Not before."

"What do you mean, maybe? You said 'then maybe —'"

He interrupted. "I meant then I will settle back here, but I have to see what I can do."

She saw that he was getting carried away with his convictions. If she wanted to get anywhere before the dance broke up in an hour, she'd have to hurry the pace along. "Do you love me, Aysop?" she asked. She punctuated this with, "darling."

She had never called him that before. He looked at her wide-eyed, as though the question confused him. "Of course I do," he said. "But do you love me?"

"Oh, darling, need you ask?" The truth of the matter was, he did. Being the most beautiful girl in the village, she could pick and choose among the many available young men, and he had always wondered whether she had really cared for him or was simply charmed and beguiled because of his position. He knew he was naïve and that he thought more about backhands and drop shots than romance. But she could still love him. He started awkwardly for her mouth and kissed her sloppily on the lips. He felt that her lips were soft, and so he relaxed his own. The fluttering of her tongue he matched almost instantly, disguising his utter lack of experience. He was mystified at how naturally his reactions came. *What a wonderful way of showing you care for someone*, he thought as he explored the moist recesses of her open mouth with his tongue.

As Natashe had decided with Anna, her best friend, this was her final hurrah. The course she plotted now would have to "bag the prize bull or risk losing it in the field of heifers beyond the gate." (Living on a farm had influenced her rhetoric.) No, it was all or nothing. She would quite bluntly seduce him and hope he enjoyed it enough to come back later for more. Then they would marry. She had it all planned. He was naïve, true, and hellbent on tennis. But he was also considerate, well spoken, and good-looking. The fact that he was Russia's number-one tennis player and destined to a life of luxury didn't hurt either.

She withdrew her head to speak. He kissed awkwardly at the retreating lips. She told herself to relax. Although they hadn't done much in the way of sex for the five months they'd been together, she hadn't expected him to be quite so inexperienced. She forced a smile. Her arms parted.

"Natashe," he said, exhaling. His groping hands made for her breasts and he began fondling them wildly. She pulled up the sweater and brought his head closer in the hope that his lips might be more gentle than his hands. She jerked backward in reacting to the feel of his capped teeth on her nipple. Then she slipped off the bench, taking him with her, and landed on a stone on her buttocks. It took her a moment to assess which was worse, the lacerated nipple or the bruised left cheek. She felt like crying but instead pulled him on top of her. "Oh, Aysop, you're so good!" she cried, capitalizing on the tears already in her eyes.

Aysop had never felt quite so possessed by any one emotion. He had to have her, and soon, before he exploded in his trousers. Tears continued to seep from her large eyes as she imagined what the mud was doing to her new woolen skirt. She considered jumping up and running away, and she might have, had he not been on top of her. "Get off for a second," she said angrily. He moved to his knees, almost castrating himself with the suddenly cramped erection. He watched, mesmerized with glee, while she threw back the skirt and jerked down her underwear. The reverberations of his heartbeat in his head drowned out any sound of her words. Sign language would do nicely.

His pants crumpled to his knees. Frantically, he stripped down the undershorts. He found they were stuck so he ripped at them with all his strength. A great tearing noise preceded his groan as he maneuvered himself into the warm orifice. He ejaculated immediately. She kicked him off and wriggled out away from under him, feeling his seed as it leaked from her onto her thighs. She was crying.

"That was wonderful, Natashe," he said between audible swallows of air. "Marry me."

"Oh, dearest, when?" He was even more naïve than she thought.

The dark stranger closed the door partway behind him and moved straight to the bed. Unceremoniously, he withdrew the cumbersome automatic from his sport coat and attached a silencer in a half twist. By the time Vladimir saw it, it was too late.

He awoke with the alien sensation of a gun barrel in his mouth. "Huh? What is the meaning . . . ?" his fat terrified mouth managed to say before the gloved finger contracted and forced him to swallow two bullets. Traces of his once shrewd mind splattered in crude chunks upon the headboard. His neck arched in a tight spasm and he died.

The two beside him, his partners for the night, were not so lucky. Their deaths followed the gesture of a struggle their instincts insisted upon. The first to rise, a slender blond woman, sprang up and ran directly for the door to the sauna. He shot her once as she turned. A spot the size of an American dime appeared on her suntanned breast. A space the size of a dollar bill opened up on her back as the dumdum bullet exploded. She sank down onto the thick pile carpet.

His lingering eye paused to examine the fur triangle located within the larger triangle of her bikini line. Her insides were showing, glistening warm in the hot summer air.

The muscular youth was on his feet tearing at the lock on the sliding terrace door. Vladimir, in his infinite insecurity, had kept it double-locked at all times. The man raised the gun, then dropped it again, granting the naked man a short reprieve. He dared not shoot lest he break the window and alert the other guests in the hotel. Moving casually on the toes of his rubber shoes, he signaled for the youth to back away. The boy screamed and dropped into a squat; he was still before the glass doors. The man walked by him to the door and flicked the lock. The door slid open. He bowed pompously and gestured with an open hand for the naked man to take his leave.

Suspiciously, the naked bodybuilder rose. Three shots hit him as he entered the rectangle of glassless space, bursting an artery in his heart.

Smoke languished from the barrel of the gun as he held it up. He felt its powerful heat as he kissed it. He holstered it and moved onto his haunches to drag the body back into the room. This was difficult, as the man was heavy but he managed. A pail of tap water was thrown over the entrails on the iron railing outside the sliding door. He closed the door and drew the curtains.

He lifted the phone and dialed a number from memory. His eyes rested on one of the original holes in the dead woman. One put there by nature. "What a waste," he whispered. The phone rang four times. He spoke first in perfect French: "I have talked with Vladimir. He has seen it my way. Sadly, so have his two bedmates. Let's celebrate." He hung up. One cursory glance about the room. Then he left as quietly as he had arrived.

Viktor was in suite 17 at the opposite end of the

same ground-floor wing. While the assassin ran a mental picture of his large countryman through his head, he remembered he had only one shell left in the gun. What if Viktor got nasty? he wondered. Then he consoled himself with the knowledge that Viktor was a reasonable man. He had too much to gain to take chances, unlike Vladimir, whose greed had led to an early and forced retirement. *Imagine*, the rangy assassin thought as he glanced at Vladimir, *risking it all for two million American dollars*. He could have had quadrupled that in only half a year if he'd waited. Silly, greedy, little dead man. A soldier of fortune who had lost it all.

Viktor climbed stiffly out of bed. He drew the curtains and glanced at the Rolex on his huge wrist. Five-forty-five? What was the meaning of this intrusion? He still had one full hour of rest. What imbecile had awakened him? He slid the seersucker robe over his giant hairy shoulders and pulled the sash around a washboard stomach. Despite his fifty-five years, he was the exact same weight and as muscular as he had been thirty years before when he came in second in the French open. Only his height had changed. He had shrunk from the towering six-feet-three he was then to the six-feet-two he was now. He threw the door back, startling the deliberately cool KGB agent. "What do you —" Viktor stopped as he recognized Joseph. The wrinkles etched deeply into his handsome face disappeared as he frowned. "Come in," he said to the assassin.

"Thank you." Joseph preceded him into the room.

Viktor left the door open an inch. "Aren't you going to shut it?"

"You can talk with the door open. Talk," Viktor said shortly.

Joseph's thoughts volleyed between the single shell in the gun and the open door. Reflexively, he obeyed Viktor's command. "Okay Viktor, have it your way. I came here this morning to discuss the Wimbledon dossier." Viktor grunted. "Do you know it?"

"You know I do," Viktor said flatly.

"Good. I'm afraid Vladimir knew it, too, and chose to betray his nation in exchange for financial gain." His tone was at once a statement and a question. He looked to Viktor for his reaction. The gray eyes betrayed nothing but the contempt they held for the uninvited visitor. Joseph elaborated: "He was, we understand, preparing to divulge vital information concerning the Wimbledon dossier to members of the Whiplin Company in America. We gather he planned to exchange pieces of information such as who was to be involved and the extent of the scandal. In return, the company would deposit a substantial seven-figure sum in his account in Lichtenstein. Then they would relay the news to the CIA and F.B.I., who would quash the operation before it began."

"So," Viktor said, obliging him with a reply.

"So?" Joseph's frown evaporated into a look of amusement. "My dear Viktor, that would not only defeat our intentions, it would be doubly destructive by undermining the entire point of the operation."

"I don't see the point. Soviet tennis will find its

way to the top, as it has in everything else. It is only a matter of time."

He digested Viktor's words, then spat, "Bah! There is no motivation. We want to win the Olympics, and we do, for with that comes a source of national pride. But tennis is different. The money-hungry West will always vanquish over our pure desire to compete. It will take time before we attain the level of greatness we need . . . I mean *deserve*."

Viktor looked at him. He had suspected something was amiss from the very first time he had met Joseph some months ago. The Soviets were a proud people. There was no need to rig competitions for the sake of hollow achievement. Granted, certain misguided competitors popped the odd hormone pill, and occasionally they took oxygen before their contests. But this was little league compared to the effects of the Wimbledon dossier.

He had seen a sketch of the dossier on some of the top players from the West; a dossier so replete with lies and deceit and choreographed half truths that he had contemplated going to the authorities himself to report it, if only to save face for Russia. Russia was not behind this, not even the KGB, he suspected, but some other self-motivated force he could not identify.

"It is not, I'm afraid, an issue for debate," Joseph continued. "We are proceeding as scheduled. Either they withdraw from the competition, or we release the Wimbledon dossier to the world press. And that, Viktor, will bring an untimely though deserved end to the capitalists of Whiplin and the reputation of tennis in the West." Joseph withdrew a cigarette from his shirt pocket and tapped it against his gloved hand. He stared at Viktor, then lit it. He offered the pack. "They're Cuban, very nice blend." Viktor shook his head. "Oh, I forgot, always the athlete."

Joseph flicked the ash provocatively on the carpet. "I must say that I am relieved to hear you've been sensible; otherwise, it might have been very unpleasant for you. Just ask Vladimir. There is one further thing, however, that I forgot to mention during our last meeting. The Crimea racquet will be made available to Chekow tomorrow. See that he practices with it immediately." Joseph licked his lips. "He will use it to win Wimbledon."

Viktor felt a sharp pain in his stomach. He swallowed. "That is impossible. He has just five days before the championship. It is too much to ask that he change for this tournament. Let him wait until Houston," Viktor said, meaning the Houston, Texas, indoor championships three weeks after Wimbledon.

"Nothing is impossible, Viktor. You've proven that. It's not every man who can take a Russian peasant and turn him into the second-seeded player at the most prestigious tennis championship in the world. But you have. And in a very short time." His smile returned. "Come now, I don't think we ask too much. Indeed, we're making it very easy for you by taking away most of the competition. All you have to do is win Wimbledon with the Crimea racquet. Then . . ." he hesitated.

Viktor filled in the gap, as was expected of him. "Then what?"

Joseph eyed him closely. "What better gift can we offer you and Chekow than that which allows you the luxury of life? Then you live."

Viktor heard the door slam and went over to open the sliding doors to air the smoke from his room. He sat down on the silk-embroidered bedspread and thought of Russia and cried.

Chapter Four

Joseph released the clip of the Smith & Wesson. He removed the spent shell casings into his hand and set them beside the final unused slug. Using a manila envelope from the bureau drawer, he held the open end flat against the bureau top, while he scooped in the evidence of the shooting. He added the leftover shell as he habitually did, yielding to his superstitious nature. From a paper carton in the back of the same drawer, he took a fresh clip and jammed it into the empty automatic. A snap of the wrist and the gun was locked and loaded. He kept the safety off. He knew the split-second wasted to disengage the steel button could distinguish between a battle won and lost. There were too many close calls in his business as it was. Besides, he thought as he refit the gun revolver into the virgin leather of his shoulder sling, one was never really safe. The leather squeaked as it accepted the automatic. He stepped out of the windbreaker and confronted the full-length mirror in the room, wearing only the holstered gun, a black turtleneck and trousers, and a pair of rubber-soled loafers he had picked up at a local shop. He stood perfectly still, then altered positions with terrific speed. The barrel of the gun was now poised at the heart of his alter ego in the glass. His gloved hand fondled the half-moon trigger with a reverence most men reserved for a beautiful woman. "Bang! Bang!" he said aloud.

The job had gone well and without a hitch. Vladimir had it coming. He knew the stakes and had chosen to gamble and got burned. A smile passed over Joseph's clean-shaven face. Vladimir's expression the moment before the dumdums drove home, he mused, had given new meaning to the phrase "A picture is worth a thousand words." In Vladimir's case it was worth a fucking million. It was at times like these that he truly appreciated the devastating power of the simple hollow-tipped shell.

The dumdum bullet, banned by the Geneva Convention, had originated in the town of the same name in India during the heat of the British Raj. To combat the seemingly endless onslaught of opium-crazed Indian patriots during the wars, the British had been forced to develop a weapon more powerful than the conventional bullet, but one that could still be fitted into existing weaponry. Enter the dumdum. The soft hollow-tipped shells, instead of passing through the victims, exploded on impact, savaging whole limbs and often killing victims instantly. What earlier might have constituted a minor injury now meant death. Advances in technology had voided the question of accuracy. He could hit a goat's belly in full stride at seventy-five yards.

He grabbed a beer from the refrigerator and turned the air conditioner on full blast. He lay down on the bed fully clothed and sipped listlessly at the Kronenbourg. After a minute, he lit a cigarette and filled his lungs with the ethereal bitterness of the filter-free Gitane. His was a good life, he reflected. How many Russians rebounded from a KGB dishonorable discharge to a position of such power and prosperity? Not many, he thought. He'd been impetuous, and they'd thrown him out of the organization and blacklisted him from any other government position. So what? He didn't need them. Shit! He'd proven that. He didn't need the wife and three kids who left him as a consequence of his disgrace and sudden poverty. Fuck them all. He had been broken and personally had pasted the pieces back together.

He drew a lungful of smoke and flicked the ash into the ceramic plate resting on his crotch. How was he to know the American was one of them? He'd had no indication, no intimation whatsoever from his superiors. Big deal, he had disposed of him in a back street in Moscow. At least it hadn't made the wire service to the West, as so many of these fucking things did. Joseph remembered the assignment that had turned out to be his last. The tough-looking American had conceded so easily. Almost as if he welcomed or expected it. The look of callous indifference exuding from the man's soft brown eyes as Joseph held the gun to his temple was evidence enough at the time. It had confirmed Joseph's suspicions: the American was obviously a mark and had to be eliminated. Everybody made mistakes, he thought, exhaling the cigarette smoke.

Then they had notified him right out of the fucking blue. A *non sequitur* diversion from his daily jaunt to the breadline near the warehouse on the river. Would he meet them for drinks that afternoon? Did Joseph know the address. Yes, of course he did. He had lived across the street from it for each of the five years he held his Internal Media Affairs post with the KGB. Could he be there? Bet your left nut, he could. He could be anywhere for a price, any price. Just say "Jump, comrade," and he'd ask how high.

There were four of them in the small high-ceilinged room. A haze of smoke hung in the warm air and dulled the shine of the seventeenth-century oak paneling. A bottle of vodka, the good stuff used for export, was before his place at the table, and next to that was a cut-glass tumbler. Ice reflected the overhead lighting from its berth in the silver bucket. Joseph entered cautiously, grasping his frayed cap between soiled hands. He wondered if his destitution showed. Could they see the vinyl belt and how he'd been forced to pull it tighter by two knife-inflicted notches to assuage the pangs of hunger?

"Have a seat, Joseph," the largest of the four said. The tone was relaxing. "Have a cigarette." The man used a ruler and pushed the pack across the large walnut table to him. Joseph pulled the paper from the packet and loosened one. His fingers shook as he tried to light it. "Rolf," the large man commanded. A small man with glasses and thinning hair crossed the room and extended a tiny cube of gold. A two-inch flame leaped from the cube. Joseph fired life into the stick of tobacco.

The big one (whom he'd later come to know as Popotov) took a pencil from his coat pocket and touched it to his lips unthinkingly. "Take the pack." Joseph took it and stuffed it into the pocket of his greatcoat. His eyes remained on the men, studying them from left to right. The big man raised a large hand and poured from an imaginary bottle. The small man, Rolf, interpreted the pantomime. He filled Joseph's glass and returned to his seat.

"It is said you were a good man before you wasted that American and they had you expelled. Is this so?"

Joseph tilted the glass to his parched lips. The sting of the vodka relaxed him immediately. He took the liberty of pouring another. The big man smiled and condoned the initiative. "I was good then, and I still am," Joseph said quietly.

Popotov nodded. "I bet you are. In fact, I'm sure of it. That's why we brought you here today. We'd like to employ you." Joseph's eyebrows rose in reaction. He sucked in hard on the cigarette. His hand was no longer trembling as he started on his second drink. "You see, we've got a problem. We three gentlemen have a problem. And as you're fundamentally equipped both mentally and physically to handle our problem, we would like to hire you, like old times. A mission. Just name a price and then perhaps we'll discuss your capacity."

"In dollars?" Anything requiring his services would be of an international nature; hence his request for dollars. He could exchange them on the lucrative black market at fifty times the fixed rate.

"Of course." Popotov raised his head and regarded the man with a look of anticipation.

"Two hundred," Joseph said tersely. He monitored their expressions. They looked at one another uncertainly. The fourth man, Rolf, was kept perceptibly at bay to one side. Probably only the secretary, Joseph decided. He waited for their answer.

Popotov hadn't dropped his stare from the thin unshaven man. He had already decided. "Very well. Two hundred it is. I'll see the money is kept on account in Bern. When you provide us with the goods, you will be informed as to the account number. Will the dollar equivalent of two hundred thousand in Swiss francs be acceptable?" It was all Joseph could do to nod. He had asked for two hundred dollars. They had automatically multiplied that by one thousand. His hand was trembling again as he reached for the vodka. "Very well." Popotov withdrew an envelope from inside his well-tailored tweed jacket and flopped it onto the table. In a separate motion he slid it across so it landed against the vodka bottle.

"Get some new clothes and a bath. We will meet

again in two days' time. There is a little matter of a trial session for you. Nothing major, of course. However, we've got to be sure our money is not foolishly invested. Do you have a weapon?"

"*Nyet*."

"I'll make sure you get one. We have booked you into a rooming house off Molotov Square. The address is in the envelope along with your instructions. See that you go there, have a good meal, and catch up on your rest. We will call for you. I would advise you upon purchase of your clothes not to go out of the rooming house. The landlady, Mrs. Petrolovik, has been instructed to see to your needs."

One of the three principals squirmed in his chair. He ran a hand over his toupee and said to Popotov, "Ask him about the files."

Popotov turned and addressed him matter-of-factly. "Oh, yes, Joseph, during your function as Undersecretary to Internal Media Affairs Director Volchinko, was Aysop Chekow, the tennis player, involved in just one incident of murder?"

The question was a coy one. They were picking his brain and he knew it but didn't give a shit. The old exchange of values. "It was just one incident but two died. Onegin and that trainer fellow," Joseph said, providing them with confirmation of what they had only speculated on.

"Then Viktor Godon merely cooperated in the coverup?"

"Of course. But with our approval."

"Then he didn't kill anybody, he just assisted Chekow?" Popotov asked.

"That's correct."

"Fine." Popotov took a cigar from a long silver case in his jacket and cut the tip with a device on the case. He tapped it on the tabletop, deep in thought. He remembered Joseph and addressed him as he lit up. "Thank you, Joseph. We will see you Thursday as arranged." Joseph reacted to the finality in the big man's words. He rose slowly and, for wont of something better to do, bowed. He backed out of the room.

Popotov turned to his two partners. He withdrew the cigar from his mouth. "Leopold, Alex, does that answer your questions?" It had been a painstaking task tracing Joseph. It was difficult enough trying to find anyone without the authorities' knowledge in Moscow. That Joseph happened to be an ex-KGB man complicated things all the more. But for a price they had located him and contracted him. The two hundred thousand might appear an exorbitant amount on the surface, but in the brief seven minutes they had addressed him, he had relinquished information of little value to anyone else, but priceless to them. With Chekow and Viktor in their pockets, they could proceed as planned.

It took Joseph time to recover from the shock of the encounter. It was all behind him now — the deprivation, the cold sleepless nights in the doss houses of the capital. He stood in the entrance hall to the fine building and rifled through the envelope. He counted the money slowly and savored the dry touch of each crisp ten-ruble note. He counted out fifty of them, then returned the notes to the envelope and laboriously repeated the whole counting process. Five hundred rubles. If it had been a hoax, a dream, or whatever, it didn't matter. He could last two months with superior food and lodging, plus buy the new clothes he so desperately needed. Tears welled up in his bloodshot eyes.

Standing in the doorway of a café, he exulted in the knowledge of the delicious food available within its doors. His short breaths frosted in the chilly October air. He wiped his nose with the back of one of his fingerless gloves. Determined to exact a reposed façade, he managed the entire three helpings of beef goulash and fried black bread without a single drink. He sat back and crossed his legs and picked at his yellow teeth with a toothpick. When he paid the bill some twenty-five minutes later, he left a gratuity of two rubles to the big-breasted waitress. She opened the door and watched him as he moved down the street. He pivoted, took in her accommodating smile, and just laughed and walked on.

He chose a plain flannel suit with an extra pair of trousers, two cotton shirts, some socks, underwear, and a pair of real leather shoes. The overcoat he bought was of a particularly heavy fiber and useful for insulating him against the icy temperatures of Moscow that he knew so well. The bland cut of the cloth and the dark color were intended to make him as inconspicuous as possible. He discarded his cap for the type of warm fur muffler he had worn during his properous days. He paid cash and left with the bundle under his arm.

Once installed into the small but tidy room of the rooming house, he washed in the communal baths. Thoughtfully, she had provided him with all the necessary toiletries. He used them to shave and clean his matted hair. He toweled briskly and stopped to admire his lean and hungry torso in the mirror. The muscles had worn away, but their foundations still lingered. Two weeks back on the exercise regime practiced by the KGB and they would fill out. He wrapped the towel around his waist and knotted it. Forcing open the window, he nonchalantly fed the filthy clothes into the frosty night air. He closed the window and went downstairs to sleep.

Two days later a large black car collected him and headed west across town. In his fresh clothes he was no longer the groveling little beggar they had plucked from the anonymity of the breadline. Sitting there in the thick blanket of his overcoat, smoking a Cuban cigarette, he could have been one of them. He took a final drag on the half-smoked cigarette and crushed it out extravagantly in the ashtray on the armrest. Only three days before, he'd have killed a man for that still-potent stub of tobacco. *How quickly we forget*, he thought and sighed. He corrected his posture and sat erect.

Another man had replaced the secretary, Rolf. This one was a youngish fat man with a near bald head and a pleasant face whom he would come to know as Vladimir. Vladimir pushed down the turn signal and maneuvered the car off the main road into a residential district.

Popotov was seated beside Joseph. He leaned over

and removed a leather valise from the floor of the car. He laid it on his lap and unzipped it. When it flopped open, Joseph recognized the sleek blackness of the MIG .357 automatic. Elongated clip. Nine .357 Parabellum shells with spring-sensitive firing pin. Adaptable to silencer with no loss of accuracy. He knew it well. He had used it in his ill-fated execution of the American four years earlier. "Take it," Popotov ordered.

He filled his hand with the cool block of steel. It felt nice, so very nice. He brought the gun close and examined it. His gloved hand caressed its hard lines. He depressed the release and caught the clip as it slid out on a well-lubricated track. He set this down and grasped the manual chassis and snapped it back, catching the ejected slug in the flick of a hand. Popotov drew back a piece of felt in the valise. "Here, you'll need this."

Joseph saw the cone of the silencer. He picked it up and snapped it in a half twist onto the barrel of the automatic. "Nice," he said softly. The others were watching him curiously. Even Vladimir eyed him through quick glimpses in the mirror. He positioned the clip into the track and slammed it in loudly with the fat of his hand. Two of the men in the car jumped nervously. "It's been a long time," he said to Popotov. A trace of a smile decorated his lips. His stare grew level with his employers.

With one finger Popotov calmly redirected the position of the barrel away from his stomach. *Very smooth*, Joseph thought. *Didn't even blink.* "We'll be letting you off at the building up ahead." Joseph craned his neck and caught a glance of the red brick high-rise on his right. "You're to proceed directly to the sixth floor and follow through until you've come to the accounts department in room 605. There are three offices inside. Choose the northernmost one, or the one to your extreme left. There will be a gentleman seated there at an inclined desk. He is built similarly to you and wears tinted box-frame glasses. See that he is eliminated. He won't be expecting you, so you'll be all right. He is unarmed." Popotov looked up at the skyscraper.

The car cruised to a stop. Joseph could see Vladimir's leather-covered fingers fidgeting on the polished wood steering wheel. The others, including Popotov, were looking away. If this was a setup, he thought, he'd prove them wrong by eluding it. They had chosen the right man for the job. Until the money started rolling in, he had absolutely nothing to lose. He tucked the automatic into a space in the overcoat and waited for further instructions.

Popotov looked at Joseph with an expression of sheer disdain. He might have been looking right through him. "That is all. When you've finished and it's successful, we'll find you." He got out of the car and walked calmly up the marble stairs to the big red building. Back inside the car Popotov gestured to Vladimir. "Drive on."

Joseph turned at the head of the flight of stairs and paused to light a cigarette. He cupped his gloved hands as he lit up. His eyes followed the trail of the black car until it turned a corner at a traffic light.

"Hold it. Excuse me, sir." Joseph felt the nerves pop in his thin frame. Then all at once he remembered the feeling and relaxed. He was fully prepared to shoot the elderly guard and walk away from the assignment, leaving it for another time. The old man pointed to a sign overhead. "I'm sorry, sir. No smoking once you are inside. The chemicals." He gazed at the block lettering of the sign.

"Sorry," Joseph said pleasantly. He crushed the cigarette in the dish of sand near the elevator and in one fluid motion pressed the extinguished cigarette into his palm. He entered the elevator, waited for the doors to close, then deposited the stub into the pocket of the coat. Not many locals could afford the expensive blend of the Cuban cigarette he smoked.

It occurred to him, as he stood there waiting to be deposited at his destination, what the guard had said about chemicals. He once knew a man who worked in a petrochemical plant. But that was long ago. The thoughts left his mind as he sauntered out of the now temporarily disabled elevator. In his pocket beside the Cuban butt lay the fuse to the elevator, where it would safely rest until he needed it again.

He walked knowingly in full strides through the opened door of room 605. The deliberate appearance of his gait evoked a minimum of interest from any of the half dozen clerks seated about the room. Joseph turned northward to his left and pushed open the glass door to the accounts office. Something struck him as unusual as he entered the small ten-by-twelve-foot room. Then it came to him and he grinned. They were smart sons-of-bitches, he thought. He'd give them that. He pointed the muzzle of the automatic at the chest of the lean dark-haired man stooped over the drafting desk; he hadn't even turned around yet.

"Olga, bring me the papers from . . ." the man said trustingly and turned away from the paper-littered desk in time to be perforated by the hail of rapid-fire slugs. The chair slid backward until he slammed into a filing cabinet behind him. His glasses askew, he slumped against the metal cabinets and stayed that way. Joseph studied the man's face for the time it took him to holster the automatic in the coat.

He thought of Popotov during his descent in the elevator and smiled again. He nodded "good day" to the guard and pushed through the revolving doors, still smiling. He had never liked his brother much anyway.

They had traveled north, so he headed south and moved openly along the main street. He had gone two miles before Olga, his brother's secretary, dis-covered the fruit of his labors and sounded the alarm. They passed him going south in the limousine and took him to lunch.

For two hours Chekow practiced his service against Lorsch, the Czech who was also in St. Tropez preparing for the tournament. Lorsch wasn't much, really, but he served as an ample sparring partner with his consistent shots and above-average returns of service. And at number forty-seven in the world, he could conceivably pull something off at Wimbledon. It was dubious, as Lorsch wasn't seeded, and even more dubious now, twelve days after his humiliating defeat to a fifteen-year-old at the Stella Artois tournament at Queen's Club. But normally Lorsch was good on grass. For this reason Chekow practiced against him regularly before Wimbledon.

Chekow wiped the sweat from his forehead and out of his eyes. The sun was bright this morning and the Mediterranean breeze was nonexistent. Usually there was the slight hint of the mistral rolling off the bay at this hour, and it usually picked up steadily throughout the day. Like Viktor, it had yet to materialize.

Behind the green of the three grass courts, one-half mile down the slope lay the Gulf of St. Tropez. It was alive with the activity of one hundred tiny boats all tacking toward some prearranged destination. The sun gleamed across the vast stretch of water, making it difficult from where he stood to see even Port Grimaud, the next significant landmark.

They had rented the innocuous stucco apartment for the second year running because of its practical position adjacent to three of the dozen grass courts in St. Tropez.

Viktor had always preferred the Côte d'Azur to other parts of Europe at this time of year. The weather was good and the temperature was hot enough to ensure a tough workout and good conditioning for Wimbledon. They had stayed here once last year before Wimbledon and once already this year before the French Open, in which Chekow had defeated McLaren in five sets. Viktor saw this as a good omen and decided to return to St. Tropez. What he hadn't mentioned was his penchant for the banana daiquiris at the Byblos, where he stayed, and the high quality of the girls available at the Papaguya where he drank. The perks of the trade.

As overseer of the generous expense account allotted by the Soviet Sporting Federation to him and Chekow, Viktor could afford to live well. True to the tradition of Soviet athletes participating in professional sports, no prize money was accepted. Not overtly. Instead, all traveling expenses, cost of equipment, and food were paid for by the committee of the tournament, provided, of course, that these costs did not exceed the prize money earned. Or, in keeping with the spirit of the Soviets, the prize money not earned. In other words, one could have a fuck of a good time while touring.

During the past two years, since Chekow's unwavering ascent to champion status, Viktor had enjoyed a subsequent rise in living standards the likes of which he had never dreamed. It was estimated that in the last two years Chekow had won nearly four hundred twenty-five thousand U.S. dollars in straight prize money. With that fountain of money to draw from and put against expenses, Viktor could order a lot of daiquiris.

The catch was — and there always was a catch — unless he was prepared to collect receipts every time they stepped into a cab or had a beer at a passing bar, he would eat into the lump sum allotted by the state. In appreciation for his progress with Chekow, the Soviets had doubled the allotment each year. But for every ruble spent in some sidewalk bistro, that was one less he could deposit in the two bank accounts he maintained in Zurich. One for himself and another for Chekow. Chekow didn't know it, but he was worth nearly ninety-thousand dollars, nearly half of Viktor's personal assets.

Among the more obvious attractions of the Byblos Hotel — the haute cuisine, the starlets, the champagne on tap — Viktor had succeeded in establising a lucrative financial arrangement with its manager, Pierre. An extra three thousand dollars, added to the hotel bill and willingly met by the tournament chiefs in question, was divided 50-50. The arrangement allowed Viktor pocket money for his own after-hour escapades. The relationship was so well established, in fact, that he could demand a cash advance upon his arrival at the hotel.

Viktor often recalled that first trip to Zurich when Chekow was playing in an exhibition for some since-forgotten cause. He had been carrying around with him fifteen thousand dollars in cash and another ten thousand in French francs for more than a month. Uncertain about what to do with the cash — as his generous expenses were now being met by the sudden influx of prize money — he had taken a seat at the bar of the hotel restaurant. There beside him was a copy of the French daily, *Le Figaro*. He picked it up and paged through it idly, starting as he always did with the sports section. The lead article for the day, he remembered, dealt with the question of arms proliferation and a limited nuclear war. Limited nuclear war? Farther along the page another article speculated on the Islamic bomb. Page three reported that India had achieved nuclear capability and had begun undersea testing in the Indian Ocean. He had lost his appetite by the time he put the paper aside and assessed the future of mankind all the way to the bank. There would be somewhere to run during the inevitable confrontation when East met West. The Swiss currency in his newly opened accounts would enable both him and Chekow to run there.

Viktor pulled the rented Citroën between the space in the bracken, then got out and reached inside for a tennis racquet and basket of balls. He noted the conspicuous absence of any breeze and discarded the jersey of his track suit on the seat of the car.

"Volley and follow through. Attack that net, it's your net!" he yelled, as he had a thousand times before and would probably yell a thousand times more.

Chekow's sudden smile turned to a look of bemusement. "Five days to Wimbledon and you're three hours late?"

"Keep your shirt on," Viktor said in the cool smooth voice of the eternal patriarch. "That just makes the time we have to practice that much more valuable. So let's get going."

Chekow looked at him peculiarly. Something about his tone was different. He couldn't place it, but the enthusiasm seemed stifled this morning. He walked back to the baseline and watched Viktor slip out of the red track suit pants.

"Good morning, Lorsch. Let's see if you can give this boy a workout today. Let's work on that return of yours," Viktor called. "Limber up with a dozen to each side. Take the net for half of them," he told Chekow. He slid the cover off the aluminum racquet, an "Ibios", made in Yugoslavia and traded within the Soviet bloc. It was okay, but nothing special. Free, if nothing else. He was too old and his reflexes were too slow for him to worry about which racquet he used. The variance between the pounds of evenly displaced pressure meant little to him now that his competition days were over. In Chekow's case, he could understand why he chose the metal American model. Whiplin knew its tennis racquets.

Chekow lofted the yellow ball up and behind his head by eight inches. He stepped into it with his full weight. The ball spat over the net and disappeared behind a cloud of chalk. "Ace!" Viktor shouted. "Next time let's see it inside the square. Chalk is for artists."

Chekow nodded to Viktor and stepped back this time to the left of the service mark. His right hand repeated the movement of the ball, while his left hand swung around using the leverage of his six-foot-two frame to its best advantage. The ball left an instantaneous indentation in the grass within the square and eluded the path of Lorsch's racquet by a tenth of a second. "Ace," Viktor called calmly. Then he added sarcastically, "Not too bad. How about if next time you take the benefit of the doubt and get that ass of yours to net?" Chekow glanced at Viktor coldly and smiled inside. That was more like it. That was the Viktor he knew.

They had practiced together six hours with a break for lunch. This, combined with the two Chekow had already put in before Viktor's arrival, totaled one long day. Perhaps, Chekow thought, that was why they were eating somewhere new this evening. Somewhere nice. He had passed the restaurant, La Ponche, many times while footslogging after hours through the streets of the picturesque town. Chekow avoided St. Tropez during its peak hours between nine in the morning and nine at night. As crowds went, those who flocked to the resort town were as rude and uncivilized as the village was quaint. Never before had he met such unattractive, loud people. It seemed to him a sort of Mecca for the social pariahs of the world. With his newfound fame, particularly in this week before Wimbledon, he found the crowds especially offensive. Even the exceptionally ignorant and uninformed had recognized him and badgered him for a reaction. Viktor's adeptness at firmly ushering these people away had saved Chekow from marring his talented hands on the teeth of more than one heckler. His usual relaxed nature became defensive and sometimes he felt himself looking for fights to vent his anger.

He sat back and nursed the one glass of wine Viktor allowed him on nights before a tournament. The strips of yellow bulbs strung along the canopy above them fluttered and sank in reaction to the mistral, which had finally come. The outdoor restaurant had always been his favorite. The way it was nestled within the two houses of period architecture with a ruin of a stone wall separating them from the sea reminded him of home. Much could be said for Western life, he surmised, yet none of it could compete with the secure grace of history. Unlike most parts of the West, Russia abounded in long-surviving customs and a heritage traceable thousands of years to the migration of the first Slavs from Prussia and the Ukraine.

Viktor poured himself another glass of the remarkably potable wine, then leaned over and emptied the bottle into Chekow's glass. His resonant voice interrupted the cacophony of cutlery and conversation. "You're ready for this one. I can see it in your practice."

"Yes, I can win."

The waiter arrived and served their food. Chekow had chosen avocado prawns and what Westerners termed chicken Kiev, his favorite.

"*Encore un bouteille*," Viktor said to the waiter, who bowed humbly, stole a glance at Chekow, and backed away. "The bloody waiters in this country," Viktor said, "all fairies." Chekow laughed. His angelic good looks had made him prey to the many homosexuals who frequented the coast. "Of course you could very easily win," Viktor said, returning to tennis. "You've proven that twice when you beat McLaren. Wimbledon will be no different if you keep your nerve."

"I was ready even last year. If I hadn't gone out

early I could have won. I was thinking too much about Natashe maybe," Chekow said.

"This happens. Women have a way of taking one's mind off the more pressing things of life," Viktor said philosophically.

Chekow rolled the wine around in his glass. "Were you ever married?" The effect of the wine had allowed him to squeeze out a question he'd been meaning to ask for years.

Viktor appraised his food. Finally, he said, "Many times in spirit. Once in the ways of the mosque." He stared at Chekow. "We are too free-spirited to tie ourselves down to any one woman. Life has too much to offer. You should be relieved that Natashe saw fit to marry that sailor. You and I share many things, and one of these is the wandering heart." He struck the area of his heart for emphasis.

Unthinkingly, Chekow finished the glass of wine. He felt a slight tinge of remorse when he realized he'd drunk his ration. "Good wine," he said stupidly.

Viktor regretted mentioning Natashe. His voice came with an added pitch meant to distract Chekow. "Always when you come to France when you are older, always buy the Corton Charlemagne. Sixty-nine was very good. Should you be poor, the Bandol Rouge is also drinkable." Earlier Chekow had linked the bottle on the table to the wine list before him. One hundred twenty francs? Was it possible? It wasn't his birthday, nor Viktor's. Maybe somebody died, he thought. "Did you ever wonder what you might had been if it weren't for tennis?" Viktor asked. He arranged his calamari before him and began to cut it.

What an unusual question, Chekow thought. "No. A hockey player maybe. I don't know, I've never thought about it."

"No, not necessarily sports. Supposing tomorrow you had to find a job, then what would it be?"

"In Russia?" he asked through a mouthful of avocado. Viktor nodded. He lay down the spoon and shrugged. "That's a good question. I don't know . . . maybe work in the mill with my father. I'd hate it, but there's not much I'm qualified to do." The stark truth in these words demoralized him some. He honestly had never considered the question. Wouldn't tennis go on forever?

"No, you wouldn't. I know you, and you're too much a tennis player to be a mill worker." Viktor started on his filet mignon. "No," he said between chews, "you'd be coaching like me, or maybe doing public relations for Soviet tennis. Why did you say mill worker?" The thought of young Chekow toiling on the production line in a paper mill had depressed him. His prodigy must never be allowed to sink to such levels. Even the fate that he had been promised for refusing to cooperate with the Wimbledon dossier might prove more humane.

"It's the first thing that came to mind. There's no point in thinking about it yet. It's not like it's all going down the toilet tomorrow." He laughed.

Viktor just nodded and Chekow thought he detected a look of compassion in the narrowed gray eyes of his coach. The waiter returned with a fresh bottle of wine. He stabbed it with the pneumatic corkscrew and withdrew the cork easily. Viktor thanked him and waved him away without tasting it. He poured the half-inch of cork recesses into his own glass and moved forward to fill Chekow's, ignoring his look of surprise.

There were always the burgeoning Swiss accounts, Viktor thought. He filled the glasses and knocked back the wine. But what good would those accounts be without out-and-out defection from Russia? Lately this had seemed the only solution to his disillusionment with his homeland. If Joseph spoke the truth, he decided, his native land held no place for him.

Although he had nearly nine weeks to grasp the implications of what Joseph had said since their drinking session in Monte Carlo, Viktor still didn't know for sure. Despite his instinct to disbelieve Joseph's words, some of what he said made sense. Russia was in a bad way both domestically and on an international level. This had become apparent since he first started giving credence to the articles in the Western press two years earlier. The troubles in Poland had never seemed nearly so acute when reported in *Pravda*. Similarly with Afghanistan. Could it be that the Russian-backed Kamal regime was really turning into a Soviet Vietnam? And the massive subsidies for Castro's government. He had never known quite how much aid was being funneled into that tiny country. Yet even more startling were the reports of widespread social and economic unrest in his own country. This he had viewed empirically on a small scale in the major cities, but could people really be starving in the eastern regions? Was the harvest that bad?

Joseph's claim that the Soviet Union was embarking on an international economic program more powerful than he could ever fathom gathered weight beside these other manifestations. Spearheading this quasi-capitalist assault on the West was the marketing of sports equipment. As the Soviets already possessed the capabilities to manufacture goods of this nature on a massive scale, sporting goods would logically lead the way. An assault on the American monolith of the automobile industry would come next, and, after this, basic military hardware and processed foods. It had all been worked out, Joseph said.

The proceeds from this assault on Western industry would help deliver the Soviet state and its people from the abject destitution it was destined to know. Russia would besiege the world with cheap subsidized goods that would soak up some of the Western riches, while forging life into an effete and expiring ideology. The price for failing to espouse the vital program would result in the death with which Joseph had threatened them. It was that simple; it meant that much.

Such a concession to the ways of capitalism, Viktor thought, would certainly mark a gradual end to Marxism and its credibility. "Could it be all going to hell?" he asked aloud.

"What?" Chekow asked.

Viktor dismissed the question with a wave of his fork. He ate on, although he had lost his appetite, and forced himself to think of tennis. "How is Lorsch looking forward to next week?"

Chekow set down his empty wineglass. Astonishingly, Viktor refilled it. Chekow tried hard not to let his appreciation show. "He's always optimistic. You've got to be when you're at his ranking. I would have said he had a chance before Queen's Club. He lost in three sets to a little kid."

"I know. That's not going to help him much," Viktor replied flatly. He emptied the bottle and, by raising it, alerted the waiter. He washed down the last piece of food with the dregs of wine.

Chekow made a conscious effort to rally the desultory conversation. "Did you see there's an airline hostess convention in town? I think they came down from Paris on holiday. Some were carrying tennis racquets. Do you think we should offer them free lessons?" Chekow winked. When he got no reaction from his coach, he tilted the contents of the full wineglass into his mouth. His cheeks puffed momentarily before swallowing. He allowed his gaze to wander through the restaurant and made eye contact with a middle-aged brunette and then her daughter. Chekow smiled and burped and tasted avocado.

Another bottle materialized on the table and Viktor distributed its contents between them. "Thanks, Vik," Chekow said cheekily. His words echoed in his head and he realized he was mildly drunk and laughed belatedly.

Viktor watched him with a tolerant eye, then turned curiously to examine the object of Chekow's interest. He saw the pair of women watching them from their table. A balding male, whom Viktor rightly took for the husband and father, respectively, had his head dipped over a bowl of bouillabaisse. The older and more painted of the two women reacted to the gaze of the handsome silver-haired Russian. She batted an eyelash his way and imitated a landed fish as she puckered her fluorescent lips. He'd seen whores with more class. He returned to Chekow grinning. A little comic relief did him good. Another glass of the red elixir to ease his mind and he said to Chekow, "When was the last time you got laid?"

Chekow almost choked on the wine moving down his throat. He backhanded the purple smear from his lips and smiled. "I don't know — a couple weeks, maybe. I forget, actually," he said, trying to sound casual about his limited encounters. He could count his conquests for the year on two fingers.

Viktor saw through his bluff but ignored it. "I think however long, it's been too long. It'll do you a world of good. Help your concentration."

Chekow looked away from the face of his coach to the two women. He lingered on the younger one long enough to make his intentions clear. She returned his stare with an expression as subtle as a karate chop. In deference to the call of the wild, the elder woman, Chekow noted, shimmied back in her chair and dropped out. Better one of them got it than neither, she must have concluded with a sigh. "But do you think I can?" Chekow asked him. He hadn't meant for it to sound the way it did. "I mean, of course I can, but will she let me?" Viktor ignored him. Chekow peered over and watched the girl sensuously chewing her meat. He felt an unquenchable heat rise in his shorts.

Viktor stood up slowly. He stretched his long arms. He was in no mood to linger. Relief would come through large doses of a potato derivative that wasn't served here. His copious hand disappeared into a pocket and reappeared with a roll of French francs. He peeled off two notes, then thought about it, and lobbed the entire roll onto the table. "It's been a trying day. I shall leave you to do your own dirty work and start home," he told Chekow. Then he intoned seriously, "We've something very serious to discuss tomorrow, so don't get too torn apart." He held back his smile. "That should see you through. Have a good time for a change, son, you deserve it."

Chekow realized Viktor was leaving. He reached out in a panic and took his arm. "Viktor." Viktor stopped and stepped back. He bent over with one hand on Chekow's shoulder. "Viktor," he slurred, "do you think I might score?"

Viktor crouched forward. The breeze toyed with his hair. He was smiling. "I think, Chekow, if you play your cards right, you'll have both of them on the floor." He slapped Chekow on the back and took off for home via the Papaguya and its prodigious stock of vodkas.

Chapter Five

James awoke feeling weak and drained from the incident in the nightclub bathroom. He judged the time by a wedge of light cutting through the curtains. It was still morning. He drew a hand over sailorgirl and verified the time with his watch. Eight-fifteen; he'd slept for five hours. He could have a leisurely breakfast downstairs and still make it to Hurlingham by nine-thirty. Give or take. He lay back and sank into the pillows. Suddenly, he remembered Pam and craned his neck for a glimpse of her sleeping figure on the opposite end of the king-sized bed.

Upon their return last night she had showered and put on a pair of his pajamas and crawled into bed with them. A sort of sterile *ménage à trois*, he had thought at the time. Explanations were superfluous. All that mattered was that she was safe. James and sailorgirl had listened to Pam's tearful recollection of the orgy, and of how she had been coerced into taking part. It was nothing to be ashamed of, James had said, and recounted a vaguely similar experience of his that had taken place in Monte Carlo not two months previous. In light of this, he told Pam he understood. At least he thought he did. He knew the reputation of women players on the circuit. Christ! Lesbian affairs were commonplace, especially with the infamous Super Six. Part of him found it difficult to comprehend Pam's ignorance on this issue, but he was a man, he told himself, and his perspective was different.

What had surprised him most was the ability of sailorgirl — alias Olivia — to console and comfort Pam. Such a lovely feminine trait, he thought, as he watched his new love comb Pam's long hair and utter the words from which she had drawn her compassion. She was just three months into her sixteenth birthday. Yet Olivia had said all the right things and known what to do.

Unthinkingly, he rechecked his watch and allotted himself five more minutes. Suddenly, he felt the warmth of Olivia's leg as it passed over his knee and draped across his crotch. She edged closer and threw an arm around his chest, hugging him. Their mouths found each other. Conscious of how his breath must be, he drew away and kissed her face quietly. Unlike Janie, his girl friend in America, Olivia had eyes that sparkled at this hour. She rubbed her leg back and forth over him and brought life to his loins. She humped his side slowly and squeezed him in her arms. "I love you," she whispered.

He reacted to the fluttering tongue. His arms reached out and embraced her. He rolled over on his side and pressed his erection against her belly. With his left hand he encircled her breast and worked it. The small pink bud came alive. Her young hips ground into him. He kissed her hard on the lips, then asked, "What about Pam?"

"She's asleep. She won't know." Olivia smiled wanly. "I won't tell if you don't."

He grinned. "Yeah, and I'll show you mine if you show me yours." He held her still and interrupted her stream of kisses. "Move over onto the floor." She obeyed instantly and disappeared over the edge of the mattress. James checked Pam closely. Her tight fetal position and steady respiration indicated she was deeply asleep. He shuffled off the bed carefully and slid up beside Olivia. She caught him around the waist and nuzzled him there. He felt the heat of her tongue. Jesus! She began to stroke him.

"You're leaking," she declared innocently from behind the sparkling eyes.

"I'm aroused," he explained. His hand found her and eased her open. She lay back, still clutching him, and closed her eyes.

"Oh, God, it's nice," she said loudly. He quieted her with a cupped hand, while she pumped against the pressure of his fingers. He rolled her over, gently separating those wonderful long legs, and mounted her from behind. Soon there followed the whimpers of a satisfied female echoing within his cupped hand. He came with great intensity in full, bucking thrusts.

When he had gathered his wits, he crawled up so he was facing her and tickled her neck. He kissed her cheek and she licked him. "Yuk!" he said, grinning. He traced the line of her buttocks while he spoke. "I've got something even more important than this to do if you can believe it."

"What's she look like?" Olivia inquired. Her soft brow hardened as she mimicked being jealous.

"It's soft and covered in fur and answers to the name of tennis ball." He pinched her bottom and she jumped. "Don't be so possessive. I've got to practice this morning and again before dinner. How about lunch in between?"

"That sounds sexy," she purred.

He laughed. "I'll meet you outside Langan's at one o'clock for lunch."

He leaped up without waiting for a reply and made for the shower. She joined him. They took turns soaping each other, rinsed, and practiced the same arrangement as they toweled. He rubbed her curly hair roughly under the towel and then patted her back. By thinking of all the things he had to do today, he succeeded in staying off the floor for the second time that morning. In the hard white light of the fluorescent lights, she looked good enough to eat. He told her this and she called his bluff. He smacked her bottom again for being crude and started to shave. She watched him closely in the mirror. Five minutes later they closed the door quietly behind them. He looped the Do Not Disturb sign over the doorknob, kissed Olivia at the elevator, and bounded down the stairs for breakfast.

They gave him the table by the wall, as requested, and complied with his request for a telephone. His papers were there waiting for him on the silver tray next to his mail. He sat down and threw back a glass of fresh-squeezed orange juice as he sorted through his correspondence. Then he picked up the phone and set it in the croock of his neck. His first call was to good old Sidney Hughes at the Dorchester. He listened to the eight consecutive ringing noises and smiled at the sound of the drawling American voice. "Good morning," James said cheerily. "It's Mr. McLaren. Why aren't you up? It must be nearly eight-thirty." He cut off Hughes's response. "Did you get the measurements?"

Hughes cleared his throat. "Yes, James, it's all taken care of. You have an appointment at twelve-thirty at Kirk's. Ron sends his regards."

"Call him back and cancel it," James ordered. "Postpone it until at least four. Wait a minute . . . there's two other things I need." James lifted his mail.

"What's that, James?" Sidney asked. His voice was heavy with sleep.

The first telegram made him laugh. It was a confirmation of the deal he'd made the night before over dinner. The message from Norm Feldman read:

DEAL ON STOP PAPERS READY IN NEW YORK TOMORROW STOP HOW WAS SHE?

He crunched up the telegram and discarded it in the ashtray.

"Hold on a minute, Hughes." The second telegram came from Brice Evans congratulating him on the deal and telling him he'd square the details and sign the necessary papers tomorrow. The message ended:

ISN'T FELDMAN RIOT?

James tore open the third message. He pressed it flat on the table. His eyes scanned it and caught the words JANIE and TOMORROW HEATHROW and he suddenly felt slightly nauseous. His face flushed. He would save this one for later.

"Yes, Hughes. You still there?" he asked casually.

"I'm here, James," Hughes replied.

"Good. Get in touch with somebody from Whiplin-Aristocrat. Have them send over two medium-grip Aristocrat racquets to the Hurlingham Club as soon as humanly possible. Can you do that?" He drove on without awaiting an answer. "Also, if you would call Citibank. Tell them I plan to withdraw some money this morning." He lifted up the copy of *The Guardian* and leafed through it. The rate of exchange had improved during the night. By waiting until today to withdraw the money, he had saved himself five thousand dollars. He had guessed the higher interest rates in America would strengthen the dollar. "Hughes, warn them I'm withdrawing two hundred sixty thousand pounds out of my account before lunch. Two hundred sixty thousand. Can you do that?"

"Sure, James, but what will it matter if I call?

They don't know me." Sidney was beginning to whine.

"Organize it somehow, Sidney. Christ Almighty! That's what you're paid for." He thought about it and raised his voice. "If there's a fucking hassle, call Brice in New York. He'll straighten it out. But do it this morning." He pictured his agent's face when he learned why he was dragged out of bed at four A.M. and grinned. "If he asks, tell him it's for heroin." James hesitated before slamming the phone down. He returned it to his ear. "Oh, and Sidney, thanks."

He lit a cigarette and drew three quick breaths before extinguishing it. Sidney wasn't such a bad son-of-a-bitch, really, he thought. He could have done worse. At least he was halfway competent. James made a mental note to thank Hughes in person.

Before he tucked into his breakfast of eggs Benedict, ham, sausages, and a quart of orange juice, he rang the hotel desk and had them deliver a bouquet of flowers outside Pam's door. He felt a bit silly dictating the inscription on the card to the young guy on the line:

To a special lady, in hopes that she might begin this fine day on a happy note.

The guy read it back the way Shakespeare might have.

James interrupted: "Yes, just send it and bill me." The waiter took the phone away as he began to eat.

He shoveled down half the food, then sat up. *For*

Christ's sake, relax! he told himself. He spied his watch. It was two minutes to nine. He thought about the UPI photographers waiting to make him marginally richer at Hurlingham. *Jesus! They're waiting to make a buck, too,* he thought. *They'll wait.* He began to chew his food and with his free hand grabbed the stack of newspapers.

Predictably, his smug little face was splashed in glorious black-and-white across the front page of each of the six London papers. Only *The Herald Tribune* carried a photo that looked remotely like him, he decided. Was his forehead really that big? He glanced over the text of the articles and found no mention of the one-million-dollar lawsuit or the threatened N.U.J. boycott of Wimbledon. *Brice must have done his job,* he thought contentedly.

The restaurant had begun to fill up with people who had learned from the newspapers where he was staying. Most of the diners carried newspaper likenesses of him under their well-dressed arms. James fumbled and drew from his back pocket a cigarette stuffed with reefer. He lit it and sucked in hard. There was always the distant chance that some drug-oriented fans would stroll up to his table and request an autograph. Their discovery as they recognized the pungent-smelling herb would provide the next installment in the history of his vices in tomorrow's dailies. "*So what?*" James said aloud. He killed the joint and placed the two inches that remained of it into his wallet. He left two pounds for the papers and left the restaurant, alone except for the fifty pairs of eyes glued to his back. He headed for the exit and the first available cab for the Hurlingham Club.

He got as far as the cab queue outside when she saw him and yelled, "James! James!" Her tone was reproachful. He looked back and saw Stephanie sprinting down the hotel steps. Christ! He wondered if he could duck into the cab and lose her. He glanced about: too many people were watching them.

"Shit!" He leaned in the open doorway of the cab.

"James, I want an explanation for last night, and it'd better be a good one, or else."

"Or else what?" he questioned dryly.

"Or else we're through and I'll never speak to you again as long as I live." She was serious. He couldn't believe it.

He moved to duck into the cab. "Have it your way."

"James McLaren, you come back here this instant!" she wailed.

He popped back out and took in the small crowd of voyeurs congregating at the top of the hotel steps. Among them were two eager-looking Japanese wielding cameras. Christ! He was in enough trouble as it was with Janie due to arrive tomorrow. If this fracas was photographed and got into the papers, he'd be screwed. But did he even want Janie? Jesus! He stared at Stephanie contemptuously. "Look, I'm late . . . ." He stopped as the little Japanese man removed the lens cap from his Nikon FM. "Get in, for Christ's sake."

They headed down Hyde Park Gate for the river

and the Hurlingham Club. He'd ditch her somewhere in between. He sat as far away from her as was possible in the cramped enclosure. He reached out and closed the Plexiglas separation between the driver but saw it had ventilating holes in it, so he sat back, sighing. "Say what you have to say, okay? I've got a big day ahead of me and don't need you around to complicate it." His mood needed no interpretation.

"James, please." Stephanie crossed her arms and pursed her lips. "James, I want to know what happened last night. If you've got a good explanation, all's forgiven."

He chewed on the ultimatum. Was she for real? "Nothing happened. I met an old friend, so I fucked off," he stated categorically. He patted his pockets instinctively for the joint.

"But what about me? I was dumped there all alone," she said, complaining. "How do you think I looked? Huh? I had lots of friends there who noticed you'd left. I might even have gotten raped."

He turned his head from watching the street and observed her coldly. "I doubt it." He felt himself losing what little patience he had left.

"But all my friends noticed you dumped me."

"Who gives a shit?" he exploded.

"James, don't you dare talk to me like that. You're damaging what we have. Please, James." She must've taken diction lessons from a Sunday-school teacher, he thought. Her tone was that severe.

He was tired of toying with her. "What we have?" he repeated incredulously. "What we have is some possessive cunt of an English chick who doesn't know if she's coming or going or already arrived. I'm sick of people assuming things about me. I don't owe you anything. I'm not attracted to you, so why bother pursuing it? Okay? Leave me alone." He saw he had hurt her.

Anger flashed in her heavily penciled eyes. "How dare you speak to me like that! God!" she spat. "My friends are some of the most influential people in England. I can see they make your stay here your last. I'm a cousin to the Queen!" she cried emphatically.

He wondered if she was crazy. The cab driver seemed to have similar thoughts as he made eye contact with James through the rearview mirror. James almost laughed. He pulled a hundred-dollar bill from his pants pocket and waved it like a flag before her nose. "Listen, whatever the hell your name is, this is my friend, the dollar bill. And I've never yet seen anything more influential than it. So don't shit me about your friends." He calmed himself. "This is crazy," he said to no one in particular. "Look, what do you want from me? We had an encounter in a taxi — that's it, it's over now."

"James, I don't want anything from you. Nothing but to be with you, and to show you how much I care," she purred. Her hand shifted to his crotch. This made him madder.

"Pull this thing over!" he yelled to the driver. The driver reacted as though he'd been expecting the order. The cab drew parallel to the curb and screeched to a halt. James leaped out and slammed the door quickly behind him. It was nine-twenty-five. In the distance he could see the club grounds. Thrusting his hand into the open window, he dropped the one-hundred-dollar bill. "Here, take her where she wants to go, will you?"

"Right, mate," the cabbie said. The cab lurched away.

James saw her pressed against the back window of the cab, and for one brief moment he regretted having handled her so roughly. Then his anger returned; she'd made him late for his meeting. "Silly starfucker," he muttered.

Fifteen minutes later James jogged onto the Hurlingham courts, swinging the two Aristocrat racquets as he limbered up. His coach, Hal Jimson, had left a message at the desk that he'd meet James for practice between eleven and three on the same courts. He folded the message and threw it into the trashcan near the desk. So much for Olivia and lunch at Langan's, he thought. He took a deep breath. It occurred to him that since his arrival in London yesterday, he'd allocated tennis to the number-three spot, behind business and "sexual gratification," as Hal called it. His coach was always after him about that. "Don't put tennis behind your "'sexual gratification.'" *He ought to preach that to some of the dykes on the circuit*, James thought.

He walked out to the court to pose for the boys from UPI and the thought of his recent behavior stayed with him. All of the contracts for sponsorship, endorsements, and the like came as a consequence of his prowess on the court. Not the other way around. Lately, in the atmosphere of million-dollar dinners and relentless adulation from his fans, he'd been getting it ass backward. That's where Hal Jimson came in, he reminded himself.

At number one in the world, he didn't need a coach as such. His dad was enough of a tennis aficionado to comment on his form. But his dad was his dad, understandably subjective and prone to placate James when he was playing badly and felt like slamming the racquet over his opponent's head — something he had done when he was twelve years old. Hal Jimson, on the other hand, didn't give a goddamn if he upset James. In the three years since James had been coached by Hal, his career had progressed spectacularly. And he was sensible enough to realize it was not all his doing but due with thanks to Hal. The ex-Davis cup coach had broken him like a colt and harnessed his genius. For this he got a hell of a lot of thanks — his face in tennis magazines, and fifteen percent of James's prize money. So it was four hours of work with Hal this afternoon and no lunch with Olivia.

James got as far as the courts and nodded to the photographers, when he remembered something. He pivoted and ran back into the clubhouse, where he had seen a buxom little blonde buying a cola. She was still there, standing by the bulletin board.

"Hey! Excuse me, but are you free for fifteen minutes?" he asked her. She returned his smile and laughed nervously at her friend.

Looking at him, she asked, "Why? Would you like to give me a few pointers?"

He laughed. "Yes, if you'd let me. I've got some people out on the court waiting to snap some pictures for the world's press. How's you like to come along and smile for the cameras?"

She sought counsel from her friend. The plump redhead prodded her encouragingly. "Go on, you're the actress."

They passed through the gates outside and onto the court. At this early hour the courts were still relatively empty. "You're an actress, are you?" James asked her.

"Well, I'd like to be. I'm a member of Equity, but no jobs as yet," she said modestly. "It takes time, I guess."

"Super. Take this and act like a tennis player. Can you do that?" He handed her the large Aristocrat racquet.

"I know." She grinned. "There are no small roles."

"Beautiful. You'll do."

Three photographers from three different services spent fifteen minutes snapping pictures of the athletic couple. James did his best to go against their suggestions, to try and blur their shots by suddenly alternating speed. He unleashed his usual repertoire of bad manners, which they expected and loved and knew sold newspapers. They finally coaxed him into a two-shot against the net, one arm around the actress's shoulder, the other clasping the Aristocrat racquet against his chest. If necessary he could always pawn the girl off as a promotion model, should Janie press him, he decided. He thought about this. Fuck Janie. He clenched the blonde closer.

In response to their questions, the girl's name was Kim Cornway, and yes, he liked the Aristocrat racquet and thought it had a tremendous future. As always, Brice had outdone himself; the photographers represented the three largest agencies in the world: AP, UPI, and Reuters. The fee received for each "exclusive" would be divided by three, but James would get three times the exposure. After a quarter of an hour he walked off the courts with the actress without acknowledging the photographers. "Typical McLaren," the men said, loving it.

He thanked the actress and gave her the racquets and the phone number of a theatrical agent he had met at a party. He obliged her by signing his autograph on her short-shorts. He swore he could feel the heat of her twat as he slid his hand under the cloth to write against it. Within twenty minutes he was on court number three practicing with the club pro, and cheating two novitiates to the game out of their hour's lesson. The pro was passable, as tennis club pros went. He had made some ambiguous assault on Wimbledon fifteen year ago. James battled on despite his dislike for the man's stubbly little ground strokes and uncertain backhand. *Wimbledon, my ass*, he thought.

It was hot out, so he took a break after half an hour and spent ten minutes swimming in the pool. Twenty laps later he rested in the water, wrapping his arms elbows out over the stone lip of the pool. The heat of the sun, absorbed by the cement, warmed him and he lay that way for a while.

He returned to the courts, having showered and changed. He moved down the aisle, past the finely manicured hedges accompanied by the sounds of tennis matches being played all around him. The perfect summer day had lured the players to beat the hell out of rubber balls at Hurlingham. All along the hedges, players, waiting for courts, viewed these matches with the stoic indifference that came from knowing they could do better. Their affected apathy took a backseat when they spied McLaren's white-haired coach. "That's Hal Jimson," someone whispered.

"I wonder if McLaren's here," another speculated.

"I saw him on number-three court earlier," a third intoned.

Jimson, the weathered veteran of countless battles on court, waved a greeting to a group of friends. He slipped the training bag from his shoulder and put it on a bench at courtside. After he unzipped the bag, he withdrew a Thermos of diluted lemonade and a pair of prescription sunglasses. He checked his watch. It was eleven-o-one.

McLaren entered through an opening in the hedges carrying three racquets and a towel. He wore the nylon Davis cup jacket he owned that had his name stitched in sprawling moronic script over one breast. The eyes of the gathering crowd were upon him instantly.

Hal Jimson waved. He raised a hand to shield his eyes from the sun. "There he is, this year's Wimbledon champ. Right on time as always."

James smiled. He strode onto the court and closed the gate behind him. "Greetings. I got your message."

They shook hands heartily. "So it seems, James. How's London treating you?" Hal leaned over and examined James's left hand. Held it and turned it over while he assessed each side for damage. "Looks okay," he mumbled. "From the report I received, I thought maybe you'd be playing right-handed." He smiled a slow, economic smile.

"Oh. The fight," James said, embarrassed.

"Yes, the fight." Hal's tone was vaguely reprimanding.

"It wasn't so much a fight as a punch. I hit him once because he asked for it. And I'd do it again." James turned away and admired the accumulating clouds. "You must've seen the tape by now, Hal. You know what these journalist pricks are like."

"Only too well, boy. Sometimes you've got to hold it inside, though. You know how I feel about this sort of thing."

"Only too well," James echoed.

"However, I did see the tape. Personally, I would have aimed for the jaw."

James followed his coach to the fence and dropped his racquets beside it. They removed their racquet covers in silence. "Aside from your first-round knockout, how's everything else? Ready for Monday?"

James bounced his fist off the Whiplin racquet. "Almost. Little jet lag still, but I'll get over it," he said.

"Good. I spoke to your family yesterday. Your father said he tried to get through but couldn't find you. They're coming over tomorrow with Janie." James winced slightly at the mention of his American girl friend. "How's everything between you two?"

"As always, finē," James said.

"You sure? I mean, if there were something wrong, you'd know you could tell me."

"I know, Hal, thanks. But don't worry about me." James started for the opposite court.

"That's good news, because, as you know, heartaches and tennis tournaments don't necessarily mix."

"Christ, Hal, I know. 'Gin-and-tonics mix, heartaches and tennis tournaments don't.' I've heard that line. You're beginning to sound like the press in this shitty country."

"Relax, boy. Remember last year. You can't blame me for being concerned. I want that title again." Hal's fatherly tone both controlled and consoled James.

"Yes." He shrugged.

During the drama of last year's victory, James's first ever in the singles, Janie had decided to play mind games. After she had suddenly learned of his two-day affair with a young South African player some weeks previous, she had faked illness and left England in a huff. Naturally, the press had leaped on the rift and featured it on the front page of all the tabloids. Even the post-tournament press conferences were marred by reporters' questions about his love life. His thoughts returned to Olivia, the sixteen-year-old girl he'd screwed twice in the past twelve hours. A smile drifted precariously onto his lips as he tried to disguise it.

James carried a can of fresh balls onto the court, removed the plastic lid, and popped the seal. Prying the steel tab back, he threw it into a wire can near the fence. He emptied the can and supported the balls on his racquet face.

Hal remained at the opposite end of the court and practiced hitting deep base line shots to James's backhand. Each shot James took effortlessly as he loosened up. Crouching with his shoulder down, he cocked the racquet out behind him, meeting Hal's shot with a solid follow-through, putting plenty of top spin on the ball. On each approaching shot James hustled into proper position to combat the speed with which the ball careened off the grass. Unlike clay, the ball sprang off the grass surface faster and less predictably. In order to compensate for the nuances in bounce, it was essential to achieve perfect positioning to receive each shot. James's slender calf muscles rippled and relaxed as he danced across the court.

After a dozen hits, James drove the ball down the sideline to Hal's backhand. He pointed to his forehand court. Hal obliged him with as many shots to his forehand. Then they switched tactics. Hal charged the net and returned the ball to the extreme corners of the court. James sprinted from side to side and returned each shot with a perfectly executed lob just over Hal's head. His coach would step back quickly on nimble legs and slam the ball into either of the far corners. James's concentration was diverted by a couple of loudmouths who had joined the crowd of spectators. He punched the approaching hit purposely deep to Hal's backhand. As expected, Hal returned the ball in a shallow cross-court lob, which James intercepted and smashed off of the base line chalk.

Hal responded to James's beckoning. He approached the net. The spectators were clapping. "What's up, James? The crowd?"

James cocked his head around and viewed the one-hundred-strong mob of ardent tennis fans. "Jesus! Even Hurlingham's got groupies. You'd think we were winning the war or something," he said bitterly.

"You know what Wimbledon does to England," Hal said, soothing him.

"Yes, but not at Hurlingham."

"Especially at Hurlingham," Hal retorted, "although I'll admit I've never seen it quite so bad. It's a good thing they're on the side of the law."

"Assume nothing," James quipped. He waved to a crowd of bandy-legged old men. "Hello, pops . . . how's the old lady . . . are you getting any lately?" The old men waved back cheerily.

"Come on, James, it's not that bad. If it bothers you, we'll move on. I suppose we could make do with Bishops Park for the day," Hal said.

"No, I'm okay for today, but tomorrow let's go to Queen's and use the indoor courts. You know I don't mind this sort of crap during the actual tournament. I mean I do, but I can put up with it, but not at practice."

"I understand. I'll get Queen's Club for tomorrow, then."

"Thanks." James moved to the base line. He confronted the crowd and clasped the front of his shorts and jiggled his genitals at them. A couple of older ladies voiced their disgust and James smiled.

They worked for an hour and a half on different shots. The rhythm was back in James's game. His ground strokes, overhead shots, and volleys were all solid and accurate. His service, the part of his game most susceptible to fatigue, was consistent and powerful. It was all Hal could do to return the blazing serve back over the net. The last fifteen minutes of the session consisted of a succession of what Hal termed "power hits." This was essentially an opportunity for James to swing as powerfully and freely as he did during a match. They assumed spots behind their respective base lines by two yards and filled the air with the blistering pop of new balls as they carried in exaggerated arcing spins over the net. At his very best Hal could manage two, maybe three, rallies before ceding to his pupil's superior strength and agility. Then he would start another ball and repeat the process.

They broke for a drink of lemonade. "Not bad at all, James," Hal called. "Remember to punch and recover all in one motion." James picked up a towel from the ground and mopped the sweat from his face. He was toweling his grip when Hal said pleasantly, "All things considered, James, I've never seen you look sharper. Never."

James dried his hands on the towel. He stared at the crowd at either end of the court. "That's good to hear. I want it this year even more than last," he said.

"If you keep this level up, I can't see anyone who's going to get close." Hal thought about his remark. "Having said that, James, one lapse and we'll be on the first flight to New York. Wimbledon's funny that way."

James picked at a callus on his palm and thought of Olivia and then Pam. "What's the time?"

Hal realized he was being ignored. He glanced at his watch. "Five past one. Am I keeping you from something?"

James grinned. "Yeah, but don't worry, it doesn't matter." His first scheduled date with Olivia and he was standing her up. He tried to imagine her standing alone in the doorway at the restaurant. A concerned look played across his face.

Hal laughed. "The millionaire martyr. I'll tell you something for free, pal. Just give me the next two weeks of your martyred little life. I'll make you a million and then set you free to sow your oats or whatever you had in mind. Okay?" he asked. James shrugged thoughtfully. Hal continued. "I need four hours tomorrow and then you're on your own."

After they had taken a breather, they returned to the court in preparation for two and a half hours of solid play, interrupted only sporadically as Hal discussed strategy. James burped up a salt pill he'd taken and with it tasted the gin from last night. He lobbed up a ball and stepped into it as he served.

His lean body contracted in a half arc and the ball spat off the surface of the racquet into the serving square.

Across town Pamela awoke with a terrific headache. She raised herself on shaking arms and stared drowsily about the strange room. Memory came to her in slow throbs of her tired head. A feeling of claustrophobia seized her. She flung back the covers and spun her legs over the edge of the bed. Her hands, wet with the perspiration of fear, massaged her temples. Had last night really happened? she asked herself. The respite from her troubles provided through sleep quickly disappeared and the sudden vivid recollections of the night demoralized her. She opened her mouth to cry but the tears weren't there. She had used them up.

She found the phone and dialed the operator. A voice told her it was twenty to two. Twenty to two? She had to be at the All England Club to practice with Mr. Barrat, her coach. She leaped off the bed and tore at the curtains. The sunlight warmed her skin and had a calming effect. She went to the window and regarded the bit of Hyde Park the view afforded her. Maybe today she would just lie out in the park and enjoy the sunshine. This way she could catch up on some much needed rest and at the same time avoid the people from last night. Her thoughts returned to the orgy and a sense of panic swept through her. "Why?" she cried aloud. "Jesus! Why me?"

She rose and fixed herself a vodka from the bar

she knew James would have on hand. She sucked at the drink as she dialed the All England Club. Had a Mr. Barrat left a message for her? He had? A clerk told her she was to meet him at three for a three-hour practice on court six. She hung up.

Good, she thought. At least Mr. Barrat had rescheduled it. She finished the vodka and immediately felt better. The alcohol from that one drink merged with the alcohol already in her bloodstream from last night. She felt giddy. She dressed hurriedly and folded James's pajamas at the edge of the bed. She thought of James and Olivia while she glimpsed herself in the bathroom mirror. They had been so incredibly kind and understanding. She ran a comb through her hair and scribbled a thank-you note on a pad by the phone.

Outside in the hall she stopped to read the card on the flowers. Pam brought the flowers closer to her face and inhaled. The fresh scent transported her back to the days of her first amateur matches in Utah. Her mother had liked flowers. "Things will work out," she said, invigorated by the wonderful flowers and the memories they invoked. "Of course they will." She felt revitalized as she sprang down the stairs clutching the bouquet.

The taxi deposited her in Wimbledon at the corner of Fawn's Way and Astor Street in front of the white-washed block of flats. She froze in the taxi. In the drive was Sheila's metallic-blue BMW. She was home. Pam paid the driver and unthinkingly collected her change without tipping him. Cautiously, she trudged across the patch of lawn to the concrete steps. Her knees weakened as she heard voices from inside. She slid the key into the lock and leaned into the door.

"Is that you, honey?" Sheila asked from her bedroom.

Pam debated keeping quiet and fleeing the apartment, but the vodka fortified her and enabled her to react rationally. She would have to face them eventually, and the sooner the better. Then she could return to the business of living and playing tennis. "Yes, hello, Sheila." She crept automatically for the bar and poured a whiskey. A moment later she returned the empty glass to the tray.

Sheila appeared around the corner clad only in a brassiere. Pam leveled her stare at Sheila's forehead. "Hello, Pammy, darling. Cheryl and I are just trying on some new outfits for tomorrow. Come have a look."

The exhibition match at Hurlingham; Pam had completely forgotten about it. Last year she had played in it and done reasonably well. The matches, if one could call them that, consisted of one hard-fought set, the proceeds going to the Society for Spastic Children. In the commotion of the past few days, she had completely forgotten.

"Come have a quick peek. They're really a riot," Sheila said.

Pam followed her around the corner. "Hey, Pammy, what do you think? Aren't they great!" Cheryl asked sarcastically. She walked toward Pam, smiling, her brown legs tightly defined in the skin-tight shorts.

"They're great, all right," Pam said hollowly. The

outfit was nothing more than a better-cut rendition of what the men wore. Her eyes volleyed to Sheila and darted momentarily to the dark patch of hair between her muscular legs. She felt herself blush and looked quickly away.

Sheila sensed her uneasiness and wrapped a towel around her as she worked to spark the conversation. "The Parisian designer swears these will be the latest fashion in women's tennis. He's offered nearly everybody in the top thirty free tailoring for life if they wear them at Wimbledon. Can you believe it?"

"He'd have to offer at least one hundred thousand dollars on top of that if he wants anybody I know to wear them. They're abominable," Cheryl said dramatically.

Pam laughed. "I think you've got a point. I wouldn't be seen dead in them," Pam said. Some of the tension disappeared as Pam began to unwind. *Perhaps they're as uneasy as I am* she thought. *After all, simply because they were involved in one orgy doesn't necessarily make them lesbians for life.* By giving them this benefit of the doubt, Pam found she could unwind in their presence.

"They're all as bad as the next. Look at these." Sheila handed Pam a pile of brightly colored cottons, all of which more or less conformed to the original pattern Cheryl wore. Sheila asked, "And where were you last night, young lady? Did you finally manage to catch up with Prince Charles, or was it his brother Andrew?"

Pam watched as the shorts fell from Cheryl's tight bottom to expose the whiteness of her flesh. The color of her panty line conjured up memories of the previous night. "What?" she asked vacantly.

"Not what, *which*," Sheila intoned cheerily. "Which one did you get — Prince Charles, or Andrew, or Roger Moore?"

Pam smiled faintly as she made sense of the question. "Oh." She lifted her head coquettishly and chimed, "All three." The others laughed.

It was evident, through her line of questioning, that Sheila had deliberately tried to purge Pam of any feelings of guilt she might have inside her. By injecting a heterosexual note into the conversation, she had restored Pam's sense of self-worth. Last night was an aberration. Pam recognized the intentional nature of Sheila's questioning and inwardly thanked her for it.

Pam returned to the living room and collapsed onto the sofa. The gloom was lifting, leaving in its wake only the earlier exhaustion. She noticed a pile of letters beside her on the table. Two were from America and one from England. The ones from the States had been forwarded by her secretary in Malibu, where Pam maintained an apartment. She opened them eagerly. The first contained a check from the Whiplin Company in Illinois, sent via their business offices in Greenwich, Connecticut! Benjamen Smythe, the president and part owner of the firm, had signed his name where necessary over a line in the thick green paper. Above the illegible scrawl was the practiced lettering of the firm's chief accountant. She compared the two signatures. Although she had met Smythe only once at a formal dinner — where he had tried to seduce her — she had never met the accountant but could visualize him just as clearly from his writing. He was probably tall and thin and wore bifocals. She toyed with the idea of handwriting analysis as she folded the check. Maybe she'd have her own writing analyzed to see if she could find out anything about herself she didn't already know. She slipped the eight-thousand-dollar check into the envelope and set it aside.

The second letter was from her youngest sister, Elizabeth, who was a junior at Westtown School in Pennsylvania. She had enrolled Elizabeth there three years ago after hearing of the school's reputation through a friend on the circuit. The rigid, though compassionate, policies of the Quaker school would, she hoped, prepare her sister for the trying times in the outside world.

She read the first three lines of the letter, then folded it and put it away. She was too exhausted to appreciate it and would save it for later. The first lines were enough to stress the point that next year's tuition had not yet been paid. As an afterthought, she tucked the check from Whiplin into the letter from her sister.

Then she went into the bathroom and stepped under the shower. They icy water buffeted her tired limbs and rid them of the lethargy that had been with her all day. Instead of packing her tennis uniform into a shoulder bag as she usually did, she slipped directly into her uniform. If she avoided the locker room at the club, she could evade any further confrontation with the Super Six, she reasoned. She could face them one at a time. Hadn't she proven that through her deft handling of Sheila and Cheryl? After confronting each individually, she could return to the locker room without feeling self-conscious, she decided. But not before.

Pam's anxiety to get on with the business of tennis found her at court number six twenty minutes ahead of schedule. She stood before the fenced-in enclosure and watched two balding and overweight men undo eleven months' worth of intricate grounds keeping on the court. Great brown divots in the turf mapped an obvious path from base line to net on either side of the grass court. In each man's struggle to win, they both played furiously, as though their lives depended upon it — and not just the five pounds they had wagered. Fat white sneakers clumped their way after every shot no matter how obviously returnable or decidedly out of bounds. The commencement of the tournament in five days and the four-day grace period preceding the tournament, during which time the courts were closed, couldn't come soon enough, Pam thought.

Pam hooked two fingers idly through the fence. She eased her full weight back and peered at the sky. Vast patches of clouds set up a barrier from the comforting rays of the sun. It was not dark out, nor was rain likely. Earlier trips to Britain had acquainted her with the habitually melancholy weather. She had often expressed her desire to live in England were it not for the weather. The people were generally civilized and the pace much more relaxed than in the U.S. But in her profession the weather meant everything. She could bear the rain — there were indoor courts — as long as it was only temporary. But in England it rained almost as much as the sun shone, and she found this uncertainty depressing.

A pair of sunbleached arms draped against the fence beside her. "And how is Pammy today?" The tone of the voice was almost provocative.

She turned around nervously and recognized Marge. A week ago she would have felt relieved — Marge was the most affable of the Super Six. But since Marge had been the first of her sex partners at the party, Pam panicked. "Marge," she said awkwardly.

"What have you been up to, you naughty girl?" the platinum-blond Australian asked.

Marge's disheveled appearance indicated that she had already had a practice session. *Perhaps she's on her way to the showers*, Pam thought hopefully. She returned her attention to the two men on the court. They had finished and were preparing to leave. "Not too much. I'm waiting for my coach."

"I know, lovey, that's why I came over. Janis, who works at the desk, is an old mate of mine. She told me about Barrat's message. I just finished on court five, so I thought I'd come over to watch and perhaps offer a few pointers. Not that you need it. You played bloody well at the Stella Artois."

"Thanks, Marge," Pam said suspiciously. Pam was still unsure of Marge's reason for visiting. *Maybe she only means it as a peace offering, one friend to the other*, Pam mused. *Maybe it's her way of downplaying the awkward situation, as Sheila and Cheryl had.* By reserving any reference to last night, Marge could be inferring it was all history. Pam's thoughts were shattered by Marge's next line.

"I really enjoyed you last night," Marge said matter-of-factly. "We went well together; I mean super well." Both women stepped back to allow the large men through the gate. They ignored the flirtatious eyes of the slightly less fat man. Not having recognized the women, he must have thought he possibly had impressed them with his prowess on the court. Pam was blushing. She leaned forward and supported herself against the fence. Her throat was dry. She wanted to run.

"Don't feel ashamed. I know you enjoyed it as much as I did. Your orgasms were that strong."

Pam shut her eyes. She bit her lip and reopened the slight wound where the Argentinian had slapped her. She fought back the tears. She would not cry, she resolved. It was not her fault. She was drugged and they took advantage of her. Marge edged closer. Her long arms linked into the fence beside Pam so that their elbows brushed together. The fence buckled out under their combined weight. Pam shook her head. "Get away from me."

"Pammy . . . don't be like that. You're not alone. We all felt bad at first. Do you feel any less a woman because of last night? Wasn't it even a little bit romantic?"

"No way, not at all," Pam said adamantly. She raised her head and eyed the empty court. An attentive grounds keeper was busy repairing the divots.

"Darling, I know exactly how you're feeling. When I was your age, I had my first affair with a woman, and I remember how mixed up I felt. I felt guilty because I enjoyed every minute of it. I loved being sucked by a woman for the first time." Marge stepped closer, her tone matronly. "Now why don't you let me comfort you? I promise not to let any of the others muscle in. You'll be mine and I'll be yours. Just us two. I promise." She rubbed against Pam's shoulder.

Pam's reaction was instantaneous. She leaped back and leered coldly at Marge. "Don't touch me, don't ever touch me, you dyke. Last night was a mistake. I was drugged. You knew I was drugged, and you took advantage. I want nothing to do with you or any of the others. They sicken me."

Marge hit back with the passion of a jilted lover. She had honestly liked Pam. "What do you mean 'they'? Don't kid yourself. I saw you, saw your face, saw how you enjoyed it. You loved every obscene minute of it."

"I didn't; I like men," Pam insisted. Her fingers tightened around the chain link fence.

Marge's laughter was the caustic, indulgent laughter of redress. It was her turn to hurt. "You like men?" she repeated. "For what? Just wait till this 'I like men,' gets out," she said, laughing. "You had a chance to be accepted as an equal by us, but now you've fucked it up. It's happened before; twice ladies like yourself decided to go the other way. Can you guess where their careers went, honey? Straight down the tubes. They couldn't take the pressure of having us against them. Up theirs, and up yours. There are plenty of girls who would welcome the opportunity to call us friends. Plenty who want to climb to the top, and I don't mean on top of a man."

Pam wanted to get to the top. Did one negate the other? "So," she offered weakly.

"So, *they'll* make it. You won't. It's as easy as that," Marge said sharply. Then her tone softened somewhat. "Of course, should you change your mind before the others hear about it, maybe we can salvage something, but that's a big maybe."

The voice of Mr. Barrat interrupted the conversation. "Afternoon Marjorie. Are you here to spy on my future number one in case she draws against you next week? Hello, Pamela, I'm glad to see you could make it after all."

Pam did her best to resurrect an empty smile. She mumbled something and walked past Marge onto the court. "What's with Pam?" Barrat asked.

"Search me. Maybe a late night. She seems tired," Marge said.

Barrat watched his protégé move across the court. He switched his attention to Marge. "Tired, is she? That's not the case with you Aussies. You're all health nuts. That's why you're so well preserved."

Marge noted the admiring stare of Barrat at her bosom. If only he knew who was sucking on those tits the night before. She smiled whimsically.

They parted amicably as Barrat entered the court and dropped his kit against the fence. Marge languished at the fence for nearly a minute, then left. Pam composed herself as she watched the Australian head for the clubhouse.

Their practice session lasted only two hours due to a light rain that came in from the north. Pam worked extra hard, relishing each moment of instruction during the shortened practice. She would prove Marge and the others wrong; she could make it! Her shots were there, even her cross-court backhand, which lately had been giving her problems. They concentrated on this shot, then switched to her service and then her ground strokes. Pam failed to notice the congregation of well-muscled women outside court six. It started to rain more heavily.

"I think it's coming down too hard," Barrat called to Pam. "You've had enough of a workout for today anyway."

Pam jogged nearer and cupped an ear. "Is that it?"

"I think so, unless you want to work on anything in particular. I suppose we could move over to Queen's for an hour or two after dinner. I booked an indoor court, which we could share." They met at the net.

"I don't think so. It felt fine," Pam said.

Barrat drew a line across his forehead and snapped the accumulated rain from his finger. "Okay, in that case let's meet tomorrow and get an hour in before Hurlingham. And bring Sheila. You two had better get some time in together if you want to do anything in the doubles next week."

The doubles. Pam had completely forgotten she'd

signed up to play with Sheila. The sensitive question of using Sheila as her partner took on a new significance. Did she want the intimacy of an on-court relationship with Sheila? Barrat said something but the words were muffled by a passing jet en route to Heathrow. She cupped an ear and leaned closer. Then she saw them. Tony, Julia, and Marge. They were poised against the fence staring at her, their expressions tight-lipped and rather grim. She realized then that Marge had told them. They knew Pam wanted out, wanted out before she was in, and they resented her for it. She felt suddenly nauseous.

"You've got a regular fan club around this place," Barrat grinned. The girls waved a spurious hello, lest Barrat read something into the entourage.

"Yeah," Pam said quietly. By the time she had collected her gear, the girls had moved on. Pam walked across the gravel paths to the clubhouse with Barrat beside her feeling utterly alone.

By three-ten James had showered and changed and caught a cab to go to the Westminster branch of Citibank. He had intended to head directly to the West End to withdraw the money from a branch there. This would have given him that much less area to cover with the cash before he spent it again. Also, he'd have been able to check the area outside the restaurant to see if by some remote chance Olivia was still waiting for him. James had neglected to get her telephone number and would just have to wait for her to call to organize anything for tonight.

He called Citibank headquarters in Westminster

and was told he could not withdraw the money from a branch in the West End. James found it difficult to conceive that one of the largest banks in the world could only dispense overseas cash through a single London branch. "If not, why not?" he had hammered at the manager over the telephone.

"Mr. McLaren, such a large sum of money on such short notice makes it necessary to handle the withdrawal through our headquarters and international branch. We only received clearance this morning," the manager said arrogantly.

"That's not my fault."

"It's nobody's fault, sir, but this is company policy. It's well known in banking circles."

James found the guy's arrogance abrasive. "In banking circles?"

The man interrupted him. "I realize you not being a banker yourself, you are not —"

James cut him off. "Thank fucking Christ for that. Listen, you have the money ready in fifteen minutes. If there are any more problems, I'm notifying my accountant tomorrow to transfer every cent I have the hell out of there."

"Surely, Mr. McLaren, you —"

James hung up.

Behind his teak-and-leather desk, the suntanned figure of Edwin Parsons, the ambitious young Citibank manager, mopped his brow with a handkerchief. *That's all I need*, he told himself. *Lose the McLaren acount and I'll be back in Pimlico supervising overdrafts.* He ran a hand over his wavy locks and loosened his tie. He was on his third whiskey and reminiscing about his fortnight in Barbados when his buzzer sounded.

"Mr. McLaren to see you, Mr. Parsons."

"Thank you, Alison, show him in," Parsons said with the poise engendered by three whiskeys on a soon-to-be-ulcered stomach. He stacked the money in the tiny leather suitcase for the seventeenth time as the door opened.

James sauntered in wearing a T-shirt and jeans. What remained of a five-year-old cashmere sweater was tied around his neck. He surveyed the office and spied the open valise. He made eye contact with Parsons, then returned his gaze to the money. James ignored the banker's outstretched hand and managed a smile. "Is it all there?" His voice was without expression.

"Yes, Mr. McLaren, sir. Would you like me to count it for you?" Parsons offered.

James eyed the young bank manager curiously. He could tell from his look of utter piousness that the banker had meant nothing by this remark. Sarcasm had yielded, as it always did, to the influence of money and the threat of job security. "No," James said. "You've got a trustworthy face."

Parsons smiled feebly. "Keep the suitcase with our compliments," he said and shut the case. He depressed the twin brass locks. "If you wish, I'd be happy to provide you with a security escort until you reach your destination."

"That's not necessary. I haven't got far to go." James lifted the valise and slung it over his shoulder in a way that suggested its contents were equal in value to the pair of worn track shoes on his feet. He spied the clock on Parsons's desk and thought of Olivia. "Maybe in the future we can dispense with this charade. There's no reason why this couldn't have been delivered to a location somewhere in the West End."

Parsons had never thought of this before. He had never had to. He combed his hair nervously with his hand. "Yes, you've got a point. I'll see this sort of thing is worked out next time, to save you the inconvenience."

"Okay." James nodded coolly.

"Good-bye, Mr. McLaren. Good luck next week," Parsons called after him. He remained bowing until the door clicked shut. "Hallelujah!" he whispered. For the time being he retained the McLaren account. He thanked God and rang Harrods to order the furniture for his new house.

James caught the first cab heading west and got out on Grafton Street. He removed the sunglasses from under his belt and slipped them on. Twenty steps later he came to the picture windows of the Dreyfuss Gallery. He didn't see them at first, so he walked on. Had Brice been accurate? he wondered. Had the gallery really acquired the set of three Modigliani oils? According to Brice, it was the very set that had been snatched up from Sotheby's lot 233 a year earlier. For three years he had admired the work of the famous Italian Impressionist. What began as a mild infatuation with the artist's simple, exaggerated figures had steadily progressed into genuine reverence for his unique style. James's collection, which started with a lithograph from a New York gallery, now comprised six oil paintings, two watercolors, and a portfolio of sketches. He had seen the series of three figures — portraits of three sisters — in the Sotheby's catalogue and dispatched Brice Evans to Paris to bid for the paintings on his behalf. Evans bid for him, but the amount that James had sanctioned, two hundred thousand dollars, had been matched and bettered by an Italian movie producer. Evans had returned to New York empty-handed. James spent the next two weeks berating himself for not providing his agent with a blank check or, more importantly, the okay to buy the things at any price.

Evans had redeemed himself this past month by presenting James with a newspaper clipping indicating the death of the Italian producer. With the obituary came the news that a major London gallery had negotiated the purchase of the paintings only days prior to the man's death. Art sources confirmed this. Two weeks later Evans received a phone call from a London associate; the Modiglianis had been bought as a set by the Dreyfuss Gallery and were now gracing that establishment's vitrines.

All of this made for good reading and better listening. James had been intrigued. The set of canvases, which had realized two hundred sixty-five thousand dollars the year before at Sotheby's, were now being peddled at exactly the same price. Only the form of currency differed. Instead of dollars, the stakes had been raised to two hundred sixty-five thousand pounds, including V.A.T.

Yet the saga did not end there. Six hours after the call from London to confirm the locale of the paintings, Brice Evans's phone rang again. "One further note, Mr. Evans, which I thought would be of interest to you and your client," the voice said in its clipped British accent. "My suspicions have been confirmed this afternoon. Inland Revenue is indeed carrying out a full-scale investigation into the accounts of the Dreyfuss Gallery. It seems one of the directors got greedy and began fiddling with the books. They may have to liquidate."

James strode up the marble steps and pushed through the glass doors to the gallery armed with a suitcase of money and the knowledge of the company's financial bind. He sidestepped two bronze torsos and a piece of stone on an elevated plate and spied the paintings behind a velvet rope. They were well displayed upon an eighteenth-century Louis XIV table.

The paintings had lost none of their attraction in the fourteen months since he'd first seen them gracing the cover of Sotheby's catalogue. True to the cliché, their absence had increased his affections for them. He stood there chewing gum and admired the ineffable quality of their beauty. The figures themselves were classic Modigliani, dramatic and elongated with stark expressive faces that attributed much of their evocative power to their eyes. Bands of auburn sunlight rippled from east to west across each of the three canvases. Individually, the works, though fascinating, appeared disjointed. When mounted side by side the sunlight swept across the canvases in one decisive wedge and illuminated the features of the three little girls.

A fat finger nudged his shoulder and James turned to see to whom it belonged. "Please, sir, kindly refrain from pushing against the rope," a middle-aged man in a coal-black wig said dryly. "It was put there for a purpose."

"Oh really? Well, you learn something new every day, don't you?"

The man raised a plucked eyebrow. "Yes," he said slowly, as though unsure of how to interpret the remark.

James edged back a few inches and resumed his appraisal of the works. He dissected the paintings collectively, then as separate entities. He heard noises from behind him, then felt the fat finger return to his back. He ignored the gallery owner's bad manners but the finger persisted. Suddenly, he stepped forward, then back again quickly, jamming the finger against his shoulder.

"You did that deliberately," the owner said. He clutched the finger in a fatter hand and massaged it vigorously. His corpulent face wrinkled into a snarling ball. The well-mapped countenance reminded James of a piece of shoe leather.

"Did what?"

The wounded owner stood before a group of Iranians lucky enough to have gotten out of Teheran before the Ayatollah's arrival. They clutched a list of *objets d'art* featured by the gallery. The Modiglianis were next on their list. The owner realized he had upset his potential clients and smiled obligingly. "Please, sir, if you don't mind, others would enjoy seeing the Modiglianis, too."

James feigned ignorance. He remained at the rope. "Sure."

"Well, if you would kindly slide down, our friends from across the sea can have a better look."

James viewed the group with a look of resigned contempt. Suddenly, he smiled and stepped aside, bowing. "How terribly rude of me."

"That's more like it," the owner said.

"Peasant," one of the Iranians murmured.

James nearly suggested the group return home wearing T-shirts of the Shah. He listened as the bad-mannered man launched into his customary spiel to his "friends from across the sea." He touched upon the more significant historical and biographical aspects of the works. Obsequiously, he removed the rope and bade them to move closer to get a better look while he elaborated on the scenario and the style.

The well-rehearsed sales routine was over in four minutes. The owner crossed his arms idly and awaited any questions the men might have. In keeping with the Moslem custom, their women just stood there looking bemused. The three Iranian men beheld the canvases with steady and knowing eyes. James noticed this and slid possessively closer to the rope. The paintings were his, and he'd be damned if he'd allow a herd of Persian Philistines to half-inch him.

Although he had the sufficient funds, in cash, he hadn't seriously intended to pay the asking price, particularly to a gallery in such dire financial straits. Any qualms surrounding the potential Iranian purchase of the works were quelled with the Persians' next question.

The leader of the group, distinguished by a surfeit of jewelry and hair, discussed the matter with his cohorts. He exchanged a brief remark as he glanced at the paintings. A conclusion was reached. The leader turned. "Is he very famous?" he asked in a thick Levantine accent. "The artist?"

Even the obsequious owner was taken aback by the question. He quickly surveyed the group, reassessed their imaginary net worth, and smilingly intoned, "Sir, he ranks among the foremost Impressionists of his period. He is comparable in every respect to Chagall, Picasso, Monet." He looked at the Iranians to see if those names meant anything to them.

"How much for one?" the spokesman asked. He pulled at the line of hairs sparsely adorning his upper lip.

James turned around to get a better look. He was grinning. Like the owner, he assessed the possible worth of his rival purchasers. The gallery owner's look of benevolence was retreating ever so slowly; he cleared his throat and lifted his good hand to his chin. "Perhaps, sir, you misunderstood me. The three canvases go as a unit. It would be a crime to separate them. No, I'm afraid I really couldn't consider letting them go individually."

James could see the owner was growing disillu-
sioned with the Iranians and their promise of petro-
dollars to take the masterpiece off his hands. He
glanced furtively about his gallery. The two security
men at the door acknowledged his stare, then
resumed their debate on how to win at the track.
Other potential customers cruised unattended among
the well-exhibited works of art. The only other sales
staff in the gallery, a young girl, was occupied with
an elderly woman. The owner looked past the Iranians at the prospective buyers strolling alone in his
gallery.

"Okay, but how much, still, for everything?" the
dark man inquired. James and the owner closed in
on the man. The owner tilted his head and asssumed
a pose of complete indifference as he said, "Two
hundred seventy thousand pounds is the gallery's
asking price, but confidentially, I think we might
be persuaded to bargain some."

*You'd be willing to bargain your left nut if it would
save you from going under*, James thought. Would
that the Iranian knew as much as he. James was
getting bored with standing around being diplomatic.
He monitored the Iranian's face for signs of stress;
it surrendered nothing and James wondered if the
man was on the level after all.

"Does that include the frames?" the Iranian asked.

The owner retaliated with a simultaneous lifting
of both eyebrows. "Yes," he said tartly, "and tax."
He crossed his arms and peered at the ceiling. He
was no longer interested. More to the point, he was
no longer interested in pretending to to be interested.

The Iranians sensed this and, like a flock of wayward sheep, congregated and humbly trod away.

"Thank you, but no," the leader called back apologetically. The women followed their men on the trail to the door.

James had had enough of this bullshit. He confronted the owner and stood squarely before him. For a moment the gallery owner looked irate. The young man's look of determination cut through him to the bone and shut him up.

"I'd like those Modiglianis and am willing to offer two hundred thousand pounds in cash now," he said crisply.

Wrinkles appeared on the fat man's forehead. He brushed nervously at his black wig. "What?" he asked, although he had heard perfectly well.

James purposely waited a beat, then said, "I'm in rather a hurry to get out of this shithole. I have two hundred thousand pounds in cash, here in this suitcase." He raised it. "You have the Modiglianis. I would like to exchange one for the other."

The owner had yet to see the money. As the chances were that the scruffy youth did not have two hundred thousand pounds in a suitcase, he resumed being his inveterate bad-mannered self. "Sir, this is a very serious establishment. If you think we have time and patience enough to endure the charades of every passing tourist, you are very much mistaken."

"This is a very serious, very pompous establishment, which, very regretfully, from your point of view, has been caught with its pants down or finger in the pie, or whatever the fuck you want to call it. Your ass is one inch from the flame, thanks to the Inland Revenue, and you're overextended as hell because of those paintings and one like them. I'm offering you a chance to get your investment back." James set the suitcase between his legs. He ignored the No Smoking signs plastered to the red damask walls and lit a cigarette.

The owner's words came in a dry staccato, belying no inner composure. "Two hundred thousand — that's what we paid."

"I doubt that. However, I'm offering you a chance to recoup a stupid investment and appease the Inland Revenue. I'm sure you, if anybody, must realize you'll never sell these paintings at their present price. Sotheby's only just got rid of them last year for two hundred sixty thousand. Dollars." This was accurate but not entirely true. There were other buyers and dealers who would have picked them up at this price.

This seemed to convince the owner. The young American knew too much to be anything but genuine. He checked to see if James was laughing in case it was a hoax. He wasn't. "Follow me, please."

They passed through a door marked PRIVATE at the far end of the gallery. A cement foyer led to a thick oak door with gold letters proclaiming the name of the fat man. James was ushered into a finely paneled room full of antiques. A miniature pewter chandelier was switched on. Its light illuminated the oil paintings on the wall. James glimpsed a Frick and a Paul Nash before the owner spoke. "Would you care for a drink?'

"Yes."

The fat man poured him a whiskey and handed it over. The man's tired eyes grazed over the suitcase. James continued standing as he sipped at the liquor. "Very well, Mr. —"

"Call me Ayatollah."

He frowned. "Very well, Mr. Aiola. I think we can do a deal," he said. The Iranian allusion passed him by. "Exactly what are you prepared to offer?"

"Let me reiterate. Here's the two hundred thousand. I'm about to walk out that door. Either I take the paintings or the suitcase. I don't care much either way. I don't feel comfortable here. You make up your mind or I walk. It's in your court." James wondered if his ultimatum was too severe. It wasn't his intention to scare the guy off. It occurred to him to show the owner the money. Placing the suitcase on the desk, he snapped the brass locks and opened it.

"Two hundred thousand pounds?"

Jamed ignored him. "Deal?"

"I've thought about this before, you know," the owner began thoughtfully. "Many times I've wondered what I'd actually take for the Modiglianis when push came to shove. You appear to know rather a lot about our present predicament with the government, and you are quite right. But as a matter of principle I couldn't let these canvases go for less than I paid for them. Zacovetti was a shrewd businessman," he said, referring to the Italian producer. "I will, however, accept an offer of two hundred ten thousand pounds in cash."

James smiled contentedly. He had called the old boy's bluff and won hands down. He finished the whiskey before he spoke. "Okay." They shook hands. "Two hundred ten thousand pounds."

"Can you have it here tomorrow morning?" he asked. "The extra ten thousand pounds. Can you be here with it tomorrow morning?"

"No, my mornings are busy enough. I'll give it to you now, unless there are some objections," James said. The owner sat back in his chair. He looked perplexed. James sorted through the valise and withdrew five wrapped stacks of ten thousand pounds each and one of five thousand pounds. He stuck these under his arm and unceremoniously dumped the remaining two hundred ten thousand pounds onto the leather desk blotter. "Count it if you like. Then write me a receipt." He positioned the valise under his arm and let the fifty-five thousand pounds drop back into it. He closed it again and set it on the floor. A minute later a receipt was relinquished.

"When would you like them delivered, Mr. Aiola?"

"The name is McLaren, and don't worry, I won't need them for at least two weeks. If I do, I'll have one of my aides contact you. I've got the receipt," James responded. He took one final look about the office. "Good luck to you, mate. From what I hear, you'll need it."

"Thank you, Mr. McLaren." Then the owner recognized the brash American from a magazine he'd read that morning. It suddenly made sense.

James left the gallery in a cab to go shopping. He reminded himself to have Evans reward the English contact who'd provided him with the inside information on the Dreyfuss's tax problems; five thousand pounds would keep him happy.

It was growing darker. The earlier sunlight had all but vanished beneath a cloak of threatening clouds. The air smelled remotely of rain and the breeze had picked up to displace what litter and leaves decorated the sidewalk in this part of town. James checked his watch: four-thirty-five. If he pressed it he could be in Knightsbridge before Ron Kirk retired to the pub across the street. All he really had to do was have a quick word with Ron to discuss which cloth he wanted for which suit and how he wanted them cut. The few odds and ends the tailor had fashioned for him in the past had fit and looked superb.

En route to Beauchamp Place, he made a quick stop at Turnbull & Asser in St. James's. He thought about not letting the meter run as he got out, then dismissed this with his usual "fuck it." After his coup *chez* Dreyfuss, he could afford it.

He was back in the taxi in a quarter of an hour with another receipt, this one bearing the prestigious logo of Prince Charles's shirtmaker. He had ordered one dozen shirts to be picked up in two weeks and had bought the cab driver a striped silk tie as a tip. They hurried back on to Piccadilly Street, through the traffic to Knightsbridge. He paid the guy off and climbed up the stairs to Kirk's.

Ron greeted him with a tape measure around his neck and boomed an enthusiastic hello. They exchanged the usual small talk, compared notes on the last time each of them had gotten laid, and shared a bottle of vintage white wine. It transpired that old Sidney had been awakened from his slumber for nothing because Ron chose to ignore the phoned-in measurements. He didn't trust thirdhand information and preferred to measure James himself. James shuffled around the tiny room while he examined the various bolts of cloth. Ron pursued him with the tape in one hand and a wineglass in the other. It took half an hour and a second bottle of vino before James reappeared on the pavement below with the suitcase under one arm and Ron on the other. He deposited his friend at The Bunch of Grapes pub directly opposite, waved good-bye, and about-faced for Brompton Road in search of a cab. With his shades off, he was no longer anonymous and was forced to sign six autographs and pose for a picture — something he rarely did — while he waited for a taxi.

Predictably, Olivia had telephoned and left a message saying she'd call again on the hour. James was stretched out in the sitting room smoking a reefer with the video on when the telephone rang. His spirits soared at the familiar sound of her voice. He bounced off the rug and sank into the bed clutching the phone. "Hey, baby!"

"How did you know it was me, James?"

"I know these things." He drew in on the reefer. "Hey, before we go any further, I'd like to apologize for breaking our date. I had to practice and I couldn't call you because I didn't have your number."

She laughed. "Our date? I thought it was tomorrow."

"Tomorrow? You mean if I had been there, you wouldn't . . . I'd have been stood up? Jesus! a sixteen-year-old standing up the reigning Wimbledon champion."

"James, you really fancy yourself," she said, teasing him. "Did anyone ever tell you that?"

"Regularly. Listen, how about dinner at nine, Chelsea Arts Club. Do you know it?" James asked.

"Sort of; actually, not really," Olivia admitted.

"It's on Old Church Street, a big white building, a bit like a barn inside, but the food's good."

"What should I wear?" she asked. "Is it smart?"

James snickered. "Look, it you have any old sweaters with holes in them, wear one. It's Bohemian."

"Okay James, nine o'clock. Oh, and James . . ."

"Yeah?"

"I think you're wonderful."

"I get enough ass kissing from everybody else without having to take it from you." He paused. "But while we're on the subject, the feeling's mutual. Nine o'clock." He hung up on her and lay back in the bed. He pulled his legs into his chest and sat up against the headboard. Beside him was the note from Pam. He looked at it, then picked it up and reread it. "Poor naïve son-of-a-bitch," he said. He lit a match and held it to the corner of the note. The dry paper flared. He extinguished the tiny flame and dropped it in a trashcan.

In the sitting room he drank one beer and opened another. On the video Sean Connery was doing his goddamnedest to keep his wig in place while he battled a giant black for the future of mankind. The Bond film, like everything else in the room, came compliments of the hotel. He switched the tape off with his foot.

Tomorrow would be "D" day, he thought. *The road show comes to London.* Mom, Dad, and their surrogate daughter, Janie. He didn't mind his parents so much. Although their presence often unnerved him, the moral support they offered was comforting at times, particularly at Wimbledon, where the English press had a vendetta against him of such extraordinary magnitude that he was surprised they hadn't actually put a gun to his head and fired it. *That's the one saving grace in this godforsaken country,* he thought. At least the nuts were forbidden to carry guns. Aside from that, there wasn't too much he liked about England, except maybe the grouse, and that came from Scotland anyway. The talent wasn't too bad, ladywise. This occurred to him as another consolation.

No matter how disgruntled he was with England, it didn't alter the fact that tomorrow three people he knew very well would be arriving via the Concorde to spend the tournament with him. Why had Janie come? he wondered bitterly. She knew things were more or less finished between them. Christ! They hadn't made love more than five times in the last three months. Lately their only link had been the narcotics they'd indulged in to wipe away their cares and cushion them from the pain of their inevitable split. He had felt genuinely saddened when he first realized they were drifting apart. For a time he had refused to admit it. After all, Janie did still love him as deeply as ever. The idea of hurting her distressed him, but it had to happen. The drugs made it easier. Janie sought a similar sanctuary for her broken heart. For several months they stayed together in this way — hiding in a sort of drugged euphoria. Notwithstanding the regular session of one-night stands, there had been no other serious love for James. Janie seemed happy.

The illusion they were living ended abruptly after James's arrest by the East Hampton Police Department for cocaine possession. A simple drunk-driving rap escalated into a major drug bust when James was discovered with one lousy gram of uncut cocaine in the glove compartment of his car. It was Janie's stuff. In her desperation to salvage what little they had, drugs had ironically marked the ignoble end of their relationship. James blamed Janie for the bust and now felt nothing but contempt for her. Suddenly, their history together meant nothing and he no longer gave a damn what she felt.

Thank God for Olivia. With her beside him, the prospect of ending it with Janie was not as bad.

Olivia clasped the wine bottle by the neck and tilted it closer. "Is this a good one?" she asked, reading from its label.

James spoke through a mouth full of chicken. "I shouldn't think so, knowing his place. It works, though." He raised his glass in confirmation and drained it. An alert waitress brought over another bottle and set it down on the bare wood table. He thanked her.

"What's wrong with this place? I like it," sailorgirl said. She looked around. "It's cozy."

"That it is," James agreed. "That's why I joined. This dim lighting lets you cop an odd feel without making a scene." He reached under the table and squeezed her thigh.

"James," she warned. They met halfway and kissed.

"What?"

She stroked his hand. "Nothing."

"There's something I have to tell you. It's your classic good news/bad news story," he said as he filled his glass.

"Uh-oh, here it comes. It was great while it lasted, but . . ."

James stabbed her playfully with his fork. "Shut up. It's not like that. It'd be easier if it was."

"You mean you wish it was." Olivia tried to look dismayed.

"I didn't say that. Look, shut up or I'll make you sit on the floor and eat." He pointed to the floor with the fork.

She rolled her eyes and smiled again. "What is it?"

"I'm trying to tell you. Tomorrow poses a little problem. My parents are coming over. All right?

But they're not coming alone. They're bringing my ex-lady."

"What's wrong with that? I'd like to meet her," she interrupted.

"Hold on. She's my ex-lady, but she doesn't exactly know it yet. That's the bad news — how to tell her it's over." He spoke the last sentence through his wineglass.

"Charming. Then what's the good news?"

"The good news is you've been chosen by a panel of judges to be my new lady."

Olivia almost knocked over the wine as she kissed him. "Oh, James, I love you."

He ran a loving finger down her cheek to her throat. "Maybe you do — yes, I think you do. But that doesn't solve the immediate headaches." He tried to picture Janie's face when he finally broke the not-so-exclusive news. "It's bound to be a little sticky. But there's 'fuck all emotion' from my end, so it shouldn't be that bad. It will take time, though."

Her pretty face looked confused. "Why?"

"Trust me, little lamb. I'll need a few days to work it out."

"A few days in bed, you mean."

James laughed. "I'm warning you, you're going to be eating on the floor. For your information, we haven't touched each other for over a month. She's frigid anyway. So trust me to end it my way. Like the song."

"Screw the song," Olivia said, frowning.

"The reason I mention this now is to let you know why I might not be available for a while." He took out a cigarette and threw one across the table to her.

Her mouth puckered as she said, "You said a few days; now you say a while. Which one is it?"

"Either. Just let me be free to do it the easiest way." He clasped her tiny hand. "And no matter what happens, don't believe any of the bullshit that gets into the papers. Promise?" he asked.

"Promise me you'll never do this to me."

He opened his mouth and said nothing. He gazed into the perfect round eyes of the sixteen-year-old. Laden with mascara as they were tonight, they looked curiously older. They could have been the intelligent eyes of a thirty-year-old. The candlelight highlighted her features alternately. Her teeth were almost phosphorescent in the darkened room. She had asked him to make a promise and, by so doing, had asked him to ponder the depth of their relationship. The sudden chill left him and he winked at her. Promises and declarations came easily under these conditions. "I will," he said softly. "I promise."

Chapter Six

April — Monte Carlo

Rain beat down upon Monte Carlo in fat, capacity
drops that bounced knee-high on the ubiquitous
cement, making tiny splashing sounds. In the precious few spots where the earth had yet to be covered
in concrete, the rain fell less audibly. It had waited
until the exact hour after the tournament to begin.
McLaren had won, as was expected. The crowd had
behaved predictably, exhibiting all the decorum of
spectators at a cockfight. Wolf whistles competed
with shouts and cat calls. Aggressive clapping inter-

rupted play intermittently. McLaren, of course, failed to retain his own composure and lashed back at the audience. He was rebuked by the umpire and this angered him and delighted the crowd. McLaren directed his wrath at the linesmen and then at his young South African opponent, who, in his opinion, shouldn't have made the finals anyway.

The South African, aware that he had the crowd behind him, would rally to within striking distance of McLaren, only to be slammed back down in defeat: It was not ordained to be. Only rarely did the script afford for an upset against the world's number-one champion. And on these occasions McLaren was nursing a hangover or sore limbs from having screwed about all night. He rarely lost as a consequence of lack of ability. Monaco had proved no exception.

He won. The spectators shut up, the South African slunk off, and he prepared to go home. But something got in his way. That something was five-feet-five with a full derriere and breasts that could be used as a ski slope. She was smoking reefer within clear view of the press corps clustered outside the locker rooms. Somehow she had secured a press pass: McLaren saw her over the heads of the media. He could smell the pungent-sweet aroma of the pot. Her narrow lips parted as she smiled. She was dazzling and, in a way, he had expected her.

He gave a brief three-sentence statement to the press before acquiescing to the impulse in his loins. The sea of newsmen parted to let him pass and he went directly to her. They started for the street and looked for a cab. She leaned into him and laughed accommodatingly, then inserted the reefer between his lips. The smoke from the joint was smothered in the rain. She shimmied closer and rubbed her head lovingly over his shoulder. Her full blond hair smelled of cigarettes. Beneath this he detected the scent of the cheap tangy perfume that she had bathed in that afternoon. He found the scent only a tiny bit curious; none of the women he habitually slept with would wear anything so cheap, and this intrigued him. She smelled . . . sexual. He had strolled through the familiar seduction scenario too many times to let this aberration faze him. He was openly available to the women of the world — rich or poor, black or white — providing they had the looks and were willing to book him on a one-night basis.

Yet this encounter would be different. Like his victory on court, it was predestined. However, of all his varying escapades in every corner of the globe, he had yet to be provided with a fuck at the expense of a total stranger. This stranger was not even a fan. In fact, he loathed McLaren and everything he represented. And the accommodating blonde in the locker room had never even heard of him. Hers was a world of back streets and sweaty smoke-filled rooms. Her sympathies stemmed from, and remained stolidly founded upon, the ten-thousand-franc remuneration she would receive for her role in the seduction. Like the deadened vein of a career junkie, her emotions and had long since dried up. Love, hate, friendship, and despair had been relegated to a corner of her mind she no longer consulted. All she knew was the insatiable hunger of the heroin that fueled her. And, of course, the fear.

The tall hollow-eyed man with the Russian accent had learned of her reputation through random inquiries among her fellow junkies. Even before they met, the Russian had seemed to know all there was to know about her and her addiction. The way he demanded to know if she was available had surprised her. Of course she was available, if the price was right. What did he think she was, after all, a fucking princess? *This is Monaco*, chéri. *There are only two princesses left. Money rules. Don't show me the size of your cock, just the size of the denominations.* She would do the rest.

The pained-looking man shoved her under an alcove to a derelict café. He eyed her indifferently, yielding nothing and showing no emotion. Something about him unnerved her. His perfect French yielded an inner cynicism that transcended the boundaries of any language barrier. "I've heard very much about you, Claudette. You seem to be exactly what I'm searching for." She saw he had cut himself shaving and was examining this when his voice cracked. "Well, my little Gallic slut, is it true? Are you what I'm searching for?"

Her eyes darted instinctively to the dark stretch of alleyway behind him. She needed an escape route in case he got violent. She looked up and tried hard to smile. "I'm whatever you make me — if the money's right. No questions, no involvements, no shit."

He struck her savagely across the bridge of the nose. The deliberate blow was not quite strong enough to break the sliver of bone. She recoiled and drew a hand up to the ringing numbness in her face. Her eyes teared. Rage echoed through her. She stood erect suddenly and jabbed a knee into the Russian. He deflected it deftly with his fist. His free hand chopped into her esophagus. She crashed back against the door to the café and gulped hungrily for air. After a moment her wind returned. "Are you available for a big fat price and one day's work?"

She responded coolly. Her actions stemmed from an inner will to live another day. "I told you, if the price is right, then I'm your girl. Business is not exactly booming tonight," she said hoarsely.

This amused him. He touched her affectionately with the back of his hand. She tensed, then relaxed as no harm came to her. There was no need for superfluous violence now that a proper employer-employee relationship had been established. She sensed this immediately. It was much the way her Parisian pimp, Jean Pierre, had treated her. "Ten thousand francs says you're available, slut," Joseph said between clenched teeth. She nodded appreciatively. Ten thousand francs would take care of her habit for the week. She knew he knew he had her now. It was only a question of saying it. She'd ask where.

"Where?" she asked automatically.

She found it difficult to meet his icy gaze and allowed her eyes to drop to the front of his khaki overcoat. She kept them there. "Not where honey, *when.*" He hesitated. She heard him smile. "I have you booked for tomorrow. Hôtel St. Etienne. You're to pick up my client inside the sports stadium, V.I.P. dressing room. When I say pick up, I mean pick up. He knows you want him, and your intentions. He hasn't yet made up his mind. I'll give you a pass so you have access to his room."

She saw him slide a hand beneath his coat. For one second the distinctive Burberry's plaid shone through. The hand seemed to be clawing at something in one of the pockets. It remained there. She looked up. "I don't get it."

"Then listen carefully. If you fuck up, I scatter your pussy across the Champs-Elysées." She saw the hand jump from the coat, preceded by the squat barrel of an automatic. It settled tightly against her pelvic bone and slid down to her vagina. She braced herself against the door and tried valiantly not to piss. *Nom de Dieu!* she whispered silently.

He kept the gun in position and continued. "My client's name is James McLaren, the tennis player. Do you know tennis? I hope not. It would complicate things if you did, and I'd be forced to pull this little trigger right now and put your pussy out of its misery." He laughed his cynical laugh. "I think Claudette believes me." His statement warranted an answer.

"Yes, she believes," came her stilted reply.

"Well, then, does she know tennis?"

"What's tennis?" she asked sarcastically. She unwound marginally as she realized he was unlikely to shoot. He needed her. Six years on the beat had endowed her with an uncanny resiliency. She could be struck down, trod on, snatched up, and dumped again, but she'd still wind up on her feet. She would be fine as long as she quelled the fire of her heroin habit. The Russian had startled her momentarily. His sincerity was not in question. He meant business. With six years of experience behind her, she could handle him.

"Very good, slut, you humor me." He batted her with his free hand. It was not a particularly hard blow, but meant only to solicit her undivided attention. It did. "You are to wait for my client tomorrow afternoon at this address." He pulled a passport-sized photograph and a press pass from his pocket, glanced at them, then handed them to her. "That's him, James McLaren. Once he leaves the locker room, you make the pickup. It won't be any great surprise because I'll have set you up as best I can. No fuckups." He wiggled the automatic.

For the past four days since he'd launched the scheme, Joseph had been bombarding McLaren with a stream of cards and letters professing Claudette's undying devotion and lust for his body. He had discovered McLaren's plans to spend the few days prior to the Monaco Open at the Hôtel de Paris. This was significant. The advance notice would enable him to implement his long-drawn-up plans. Infinitely more significant was the discovery that neither McLaren's parents nor girl friend would be accompanying him due to previous commitments. Joseph had opportunized on their absence and began baiting his prey the minute James stepped onto the baked tarmac of the local heliport. The phantom female admirer, a character created and perpetuated by the Russian, had expressed her affections with an enormous bouquet of flowers at the heliport. Spicy love letters and a wicker picnic hamper filled with Stolichnaya vodka awaited him at the Hôtel de Paris. More letters followed and eventually a phone call was put through with the aid of the chambermaid at Joseph's less grand hotel. Would he meet for a drink? He couldn't? Why not?

James laughingly shrugged off the amorous suggestions. He was worn out from a bout of flu and genuinely needed the rest before the match. Would he be available afterward? A date was set, tentatively for after the match. James promised to keep an eye peeled for the eager blonde known only as Jeannette.

Joseph picked at the scab on his neck where he had cut himself shaving. His grip eased on the automatic, then tightened again. He persevered. "You start work when he gets off. The match is scheduled for two o'clock. Be there by three just in case. Proceed with him to the Hôtel St. Etienne. There's plenty of vodka and gin in the bar in your room. Make sure he drinks some." He paused. "Then go for it." He returned the automatic to his pocket as he stared at her. "Don't be surprised if you get a little company. Keep thinking ten thousand francs and do your number." His hands jerked from the coat. She anticipated the cold steel of the automatic dildo but was disappointed.

"Here, slut." He tossed her a clear plastic bag containing two ounces of green, fibrous material. "I trust you can roll a joint. Roll some and smoke them with your client. It's been treated to make it work extra hard." A frugal smile hung on his lips, then spread to form the cynical grin that was his trademark. He extended a clenched hand palm downward. With his free hand he reached and took her by the finger, then twisted her hand until it formed a cupped surface. His clenched fist relaxed over hers and she caught the tiny sachet of heroin. Animation leaped into her pretty face.

He noted this and smiled in earnest. Her addiction would play into his hands. She needed what he supplied and, therefore, indirectly, she needed him. She could consequently be trusted to act out her part in the choreographed charade. Inherently, he trusted no one. Too many times in his life he had found himself on the wrong end of a conspiracy. When he needed to enlist the services of another, it was imperative that he render that individual trustworthy through whatever means. This explained his reasons for footslogging it around the red-light district of Monte Carlo, asking very definite questions to random whores. The ability to uncover weakness in others was, ironically, one of his strengths.

"Thank you," Claudette said feebly. Her palms glistened with an instant sweat and her whole body began to tremble gently. She hadn't realized how much she needed a fix. Already her brain worked feverishly to locate a suitable vein for the drug.

Joseph had to stop himself from laughing. He would have no problems with Claudette. "Not so fast, slut." He snatched the sachet from her fingertips.

He squeezed it. The quarter-gram of powdered lactose and heroin cut 70–30 would keep her going and ensure that she would be in good form for the succeeding day's events. He waved the packet casually in her face. "Consider this an advance toward services to be rendered. You'll receive your fee tomorrow night if everything goes smoothly. If it goes any other way, I've booked you a one-way passage to a faraway land where money buys shit" — he slid his tongue over the chapped surface of his lips — "unless they sell smack in hell, Claudette." He let the sachet fall to the street. He lit a cigarette as he walked away.

The acrid smell of the Gitane wafted back on the sea breeze. Claudette watched him until he rounded the corner and the sound of his footsteps had faded from the cobblestones. She crouched and retrieved the small white packet. Her painted fingers wiped the grit against her lips and cheeks. Her heart raced as she reveled in thoughts of the warm, tingling satisfaction the powder would bring. Then she remembered his threats and her instructions. She placed the heroin carefully in the small hollow of her breasts. The tight-fitting T-shirt kept it there. She folded the manila envelope with the scrawled details of the seduction and slid it into her purse.

She forsook the luxury of her one-room apartment and the seclusion it would offer. There was always the chance that Marie would be back with some of her friends, and Claudette knew that her roommate's voracious habit would make short work of the powder. It was meant for Claudette alone. She had stood the abuse, accepted the threats, without the help of anybody else.

She hiked the arduous slope leading to the monument. She had decided to shoot up while watching the coast. From there she could see what boats had entered the harbor. She was perspiring fiercely by the time she slumped onto the bench at the base of the monument. It was not a particularly conspicuous piece of concrete and marble. But, unlike the monsters that besieged the tiny island, its slabs were inscribed with the names of the two hundred long-obscured souls who had died during an equally obscure war. She sat so that her head rested exactly below the words "Vondecoeur, Paul, Pierre". She peered out over the incline past the rocks and buildings into the sea. The myriad-colored lights of the ships formed a deceptive illusion of an extended coast.

Her thoughts returned to the heroin. She broke the packet with her teeth and tasted the powder. It was both bitter and sour. Her knowing tongue weighed the potency against the roof of her mouth. It was active, at least. This she could tell. The silver spoon, with its tarnished bottom and handle fashioned into a hook to facilitate a steady hold, was filled to capacity. She flicked the fat head of an all-weather match. It erupted with a sizzling sound. Its tongue of smoke lapped at the already blackened underside of the utensil. The powder dissolved under the heat of the third match. This was transferred into the syringe via a narrow groove filed in the spoon. She checked the level. The elastic tourniquet raised a vein on the fleshy side of her calf. She clasped the syringe in two hands to steady it and inhaled sharply, biting on her breath as she injected. The glow took hold of her leg and moved quickly to her head and limbs with the acute effervescence known only to the addict. She might have orgasmed had she remembered to touch herself. Her head slumped and rested as it did after the hit against the engraved names of the war dead, exactly under the name "Voleneau, Alex Cocteau". Her senses digested the sounds and sights of the harbor. She saw everything and nothing at all.

Joseph rented the video equipment from a little shop that made its money developing tourists' film in two hours. He left a cash deposit for the two video porta-packs complete with zoom lenses and microphones sensitive to ten meters. He paid cash for the tungsten lamps and tripods and stowed the gear in the boot of the Citroën saloon he had rented for the week. A brief visit to the more sophisticated camera shop across the street unearthed a selection of adaptable infrared lenses. He bought two of these.

Next stop was the upscale, three-room suite that, like the car, he'd taken for the week. The management of the Hôtel St. Etienne knew him as a Yugoslavian press attaché that he alleged to be. They also knew him by his wallet and the swarm of French notes it deployed. He wore sunglasses perpetually — even on cloudy afternoons — and none of the staff could recall seeing him at night. He surrendered his car to the valet in front of the hotel and accepted the assistance of an obliging porter. All the porters recognized him and instantly leaped to unburden him of any luggage or little crisp notes he might be carrying. He thanked the moustachioed-Arab porter who helped him with the equipment. He tipped the usual amount in an attempt to attach no importance to the instruments and the act of carrying them.

The hotel suite was ideally laid out to situate both the orgy he had planned and the camera equipment. The first room beyond the door was small and ordinary. Probably meant, he thought, to accommodate an overflow of guests for the night, or perhaps children. The second, a sitting room, was quite large and symmetrical in shape. An adjoining bathroom complete with the vulgar accessory of a sunken tub led off from the right. The third and final room was accessible through the hanging archway. Consequently, the master bedroom could be partitioned off with the use of blankets or cardboard to create the illusion of a wall. By moving the bed and the bookcase into the sitting room in front of the flap of blanket, he had masked any hint of a past violation. It looked like another wall.

As the archway was of a considerable length, he could put each of the cameras at the extreme corner of either end and that way obtain a greater range of angles with the cameras. Employing tight focuses for greater clarity of image, he could effectively film every inch of the room. He mounted one of the cameras with strips of wire and a dozen finishing nails. The second he was prepared to hand-hold during the actual escapade. He secured the tungsten lamps on tripods and extended them to their full height. These were to be employed as a precaution if the infrared lenses failed to work. He reckoned by checking the respective light meters on the camera porta-packs that he could determine whether the lenses were working and the cameras recording.

His last chore before the arrival of the hallowed and as yet unscandalized guest — and the menage of unemployed actors and actresses — was to attend to the refreshments. He knew from his investigations that McLaren drank and favored vodka. He arranged a bar against the wall in the center room. Each of the half dozen bottles of assorted liquor was opened and one-third of the precious liquid was poured down the bathroom sink. A year before he would have thought such an exercise totally impossible. He smiled as he remembered. Moscow had been so cold and uninviting. In place of the deleted booze, he added his own concoction of wine treated with a Valium derivative. The effect of the contents taken even in moderation was guaranteed to have the imbiber seeing planets that were yet to be discovered. He'd read about McLaren's coke bust and obliged him with three grams of pharmaceutical-strength cocaine.

Claudette finished the advanced payment of heroin for breakfast. She bathed and dressed and spent the rest of the morning chewing chocolate bars and smoking cigarettes while watching the T.V. She even caught a few games of the women's finals match. The commentators spoke constantly about the men's finals following directly afterward and of McLaren. She switched to a Cary Grant movie. To her the world's top-rated tennis player was just another client. She'd get his rocks off just like the guy before and the guy after. She had been waiting for nearly three wonderfully opiated hours outside the sports stadium when he emerged.

They took a taxi to the Hôtel St. Etienne. James surprised her by being so utterly seducible. The persuasion the Russian had alluded to simply wasn't necessary. If anything, she would have to deter his advances lest he shoot his load in the cab.

He pounced on the reefer and fueled it with the powerful bellows of his athletic lungs. She noticed the exceptionally strong dope taking over. It had a calming influence. His hands were still down her jeans. They were just scratching about less frantically.

Nobody recognized him as he moved with her through the dark side entrance into the hotel. In fact, nobody even saw him. They proceeded arm in arm to the second floor. Claudette twisted the knob of the first door. She led James inside and licked his ear provocatively as he brushed by her. She shut the door and locked it with the type of tiny chain lock that looked stronger than it was. By the time they neared the bar, his pants were down around his ankles and he was sucking her through her brassiere.

Joseph was filming from the start; the entrance and then the impassioned advances by McLaren were all captured on videotape. He had learned a lesson through his experiences filming the girls on the circuit: Keep the camera running; never miss a trick. In the spontaneous environment of covert photography and big-league espionage, there was no way of predicting who would do what to whom and when. The outing in the Hôtel St. Etienne marked his eighth and final leg in a blackmail scheme that had taken him around the world in pursuit of the professional tennis champions.

The evening went beautifully. The infrared lenses were functioning. He was able to film everything from McLaren's first line of cocaine to his first of six vodkas. Joseph captured for posterity the first inkling of sexual foreplay and the mutual undertaking of oral sex. As the stable of actors and actresses entered on cue from the bathroom, he filmed them. He even caught McLaren's only brush with homosexuality as the half-conscious tennis star allowed one of the naked actors to suck him off. It was all over in two hours. The bit players quietly took their leave, still blissfully unaware of the actual meaning of the encounter. They each collected their four hundred francs from Joseph in the hallway outside and left the hotel.

James remained in the fetal position on the bed enjoying the sedated slumber of the Valium-laced booze. Claudette had managed to retain her sense of awareness. She confronted Joseph and asked him for her cut. She was told quietly to be patient and helped him pack the video equipment. This was arranged near the door. All of the liquor was fed to the bathroom sink and the bottles were rinsed with soapy water. The tap was allowed to run on boiling-hot for five minutes.

They crept stealthily down the fire hall, through the doors, and onto the street. The Citroën was parked at the curb five yards away. She helped him deposit the gear. They drove off.

Joseph reacted to the pop of the ejected cigarette lighter in the dash. He lit two cigarettes, one for her. The cool, unfiltered tobacco of the Gitane circulated within his lungs. He was content and reached over to touch the four hour-long tapes with his fingertips; they were really there. Tomorrow he would rent a VCR and a television and edit the film. He would make two copies of the finished version. One would be placed in his safety deposit box in Geneva. The other would be played for Popotov and the others when they met to monitor and discuss his progress. He had them by the balls now. The Wimbledon dossier had been compiled and he alone had access to it. True, they had fished him out of the gutter and given him a reason to live. He admitted this. But that was old news. He'd renegotiate a better deal now that he'd gained the necessary leverage. There was nothing wrong with a little honest bartering. He still intended to play their game. He was merely rewriting the rule book.

Joseph remembered Claudette was there when she asked about her fee. "What? Oh, certainly, slut . . . I mean Claudette. You've waited long enough." He drove the car to a parking berth on the road to the sea. Light from a streetlamp cast a crooked shadow over the nefarious pair. He arched around and withdrew a large paper bag and settled it on his lap while he extracted her reward.

"I believe this represents a fair exchange." He threw her the plastic bag full of white powder. It landed on her knee. She weighed it instantly. It must've been at least a pound. Even if it was cut up as much as the earlier batch, it was magic. Was she dreaming? Could it be true? He cut her off before she could speak. "Don't thank me, you've earned it. Besides, I deal in this shit. I run out of cash occasionally, but never this."

"What's cash?" She smiled. Her smile was radiant.

His hand came out of the overcoat, clasping another sachet between the fingers. "Here's a leftover from last night. I was afraid if I gave it to you, you'd have shot it all up at once." She was speechless. He eyed her gamely. "I'll tell you what — seeing how I've done so much for you, give me the pleasure of seeing you enjoy. It's rare that I get to witness the fruits of my labors. Please?" She was calculating how much smack sat on her lap and what it would fetch at present street prices and how long it would last.

"Oh . . . what . . . er . . . okay. Sure, Daddy." She was into the sachet instantly. Two minutes later she glanced up as she removed the hose tourniquet. Her gaunt and smiling face registered mild surprise at the alien sensation. Her fingers, which were pressing the point of injection in her arm, rose to her throat. Her mouth snapped open and her tongue was out. Joseph took the half-empty sachet from her lap and with a strong arm pinned her to the seat. He drove on for five hundred yards before shoving her lifeless body out of the moving vehicle. She landed with an abrasive thud and rolled into an accumulation of bushes. He threw the strychnine-laced sachet after her. " 'Night, slut. My regards to the reaper," he said pleasantly in Russian and drove on.

A mile passed before he dumped the powdered milk out the car window across the street. It was dispersed in a swirl of eddies by the sea breeze and scattered to merge with the damp gravel of the road surface.

SwissAir flight 602 taxied to a halt opposite terminal seven at Geneva's International Airport. Among the passengers disembarking on the gangway into the awaiting SwissAir courtesy tram was the slim Russian with the hollow eyes. A flight bag was hooked over his shoulder. It contained the usual things: passport, visa form, magazines stolen from the plane rack, plus two videotapes. Joseph had edited the film the day before in his hotel room. Two copies were made and the edited bits had been destroyed. The shoot had been successful enough. The tight focus of the mounted camera had recorded some very clear, very graphic closeups. The hand-held camera had pursued McLaren about the room, filming the other actors and taking establishing shots of the hotel suite. Together, the two cameras had recorded some extraordinarily compromising activity. McLaren's career both as a competitor and an endorser of products was essentially over, Joseph thought. Unless, of course, he agreed to their terms.

Joseph passed through customs and hired the driver of a maroon Mercedes to take him to the Hilton. His bags, recent purchases from France, sat behind him in the trunk. He spent the next half hour checking into his room and organizing his schedule and possessions. He placed three phone calls, masturbated, and took a shower. He was shaved and dressed within the hour. He double-locked the suite door and waited for the elevator with the two identical sets of tapes in a valise under his arm.

The security guard at the uptown branch of Bank of Geneva escorted him to the safety deposit hall in the vast modern edifice. Joseph watched the man as he unlocked and withdrew his steel container from the wall. He was then directed to a private area composed of elevated mahogany tables with curtained enclosures for privacy. He took out a bundle of tapes and laid it in the steel container. The box was reshelved. He watched the guard lock it in place, thanked him, and returned to the cool spring air of the Swiss avenue.

The light at the top of the elevator doors indicated his arrival and a belated chime echoed down the spacious corridor. Joseph crushed a cigarette dead in the hall ashtray and wondered how Popotov would accept the news. There was always the chance they had prepared for it and were waiting in the office ready to throw him out the window; being Russians they were not beyond such crudity, he thought. They were mostly old boys with old-boy reflexes, and if it came to physical violence, he could give them a hell of a fight. Rolf, the timid male secretary, probably didn't even carry a piece, and the only one he really had to watch was Vladimir, the baby-faced front man whom Joseph instinctively mistrusted.

He threw open the door without knocking. His pocketed hand rested on the half-moon trigger of the loaded automatic. One quick survey of the room and he realized they hadn't a clue. It was just his paranoia showing, his survivor's edge. He stared at them: all lined up like a goddamned human shooting gallery. Joseph could have picked them off in the time it took to yawn and still collect the Kewpie doll for hitting the hearts. He laughed uncertainly. He withdrew his hand from the pocket. Closing the door, he made for the picture window at the end of the table. It struck him how uncannily similar this room was to the one where they'd first met in Moscow. Perhaps they wanted it that way, he mused. The image of Moscow quickly dispersed his smile.

"Hello, gentlemen, how's every little thing?" He paced closer to the window and kept his coat on. He viewed the panorama of skyscrapers and city streets and trees with cherry blossoms. The river darted between an interruption in the buildings.

"Have you got the tapes?"

Joseph was surprised by the source of the question. It came from the little pockmarked fellow with the toupee, and the only one in the group who had yet to speak in his presence. There remained a third and equally silent member, an old man with a squint and long wispy tendrils of white hair beginning in a thicket on his forehead. Joseph suspected these two were the money men who had financed the enterprise. They also stood to profit the most from the scandal. Popotov commanded the head of the rectangular desk between the money men. Rolf hovered on the periphery awaiting orders from someone. Vladimir divided his attention between glances at the picture window and bemused looks at the men around the wooden table.

Popotov's large head turned to behold the ex-KGB man he'd dragged from a Moscow gutter. He poised his bristly crown toward Joseph and managed a look of the greatest sincerity. "Have you?"

Joseph then noted the video machine on the table in the connecting room. It was plugged into a television set and ready to roll. He decided to dazzle them with his nonchalance and stared idly out the window before replying. Vladimir curiously followed his stare. So did Rolf. Finally, Joseph nodded.

"What the fuck's that supposed to mean?" Popotov demanded.

Joseph stared at him and grinned. The smile was tentative. The shadowed corners of his eyes grew narrow. "Relax, Papa, they're right here." He raised the valise.

"Let's see them," the white-haired man said dryly.

"Okay," Joseph said. He started for the video. A grip of steel in the form of Popotov's large hand took him by the forearm. He twisted free.

Popotov pivoted in his chair. "I shall put them on." He stood up to his full height of six-feet-four. His attempt at bullying the younger man failed miserably.

Joseph glared up at his employer and laughed.

He lofted a hand to his shoulder and forced him back into his chair. The look of utter intensity on the younger man's face suggested to Popotov that he behave himself. Popotov had everything to live for. Joseph, Popotov seemed to remember, had nothing. "Relax. This is my handiwork. Please allow me the honor of presenting it to you," Joseph said flatly.

There followed a void in the conversation. Rolf's eyes volleyed between Joseph and Popotov as though wondering who would yield first, for the ex-KGB agent had forced a showdown. The white-haired man sensed the possibility of violence and alleviated the tension by butting in. "Put them on, then, young man. You are wasting our time." He patted Popotov's arm consolingly. "Let him show us what he has accomplished."

It had taken nearly fifty thousand dollars in expenses and three months to produce the two hours of edited tape he had in the valise. Joseph slid the first cassette into the machine and switched it on. "*Voilà!*" he said sardonically. "The Wimbledon dossier." He took a seat at the table. Rolf flicked off the lights.

The first hour of tape featured the glorious color antics of the lesbian professional tennis players at play. The tape was a distillation of seven separate orgies and included virtually every woman in the top twenty-five who was either lesbian or bisexual. Only a handful of younger girls or married players were absent. All the regulars were there in all their iniquitous splendor.

These sessions, because of their frequency, were

relatively easy to record. All Joseph had to do was organize a lesbian party, invite some of the notorious local girls, then let the word leak to the various players. Because not all of the lesbians attended every party, he had to repeat this maneuver a total of seven times. The tape they were watching represented the highlights of six and one-half hours of actual filming. The Russian men spoke their satisfaction through a lack of criticism. Even the volatile Popotov surprised Joseph by remaining silent. They sat breathless without flinching and sprouted five erections that lasted for the duration of the film. The McLaren tape, all forty-five minutes of it, was inserted into the machine after the others. Judging from their expressions, they enjoyed this pièce de résistance even more than the other.

Light returned to the room. Joseph collected the tapes. He smiled secretly as he placed them on the table. The elderly pockmarked financier was sweating perceptibly, as was the other money man, to Popotov's left. The distinguishable odor of lust hung in the air. A sure sign of success, Joseph thought.

"Very well," Popotov said coolly. "You've done your job. All that remains is for you to put these tapes to work for us. If we achieve the anticipated results, then you shall be paid in full for your efforts. At present we're willing to release a further seventy thousand dollars in Swiss francs. This will give you a total of fifty percent of the agreed price."

How generous, Joseph snickered. He swallowed the accumulation of saliva and mucus in his mouth. "Thank you," he began humbly. "However, there is a slight snag, which I'm confident will not prove insurmountable."

"What snag?" Popotov's face, red from chronic high blood pressure, went redder. His knuckles stood out upon his hand as he gripped a pencil like a knife.

"Just a slight one. You see, gentlemen, I was forced to appropriate a considerable sum of my own money in order to get these films made. Quite a bit, actually."

Popotov snapped the pencil in half. He should have expected as much. His hand moved protectively toward the tapes and slid them in toward his chest. Joseph detected an abrupt communicating nod from Popotov toward Vladimir. Vladimir shrugged in his seat. "How much more?"

"Rather more than you anticipated, comrade. I think three hundred thousand dollars in a cash advance plus a guaranteed ten percent of the profits would appease me."

"Oh, would it?" Popotov retorted bitterly. Ten percent represented nearly one-half his own cut. He couldn't help smiling at the man he'd rescued from the gutter. Once a loser, always a loser. He monitored the expressions of the others. They registered similar looks of amusement and incredulity. "You amuse us, Joseph," Popotov said.

"Do I? I don't intend to. In point of fact, I had expected a much more distressful reaction," he said. He watched Vladimir cautiously from the corner of his eye.

Popotov laughed openly. His resonant bear laugh was contagious. Even Joseph was smiling. "Sorry to disappoint you, but it's a little late. We've got the tapes, and you've got our word we'll come through on our part of the bargain." Popotov said this spitefully. "Enough of this revelry." Joseph rose to leave. The men found his altogether reposed façade both curious and disturbing. Vladimir itched the handle of the Heckler & Koch pistol in a holster on his calf.

Joseph stood very still. "I'm afraid you're slightly wrong there, gentlemen. However, time will surely tell."

"What?" the white-haired one inquired. "What are you up to, for heaven's sake? You've given us the tapes. We've seen what's on them."

"You've got the tapes, all right, but there's not much on them of any use to you," Joseph said knowingly. He began again before they could interrupt. "I took the liberty of erasing the tape during the projection. What you've got there, Popotov, gentlemen, is two hours' worth of . . . of air."

"What?" Popotov roared. Vladimir was fidgeting with the revolver on his leg.

Joseph took the initiative. "Allow me." He strode brazenly forward, swiped up the closest tape, and shoved it in the machine. Grainy blank tape filled the screen. He let it run. "You see, boys, dead air."

"You son-of-a-bitch," Popotov said.

"Bastard!" the pockmarked one exclaimed.

"Not so fast with your denunciations. You might force me to double my price."

Eyes met eyes in a furious wordless conference. Even Rolf appeared nonplussed. Only the white-

haired boy retained his composure. "You scumbag!"
Popotov spat. "I personally pick you off the street,
give meaning to your worthless life — to be rewarded
with this."

"Keep it in your trousers, comrade," Joseph replied. "The game still goes on. We just amend the
rules some. As I see it, you haven't got a goddamned
leg to stand on. I have the tapes. You want the
tapes. You haven't got the time or know-how to
refilm them. We can work out a compromise." He
paused. "Surely, if the tapes mean as much to you
as you profess, then an extra three hundred thousand
plus a fair percentage is not exorbitant. Think of
what you stand to earn." They did. Their rage
mellowed.

"You gutter rat, you've crossed the wrong men."

All eyes rested on the pockmarked financier. He
alone pursued the invective. Popotov shut him up
with a slicing glance. Vladimir was looking remotely
amused by it all.

Popotov began scribbling figures on a tablet in
front of him. "And if we meet your terms, then what?"
he asked.

"Then we proceed as planned. You see, I, too,
maintain a certain level of what Westerners refer
to as 'ethics.' I don't want it all. Just a piece of
it — my piece."

Popotov asked, "When do you deliver?"

"When would you prefer?"

"One hour."

"Sold to the old boy in the crewcut," Joseph joked.
He delighted rubbing salt in the wound. He'd show

them just what a scumbag could accomplish. "Whomever you choose to deliver your end of it, have them meet me in the foyer of the Bank of Geneva, Curzon Street branch, in one hour's time. Have them there alone, with the money in cash — and a contract of some sort drawn up by your solicitors and declaring my ten percent." He cleared his throat. "I realize, of course, that this formality is only as binding as you choose to make it, though I'll take my chances. You'd hate me to blow the whistle, wouldn't you?"

"And you will have the tapes?" Popotov asked through a cloud of cigarette smoke.

"Of course."

"How do we know these are the only copies?" the pockmarked man demanded.

"You have my word, as a gentleman."

"A gentleman? What good is your word? You've already proven your duplicity. What if you choose to trick us again?" The little financier was near hysteria.

Joseph wondered if his bargained ten percent was to be taken out of the pockmarked man's pocket. The way he was behaving, one would think so. "And the meek shall inherit the earth," he said philosophically, ignoring the questions. "God help us."

Popotov nodded. Something resembling respect played on his hard features.

Vladimir would do the honors. The baby-faced assassin was in the center of the maelstrom of phone calls and solicitor's instructions that began the instant Joseph left the office. A contract stipulating Joseph's ten percent was drawn up by proxy over the telephone. The family firm of Freidrich and Glass saw to this from the haven of offices overlooking the Rhône. Within minutes the contract was signed, put in an envelope, secured with sealing wax and their stamp, and was sent by messenger to the Bank of Zurich. Vladimir and Rolf were to rendezvous at this, their consortium's own bank. Rolf had acquired over his years of service his superior's trust and respect in all business matters. He also had power of attorney over all legal affairs. In addition, he was a certified accountant and an expert on world commodities and might have gotten ahead in life had he not lacked the balls to cross the street alone.

At the Bank of Zurich Rolf broke the envelope seal and spent the next ten minutes scrutinizing the contract before pronouncing it sound. He signed each copy twice and handed the extra to Vladimir. The dollar equivalent of three hundred thousand in Swiss francs was withdrawn in cash from the consortium's account. Normally a bank draft would have sufficed, but as this would be traceable to Joseph's own account, Joseph had demanded cash. He was impetuous, not stupid. Rolf placed the money carefully in a small leather case. He counted each stack meticulously, then signed for the total amount. He handed the case to Vladimir. The contract was placed over the money and the case was locked. On impulse, Rolf shook hands with Vladimir and wondered if the baby-faced chauffeur was headed for the Bank of Geneva or Mexico City.

The thought had occurred to Vladimir. Not once,

but regularly. Every time he had more than the price of a penthouse in Rio at his fingertips, he had debated absconding with it. Recently, he had dismissed these follies as little league. He was determined to stick it out for the big payday when he'd be able to commute between Rio and Paris in his own Lear jet. Lately, he'd had the feeling that day was not too far away.

Vladimir found Joseph reading a magazine in the Bank of Geneva lobby. They greeted each other respectfully, if indifferently. Joseph counted the money on a table in the middle of the foyer, dividing his gaze between the bundles of francs and the fat face with the thinning hair on top. Vladimir never moved. Joseph skimmed over the contract. It seemed acceptable. As he had said earlier, the piece of paper was only a formality. Bullshit, really, but binding if the men ever wanted to go legitimate in the free world. Having deemed the transaction satisfactory, he slid the package containing the tapes across the polished surface of the table. It rested at Vladimir's arm. The chauffeur picked it up, a faint smile blossoming upon his baby face. He waited by the door as Joseph deposited the cash into his account. They left together.

Vladimir bought the first round. Dark, stained wood and low-wattage bulbs illuminated the bar like an early dusk. It was two-thirty in the afternoon outside, but it looked like night inside. The thick smoke from Vladimir's Cuban cigar moved slowly across the booth into the aisle to the chagrin of the dozen customers.

"Thank you," Joseph said. He acknowledged the schnapps and raised his glass. "Cheers." It burned a line to his stomach, where it pooled with the leftovers of a cheese sandwich. "What's on your mind?"

"Oh, nothing really, Joseph. Think of this as a social outing," Vladimir said gamely.

"No offense, but I choose my company in my own time. I don't mix business with the other."

"No offense taken, comrade. Consider this a celebration drink for completing such a coup. Frankly, I wouldn't have put money on your chances of pulling it off."

"Are you a gambling man?" Joseph intoned.

"Yes, most of the time."

"Well, you would have lost." Joseph took out a cigarette. He lit it and breathed out silently.

Vladimir felt a little embarrassed. He toyed with the half-full glass of schnapps. "Can't win them all." He finished the drink. "Anyway, I just wanted to congratulate you on your victory, that's all."

It was obvious that Vladimir was foundering. Joseph helped him out. "Thank you, Vladimir. Forgive me. I've got a lot running through my mind this afternoon. Have another drink." The waiter poured two more. "Tell me, have you been with this crowd long?"

"Sort of, from my point of view. Two and a half years in May. I'll stick with it a while longer," Vladimir said. He moved enthusiastically into the conversation. "I'd be out tomorrow if I could pull off the big one. I don't think that's news to anybody. For the moment they need me and I need them.

As soon as one of us grows indispensable, that's it, end of story."

"The law of the jungle."

"None other." Vladimir sucked on his cigar. Smoke seeped between his teeth as he continued. "My father was in the Politburo many years ago. He gave the big one, Popotov, his break. He was a coal miner and he made him a politician. I think he feels he owes the old man something."

"He still alive?"

"Barely, last I heard, anyway. They keep him plugged full of sedatives and dust him off occasionally for press releases."

"That's why they keep you hanging around?" Joseph asked.

"That and the fact that I can handle one of these." The Heckler & Koch pistol found its way onto the table beside the schnapps. Joseph suddenly realized that this man Vladimir, with the porky baby face and thinning hair, was very young.

"How old are you?"

Vladimir ignored the question. He removed the gun from the table and crouched forward some. "Getting back to the law of the jungle, those old men mean nothing to me. For the present, they pay better than the next guy. Now, if someone came by and offered better . . ." Vladimir grinned.

Joseph noticed he was pursuing a deliberate line of conversation. He licked the liquor from his lips and nodded. "Go on, I'm listening."

"Let's assume there was an interested party, somebody who needed something they had. Or, better still, something I had. Supposing they were willing to pay for it."

"Such as?"

"I don't have to write it down, Joseph. You're a clever sort. We've got something we could pawn off tomorrow for the price of a few town houses in Belgravia." He was dreaming some. "All it would take would be a phone call to the right people . . ."

Joseph smiled from behind the cigarette. "Brother, follow the wind if it calls you. That's my advice. I'm content at present to stick it out and see what gives. There's money in tennis racquets."

"Yes, but think of the time it will take. Anyway, it's speculative."

"So is breathing." Joseph inhaled the last resolute drop of schnapps. "What's your cut?"

"Two percent, plus bonus, plus a salary."

Joseph nodded benignly. "To each his own." He withdrew a billfold and scattered a few notes across the table. "I'm going to give you a word of advice that is worth about as much as I'm asking for it. Pretend this conversation never took place. I will. In the future try and keep that tongue in your mouth. You'll keep it longer."

The grin faded altogether from Vladimir's face. Joseph reached out and patted his shoulder fraternally. "Have no fear," he said ambiguously and wondered how long it would be before the young man was found dead in some hotel room.

Rolf trudged up the final flight of stairs. He shuffled his feet across the carpet and turned toward room D-14. Everything about the quaint little Swiss inn he found oppressive and unhygienic. Why couldn't they stay at the Intercontinental or the Hilton, for Christ's sake? Did they seriously believe there were more potential CIA and KGB agents there than in the likes of the Vaud Platz? Shit! The air smelled of a combination of cedar and diesel fuel due to a faulty ice machine at his end of the hall. The four flights of stairs he found taxing as hell, especially after a late dinner. Nor was there any television. Not in his room, anyway. As chargé to Popotov — one of many functions to the consortium — he either had to put up or shut up. Besides, Popotov preferred these types of places. It reminded the consortium chief of his early, no-frills life in Leningrad. "Nostalgic old fool," Rolf said out loud. His voice carried weakly down the hall.

He unlocked the door and hastened to the bathroom. His delicate hands wrapped around the toilet base as he vomited up the contents of his four-star dinner. Popotov had forced him to attend, as he always did when he wasn't feeling horny and out on the prowl for an available woman. Rolf finished retching. The taut, sore muscles of his stomach tensed in a final purging convulsion. He gargled with the dark cedar water that came out of the tap, spat out the dregs of vomit, and repeated the action. Squeezing an inch of toothpaste onto his tongue, he rinsed his mouth out slowly. After he had washed and toweled his face, he felt better. Kara was to call tonight at eleven and he wanted to be in good form.

He poured a large tumbler three-quarters full with

vodka and sipped at it hungrily while he debated his alternatives. For months now his conscience had been gnawing at him. The incessant worry manifested itself in chronic bouts of constipation, frequent insomnia, and duodenal ulcers that caused Rolf perpetual indigestion. His ravaged stomach could no longer hold down solid food. No sooner did he eat than it all came chortling up in a syrupy bile. Yet even more worrying to him was his sudden sexual impotence. What once could be boasted of as the forte of the slight, meek man had deserted him along with all his other normal bodily functions. He was quite simply dying, although he didn't know it yet.

And all for what? This question he asked himself from the time he took his milk-and-egg-white drink in the morning to his last jigger of vodka in the evening. Why? Since the first meeting in Moscow when he learned of their plan, Rolf hadn't been the same. He had weighed the pros and cons, the motives, his feelings, his allegiances, and had come to the same stalwart conclusion: He could no more sit back and watch Russia be humiliated than give up his precious Kara.

All of the intricate preparations to bring Western tennis to its knees would inevitably come back as a major disgrace to Russia. He knew this. If the Soviets could not succeed on their own merits, if Russia's champions were not yet equal to vanquishing the West at its own game, the spoils of subterfuge would not make these gains worthwhile. It seemed so incredibly obvious. Couldn't the others appreciate the consequences? They were rich men already. Did they really wish to desecrate their mother country for the sake of financial gain? Such vaulting, blind ambition must be stopped before it was too late.

During the tape presentation that afternoon, the true unsavory essence of the scheme had been emphasized. Whereas the others had been mesmerized by lust, Rolf had sat horrified at what these men would attempt to perpetrate in the name of Russia. It had taken what remained of his strength not to vomit during the presentation.

An hour later he was nursing a bottle of vodka in the wingback chair in the corner of the simple hotel room. The tears came less easily. He wondered if Kara would call. She was an hour late already. The sound of the telephone jarred him out of the chair. She had remembered! He crawled to the phone and lifted it reverently. "Hello?"

"It's Kara," the husky voice said. The words were completely devoid of any emotion. She might have been phoning an order in to the butcher.

"Sweetheart, how wonderful to hear your voice! You can't imagine how I've missed you this week, my pet." His gay, romantic tone was blemished by the nasal sound of his earlier tears.

"Have you been crying again?"

"No, lover, honestly. I must have caught a cold last week in Leningrad. I think it's the flu."

"Yeah, well, sorry I'm late in calling. I was tied up."

He heard her giggle across the line. She was whispering to someone. "Darling, forgive me for asking,"

Rolf began hesitantly. "You know what I'm like, especially now since my problem, but is there somebody else there?" He was blushing.

"Don't be ridiculous. I'm talking to Tilly," she scolded. Tilly was their dog. Rolf beamed. He knew his Kara. She may have been flirtatious, but she would never actually stoop to cheating on him. They had all warned him after the engagement. They had said she was beneath him. A common factory worker's daughter marrying a future politician and son of a banker was unheard of. But he alone had understood Kara. He alone had known what a sweet, wonderful girl she was and what a marvelous bride she could be. He had always been a tiny bit shy. Her innate gregariousness would help him tolerate the social situations he found so acutely uncomfortable. Four months of impotence and she was still as loyal as ever. He would get her an extra-special gift this time, he decided.

Kara brushed back her mop of blond hair. She rolled over onto her flabby belly and spread her legs invitingly. The young miner she had met on the train that morning massaged the whiteness of her buttocks. He opened her and guided his penis deep inside. She wriggled with delight. He churned away slowly while she spoke. "Look, I've got to go quite soon. Mama's not well, and I promised to phone her on the hour," she said, lying. Her own hips began to match the gusto of her partner's. He took hold of her breasts and squeezed them deliciously.

"Oh, please, Kara, darling, not yet. Just a few more moments, my angel. You don't know what a week I've had," Rolf pleaded.

She slid a hand beneath her and grabbed the miner by his testicles. She led him in and out more slowly. "You're always having 'one of those weeks.' How do you think I feel when all you do is complain? What kind of a life is that?" By hurting him, she hoped to cut short the conversation. "I want somebody who's happy and confident, not some half man who cries at the tiniest little thing."

Rolf covered his face with his hand. He arched his head and bravely fought the tears. They seeped between the redness of his eyelids. His stomach gurgled and he felt terribly weak all over. Why did she have to say that? Anything but that. "Sweetheart, that's not a nice thing to say to someone," he offered pathetically. "Don't you know how much I love you?"

"If you love me so much, why can't you fuck me? You know it's hard for me. I'm a young woman." That she was seven years older than he was immaterial. The fact that she was fifteen years older than the miner was even more so. She felt the premonition of a strong climax welling in her. She kept up the pressure and increased the frequency. The miner was beginning to pant. She shushed him with a finger and smiled.

"But I satisfy you. You said so. You said in other ways I satisfy you." Rolf was panicking.

"Do you?" she asked, out of breath.

"Darling, please don't be like this. My problems

are only temporary, I swear it. In fact, I nearly felt like doing it this afternoon. It was hard and all."

"It ain't like it used to be," she said. She had to admit that Rolf in his prime could fuck with the best of them. As a gourmand of men, she fancied herself a good judge of what could be achieved between the sheets. "I want it the way it was," she demanded testily. "You can't expect me to live the rest of my life like a nun, can you?"

She made up his mind for him. It was no more a matter of courage versus his congenital timidity. It was suddenly clear to Rolf that Kara was nearing the point of no return. She would be out soon looking for greener pastures, and he couldn't really blame her. Rolf was the first to admit he was not the man he once was. She had been generous in her estimation of him: He was not a half man, but more like a quarter. A rare spurt of adrenaline rallied him. The tears receded abruptly and he began to sweat. He decided to act against them and seize the tapes. If he did it covertly, they would never suspect him. And yet the prospects of their finding out didn't worry him. Any fate was better than one without his lovely, innocent Kara.

The need to persevere with the sniveling conversation left him. "Of course not, Kara. Don't be so dramatic, darling one." He lifted his chin and sat erect. "I give you my word that I'll be normal again by the time I see you next weekend. Count on that. I've made up my mind to do something."

As he had never chosen to confide in her about

the Wimbledon dossier, she had no idea what he'd made up his mind about. She was too entrenched in the final stages of her pre-orgasmic shudders to care. "Ooh, that's nice," she moaned.

A smile crept back onto his lips. "Nice, is it? Darling petal, you'll never know how much this conversation has helped me. You've given me a new lease on life," he said warmly. It was absolutely true. She had through her impassioned indifference given him a new, albeit short, lease on life. "Thank you," he added pompously. "You are my salvation."

The miner could no longer restrain the fire. He hoisted her buttocks off the bed and slammed home. His ejaculation sparked the glow within her womb. She pressed against him and matched his furious bucking movements. The phone was swept off the bed and landed upside down on the floor as she came. This convenient act of providence had deprived her husband of the victorious cries of her climax. Rolf lingered on the dead line. An unmistakable mark of satisfaction was spread across his swollen face. Undoubtedly, she had been overcome by the emotions of his resolution and had hung up speechless, he mused. He was only half right.

He replaced the screw top to the remaining quarter bottle of vodka, and set it on the table near the phone. This is where he always set it so it would be in the right place should he need it in the morning. It took him ten minutes to change into his pyjamas, brush his teeth, and comb his hair. He was climbing into the expanse of eiderdown when he noticed the bottle. He rested on one knee on the bed, and then, bounding up, crossed the room. He took the nearly empty bottle from the table plus the two full bottles on the shelf and lugged them to the window. It pulled open easily on a ballbearing track. Leaning over the radiator, he dangled half way out the window, clutching the bottles. At this late hour the street below was deserted and there were very few cars. He moved quickly and hurled the bottles onto the pavement, savoring the long second it took for them to land. Three crashing pops reverberated along the cement four stories down. A car cruised by so he stole inside and shut the window. He flicked off the light and fell into bed, consumed by the billowing quilt. He was fast asleep before his head hit the pillow.

Chapter Seven

Greenwich, Connecticut

Benjamen Smythe stretched out of the bed and shuffled across the Persian carpet into the bathroom. He hung his silk pajamas on the golden cupid figure that his wife, Tessa, had installed on the cabinet door twenty years earlier. The figure itself had grown tarnished over the years, and part of the bow had come off to expose the flint-gray of the lead interior. In a funny way the decline of the idol as a symbol for love and beauty had mirrored the inevitable decline of Benjamen and Tessa. The gilt façade of a perfect relationship had been chipped away over time. What was revealed beneath the exterior was none too pretty and had had them straddling the door to the divorce courts for years. Thirty years of marriage had survived the threat of separation due to a number of factors, not the least of which was their mutual devotion to Catholicism.

Smythe was partial to bending the code of his Church through his endless love affairs with other women. In a way the Church condoned this, if only as a last resort against divorce. It seemed the Church was more concerned with statistics than truth. They were willing to overlook the peccadilloes of humanity so long as the actual hard figures were suppressed. The parishioners might be banging the living shit out of one another. Provided they didn't actually divorce their spouses, thereby boosting national divorce statistics, it was okay. This was fundamentally how Smythe viewed it. His life was a constant parade of morals bent, never broken.

He ducked under the shower and stepped out again, cursing because the water was too hot. He banged a fist on the metal cubicle and readjusted the temperature. It took him just over three minutes to soap and rinse and wash his hair, plus endure a final thirty seconds of an icy-cold spray. He toweled off as he made his way across the mosaic floor in the large room. An Irish granite jaw was covered in shaving cream and cleaned methodically with a double-edge blade. He brushed his teeth and combed his hair.

Smythe was truly a creature of habit. Each morning for thirty years, whether at home or away, he had risen at precisely seven o'clock, in time to sit down to breakfast by seven-fifteen with *The Wall Street Journal*. At the Georges V in Paris or a dilapidated whorehouse in the northern section of Bangkok, he adhered to his morning ritual. In this respect he might have been provincial and a touch small-minded, but he could have cared less. There was very little he cared about aside from Whiplin and his farm and maybe the New York Knicks.

He was very nearly late this morning. Vanity got in his way before the mirror. He had already dressed in the suit laid out by Franz, his valet, and was finishing with his tie in front of the mirror when his cold blue eyes zeroed in on his growing bald spot. He paused to regard the thinning area in the sea of gray. "Damn!" He experimented with the part and eventually switched it altogether by combing his hair from left to right. An application of hair oil kept the unruly bits in place. He was about to step out of the room when his senses returned to him. He backed up and pulled on the overhead light. "Fuck the hair," he said.

In his opinion, few things looked worse than a bald spot atop the old cranium, but one of these was walking around looking like the kind of idiot who was attempting to cover his balding pate with a complicated allocation of bits of hair. Such a maneuver merely accentuated the condition by making it all the more obvious. He would go out like a man. He mussed his hair and combed it the way he always did.

"Good morning, Mr. Benjamen, sir," Melba, the

portly black housekeeper, said with her indefatigable good nature.

Smythe looked up and eyed her with the gaze of a man who had been insulted. He appraised her lily-white uniform, then returned to his paper and asked, "Is it?"

"Yes, sir. Miss Tessa, she called from her mother's in Palm Beach. She likes it so much she's stayin' another week."

"So . . ." He checked himself. This was good news. He looked quizzically at Melba, then shook his head idly. "That sounds interesting. Where are all the children?"

"Why, Mr. Benjamen, sir, they's all away to school. Robby left this morning on account of he was sick last night, but the others left Sunday as usual."

He lowered the paper some. "Sick, my ass. The kid was drunk all weekend." He dropped the paper and looked seriously at Melba. "Melba, do you think I look after that boy? I mean, is it right for a fifteen-year-old to be drinking gin?"

"All children comes to alcohol at some time in their lives," Melba said diplomatically. She was backing away perceptibly toward the kitchen door.

"Don't go away when I'm talking to you, dammit, Melba!" he roared. He frowned and said, "Seriously, Melba, I'm going to ask you a question. Now, you know that above all I am a fair man and a realist. I'm used to dealing with the truth. God Almighty, I've raised five children. Nothing you say will affect my opinion of you, you know that."

"Yes, Mr. Benjamen." Her nervous state caused

her to punctuate each response with a sort of half-assed little bow, something she'd seen in *Gone with the Wind.*

"Fine. Then answer me this: Have I been a good father to that boy? I mean, have I shown him the proper attention and guidance and done all the things a father should do? Be frank, Melba."

"No, Mr. Benjamen."

"No, what?"

"No, you ain't been a good father like you shoulda."

"Who asked you?" he screamed. "Get the hell out of here and make my breakfast, and stop that silly-ass bowing every time I talk to you. The war's over, in case you haven't heard. You're free." She bowed for the third time during the tirade, then ran out of the room. He picked up the paper and shook it. "Goddamned insolent woman," he muttered. "I don't know why I keep her on." He sighed heavily and sipped at the coffee. "That son of mine needs a swift kick up the ass. Neglect, hell! His life has been one big country club. Christ only knows why I send him away to school; he probably learns it all there."

He leafed through the paper. After he noted the headlines and saw who had died and who hadn't, he would return to page one and read the paper thoroughly. He was leafing past the sports section when a certain headline over a certain picture caused him to freeze. *"What?"* The noise of this single expletive shook the contents of the room and altered the swinging door to the kitchen by an inch. The sudden shock of his yell made Melba sag to one knee in fright. Her first thought was heart attack. She righted herself and raced into the room.

"Mr. Benjamen, are you alive?" she asked breathlessly.

"Get out!" he screamed. She raced back into the kitchen with a hand clasped to her prodigious bosom. "That profligate son-of-a-bitch! What's he up to now?" Smythe bellowed. He pored over the tiny article below the photo:

James McLaren is seen here with London actress Kim Cornway practicing for Wimbledon. Reigning champ McLaren was experimenting with the new Aristocrat line of racquets. The newfangled racquet is now available for retail sale in America.

"Goddamned son-of-a-bitch!" Smythe said quietly. "He takes the option I give him on the stock. Then he turns around and screws me." He smoothed the paper down flat and finished the short article, then gazed closely at the snapshot. Sure enough the big "A" logo of the Aristocrat racquet was staring out from in front of McLaren. To highlight the visibility of the Aristocrat brand, McLaren had held the racquet tightly against the whiteness of his shirt.

Smythe looked at the picture distastefully. "Shit!" There was nothing legally he could do, and he knew this. He could sue the young prick for breach of contract for promoting the Aristocrat racquet, but there was no certainty he would win the case. The two firms were listed on the New York Stock

Exchange as separate entities, but technically Whiplin owned Aristocrat. Any exposure Aristocrat got would really be benefiting both firms. How were the judge and jury to understand that Aristocrat was designed and intended merely as a tax writeoff? Christ! Furthermore, to drag McLaren into court would dirty the name of Whiplin racquets with the millions of McLaren fans worldwide. Smythe could probably win, and have the arrogant shithead of a champion pay back his profits from the stock. But the boy would only have to answer the phone and get another healthy contract from another firm and the publicity of the case would virtually guarantee that next firm a large share of the market. "No, goddammit!" Smythe sighed. "He's got me by the proverbial balls, the son-of-a-bitch."

The phone rang next to him and he swiped at it. "I know, Whitney, I can read, for Christ's sake."

"I realize that, Benjamen, but do you realize there's nothing we can do without risking a sticky court case we might not even win?"

"Jesus! you're my vice-president and paid to do and not to think so goddamned much," Smythe said gruffly. "I know where we stand." He leaned back in the chair and called out, "Melba my breakfast, please."

"I still think —" Whitney continued.

"Don't think," Smythe interjected. "That's an order. You're my business brain. What's the market prospectus?"

Whitney, the vice-president of Whiplin, said, "Well, as you forbid me to think, I'll give you all the options. The publicity will doubtless rally the stock — how much, I can't say, as I don't really know McLaren's appeal, but this close to Wimbledon it's bound to go up. Consequently, any raise will result in a profit for Aristocrat with a dividend this quarter for shareholders. Good-bye to tax liability."

"Shit! I'll get that son-of-a-bitch someday."

"Sure, Benjamen. In the meantime, concentrate on rallying Whiplin. This little incident may actually translate into a loss somewhere along the line."

"Whitney, that's one hell of an option. I thought you said we had a choice," he added.

"I didn't."

"Well, you alluded to it, dammit!" Smythe held a hand over the phone. "Excuse me," he said to Melba. She set his ham and scrambled eggs before him along with a plate of whole-wheat croissants and some prune juice. He drank the juice, then said, "Like hell."

"The only conceivable option short of counting our losses is to sit back and let Aristocrat realize an innocuous profit, pay the tax, then sell the fucking thing."

"I'll do all the swearing around here, thank you, Whitney." He considered the proposal. It seemed a sound one. "Okay, that's what we'll do. The dye is cast anyhow, as of this morning." He took a last look at McLaren's toothy smile and the racquet in his hands. "McLaren's pulled a fast one. It will take me a while to decide how to get even. Devote the equivalent of a quarter of our projected promotions budget to this new thing."

"What?" Whitney asked.

"If we're going to make this subsidiary viable, then let's make an effort. I want some thought and money put into this thing or else we forget it. We can always sell it tomorrow to the Japs. Besides, we can put the expenses toward taxes."

Whitney saw his point. "No, you're right. We'll boost it, then sell it."

"Of course I'm right. Anyhow, it might indirectly boost our profits by drawing on some of the competition." As an expert on the state of tennis equipment manufacturers, Smythe knew the additional competition offered by the untested racquets would, if successful, draw a share of the market away from one of the other firms. Profit margins were so slender in this fiercely competitive market that such a slight shift could bring one of his competitors to its knees. His only concern was that McLaren fans might switch their allegiance to Aristocrat, then back again to the competition. "Let's hope we don't lose out. If we're lucky we'll put one of the others out of business," he said through a mouthful of ham and eggs.

"My feelings exactly. I'll report to you later on how the stock opens," Whitney said.

"Do that." Smythe hung up. He always knew that potentially Aristocrat Tennis might take off, in which case he could stand to earn a profit over and above the money saved through tax concessions. It had been his contention when he started the firm that larger-faced racquets had no future. Maybe he was wrong. McLaren had thought so, and in spite of being an A-1 son-of-a-bitch, the young man knew his tennis.

Smythe spent the next hour finishing breakfast and the paper, dispatching the household chores, and talking politics with Melba. Beneath her timid nature and general appearance of not having two brain cells to rub together, the woman was exceedingly bright. Smythe had found that nature had blessed her with a very profane though sagacious wisdom, and on many occasions he sat her down to converse about his many problems. She listened patiently, ingested the information, then expressed her views. He would shower her with praise or curse her accordingly, but he always listened.

He deposited the paper in a bin in the entrance hall, where it would later be fed into a compactor to make a paper log for the fire. He never kept a paper. The information he absorbed while reading was recorded indelibly in his photographic memory. What he found intriguing, he lingered over for an extra minute. That which bored him, he discarded instantly. In this fashion did he live his life. Decisions were made quickly and with irreversible resolve. He had a tremendous capacity to weigh any foreseeable consequences. In thirty years — from company salesman to president, chairman of the board, and whatever other laurel he chose to bestow upon himself — he had never once been wrong. As a result, Whiplin ruled supreme in the world of tennis.

The warmth of a June morning accompanied him across the lawns to the kennels. The frantic yelping of the hounds caused him to smile. Their sounds interrupted the morning air, silent except for the birds and the noise that wood made when hit with an axe. Smythe had instructed Franz to clear the debris from a tree that had fallen near the house during an electrical storm. Franz had asked to use a chain saw and Smythe had replied flatly that he could once he had left the property but not before. After all, hadn't the pioneers used axes? Franz had expected this answer from his employer; he knew how much Mr. Benjamen enjoyed his mornings on the farm. The two-hundred-acre oasis of forest and rolling field was Smythe's pride and joy. Located merely two miles from Greenwich proper, the estate was indeed a novelty, and developers had been after him for years to sell some of his more remote property. "And have you litter it with that shit you call housing? You must be out of your fucking skull." End of story.

He slid the rusty latch and let the whitewashed door to the kennel crack open. The yelping increased. "Keep your shirts on." He grinned. The steel booths were opened by the manual pull of a lever. The dogs scurried obediently to his feet and he crouched and patted each one. "Away with you." On command they sped across the lawns into the field. He would follow on his morning stroll.

En route he passed Franz chopping at a particularly obdurate branch halfway up the tree. Smythe nodded hello and regarded the effort of the handyman. After a moment he removed his jacket and folded it across the grass. He confronted Franz. "May I?" The little man bowed. Smythe accepted the axe.

He paused, then swung it fluidly over his well-muscled shoulder. The branch exploded with a thwacking sound as bits of timber sprayed the air. Smythe relinquished the axe to his stunned servant, collected his jacket, and headed out after the dogs.

Chekow and Viktor arrived in London and went directly by taxi to the Ebury Street Hotel in Pimlico.

Joseph had been as good as his word. First thing that next morning in St. Tropez, one dozen spanking-new Crimea racquets had arrived at the reception desk of the Byblos. Viktor had collected them and resignedly threw them in the car with the others. Each racquet was enclosed in an ornate plastic slip-case with the word CRIMEA painted across it in bold, contrasting-color letters. The grips varied only slightly in size to account for any compensations Chekow might have to make with the new instrument.

They practiced for five hours with the new racquets. Chekow was told to experiment with the grips, which he duly did, and found the medium six-and-a-quarter-inch the best for his unconventional Western-style grip. He interrupted play throughout the session to examine the racquet, occasionally exchanging it for another size. Chekow had many superstitions, so before any tournament he found it necessary to ensure that each racquet had been used. He felt more comfortable if he had actually practiced with it. This was commonplace with most of the championship players. A "cold" racquet was to be avoided.

Practically speaking, it was a good policy. Often

a racquet would come from the factory having been strung wrong — too loose or too tight. The strings could be misaligned. That first morning in St. Tropez, Chekow had found little fault with the aluminum Crimea. The grip on two of the racquets had begun to peel away, but this could be remedied. On one the gut had been strung too loosely. Each time he served, the center strings would be displaced a few centimeters. This racquet he would discard. By the end of the day he was left with seven good racquets out of a dozen.

Chekow and Viktor had discussed the Crimea over a dry lunch in Nice before their flight to London. Not surprisingly, Chekow had praised it for the dependable, efficient tool that it was. There was nothing fundamentally different about it. Nothing to solicit more than the typical inquiry concerning its manufacture and designer. The head had been engineered to sink deeper before the molding and this resulted in a slightly more oblong face. Otherwise, it was just a racquet. What bothered Chekow was the way in which he had come to adopt it as an order from Viktor. What perturbed him even more was that it was aluminum, not a Whiplin graphite, and that it was given to him on such short notice.

In order to compensate for the newness of the instrument, Viktor had plunged his pupil into a grueling bout of practices for each of the last four days. All the regularly scheduled practices had been cut in half, with the priority placed on frequency and not endurance. One four-hour session before lunch would be broken down into two two-hour sessions. Even during their moments off court, Viktor had Chekow clasping the new racquet constantly, gauging its peculiar weightlessness, measuring its reach and feel. There was no margin for error. Every nuance had to be experienced and logged. They had no choice. Their lives depended on his performance with the Crimea.

After installing themselves in the London hotel, they ordered a full lunch in their room. Chekow had steak and eggs and potatoes washed down with three glasses of milk and a handful of vitamins. Viktor ate scallops and sea bass and drank German lager. They ate in Viktor's room in front of the television and watched a BBC play about a blind man in Regent's Park who'd taught his dog to do tricks.

Since the early morning ultimatum with Joseph a week before, Viktor had found himself drawn closer to the young player. The rigidly structured, somewhat reserved relationship of coach and player had eased considerably. They no longer did everything individually. Where previously a dinner engagement was the exception, it was now becoming commonplace and Viktor's evening forays on the nightclub circuit had decreased, dramatically. Whether this came as a result of his meeting with Joseph, he didn't know. He suspected as much. He knew in his own way he was exerting extra and unfair pressure on young Chekow and that by spending more time with him he was atoning for that pressure.

The BBC play ended and lunch finished. The porter reappeared and humbly removed the soiled plates and cutlery. Chekow returned to his room and slept for two hours. Viktor attempted as much, but his thoughts found no respite in sleep. All he could think about was his hollow-eyed countryman and the threats he'd made on that morning in St. Tropez. It didn't make sense. Why would Russia, via the KGB, attempt such a foolish endeavor? Had they really lost all perspective? The question preyed on him. He ordered six bottles of beer to be delivered to the room. He sipped at these thoughtfully and let his mind drift.

Chekow and Vicktor arrived at the All England Club that afternoon in time to take the practice court allotted them by the committee. This close to the tournament all member playing had come to a stand-still to allow for more practice time for the competitors.

To either side of the courts as they practiced, chaos reigned. Disgruntled grounds crews were busy sides-stepping the tournament committee of old ladies in flowered hats. White-haired gentlemen with pencils behind their ears strode the grounds clutching clip-boards. Club members, some in tennis whites, some not, poked curiously between the courts in a frantic search for their idols. The sun flickered overhead in between the constant threat of rain. Occasionally during the day the sky would darken and open up with a light rain. The moisture from God was com-bined with the spray of an antiquated sprinkler sys-tem and was welcomed.

In the center of the pre-tournament commotion,

the rangy Russian boy and Viktor gave an impressive exhibition for the crowd of enthusiasts who had gathered to watch them. Unlike McLaren's experience at Hurlingham, nobody was drunk or rude or in the least bit interfering. At the All England Club, tennis was revered and was not simply a pastime to follow drunken lunches on a weekend afternoon.

They ate a quiet supper together in the hotel restaurant. Viktor apologized for being so uncommunicative and took an early leave. Chekow stayed at the table for half an hour picking quietly at a lemon sorbet while he read that morning's copy of the *Times*. He looked up between articles in search of an interesting soul with whom he might have a conversation. None appeared. Most of the tourists were too engrossed with their multilingual guidebooks of London to take notice of the suntanned tennis star. Most of the English were too consumed with being English and never so much as glanced up from their plates.

His efforts to do the crossword puzzle, the acid test of fluency in a foreign language, proved futile. He got only three of a possible twenty-eight and gave up when confronted with a nine-letter word for "antediluvian thimble." As it was not yet nine o'clock, he decided to go for a stroll before bed. He set out with the intention of cruising the immediate vicinity of Pimlico, but he was waylaid by the sight of a generous female bottom in a pair of shorts. Chekow followed her idly for fifteen minutes until she turned right at the Chelsea Barracks near Hyde

Park. He pushed and for want of anything better to do waited for her outside the gate. The two corporals on guard regarded him suspiciously from their posts. He ignored them and was about to start off again when the woman emerged. She sprang down the steps, looked his way, and smiled deliriously. His ego, which had soared, at first, now plummeted as her flank was taken up by a burly man of about his age in officer's regalia. Chekow bowed his head and proceeded aimlessly into the park.

He recognized Hyde Park from his past visits to London. He'd consummated his first affair here with a large-breasted fan from Wales. He recalled this little piece of nostalgia and turned west for the Serpentine and the Albert Memorial. His sneakered feet trod across the wispy green terrain. He leveled his stare and smelled the clean night air. To his left lay the opulent residences of Hyde Park Gate. Silhouettes shifted beyond the many curtained windows, unaware of the young Russian voyeur. He wondered if the people inside were tennis enthusiasts. He set his course for the stone building deep in the park where the art exhibitions were held. He got closer and saw on a board in bold, yet precise, lettering the words SERPENTINE GALLERY. The bosomy Welsh fan and he had made it in the shrubbery to the left of the gallery.

Light from a streetlamp licked his coal-black hair, then left him again as he walked on. He passed the gallery, with its canvases eerily dormant in the dark, and picked up his pace as he spied the pond beyond. From the distance the surface of the Serpentine looked smooth and unblemished. Available light congregated upon the reflective top like a mirror, occasionally reflecting the scalloped reaction of a passing breeze. Chekow noted only a few hardcore tourists encircling the Serpentine at this hour. Beyond the pool toward the high street a lonely figure sat crumpled upon a bench, shoulders stooped.

A cursory inspection revealed a vacant bench devoid of any of the ubiquitous pigeon shit that religiously plagued public facilities. Chekow stretched against the sturdy wood and threw his legs out. He stared at the bright lights of Kensington Palace.

Something was amiss this year that Chekow could only sense. He knew Viktor would never tell him. It wasn't his coach's nature to divulge information that he thought might upset Chekow. In times of stress Viktor was repose itself, Chekow thought. Chekow would proceed as always and do his best with the Crimea racquet. His chances were better this year. He'd broken the ice last year by battling his way into the finals and he had that experience on his side. Christ! He was seeded second to McLaren. Then what could Viktor possibly be worried about now that he wasn't worried about last year? No other Russian had gotten further. In fact, he had gone further than any Russian in history. What, then, was the problem?

He picked up a handful of pebbles from the ground and practiced flicking them into the pond, displacing the water and sending ripples across the surface in rings. His eyes skimmed the water's edge and rested fleetingly on the lone figure on the faraway bench.

He draped his arms over his knees and wondered what Natashe was up to in Leningrad. He thought about her marriage to the sailor and what a mundane little life they would lead. Why, he wondered, had she forsaken him so soon after his departure? Was it despair? Loneliness? Or had she never really loved him? They had made love once. Didn't that mean anything? His thoughts jumped to his family in Leningrad, whom he hadn't seen in eight months, a record for him. Were they all right? Were they missing him? Yuri must be nearly as tall as he by now, maybe taller. In a year his brother would be called up for the military, Chekow realized, and this depressed him. Perhaps he would be exempt, he thought. He was only a kid. He would have a talk with Viktor about this, he decided.

Chekow knew himself well enough to recognize the track of his present thoughts. He was, for whatever reasons, growing sentimental, and unless he changed his thinking, the tears of loneliness would soon follow — he knew this feeling well. Here he was, one of the top athletes in the world, reasonably handsome, popular with the fans, in his own way forthcoming and gregarious. He had it all on a silver platter, yet he never stopped wondering where he'd gone wrong. Why was he so lonely? Was it his fault? Was he less approachable than those players from the West? Perhaps he would try to alter his personality, and maybe the people he wanted as friends were just parasites anyway and he was better off alone.

Between this constant volley of thoughts, he

glanced intermittently at the solitary figure across the water. The surviving aficionado of late-night parks had risen and begun to amble in his direction. Chekow pursued the curious figure with mild interest. Whomever it was seemed so acutely alone. *Indeed*, Chekow thought, *the poor soul looks even more dejected than I*. The man sauntered past Chekow at a distance, his large head upon his chest. His hands were stuffed deep into the pockets of his windbreaker. The feet moved mechanically, lacking animation.

Chekow suddenly remembered his time in St. Tropez. He recalled the recent conquest of the mother-daughter team who had been so readily available. His jaw cracked into a smile and he laughed. As Viktor had prophesied, Chekow had indeed gotten both of them on the floor. Twice. The daughter, though inexperienced, was tighter. The passionate technique of the mother could not forgive her the size of her orifice. A bit like poking a pencil into a waste can, he thought. Resurrected memories of the night enhanced his smile. Then all at once a sort of sadness descended upon him. A gust of wind from the direction of High Street Kensington sailed guilelessly across the park, disheveling his short black hair and stirring the pond water.

The familiar steel grip took his shoulder, then released it. Chekow pivoted and looked up at Viktor. For a while his thoughts were muddled. Then he saw it, and it demoralized him. Poor Viktor: another knight with no castle. The sustained breeze mussed his coach's thick silver hair and pressed sections of it flat against his brow. Even in the half light the lines etched into his face were visible. The hard eyes were shiny and wet and Chekow wondered if this was the wind. "Yes, boy," Viktor said decisively, as though they had been discussing something and he had provided the final word. "You are not so different from me," the thick voice said.

Chekow found the familiar sounds comforting. "Yes," he agreed.

Viktor combed at his hair awkwardly. "There are often times in life when one feels left out and forgotten. It is especially hard for the young. Yours is not an easy life." Chekow nodded. The sympathy brought him perilously close to tears. "Come, boy, let's have a beer together." Viktor's great arm rested on the young man's shoulder as they set off. They walked across the grassy stretch, neither quite so alone.

James McLaren signaled good-bye to Hal. Their last practice before the championship had gone smoothly. McLaren had arranged for them to hit a few balls with some of the other players. Afterward, he and Hal had walked around the grounds to have a look at the competition. They paid particular attention to two of the qualifiers, a big American kid out of U.C.L.A. in California and a stocky Mexican. The serve and ground strokes, respectively, of these two were among the best he'd ever seen. "Good luck to the son-of-a-bitch who draws them," he muttered to Hal.

He was toweling off in the locker room when he

caught sight of Brice Evans. His jaw dropped. "Are they here, too?" he asked his agent. He knew Brice was scheduled to arrive via the Concorde with his family.

"I know we're not married, but at least you could say hello," Brice said.

"Hello. Where are they?"

The small well-dressed fellow parted his hands in a calming gesture. "Relax, James. I left them at the hotel to unpack. I knew you didn't have a car, so I thought I'd drop by, say hello, and give you a lift."

James pulled a pair of faded jeans over his boxer shorts. "What hotel?" he asked ungratefully. He continued to dress.

"The Gloucester, like I told you. I know how you feel about your privacy and steered them away from the Royal Garden."

"Good. Is she with them?" His head disappeared under a towel. He dried his hair vigorously.

Brice sat down upon one of the benches running parallel to the lockers. He ran a hand over his crop of brown hair. "Who's that, James?" he asked coyly.

James almost smiled. He looked at Brice as though ready for an argument. He opened his mouth, then shut it again. "Janie," he said finally in an obvious tone.

Brice lit a cigarette. "Why, of course, Jimmy boy. She's here, ready and willing."

Again James tried hard not to smile. His eyes hardened. "Must you always be in such a good fucking mood?" He pulled a T-shirt over the lean muscles of his back. It hugged his body and highlighted the solid shoulders and well-defined chest.

"It keeps me young, James."

"It exhausts me." James looked at the cigarette. "Give me one of those." Brice proffered the pack. James saw he was smoking Dunhills. "Are we putting on airs now that we're in London?" He took a cigarette. "What happened to Marlboro?"

Brice shrugged and extended his gold lighter. "What's eating you, Mac?"

James held the breath. His eyes moved searchingly for the exit door. "Her. What else?"

"Her who?"

"Brice, I've got a lot on my fucking plate, if you don't mind. Okay? Enough with the coy shit. You know who I mean."

"I know who you mean?" Brice echoed sarcastically. "Like hell. You're in and out of more holes than a golf ball. How should I know who you mean?"

James's stare fell from Brice to the floor. He said "Janie" distastefully, as though the word itself was repellent.

"What about her?"

"It's over, that's what. I want out," James said flatly.

Brice grew anxious. "Yes, but it's Wimbledon fortnight in two days. Couldn't you put off telling her until after? You know what you're like."

James threw some of his spare gear into the locker. "No, thank you. I want out as of yesterday. As of last year, actually."

"Are you still riled up about that coke bust?" Brice asked.

"Nope."

"I know we've discussed Janie in the past, but is now the time?"

James sat back down on the bench. He strained an arm behind him and slammed the locker shut. His racquets remained at his feet. "Yup. Let's get out of here."

Brice was seated in the passenger's seat of the Alfa Sud. James had bullied him into letting him drive. Miraculously, they made it to Kensington without an accident. James was still not used to the right-hand drive, but he had Brice beside him and the agent provided a constant source of reminders. They stopped at a bottleneck in Earls Court Road. James delighted in honking his horn at frequent intervals during the wait. The truck driver directly ahead of him was not so delighted. "Will you stop that?" Brice pleaded.

James smiled. "The tide has turned. Now look who's uptight."

"Yes, sure, anything to placate you." Brice opened the window and craned his head in the direction of the pileup. He sat back down. "Look, James," he began on a more subtle note, "what can I say to persuade you to postpone this decision?"

"Anything you like, because it won't matter to me." He tapped his hand on the dashboard as he monitored the passersby.

"Can't I say anything?" Brice was growing pompous.

"Yes," James said coolly.

"What?"

James continued his surveillance of the passing talent. "You can say 'sorry for being so fucking nosy' and shut up. Okay? I've made up my mind. Let's forget it."

"Okay. Jesus! I'm only trying to help," Brice said.

"You can help by giving me support." James turned and said confidentially, "And if you're real good, I'll introduce you to my latest squeeze."

They both started laughing. "You incorrigible son-of-a-bitch. You're beginning to make Errol Flynn seem like a monk."

The Alfa snaked through the traffic, skipped a red light, and zipped the wrong way down a one-way alley. They rambled over a piece of sidewalk behind a building and found themselves two blocks south of Harrington Gardens and the Gloucester. James saw that Brice had gone pale as a result of his Grand Prix-style circuit across Kensington. "Time and tide wait for no man," he said philosophically and smiled at his passenger's discomfiture.

They were in the elevator when Brice remembered an earlier phone call. "By the way, I received a call from Smythe's man Whitney. He says to tell you if you do anything like that again, posing for another tennis sponsor, they'll pull out of the contract and sue you."

James smiled. "Whoa! Such strong words."

"That's what I thought until all of a sudden his tone mellowed. I think they know you know you've got them in your pocket and they're trying to get back for lost pride."

The doors to the steel lift parted. James felt a familiar queasy feeling returning to his stomach. He thanked God Janie hadn't been there in the hallway to greet him. "Now or never." He sighed.

"What?" Brice asked automatically. "While we're on the subject, did you catch the latest market prices. I've a little surprise for —"

James hushed him with a gentle hand. "Come on, Brice, save it. This isn't as easy as I thought it was going to be."

The door opened and he shook hands with his father. Peripherally, he sized up the situation in the modest, though comfortable, suite. The women sprang from the couch to meet him. His mother, a shapely woman with hair piled too high on a greying crown, was preceded across the room by her favorite eau de cologne. James stooped and kissed her and thought how very remarkable it was that his mother should smell like the woman in Monaco. Janie idled forward. She'd lost weight and was sporting a tan, which suited her. James took one look and could tell she was high on coke.

"Hello," he said dryly. He offered his cheek and Janie kissed it. He had resolved earlier to play it cool from the start. It was over. He knew it. He wanted her to know it. Expressing emotions was never very easy for him. He'd be brash and unsubtle and leave no doubt in her mind.

"Jimmy, how's the arm doing?" his mother asked.

"When we heard the report and saw the film, we thought maybe you'd broken your hand," his dad said.

James appeased them and raised his hand and clenched it. "It's still there."

They all laughed stiffly. "One thing's for sure — the next reporter to hassle him will keep his distance, or else look out," Brice said. He pretended to duck a punch. They laughed loudly and forcibly this time, as though it were the funniest joke in the world. James looked to his agent and frowned.

"At least that's behind you. Was practice okay?" his father asked. "I know how you felt about last year."

James looked at his shoes. "Sure. No more problems than anywhere else." He felt sorry for having to play the heavy with his parents. They didn't really come into it, but by being here, with Janie, they were involved.

His father scratched his head and exchanged a worried look with his wife. It was her turn. "So, James, what's your schedule these next few days? Are we going to be seeing a lot of our famous son?"

It was a pretty stupid question, which he debated ignoring altogether. "Not for a while. I'm playing on Tuesday, so I thought I'd keep to myself and concentrate on tennis. I'm more determined this year than last." He didn't have to tell them that.

His father detected a glimmer of enthusiasm in his son's voice. His friendly eyes narrowed. "That's the spirit," he rallied. James thought it prudent not to mention all the time he intended to spend with a certain sixteen-year-old.

"I know you'll win it, son. I can always tell, can't I?" his mother said.

"Yes, Mom."

"Oh, and James, I thought your decision to take the option on Aristocrat was a good one. Brice tells us all you're a regular Howard Hughes."

James rolled his eyes. He knew they liked this expression because he used to do it constantly as a kid and it was his way of telling them he was still their little boy at heart. He wasn't, of course, but he liked for them to think it. He turned casually to Janie. His expression was a curious combination of stoicism and disdain. He thought of saying something in the way of a hint, but refrained. There was no cause to humiliate her before an audience. They would have their moment alone. He returned his stare to Brice and frowned at him for no reason.

"Jimmy, I think your mother and I would like to nip down and grab a sandwich. You're welcome to join us," his father said. "And you, too, Brice."

"No, thank you, I've lost my appetite," James replied.

"It's not anything?" his mother asked, worried. "Not like the flu?"

"No, Mom, I just ate a big breakfast, that's all," he consoled her.

"Yes, well, you know how we absolutely loathe that airplane food. We haven't had a thing in twelve hours," she said.

"Anything to eat, that is," his father joked.

James smiled for him. It struck him then that the three arrivals were mildly drunk. The realization gave him a kind of strength; his undemonstrative manner would seem less serious if they were slightly tanked. Janie smiled at him and brushed back her blond hair.

They rose to go. Brice took the hint and met them at the door. "James, I'll be in tonight if you want to drop by and discuss the Aristocrat option," he said.

James looked puzzled. His brow wrinkled. "What's to discuss? I thought we took it up already." His puzzled look switched naturally to one of anger. He was in the mood to get angry.

"We did," Brice assured him.

"Haven't you heard, son? Since it went public, it's nearly doubled," McLaren senior said cheerfully.

"That's nice," James said matter-of-factly.

"That's two million dollars," Brice stipulated. "And climbing."

They languished painfully in the doorway waiting for the appropriate cue under which to take their leave. James finally made a remark about the time. His parents took the hint and left, leaving him and Janie to do battle.

Suddenly, he felt he needed a drink. As no drink was available, he went into the bathroom, stood before the mirror, told himself to relax, then emerged. He felt strangely weak in the knees and sought support from the doorframe. "Janie, I'll be straight. I want to end it. It's over between us and has been for a long time."

He anticipated an outburst that never came. Janie bowed her head slightly and covered her eyes with her palms. "I know, James," she said solemnly. She looked at him, then looked away and began to weep softly.

All traces of the contempt he had harbored for so long drained out of him. Sharp pangs of remorse stirred inside him. "What do you mean, you know?" In a curious way he felt offended. Had she been plotting to leave him?

"I'm not totally insensitive, James. I've known how you felt since last year, for Christ's sake. I almost didn't come over this time." She wiped her tears on the bedcover. "I've been thinking of ending it, too. I can't endure the constant hurt."

He was stunned by her revelations and tried to construct a fitting retort, but the proper words escaped him. A sense of loss overwhelmed him. He almost wished he did love her, and an instant passed during which he wanted her back. He fought it off and thought of Olivia. "Okay. It's not easy, I agree, but it's better this way. We were growing stagnant. It's important to keep moving forward in a relationship." He scratched at an earlobe. "Am I sounding like some God-awful social worker or something?"

"Or something," she said amiably through her tears.

They went out and paced the sidewalks of Kensington walking close together, though never touching, hovering in the vulnerable limbo between past union and future separation. Any physical contact now would be their undoing. They'd willingly taken the first tentative step toward a parting, and to go back now would mean wasted pain.

Their strength came from two very different sources. In the case of James, his determination and the strength to sustain it were pulled from within and reflected the toughness of his character. Janie had surrendered, as she habitually did, to the influences of whatever narcotic she thought would make it easier. In this instance she'd opted for cocaine.

Over their second cup of watery coffee, they tried to sort out the next move. "How will I tell your parents?" she asked.

He took a generous swallow of lukewarm liquid and spat it back into the cup. He wiped a drop of coffee from the lenses of his sunglasses. "Sorry, this shit makes me want to puke."

"James, what should I do about your mom and dad? What am I going to say? Christ! they're like parents to me," she said. She had been chain-smoking since they sat down.

"You don't have to tell them anything," he said without thinking.

His flippancy angered her. "Of course I do," she snapped. "Stop being so thoughtless."

"I don't know," he retorted. "It's not my problem. They're my parents. You handle it." He tapped the spoon to a nervous beat upon the table. "Sorry."

"I'm sorry I raised my voice," she said.

"Tell them it's a trial separation and that we're just not getting along anymore. Which is sort of true."

Her spirit winked at him through her dilated eyes. "Really, James?" she asked hopefully.

He cursed himself for the ambiguity of his remark.

It was not his intention to build her up to tear her back down. Consistency was far less damaging in the long run. "No, but say that anyway. We've got our whole lives ahead of us. You'll meet somebody in a month and forget all about the pain we went through. It happens every day."

"I'll still miss them." Her eyes brightened with the next idea. "Maybe I could see them occasionally, like at matches or local tournaments."

He cleared his throat and stared at her half-smoked cigarette. Finally, he told her, "I don't think that's the best idea, at least not for a while. We've got to split for good with no ties. Otherwise, we'll never get over it."

Her breathing grew labored. She spoke with an intonation of despondency that stabbed at him. "James, I can't bear it. It hurts too much." She jumped up and started for the door. Tears streamed down her face. She clutched at her sunglasses and sobbed resoundingly.

He caught her outside the café and grabbed her by the wrist. She twisted free and withdrew her arm into her chest. Then her hands clamped against her temples. "Please, Janie," he said, "it's not as bad as you make it." Her pursued her. "You still have the memories, my parents."

"It's all so sad," she cried.

He grabbed for her again, but she clawed free and sprinted to a taxi. He remained within the throng of onlookers, pressing a hand to the place on his forearm where she had scratched him. He wiped the blood on his jeans and sucked at the wound.

It stung, though he couldn't feel it through the numbness.

James sat sprawled in the chair with the lights out and the video on. He rolled the vodka around his mouth and spat it out in a plume of spray toward the television set. Clint Eastwood's face became distorted behind the beaded wetness. James found he couldn't drink. The alcohol merely aggravated his empty stomach and begat an urge to vomit. He'd been sick twice that night already. The half dozen joints he'd smoked left a blue haze in the TV light.

What surprised him was not Janie's reaction but his own. He didn't long for a reconciliation and knew such a move would prove pointless and fatal. But he felt bad beyond the vicarious hurt he felt for Janie. For the first time in his twenty-three years he felt vulnerable.

He made his way unsteadily to the bathroom and slipped into the bath. He turned on the hot water and smiled stupidly. He thought of Janie and then Olivia, then Janie again, and started to laugh. He slid under the water and opened his eyes wide. Light undulated in strips overhead. The walls appeared to crane inward at strange obtuse angles. He tried saying "Olivia" through the water and followed the bubbles and his syllables to the surface. He sat up and wondered why he'd lost a spelling bee in the fourth grade and fell asleep.

He awoke in a sedentary position with his chin slumped over his chest. The phone was beckoning. Slowly, he extracted himself from the primordial warmth of the water and staggered into the bedroom, flatfooted. "Yes, sir," he said.

"James, it's Pam. How are you?"

He listened to her with the calm sagacity of someone who had smoked six joints. "You're upset."

"No, James. Why do you say that?" She paused. "Could I see you tonight? It's sort of important."

"I told you you're upset. What's the time?" He tugged at the bedspread and flung it over his back like a towel.

"It's eight, just past eight," she said.

"I'm starving. Are you?"

"Yes," she said hesitantly.

"Meet me at the Chelsea Arts Club in an hour."

"Are you all right, James? You sound funny."

"I am funny. So are you. Everything's funny. Haven't you heard? The world's one great big fantastic joke. That's why everything's so fucking hilarious." His words echoed in his head. He felt suddenly self-conscious. "Pamela, darling, I'm not in the best form, but if you think you could tolerate me, meet me there when you feel like it."

"Lovely, James."

"You'll know me 'cause I'll be the one wearing the green hat with no clothes on. So long." He staggered back into the tub and stood under a cold shower for five minutes. He swallowed a tablet of speed and got dressed.

They ate quietly and drank three bottles of Beaujolais in the quiet ambience of the Chelsea eatery.

Pam began quietly with the resigned tone common among friends unburdening themselves of personal problems. James listened silently through bloodshot and sagging eyes and a bobbing head. From behind he resembled a punch-drunk prizefighter on leave from the farm. His condition made it easier for Pam to make her disclosures.

"They cornered me again, James — all of them this time," she continued. "But it wasn't like the party that I chose to attend. It was right in the middle of my apartment after the exhibition at Hurlingham. I came home and found them making it with one another. They'd been back only a half hour before me, but most of them were already drunk or stoned. I tried to resist but it wasn't worth it; they were too drunk."

"Like us?" James queried facetiously.

"Come on, James, don't be like that. This is really serious. If you're not prepared to listen, I'm going to leave," she said. She surveyed the crowded room and wondered if any of her fellow diners had heard her.

James lifted the wineglass and held it against the candle in the middle of the table. He admired the purple halo and set it back down. He thought of telling her that if she wanted to leave, she'd have to race him to the door. He'd tried telling her about Janie, but Pam had dismissed the subject and the pain she had caused him with a nod of her head. Tonight was Pam's night. "I'm listening," he said soberly.

"It happened again, James. Like the last time.

Exactly like the last time." She drained her glass. "Do you think part of me is like them?" she asked. "I need to know." Her voice cracked. She breathed through her clenched fist.

"Whatever you do, don't cry. I'm telling you now because I couldn't bear it tonight, Pammy. I'm willing to listen and offer my advice and my sympathies, but that's it. No tears or I'll have to go." He delivered the warning with a steady tongue. There was no doubting his sincerity.

Pam stemmed the tears and nodded knowingly. "All right, James, I apologize. I'm really sorry about you and Janie, too — honestly I am. I thought you made a cute couple. But I'm almost at the end of my rope. That's why I'm banging on about my problems. If I can't find someone to discuss this with, I'll do something drastic."

He took her by the knee under the table. "I'm always here."

"Thanks." She sniffed. "No tears tonight, I promise."

It didn't take long for her to set the scene. Her descriptions were evocative; he could picture Pam in the small apartment with the naked members of the Super Six. They discussed areas of Pam's past that he knew nothing of before: the alcoholic and sexually aggressive father, the motherless home, her sisters. Something about her plight — the utter loneliness that was a way of life to her — James could understand. His present despairing condition allowed him to sympathize with her completely. Any advice he dispensed would be tantamount to advising himself. Consequently, he wanted her that night. He intended to soothe her through the most personal way he knew. He almost expected her next sentence.

"Make love to me, James," she said. She added an obscure though understandable postscript. "It's my only chance."

He was undressed and in bed by the time she entered the room. She approached the bed with her head bowed slightly like an angel. Her impish grin he translated as a faint show of pride over her beautiful naked body. She laughed nervously as he crawled across the bed. The inexorable passion of a first-time affair gripped him as he watched her. James remembered how he had thought of her before many times, as he watched her on court. Her long hair spread across her shoulders. He reached out and let it sift through his fingers. She bent down and drew her colt-like legs under the sheets. His breathing was at the same time resonant and shallow. They faced each other squarely. He'd forgotten how pretty she was. She stretched past him and brought her perfect breasts against his mouth and she flicked off the light. Rivers of moonlight poured through the spaces in the drapes. He moved her trembling hands to his hips, then encircled and massaged her breasts.

She could feel him against her thigh. His movements, although tender, were foreign. There was a coldness here she hadn't anticipated. What was gained through the sheer intimacy of the encounter was lost in the confusion in her head. Her concentration vacillated between extremes, the effect being that she felt nothing. Determination would prove her salvation. She would have him as they had had her, deep inside her like the rubber phallus they had inserted in her. His seed would cleanse her. Transform her. Deliver her back from where she had embarked. She was a woman. She loved men.

He was touching her there and fighting for her mouth with his. His tongue lapped at her and invited her reprisals. She acted as she thought she should and mirrored his advances. This was James, she kept repeating to herself. Lovely, sweet James. Her loyal and wonderful friend. Images of the Super Six swirled in a surreal blizzard before her. She felt drunk and opened her eyes and saw him and kissed at him. He repositioned her stiffly so that she straddled his hips. Her chest remained firmly crushed against his. He touched her again and again, despairing for a reaction. She understood this and squirmed accordingly. She bit his ear. He moved into her and she felt relieved, for it would soon be over. She thrust herself against him. Her little mouth winced at the pain. He drove into her, forcibly conquering the dry conduit laboriously in short bucks. She screamed and gripped him tighter.

Chapter Eight

Moonlight poured through a space in the curtains and Pam wondered whether things would ever be all right again. Her vagina felt sore and her breasts ached. James sighed and snuggled into the blankets beside her. His muscular legs were tucked on either side of the sheets so that his left leg lay exposed. His head shifted into the path of the moonlight and it was as though he could feel the light and draped a hand over the back of his head and sighed.

He had passed out after the first round. He slept heavily, a wine-induced sleep, content in the illusion that he had satisfied her. He had no way of knowing otherwise. Pam lay awake with her hands beneath the pillow and her eyes on the persistent beams of light, trying to remember where it had all gone wrong. She was less morose than she might have been. She had to find out for sure, and now she knew. The sobering moment of anagnorisis would return to her in the light of day when she was alone and destroy a little piece of her. She prophesied this. For the moment she felt distantly satisfied at having gone through the motions. This was, in her opinion, the next-best thing. The satisfaction engendered through the charade with James helped her; for she was a woman.

It took her no time to change. She stopped in the doorway to look at him. The light was still caressing the back of his head though, the actual spot had altered due to his movement. She would have liked to awaken him to talk; his encouraging words would have fortified her that much longer. But this was only a temporary measure. She had to distance herself from the prostrate figure and any reminder of the act she found so offensive. No, she thought, she must be alone. All alone. Always.

Sadness crept up from deep within her and weakened her. She hurried through the lobby, past the reception desk, pretending not to see the bleary-eyed porter at the door. He sat up from reading a copy of *Country Life* he'd taken from the reception desk and, for want of a better reaction, saluted her. She drifted toward the Thames, moving mechanically on sheer instinct. Twice she was nearly struck by a taxi. Her handsome head was down; she saw only the precise area before her and therefore missed the tall man in the overcoat with the hollow eyes and the stale, derisive expression.

A warmish wind was burgeoning on the banks of the river. It dragged with it the sounds and smells of the city. The thick smell of water prevailed. A familiar vacuous sadness touched her as she neared the bridge. She lingered at the dark steel walkway that ran beside the road where the cars passed from Chelsea to Battersea and vice-versa. "Why?" she asked aloud. She brushed the tears from her eyes and mounted the parapet. "Why?" Her question was stolen by the breeze and stifled. The sound of her leather soles defied the winds and rang harshly along the metal. She tried to walk more softly — she wanted no attention drawn to her — then relented as she sank back into the loud empty shuffle of the lonely. Cold graceless footsteps slapped along the parapet.

Her senses came to her in heavy throbs and rescued her from the sudden self-destructive impulse. She clung, extended halfway over the railing — the wind tugging at her lovely brown hair. Her head was pounding. She righted herself and returned to her feet. Then she groped for the railing to steady herself and peered at the frothing paddock of water. White choppy water materialized on the surface in a languorous surging reaction.

"I didn't think you would do it," a voice commented plainly.

Pam whirled around to find him. She glanced first left, then right, but couldn't spot him in the darkness. She smelled the cigarette and her nostrils flared slightly. She relaxed and settled against the railing on her elbows. Fear of strangers and subsequent self-preservation didn't rate very highly at the present moment. She felt him move.

"I said I didn't think you would do it." She pretended not to hear, so he slid through the balustrade from the road and joined her. His hands settled, entwined, over the railing, holding a cigarette. "I'm glad you didn't. That would have been such a waste."

She detected an accent. Her head moved enough to make him out. Her first thought was that he was not bad-looking. His hollow eyes were squinting against the breeze. He looked like he'd shaved recently. "Who are you?" she asked.

"Call me an admirer. I saw you passing while I was out taking a walk. You looked like you could use a friend. Then this almost happened." He fingered the cigarette and sent some of the ash over the bridge toward the river. "The water's very cold this time of night."

"It's a little late to be walking around," she said. The wind emitted a final exhalation and then quelled. She could hear him more easily now.

He pointed vaguely toward the Chelsea embankment with the cigarette. "Not really. Not when you live right on the river. I've always been a night person and function better when it's dark," he said pleasantly. He seemed to anticipate her next question. "It's two o'clock in the morning."

She nodded. His excuses sounded logical. Besides, it wasn't that late. She stared into the Thames. "I wish I had the nerve. I really do."

"No, you don't. You've got too much to live for.

You're young, beautiful, successful. Unique. In many ways like some rare gem." A flawed gem, maybe, she thought. He smoked his cigarette elegantly, his gestures deliberate. He could have been an actor. The smoke blew back around his face. He smiled. "Your fame precedes you."

It didn't worry her that he knew a lot about her. Many people she had never laid eyes on knew her and followed her career. She found his attention mildly flattering. "So you're a tennis fan, too?" she asked.

"Too?"

"I mean you're a tennis fan," she explained. She about-faced quickly and slipped her hands into the pockets of her skirt. Her back was touching the railing.

He appeared to be studying her face and something in him looked pleased by it. "That's the understatement of the bloody year. In fact, you could say I live for tennis." He thought about it. "Yes, you could say that, and you wouldn't be far wrong."

"Oh, really?" Her pride glistened under a façade of indifference.

"Yes." He nodded. "One finds so many lovely women at the tennis tournaments. I've spent most of my life trying to understand this phenomenon." He studied her, then looked off into the distant night.

"Is that what you think?" When he nodded, Pam said sotto voce, "Few things in this world are what they appear to be."

He heard her. "Few things are, my love. Take artists. I've devoted much of my life experimenting with the various arts; painting, sculpture, drawing — you name it. The original dilettante. I've come to know many prominent souls in the art world. Believe me, there is nothing sacrosanct about these men for whom the world holds such reverence. They are like you and me and the man on the corner. Nothing mysterious or exceptional. They have merely perfected the art of imitation." He spoke again with a strange tranquility. "That is all art is, of course — imitation, plagiarism of one sort or another. Nothing is original anymore."

She brushed at her hair. "I've never heard it put quite like that."

His words hung in his mind like an afterthought. Had he been too aggressive with his views? "I'm sorry if I let my convictions get the better of me," he said.

She screwed up her lips and then nodded. "No, I think your point is valid. I've never thought about it before, but you're probably right." She stared at his cigarette. "You learn something new every day."

"Don't you, though." The exchange died naturally. The reposed cadence of their words made it clear neither was going to run off. Therefore, there was no reason to hurry the conversation. After a while he said, "I can imagine what a life you lead following the professional circuit. Existing out of a suitcase is never very pleasant and a trifle lonely." He said this gently.

"That's true," she whispered. "I'm used to it, though."

"Is that why you were contemplating taking a midnight dip with your clothes on?" His question contained a curious mixture of challenge and derision.

"I don't know," Pam said coolly. "It's my business."

"Indeed, being a doctor, I think I can appreciate your feelings more than most." His assertion of being a doctor would open her up to him. Doctors invariably had this effect. They had in a sense adopted the role of latter-day priests in the agnostic and turbulent 1980s and he knew this. He withdrew a ready card from inside his overcoat and pressed it into her hand. His touch warmed her.

"Josh Boorman. Practitionner General. Paris huitième," she read. He'd had the cards printed during his last stop in Paris. "That sounds more German than French," she observed.

"Very astute, my dear girl. I practiced in Düsseldorf before making the switch to Paris. My wife's family lived there," he said ambiguously.

"Well, Dr. Boorman, what brings you to London?"

The rest was easy. He had secured her confidence through this remarkably simple ploy and the rest would follow as he had planned.

They proceeded back along the parapet to the embankment and down Cheyne Walk. She accepted his suggestion to continue the conversation, on women's changing roles in society, in his flat located on the same street. He had again drawn on his uncanny ability to identify people's character, discover their weakness or interest, and play to that. He saw she was undecided about her sexual preference, and the remainder of their talk hovered, however subtly, on sexual stereotypes and bisexuality.

He made an allusion to a wife asleep in a back bedroom when they were loitering on the outside steps. The lie seemed to convince her that she would be safe inside with him and that he was not a pervert. He shut the door and grappled with the dial for the lights. He adjusted the brightness. She saw that the flat was tastefully decorated and had a cozy, lived-in atmosphere, almost congenial. And this was the way the young couple had intended it to be before the husband got a transfer to DeBeers Johannesburg. They'd given it to an agency on Brompton Road that leased it out in three-month stints as a precaution against squatters. So far the two-bedroom Chelsea flat, on the same block as the abodes of Mick Jagger's wife and J. Paul Getty's son, had been his only real extravagance. If it went well, he thought, he might even decide to buy the place.

"Whiskey or gin?" he asked.

"Oh . . . er . . . a whiskey would be lovely." She attempted to sound as though she hadn't expected it.

He fixed two whiskeys and put on a record of Vivaldi concertos. She joined him on an oblong sofa in front of the fireplace. A window was open on the street side and occasionally she heard the rumble of an early morning delivery truck. He noted this, too, and got up to close it. He smiled at her when he sat down. All conceivable avenues of escape were now sealed off. Including the front door. When closing it, he had triggered a small spring device that made flight from either side impossible.

"But do you really think women have evolved enough in society to make it in these new roles without losing their femininity?" Pam asked the question, and a sort of glint — a lecherous expression — appeared in the doctor's eyes. She drank from her glass and looked up. The glint disappeared.

"No, my dear, not as such. As a matter of fact, I agree with your perceptions totally and utterly. Isn't that a coincidence?"

He was being strangely elusive. With his answer he had contradicted himself. Was it just her imagination, or was his accent becoming more pronounced? "You mean they have sacrificed their femininity?" She qualified herself. "I'm not sure I understand you completely." The whiskey and the late hour slowly debilitated her.

Amusement flickered in Joseph's deepset eyes when he spoke again. "I can't actually remember what I mean. Maybe I was playing truant when that chapter was discussed at medical school." She wondered if she heard him correctly, then wondered if he wasn't moderately eccentric. His next question dispelled any doubts about what he was. "Wouldn't you agree that all women are nothing but cock teasers anyway and really only want one thing?" Pam stirred uneasily and checked to see the distance between her and the door. "Janie, there's no cause for alarm. I'm simply treating you as any self-respecting doctor would. I'm interested in seeing what sort of woman you are." He stole a glance at the door. "Please excuse my somewhat unconventional manner."

Her soft brow frowned. She suppressed the impulse to look at the door. "Janie?" she asked. She wore a bemused look. "You said Janie." For some reason he was associating her with James's girl friend Janie. This confused her further.

"Yes, Janie, there's nothing to fear."

"But I'm not Janie." She thought hard, then saw it clearly. She smiled affably. "You thought I was Janie, as in James's Janie. That is funny. No, I'm Pam."

"Silence, " he hissed. "Having invited yourself up here with one thought in your mind, I now propose you put up or shut up, Janie." His jaw dropped and his uneven teeth showed. He stood up and undid his trousers, displaying his erection. The sudden terrible knowledge of what was happening stung her. She'd been trapped by a madman and he was going to rape her. The instant panic threatened to choke her and she fought to get a deep breath.

"Help!" The word scratched free from a stone-dry throat, barely sounding above the Vivaldi concerto. She tried to scream again as she sprinted to the door and tugged on it.

Joseph stepped out of his pants calmly. His wild and hollow stare cut across the room and beheld her as she struggled. "Come to me, Janie," he commanded.

"Oh, God," Pam moaned. She grabbed a book from the shelf and hurled it at him. She ran for the window. Clenched fists had no effect on the unbreakable Plexiglas he'd had installed. She raised a chair and prepared to hurl it through the glass.

"Why must they always be like this?" Joseph asked warily and reached behind him. He leveled the automatic at her shoulder. "Relax, Janie, it's just a fuck." The gun ejected a shallow spurt of hard white light. The bullet careened off her collarbone. A speck of powder erupted upon the wall behind her.

Pam rebounded off the window and back onto a table. To his annoyance, she knocked over a picture he had bought that very day from a little gallery on Kings Road. He tugged at her roughly and threw her onto her belly across the couch. She was bleeding from the cleft of flesh between her shoulder and neck. He saw it was only a surface wound from which, theoretically, she could recover.

He hoisted up her skirt and peeled off her panties. He moved into her and climaxed instantly. For a minute he remained inside while he listened to the end of the concerto. Then, using an embroidered towel from the couch, he clamped it over the wound on Pam's neck. Luckily, his whiskey was only an arm's length away. He stretched and hooked a finger over the lip of the glass and reeled it in, nursing the drink between fondles of the perfect breasts of his prisoner. They were lovely and hard and the nipples puckered at his touch. Her reflexive response excited him. He started again, humping her more slowly.

When he finally finished with her, he stripped the remaining clothing from her body. He stuffed these and the embroidered hand towel into a plastic bag. The next quarter of an hour was spent scrubbing the blood from the edge of the couch where the single .25-caliber slug had lodged quite inconspicuously in the plaster behind the Hessian wall covering in that section of the room. He swatted at the negligible accumulation of dust where the bullet had hit after grazing Pam. His hands were sticky with blood; plenty of soap and warm water returned them to their former pinkish selves. He dabbed at a crimson speck on his cheek, guessing he picked this up while fucking her.

Next he carried her slender frame as far as the bed in the next room and dumped her unceremoniously onto it. Leather belts were used to bind her hands to the bedposts. He had, as an uncharacteristically thoughtful gesture, left space enough for her to move her hands about. So long as they couldn't touch each other and undo the bonds, she would be fine. He draped a towel over her neck wound and covered her in a sheet. She stirred just as he was closing the door. He returned to her bedside and stood over her. There was absolutely no pity in his face. "How does it feel to be kidnapped, Janie? How do you think McLaren will react to the news?" A sharp blow to her temple knocked her cold. He returned the room to darkness and departed.

Chapter Nine

Geneva

The meeting had been arranged some months ago. And Rolf had been present, acting as the representative and chief organizer for the Soviets. The Americans had named the date and the place; the Dag Hammarskjöld Conference Room in the Hilton Hotel at 4:30 P.M.

Rolf was in attendance, as was Popotov, Vladimir, and the two Russian financiers. Joseph was absent for no other reason than that he hadn't been told. This in itself was a small coup, given Vladimir's chronic indiscretion. But somehow the baby-faced man managed to keep his mouth shut about the American retailers. Popotov, for one, had impressed upon Vladimir the financial importance of the meeting and how Joseph, if he knew the terms of the deal, might see fit to blackmail them. The ten thousand Swiss francs Popotov slipped into Vladimir's coat pocket didn't hurt.

The decor was classic Hilton. Angular Formica furniture with a glazed-wood veneer. Spotlighting was set in tracks on the stucco ceiling. The style of the curtains was borrowed from a circa-1969 county library. They had been pulled back to allow a panorama of the lake and the skyline. Amid this bastion of prefabricated bad taste, the Americans felt right at home. Rather like pigs in shit, Rolf had thought. Among them, the six middle-aged Americans represented one-half of the entire American sports market. The distribution area controlled by these gentlemen included every major sporting-goods store in America and its territories. Everything from the largest supermarket chain to the most insignificant merchant with a half dozen stores did business with them. All schools, gymnasiums, sports centers, and mail-order catalogues fell under their influence, and only the smallest establishments with negligible turnovers eluded their sales network. Last year alone three billion dollars in retail goods was siphoned out of the stores by sports-conscious Americans. Of this staggering total, two hundred times the gross national product of Uganda, one-half of it filtered down through the hands of the six Americans at the table. They were well heeled, even by Saudi terms.

A jovial character with bushy eyebrows and a broken nose asked Rolf for another highball. His ill-fitting tweed suit and string tie belied the chain of thirty-one hundred supermarkets he represented and another ninety-six he owned personally. At his suggestion the stores had been fitted recently with high-quality sports departments that had taken off and set profits soaring. In his home state of Alabama, rumor had it he was the man responsible for swinging the vote to Reagan during the 1980 Presidential election.

Mr. Wallis, as he was now known — having Anglicized the name from Wallicznintz after college — had been elected to speak on behalf of the Americans because of his genius for manipulating people and his innate farm-boy honesty. The Americans thought the Russians would appreciate this. Popotov, Vladimir, and Rolf would do what they could with their limited English. Words, however, were adornments in the world of international commerce and could be dispensed with to uncover the hard facts. These men would confine themselves to the figures.

The five Russians sat opposite the Americans. Rolf was to the side near the bar Popotov had had him set up. Generous plates of hors d'oeuvres were situated on the American side of the table. Vladimir caused a minor sensation when he stood up and helped himself to some of the tiny smoked-salmon sandwiches. He sat back down and munched on them. He noted that the Americans occupied the western side of the table, the Soviets the eastern side, and wondered if this was significant and smothered a laugh.

Popotov removed the cigar from his mouth and

flicked the ash in the glass bowl next to Vladimir. Vladimir was seated beside Popotov to help him with his English. Despite the young man's proficiency in this capacity, Popotov could see the son of his friend was turning into a serious liability. The boy's arrogance surged unchecked.

"How do you think?" Popotov asked the Americans. He gesticulated toward the racquets in case they hadn't understood him.

Six Crimea racquets had been deployed before the commencement of the meeting and were sporadically picked up and examined. Mr. Wallis turned to gauge the reaction of the bearded men at his left. John and Jake Hagler, both from Houston, headed the largest proportion of the distribution market with their family firm of the American Amateur Athletic Corporation. The fact that the company sounded more like an organization to benefit sport than an entity to exploit it had contributed enormously to its success. It was this firm that codistributed for Whiplin tennis products among others.

"The premise is fundamentally sound," Jake Hagler said to Wallis. "If the marketing's there, a Russian product could sell. It has a certain novelty commensurate with attendant American tastes."

"Have we the necessary incentive and space allocation per subsidiary?" John added.

Wallis said nothing. He looked away and sucked in half the highball. *Ever since those boys went to Harvard they've never been the same*, he thought. Yet the joint total business acumen these two possessed could be placed on the end of a stick. Wallis knew, as did everybody else, the Haglers' old man ran the show, and if he wasn't being operated on for prostate cancer he'd be here instead of them.

Wallis turned to his right. "You see, gentlemen, this here racquet in itself is very nice, a cute design, looks good under the arm of the club pro or the wife when she goes shopping," he said in a rolling Alabama drawl. "But as you can well imagine, that in itself ain't enough in a tennis market inundated with all sorts of similar products."

Popotov understood very little of what was said. He consulted Vladimir and Rolf and understood even less. Nonetheless, Popotov had gathered enough from Wallis's tone to recognize a problem. "What?" Popotov said. "You no like?"

Wallis caught the flavor of desperation in the question. "No, we like, all right." He grinned to make the point. "But there are many problems."

"What problems? Racquet is good, *nyet*?"

"Yes, it is good, but there are too many in America as it stands. Very much competition. These figures are not competitive enough. There isn't anything unique enough about it," Wallis said. The language barrier frustrated him. He scratched at the sheet of figures before him. "I'm afraid we've got to have a larger advertising commitment from you toward a national campaign — television, magazines. You know."

Popotov understood this sentence. He regarded the page full of numbers. "Two and half million not good advertising?" he asked in halting English.

"It's a start, but not when y'all are introducing

a new product into such a highly competitive market." Wallis spoke in broken sentences, much like Popotov. He monitored the faces of his countrymen. They looked composed enough, he decided. Why shouldn't they? They'd been flown to Geneva and put up in first-class accommodation for three days at the Russians' expense. Personally, Wallis welcomed the chance to do business with the "Ruskies." He was under the misconception that the Crimea racquet would be vastly subsidized by the Soviet state to undercut the American market in much the same way that it sold its farm machinery and vodka. Consequently, the retailers could slap on a hefty additional charge to increase their profit.

In the case of the Crimea racquets, some well-placed bribes had, in fact, procured a small subsidy from the state. But not nearly as much as had the venture been a bona fide government one. In actual fact, Russia had precious little to do with the deal. Although the racquets bore the spurious label "Made in USSR," the racquets were manufactured in Yugoslavia. The spoils of the communist system had merely been tapped and used to the advantage of the entrepreneurs. Cheap raw materials and labor had been opportunized on, with little compensation made to the system.

The two primary factors that caused Popotov and company to profess an actual Soviet affiliation in the manufacture and sale of the Crimea were young Chekow and the subsidies. Rubles equaling four million American dollars had been allotted them from the state. This had helped to get them started, but it wouldn't enable them to offer the goods at cut-rate prices, as Wallis had anticipated. Chekow was enlisted for the obvious reasons: No other Eastern European or Soviet male player — and very few of those in the West — had the ability to win any of the major tournaments. With Wimbledon rigged, the Chekow-endorsed Crimea would receive maximum exposure and more advertising than any amount of money could buy. Last year alone, five hundred million people had watched the men's finals. This staggering figure would translate into thousands of Crimea sales worldwide if Chekow won. This was the backbone of the Russians' assault on Western tennis. Of course, the possibility existed for Chekow to go out early in the tournament. The Russians were willing to admit that terrible reality. But since the odds were that Chekow would meet McLaren in a major tournament in the near future, the Wimbledon dossier could be used to their advantage to ensure victory at that time.

Popotov conferred with his colleagues. "It is apparent they know nothing of Chekow's sponsorship of the Crimea," he began. "For this reason they are hedging on committing themselves."

"Perhaps if we suggested the possibility of a victory with the racquet, then they'd agree," the pockmarked financier said defiantly.

The white-haired elder nodded. "He has a point, Popotov. Offer the goods at one-half our original asking price."

"But that's madness, Leonid. We'd be selling at a loss," Popotov broke in.

"Ah, but there is method in this madness, I assure you. What is your net worth, Andrei?" the elder asked the pockmarked one.

Andrei shifted about in his chair, stroked his toupee, then said, "You know. Eighteen million Swiss francs. About seven million dollars." He underestimated by three million.

"Is that all?" The white-haired man looked bemused. "Very well. What is yours Popotov?"

"Five million dollars." He exaggerated by one and a half million out of pride.

"Fine, fine." He nodded. "You see, together we can supply the goods to the Americans." He hurried along in case the others tried to cut him off. "We will sustain a loss at face value; most certainly we will. However, once the proper distribution is established, our young man's victory at Wimbledon will ensure a large increase in sales, whereupon we double our prices over a period of time. They will still be competitive, and in a matter of months we will have turned loss into gain. This is how the American business mind works."

"What if he loses?" the pockmarked one inquired.

"If he loses the battle, he can still win the war, Andrei. We raise prices gradually to cut our losses. There is more than one tournament." When he said it, it made sense. Indeed, it was practically the truth. But one crucial element had been overlooked even by the white-haired one. He had underestimated the caprice of the American market. Here today. Gone tomorrow. Quite frankly, if the retailers didn't receive immediate and sustained results, the distributors heeded the cries of their lifeline and terminated the options on the contract. Rather like chopping out the deadwood. In not so many other words, Chekow had to win Wimbledon or their investment was down the tubes.

They agreed on his game plan. Popotov sucked at his cigar. He waved away the smoke. "Very well. We have agreed to make the terms more attractive and have decided to halve the figures before you. This is for the first three months of operation, with a clause to increase the wholesale price marginally after that period at prearranged increments." He was confused when he received no reaction. It struck him he'd spoken in his native tongue. He began again in broken English.

Within the hour a contract was drawn up by one of the Hagler boys, who was also a lawyer, and signed. Nine million dollars' worth of Crimea racquets were ordered at the ludicrous wholesale price of roughly ten dollars a racquet to retail at forty dollars. An advertising commitment was pledged with an additional one and three-quarter million on top of the two and a half already agreed upon. All sales, including distribution costs, were on a commission basis, so that for the time being the value of the merchandise was outstanding and earning a loss in real terms when played against interest rates. For each racquet sold, the net loss to the Russians came to just under a dollar. Outwardly, this was not the most viable business arrangement. Should Chekow win Wimbledon with the Crimea, the figures would improve.

Popotov tugged the rapier of curiosity out of his prodigious belly. He had committed nearly his entire fortune and he had to know. "Mr. Wallis, sir, if Chekow, he take Wimbledon with Crimea, how good is it?"

Wallis was in a generous mood. The deal he'd agreed upon was like taking candy from a baby, or rubles from a Russian. "You mean, Mr. Popotov, if y'all should win Wimbledon with your own brand of racquet. You want to know what that means in sales?"

"Yes," Popotov said. "In dollars."

The other Americans were grouped at the door ready to leave. Wallis stood up and clutched his valise. "Well, should that happen , I think it's conservative to say you'd make . . ." — he screwed up his flat face and raised his eyebrows — ". . . taking into account your specified price increases, I'd say y'all could expect orders to increase by a multiple of ten."

The American delegation disappeared behind a deluge of smiles and bone-crunching handshakes.

Rolf waited until they'd reached the street to make his move. "Rolf, where are you headed so determinedly? You look like you're keeping some young lady waiting," Popotov said affably. Throughout the sensitive proceedings Popotov had retained his good nature. Now that the meeting was over, he was in a buoyant mood.

"Oh . . . I'm just . . . I need to do something," Rolf said, noticeably flustered. "I won't be gone long."

Popotov had often wondered how Rolf came to find sexual gratification. The poor guy was away from his wife for eight months of the year. Popotov had decided long ago that his erudite little secretary was probably a fag of some sort. Whenever Rolf chose to steal away without advance notice, Popotov assumed he was seeing to these primal needs. "Very well, Rolf, don't let me stop you." When Rolf remained standing, Popotov brushed him away with broad sweeps of his hand. "Away, away with you. I'll expect you for supper at the Vaud Platz. I'm eating in tonight."

"Yes, sir, Popotov," Rolf said, then vanished around the corner of the Hilton.

Popotov thought it strange, but had he detected a cynical edge in the words of the secretary? He shrugged it off and moved for the waiting taxi. He saw Vladimir standing by the curb. He hesitated at the door of the car. "Vladimir, what are your plans this night? Are we to expect you at supper?"

"You can expect me if you like," he told Popotov cheekily. "But I probably won't show."

"You find our company less than stimulating?"

"Well, I guess you could put it that way. I've got better things to do than to talk business all night long." Vladimir gazed aimlessly across the street as he spoke.

Popotov cleared his throat and ducked into the cab. He thought about Vladimir the whole way to the Vaud Platz.

Rolf weaved in and out of the traffic, his tiny timid head jerking conspicuously from side to side. Was he being followed? Had they anticipated his actions? He crossed the street and recrossed it farther along at a stoplight. In his haste he narrowly avoided getting hit by a Mercedes limousine. He slunk away redfaced as the limo raced past him. Despite the cool air of a spring afternoon, he kept dabbing at his brow to clean away the sweat. Nervous swipes with a soiled handkerchief had rendered this part of his face red, and any subsequent perspiration burned his chafed skin.

He finally decided that he'd lost any potential tails — an ironic conclusion, since his actions had done everything but elude attention — and hailed a cab.

The light was beginning to taper as the sun slid across that last portion of the horizon prior to its deceptively rapid descent. Rolf noted this phenomenon while on his knees in the office. Such was the measure of their trust for him, he alone possessed the full set of keys that unlocked not only the doors, but the filing cabinets. An extra set was logged in the vaults of the Bank of Zurich and could be relinquished only if all three Russian elders were there to sign for it. As far as they knew, the videotapes of the Wimbledon dossier were in the same vault in the same bank and had been put there by Rolf.

In fact, he had only pretended to deposit the tapes at the bank, but had left them in the filing cabinet in the rented office overlooking the Rhône. This was part of his plan. Sure they would berate and probably fire him once they realized he'd neglected to deposit the tapes. But fuck them, he thought. Eleven years and he hadn't once made a botch of anything. In a sense he'd been waiting his whole life to fuck up like this. He had their trust; they would never accuse him of deliberately choreographing the quagmire. Rolf considered himself above suspicion. No, if the tapes disappeared, blame would fall upon Vladimir or Joseph — but not him.

The tapes were precisely where he had left them, on the left-hand side of the second drawer from the bottom. He pulled them out and laid them quietly on the table. Using the soiled handkerchief he wiped away any fingerprints, then shut and relocked the drawer. He had time, he told himself. Moreover, he didn't feel nervous. Maybe he would even steal a peek at one of the tapes. He could surely enjoy them now, knowing they wouldn't be used in the name of his country. He could pop one in the video, play with himself, then remove it. What could be easier?

He got as far as the video machine when his senses surfaced above the lust. Jesus! He could buy a porno tape if he was that badly off. Abruptly, he observed the desire pumping strongly through his veins. He groped for and felt himself nearly shouting for joy. He was hard! Already he was improving! His beautiful bride, Kara, would delight in the attention of a sexually active husband. How wonderful life could be, he thought, rejoicing. He gathered up the tapes and left the office without switching off the lights.

Joseph rubbed his hand roughly over the crotch of the young prostitute. He inserted a finger into her vagina as he moved forward to deliver instructions to the driver. Then he froze. He gazed up across the square to the expanse of white block that comprised Kruger House. A trained eye brushed over the south section of the building. He squinted. Was he imagining it, or was the light on? He withdrew his hand from the girl's crotch and leaned over the driver's shoulder, causing him to mutter incoherently.

"Shut up!" Joseph barked. He was trying to think. Did not Popotov detest doing business after five-thirty? But it was already seven. He stopped theorizing and shouted an order. "Quickly, to Kruger House!"

The irritated driver drew up in time for Joseph to see Rolf cross through the entrance of the building and dart into a cab. Joseph felt a knot form in his stomach. "The tapes," he whispered.

At Joseph's command the prostitute was dumped on the curb and the taxi raced off after the little man. They crawled through the heavy traffic, keeping a safe, though secure, distance. Unbeknownst to the tough-talking driver of his car, Joseph would have to kill him if it appeared his prey was slipping away. He plainly couldn't risk it.

His worst suspicions were confirmed when Rolf's cab braked alongside the bridge spanning the river Rhône. The little man was disposing of the precious tapes; somehow, Joseph knew this. His taxi followed and ground to a halt near the stone staircase where Rolf had descended. He threw a wad of notes onto the front seat and set out after Rolf. The cab pulled away slowly. The driver kept a wary eye on the two men parading along the grand bank of the Rhône.

After about a minute he tired of this pastime and pushed on.

The night closed in swiftly. The spring day renounced the sun and its accompanying warmth with an unusual rapidity. The air along the bank of the river grew cold. Rolf continued at a steady pace. He buttoned the flaps of his light cotton overcoat. His short breaths frosted visibly in the air and trailed along behind him. He hugged the three separate envelopes of tapes under his arm. Twice they'd threatened to slip from his grasp, but each time he had caught them and tucked them in against his body.

As it was not yet dark, Joseph was forced to linger out of sight at just beyond striking distance. He knew if he aimed and missed, Rolf would hurl the tapes into the surging river, only yards to his left. Joseph decided then to risk it. He consumed the area between them in large measured steps, gaining ground at a constant rate. The automatic was shifted from the warmth of the shoulder holster into the large pocket of the overcoat. Joseph breathed in the crisp twilight air. The hollow cavities of his eyes formed slits against the cold wet air. Rolf was approaching an interruption in the river where the water cascaded over a small waterfall. On the south side of this terrace the river descended to a lower level and persevered with greater aplomb.

Rolf traveled along, consumed by the excitement of what he was actually doing. He was in fact saving Russia from disgrace and earning back his self-respect in the process. All his humble toiling and bowing would be discounted in one sudden action. One casual flick of the wrist and the tapes would join the rest of the shit in the Rhône — and then he would go to Kara. . . .

Rolf lowered his head a fraction and stormed through the gauntlet of chilly air. His hard-soled shoes clattered over the gritty inclined path. Occasionally, he slipped and he had to shift his weight to keep from falling. Tears welled in his eyes in reaction to the cold. He began removing the tapes from the envelopes forty yards from the dumping spot. He was singing.

Joseph sized up the distant scenario. It was time. He clasped the automatic in his cold fingers and sprang off the balls of his feet. He gained rapidly on Rolf, who, so near to his destination, had begun to slow down. The little man was examining the tapes up close with the aid of a match as Joseph aimed while still in full stride.

Rolf was aware of the foreign presence at once. His fawnlike ears detected the shift in sound. He jerked about, sighting from the corner of his eye two white flashes. The flashes were followed by a sifting sound as the slugs whizzed by inches from his chest. Yet a third flash erupted simultaneously with a stinging sensation on his jaw. Rolf swatted at it and stepped back reflexively. Two slugs filled the air where he had been. He groped for his chin and became aware of the warm sickening trickle of his own blood. The nameless horror that he had been caught in the act swelled in him and rose quickly to his throat. Breathing became arduous. *The tapes!* he thought suddenly. *They mustn't get the tapes!*

He started running. What was left of his jaw was cocked into a grisly broken smile. He would still defeat them; all that remained was for him to throw the tapes into the water. His unsteady feet scraped along the gravel. In an uncoordinated dash, he turned to face the river.

Joseph was nearly upon him. He cleared the icy tears from his eyes as he pumped shots into the small moving figure at the water's edge. Suddenly, his eyes cleared and he watched helplessly as two of the tapes, two priceless examples of his handiwork, plunged into the torrent of water. Joseph dropped to one knee cursing and put two holes in Rolf's lungs.

The little man, so valiant in the face of defeat, seemed suddenly overcome by the fire in his chest. He pressed on, oblivious to the one remaining cassette clasped between his bloodied fingers. In his mind he had won. He was the hero and it was over. He alone had saved Russia. Blood moved in reverse peristalsis up his throat. Kara would be so proud of him. It was worth it. He had righted any wrongs he'd ever perpetrated . . . he was a good boy. His mother appeared on the bank and said, "You can come home now."

A piercing scream rang across the banks of the river as the final slug from the automatic hit him. The pain in his lower back, initially unbearable, disappeared at once. Memories of the awful pain rested in his brain like a scar and would remain there for the rest of his life. Which wasn't saying much.

He was still running in great leaps and bounds, but only in his mind. The gnarled finger of lead lodged in his spine had rendered his short legs useless. He tried to crawl but soon found he had only one good hand. This confused him and he took inventory of the bad hand and realized it was clutching a tape. "Oh, no," he whispered softly as the power drained from his lungs. Bleary eyes saw Joseph crouched on one knee in front of him. He heard mumbling and saw Joseph's mouth move. He was aware of Joseph hitting him about the face before he died.

"Goddammit!" The word traveled along the banks of the Rhône and was drowned in the noise of the water. Joseph stood with his legs apart and his head bowed. "Dammit!" He had pried loose the lone cassette from the corpse's white fingers. Joseph brought the tape to his face and thumbed a gold lighter. The light flared and he read the label. "McLaren," he said aloud. He used the back of his hand to clear the perspiration and saliva from his eyes and mouth, respectively. "Thank fucking God."

He rummaged over the body and removed all valuables and means of identification. He slipped these into the pockets of his overcoat. He recognized the shirt of the dead male secretary. It was of the type sold in the finer stores in Moscow. The rest of the clothes were European in origin. He hoisted the body up while he removed the tag from the back of the shirt. He pocketed this. With his foot he rolled Rolf down the incline. The body landed with a quiet splash and was immediately sucked out by the current. Joseph watched Rolf's corpse glide across the soupy surface of the water. He turned and started for the bridge clasping the tape.

The door to room A-14 in the Vaud Platz blew open behind the force of a well-placed kick. Splinters of wood fanned out upon the rug. The door rebounded with a boom and was caught. Joseph gripped it tightly, appraised the contents of the room, then slipped inside and slammed it behind him.

Popotov's great bear of a figure swept into the front parlor from the bedroom. A burgundy quilted robe was slung over one shoulder. In one hand a book of Pushkin. In the other a revolver. His mouth broke from the snarl to whisper, "What do you want?"

He almost shot Joseph as the younger man approached and brushed by him. Joseph hesitated in the doorway to the bedroom. A bosomy black woman peeked out from between the covers and regarded him nervously. He turned back to Popotov. "Get rid of her," he said disgustedly.

"What is the idea of breaking into my room, giving me orders?" he roared. "I won't stand for this horseshit any longer!" The once tough miner had had enough of the brazen insolence from his employee. He lowered the gun and hooked a punch toward Joseph's head. Joseph stepped back gracefully. He responded to the rush of air and landed a jab on Popotov's broad chin. The jab stood him up for the split-second Joseph needed to connect with a right cross. The big man crashed onto his back a clear yard from the point of impact.

Joseph poked a head into the bedroom. "Get dressed and get out," he told the cowering woman. He returned to Popotov and spoke to him on one knee. "We have to talk. Rolf has destroyed all but one of the tapes. I had to shoot him," he said plainly.

Popotov was no longer angry. "I don't believe it. Why would he do this?" he asked, breathless.

"I don't know." He was grateful now that damage from the punch had been minimal. Ideal employee-employer relationships did not necessarily include exchanging blows. "I'm sorry about that." He indicated Popotov's chin. "I hadn't intended to use violence, but it couldn't be helped. Now can we talk?"

He helped Popotov to his feet. "Yes," Popotov replied coolly. Popotov stooped and picked up his revolver and slid it into his robe. He adjusted the garment and tied the belt. He disappeared into the bedroom and came out again, this time wearing slippers. The prostitute followed shortly. She scurried to the door and slipped out.

"Ever hear of knocking?" Popotov asked.

Joseph stared at the door. "My apologies. I'll send someone around to fix it."

Popotov crossed the room. His thick fingers slipped around the neck of a cut-glass decanter of vodka. He took two glasses from the table and filled them to the top. "Don't bother. I'm on good terms with the staff. I'll notify them as to the sad state of their security." He took a seat beside a brass lamp and crossed his legs, then took a long pull from the glass and showed his teeth. "Now talk."

"I found your man Rolf attempting to steal the tapes an hour ago. He was walking along the river getting ready to throw them in." Joseph took a seat on a table and sampled the hundred-proof vodka with a grimace.

Popotov watched as Joseph removed the remaining cassette from his coat. "Let me see." Joseph lobbed it to him. He scrutinized the bloodied cover and the word "McLaren" smeared across the label. He scraped the blood with a thumbnail. "McLaren," he said, reading it. There was a trace of scorn in his voice. "So you just happened to be in the right place at the right time. You found Rolf at the precise moment as he prepared to dispose of this final tape and killed him. How very fortunate."

Joseph responded coolly to the challenge. "Isn't it?"

"Do you really expect me to believe that? Your word against that of my loyal chargé. You've already proven your reliability." He finished the drink and got up to pour another. He calmly confronted Joseph and topped his glass. "Persuade me."

"The blood type, for openers," he said. "I happen to be blessed with type O-7 negative. Very rare. It's doubtful your man had the same. Had he not been clutching the cassette before I shot him, then his blood wouldn't have to be on it."

"Wouldn't have to be, no. But then what's to stop

you from handing him the tape and then shooting him?" Popotov touched the glass to his lips. "No, if you speak the truth, you can do better than that."

"Can I?" Joseph's tone was threatening. "I didn't come up here for a nice friendly chat with Grandpa Popotov. If you can't see I'm being straight, then good luck to you. I'll bill you for my ten-percent cut and be on my way. You'll have served me well." He lit a cigarette. His brow creased and he grew mean. "How the fuck do you think he got the things in the first place? I didn't take them out. Officially you and your 'partners' have to be present to withdraw them. How could Rolf have released them unless he didn't deposit them in the first place?"

"But why?"

"Mine is not to reason why. You know him better than I ever will. You tell me."

"I can't imagine." Popotov's weathered face registered thought. "In point of fact, he had been acting strange."

Joseph said, "The wonders of hindsight."

"Poor confused bastard," Popotov reminisced. "I shall miss him."

"You'll have time enough to mourn once this is settled. I don't suppose it alters things?"

"No, we have." He corrected himself and began again. "You have salvaged the most important tape. McLaren is our target. If and when he backs out, then our problems are mitigated. If Chekow loses somewhere along the line at Wimbledon, we simply pull out the tape and use it as insurance that McLaren loses in any of their succeeding contests. It guarantees that Chekow and the Crimea beat McLaren every time. I wouldn't call this too big a sacrifice to rescue an otherwise doomed career."

Joseph rose to go. "As long as nobody blows my ten percent, I'm satisfied. I was afraid I'd missed the news flash and that you and the others had decided to pack it in. I see now that isn't so. Again you'll excuse my somewhat dramatic entrance."

"It's forgotten. I see now why you behaved the way you did," Popotov said.

Everything was chummy enough, Joseph thought. At least he was reasonably certain that Rolf had acted independently. He smoothed the surface of the busted door with his fingertips. He smiled gingerly. "By the way, I heard about your meeting this afternoon. I hope it went well."

Popotov said nothing. There was something he had been meaning to ask Joseph, and now seemed like the time. "It appears Vladimir is destined to become a bigger liability than an asset. His vaulting ambition and regular indiscretion have altered my feelings for him." Popotov's uncertain tone beckoned for a reply.

"And?"

"And keep an eye on him for me. No action just yet. His father and I were once very close. I'll put off dealing with him until he leaves me no other choice." Popotov stood up. "I'll let you know." He walked to the door. "Would you care to join us this evening? A sort of victory dinner after a successful day."

"The Americans ate it up, did they?"
"Yes and no. Shall we expect you?"
"No, no, thank you. Good night."
"Yes, we'll talk."

Chapter Ten

London

Joseph let a week pass before notifying McLaren. As had been agreed with Popotov and the others, there was no point in flushing what was left of the Wimbledon dossier until a meeting between the two principals appeared imminent. It could, as Popotov said, always be saved for their next confrontation. Eight days into the tournament Chekow and McLaren, the two top seeds, were well on their way to a collision course in the finals. The young Russian with the Crimea racquet had served them well. His early matches — by some act of fate against the less-gifted players — were taken decisively. In each of his first two matches, he had claimed victory without dropping either a single set or service game. In his last match, the quarterfinals, he had broken serve all but three times. The opponent was a formidable one, Ken Tiernon, the sixth-seeded Australian champion, and the press made a big deal of the triumph. Much to the delight of the Russians, the tabloids made mention of the new Crimea racquet that Chekow used, and which was now available in most sporting-good stores. Joseph could see his hefty percentage taking form on the Western horizon. *If only Chekow can pull it off*, he thought.

Indeed, it was McLaren who posed the problem in the question of conquests. It was no longer so much a matter of Chekow's winning as it was of McLaren's losing. At great trouble and expense, the Russians had arranged for McLaren to lose. But not before the allotted time. Once they corraled the American into the Wimbledon center-one court against Chekow, they could be assured of the outcome. Maximum exposure would be achieved for Chekow and the Crimea. If McLaren went out early and Chekow made the final, they'd have no way of dictating the result. Just as important, a McLarenless final would draw a considerably smaller share of the tennis viewing public. Ideally, it had to be a *pas de deux* with Chekow and McLaren. Whether such an arrangement could be engineered remained to be seen.

Pam had been kept alive with about as much tender loving care as one would expect to find in a zoo. Her sustenance for her past five days of captivity consisted of Perrier water and prawn fried rice from a Chinese carry-out on King's Road. She ate very little, just enough to satisfy her captor, and consequently had lost much weight. Her fine skin had yellowed and she hovered on the constant verge of fever. If Joseph happened to be there and biology beckoned, he would unstrap her and drag her to the bathroom. There in full view of her captor she would attempt to assuage the bloated pangs of constipation.

Pam felt she was slowly losing her mind. If only she knew why he was doing this and to what end, she might retain some sense of her former sanity. Maybe this was retribution for sins not atoned for? Did she deserve it? Yes, that was it. She had sinned and this was her punishment. Her heart pounded and her eyes teared with sudden sorrow. She wriggled pitifully on the bed and felt the prickly heat rise in her as she aggravated the bedsores. The realization that she could trust neither her own nor the opposite sex had depressed her unbearably. She wanted only to die.

After he had screwed her for the second time that day, Joseph showered and shaved. He stuffed the automatic into his shoulder sling, grabbed the tape, and fitted it into the pocket of his sport coat as he went out the door. There remained hidden in the apartment four copies of the Wimbledon dossier. For security purposes Joseph had hired a video duplicator in France and ran off the extras. Against Popotov's wishes he refused to surrender the tapes to anyone else involved in the affair. Rolf's heroics had been lesson one. Vladimir's near defection was number two. Once was a mistake. Twice was a habit. He wouldn't risk a third and told Popotov and the others as much.

The Russians had come to understand their hired hand during the past few months. He was greedy and ambitious, with as malignant a soul as could be found in any penal institution around the world. But unlike many, he adhered to an ideology that decreed: "Play the game by your own rules, but at least play it." The men recognized that Joseph was playing the same game on the same side as they. In this most paradoxical way he could be trusted. Especially as he was now receiving his disposed colleague's extra five percent.

The word on Vladimir had come from within the triumvirate. One of the financiers had learned of Vladimir's intentions through a source in the Russian underground. Again the young man's loose tongue had led to his downfall. Vladimir had mistakenly confided to an associate of the financier of his plans to cash in on the Wimbledon dossier. The Whiplin Company, he was told, was willing to hand over millions for evidence of the tapes' existence. He even expected the CIA to be called in to save face for Western tennis.

In fact, he had told the associate no more or less than he had told Joseph during their drink in the bar. Vladimir simply had imparted one of his lingering fantasies. He had merely been dreaming out loud, Joseph mused. Unfortunately, the associate was marginally less discreet than Joseph had been.

The old boys had overreacted and dispatched Joseph to the Byblos Hotel in St. Tropez to carry out the death sentence. *All's fair in love and war and subterfuge*, Joseph thought as he strode into the Royal Garden Hotel.

James was changing for a quiet dinner with his parents and Olivia in Chelsea. It was not a victory dinner for taking his quarterfinals match, but a "wish me luck" dinner that he would get his act together and even make the finals. During his three-set quarterfinals match against Frazier, an American rival of little consequence, James just squeaked by. He took the first set by breaking service in the opening game and holding on to win six-four. The crowd, of course, contributed as much as they could to his discomfort, attempting to provoke him into the rage he'd demonstrated last year. Two particularly garrulous spectators were escorted out of the stadium and off the grounds.

He dropped his service twice in the second set and fell three-six after an arduous hour and seven minutes under an unusually hot British sun. The capacity audience was then treated to the very spectacle they anticipated and had flocked to see. After what James viewed as a series of horrendous "shithead" calls, he managed to incur the wrath of every single linesman and official within the stadium. He received the customary precautions, a public warning, and was penalized two hundred fifty dollars for swearing. For his efforts he was also conceded a new referee and an apology of sorts from the umpire.

The more subtle spoils of his tirade materialized in the ensuing timidity and confusion that sprang up in the mind of every official on court. Three borderline calls in the next set went his way. Frazier did his best to protest but McLaren called to him to "shut up and quit stalling." Frazier predictably lost his temper and rallied back. James resurrected a repertoire of his best shots and edged out the match five-two in a tie breaker. A recurrence of the Heathrow fisticuffs incident almost befell him as he left the stadium later that afternoon. He told about a dozen members of the press to "go forth and propagate yourselves" and brushed aggressively by them. Needless to say, Brice was none too pleased with the quote.

He was in the midst of changing for dinner and watching a taped flashback of his shaky victory when he smelled the Gitane. The distinctive scent of the smoldering tobacco was suddenly in the room with him. The smell permeated the air quickly. James found it strangely familiar, yet the association he could never quite place. The shadow of the stranger cut across the separation between the two rooms and hung obliquely across the floor. It shifted and James stood up.

"Don't be alarmed, Mr. McLaren," Joseph said. "We have to talk."

The confident pitch was disconcerting. Overwrought fans he could and did handle regularly, but the Russian's casual assertiveness disoriented him. He tried his usual response in case he had overestimated the guy. "If you have anything to say to me, I'll be in the restaurant in an hour. If you want an interview or an autograph, I'll give it then," he said curtly. "Now get out of here before I throw you out."

The thought of the slender tennis star throwing out anything besides the garbage was amusing to Joseph. He let the smirk show, then retracted it. "I won't waste your time, so don't waste mine with your idle threats. We have some business to discuss."

"You can talk to my agent. He handles the business side of it. Now fuck off," James said, interrupting him. He searched around for a suitable object to throw at the intruder.

Joseph stayed quiet. He draped back the front of his khaki jacket and let the automatic show. "Please don't interrupt. May I sit down?"

James's first thought was that this was the police and he was being arrested. But what had he done lately, in England? Then he remembered: the Latin in the bathroom. But this cop had a funny accent that he couldn't place. His eyes balanced on the drab gray face with the hollow eyes.

"May I sit down?"

"If you say so." James watched him sit. "What is this? Are you the heat?"

"Don't talk," he commanded coolly. "I shall talk. You sit down." He pointed to a chair. "You sit down and don't talk." James did as instructed. Joseph leaned forward and offered a cigarette.

"No," James declined.

"Very well, I'll be brief." He scanned the room idly before he asked, "Do you know Chekow?"

James wondered what the gun-toting stranger was up to. "Yes I know Chekow, sir," he said sarcastically with military precision.

"What do you think of him as a player?"

He let the puzzled look roll off his face and decided to dispense with the sarcasm in the hope that a brevity of words might accelerate the conversation. He thought: *Chekow . . . Chekow has the same accent.* "He's good. Two in the world. He's one of yours."

"Oh, really?" Joseph asked, amused. "How did you know I was a Russian?"

"You wear it like an overcoat. I can smell it on you."

Cordiality had no place in this suite in the Sheraton. "Don't be that way." Joseph frowned. His frown twitched.

"Okay, then say what you're here to say. I'm late for an appointment."

"What could be more important than an appointment with destiny?"

"You tell me."

"Shut up," Joseph said emphatically. "And listen to me."

James tempered his anger and listened.

"It seems likely that Chekow, number two in the world and number-two seed at Wimbledon, will meet you in the singles final. If this is so, nod your head."

"Maybe," James said defiantly.

"Should this occur — indeed, should you ever meet Chekow again in any tournament herein — you shall plainly and simply lose. Cut and dry."

"Oh, is that all?" James asked.

"Yes, and you will lose for one very important

reason, that being that I hold in my hand the fate of your career as a public person." Joseph shifted and the cassette was in his hand. He waved it at James. "Do you recall a meeting in Monaco two months ago with a young woman named Claudette? It was after the Monaco Tournament, which you won. Afterward, you met Claudette and went with her back to her hotel room. Do you recall this?"

He did vaguely, but having been through the legal shredding machine once before with the cocaine, he knew enough to deny everything. "No."

"No?" Joseph asked politely. "You forget the booze, the drugs, the sexual orgy that took place? You forget all that?"

"I don't forget it because it didn't happen."

Joseph smiled icily. "How convenient. You forget it and it stays forgotten. Would that we could all function in so righteous a fashion." He stood up. "Allow me to refresh your memory, if you will. I'm interested to see what your retentive powers make of this." He crossed to the video machine. Since he had broken into the suite on two separate occasions, he knew the layout.

James looked at him. He thought to jump up and hit him, but the rangy Russian with the automatic suggested this was not the best idea he'd ever had. He tried to picture the events in Monte Carlo. The girl named Claudette. Was that her name? He could envision her, a blond blur on his memory. They had gone on to her apartment . . . no, hotel room. It came back in bits and pieces like a forgotten dream, but told him nothing.

"*Voilà! Regardez,*" Joseph said.

James sat back and stared dumbstruck for ten minutes. After fifteen his frozen rage began to thaw. He exploded after eighteen minutes and sent a wild punch into the sinewy mat of Joseph's stomach muscles. Despite his fit condition, the untelegraphed blow stunned the Russian and he stepped back, heaving. He came within a second of drawing the automatic on the irate young man but left the piece in his holster. James came at him again with flailing arms. Joseph pivoted and delivered a heavy karate kick high on his chest. James went down and bounded up again, this time grasping a stool. He chucked it at Joseph's legs. The Russian sidestepped it, but not before it nicked him in the shin. Enough was enough. Joseph leaped. An arcing foot caught James on the temple and sent him legless to the floor. He fell with a thud and was attempting to rise when a forearm locked around his throat. He struggled and then went still. Air flooded back into his esophagus. His normal color returned.

"I have something to say to you. A bargain. No one else will have to know if you behave yourself," Joseph said in a strong whisper.

If only he had remembered to lock the outside door, his words might have rung true. Olivia stood shaking behind the curtains in the bedroom. She had witnessed the end of the struggle and hid while she wondered what to do. She could just make out the sounds of the stranger over the accented pulse of her heartbeat.

"Can we discuss this like civilized persons?"

"Yes, let me up." James refused the outstretched

hand. He stood up and shoved his way past the stranger. His inability to accept defeat was apparent at every level, even now after the fight. He poured a large glass of vodka.

"Would you mind mixing me one?"

"Fuck you. Tell me what you want."

Joseph removed the automatic and leveled it squarely at James's balls. "Very little prevents me from finishing you now. If you weren't an integral part of our operation, I surely would."

James saw the mad spark in the stranger's eyes and believed him. He shut up. Joseph holstered the gun.

"What I want is nothing short of what I've demanded. You play your normal game and do what you can. This will please me. However, when you meet Chekow — whether at Wimbledon or any other tournament — you lose. Understand?"

"Or?" James asked dryly.

"Or my home movies find their way onto the desk of every major newspaper in the world, plus a copy for Benjamen Smythe at Whiplin." He watched James devour the drink. "Think about it," Joseph said. "You have a whole minute."

"You want me to lose only to Chekow? For how long?"

"As long as we say. We write the script and you live it." He considered his demand, then said, "Probably we shall require your pledge for no more than a year."

"May I ask why?" James swigged the last of the vodka. He breathed deeply.

"You may ask anything you like. After all, I understand it's a free country. Equally, I don't have to answer."

James affected an expression of unconcern. "Oh."

"Think about the implications of the tape. Scenes of drug taking. Cocaine, no less. The orgy. Homosexual fellatio. Prime cuts, *n'est-ce pas?*"

"What happens after a year?"

"Intelligent question. After a year we sell the tape to you for one million dollars. By that time Chekow will be number one. If not, we keep the arrangement pending for a while longer." The million-dollar ransom was his own idea, his self-allotted bonus for doing the dirty work.

James sniffed at the tumbler. He had even lost the energy to refill his glass. He dragged his voice up from somewhere in his stomach. "I'll think it over."

"Will you?" Joseph asked incredulously. "Then think about the two million a year you earn for playing games. Think about what the tape would mean to your sponsors. Think about the shame. But most importantly, think about this." His hand moved. An object no bigger than a coin landed on his lap. He acknowledged the ring with a frown.

"That's right. Think about Janie. Think about what her life means to you." Joseph waited. "Why not give her a call to confirm it? I would if I were you."

The situation was almost funny. "I suppose you'll want her for a year, too, until the 'arrangement' is up?" James said cynically.

"No, James, just till next week. She's being looked after very well. She hasn't a clue why she's being held. If you play your part like it's written, you've nothing to fear. If not, you might as well kiss her memory good-bye now."

James took a deep breath, then asked, "Did it ever occur to you and your bunch of scholars that either of us might go out before the final?"

"That's not your fault, and we appreciate this factor. Janie shall be released after the tournament," Joseph said. He pouted as he scanned the room. "I have to leave you now. Keep the tape in the machine with our compliments. I hope we don't have the need to meet again. It might be unhealthy. *Adieu.*" The tall Russian walked out backward. He dropped into the shadows of the front room and closed the door behind him.

Something about Janie's plight rang untrue, and James knew this. Janie had called his parents only this morning from New York. They had told him so. She had sounded fine and reasonably happy and was on her way west with some friends for a holiday. James remembered as much. Besides, he'd never seen this ring on Janie before. Was the kidnap threat a bluff? Admittedly, the ring was familiar, but no one he knew . . . He stopped thinking. Pammy. Of course. Pammy's ring. The little gold one she'd worn since he met her. They had mistaken Pam for Janie and were now holding her. A sick, nervous feeling swept through him. He fixed another vodka, drank it down, and nearly gagged.

Suddenly Olivia was at his side, holding him, her

lithe figure trembling. James embraced her and for a long moment allowed the feelings of self-pity to sink in. It was bad enough that they had jeopardized his career, but to kidnap Pam . . . An awful sense of guilt descended upon him. Pam was his responsibility; she had been abducted to influence him.

Then, the momentary sense of despair faded. Pam's only chance lay in his keeping control and maintaining his composure. He focused on Olivia and held her by the shoulders. "How much did you hear?"

Olivia looked up — stunned by the crispness of his words. "I heard enough to know you should contact the police."

"No. Nobody else gets involved. You heard him, they've got Pammy," he said tonelessly.

"But he said they would let her go after the tournament. James, if we call the police they could get straight to work. Then when they let her go, they could move in and catch him."

"That only happens in the fucking movies." James rose and walked by her to the bar. His face was hard and cold. "I'm sorry, baby, you had to listen in. If you heard about the tape, then you'll know what kind of a position I'm in. I don't have a choice. Either I play along or lose it all. Not that that's such an awful thought."

"What was on the tape?"

He sat down with a glass of gin and lit a reefer. He sampled both. When he answered, he was staring at the floor. "How much of it did you hear?"

"Only the last bit after you were fighting. James,

was there something horrible on the tape? Tell me, James, let me help you." She slid to her knees and embraced him. He tried to push her off but relented out of fatigue. It was all getting to be too much for his twenty-three-year old constitution. *How much can a young man take?* he wondered.

"Switch it on, baby. Treat yourself to a private premiere."

She did. She watched for a minute. When she finally made sense of the jumbled mass of naked limbs in the uneven light, she moved to shut the machine off. "Step right up and see McLaren get screwed," James muttered. He was slurring his words.

Olivia shut if off. She saw he had drained his glass. "James, we've got to call the police."

Through the booze he registered the shock on her face. "No," he said plainly. "There's no use fighting them. They've got me by the nuts and they've got Pam."

"Didn't that man . . . the one who was here . . . didn't he say it was only for a year? I heard that much. If the police don't get them, it's only for a year."

He ignored her. The drink had put him on a trip to a world all his own. "In fact, I'm glad it's over. The pace was killing me. I honestly think I want the hell out. I just wonder what the hell I'll do."

She upset the silence with the shrillness of her voice. "After a year, he said he would sell you the tape. If worst came to worst, you could do that. You have the money," she said, offering her childish solution. She removed the empty glass from his hand and gripped his fingers.

He rubbed his eyes and yawned. "Am I supposed to accept his word on that? He could sell me the tape and have another dozen copies hidden somewhere until he needs more money. I'm through with it. Maybe part of me always wanted an excuse to get out, and here it is." He stood uneasily. "Now get out, and if you call the cops I'll get you. I swear it." He swung at her drunkenly but missed and followed his own punch down to the floor. He passed out.

Olivia bent down and kissed his head. She covered his prostrate figure with a sheet and was about to leave the suite. James's parents were waiting for them. She had a thought and returned to the video machine and removed the tape. She left the hotel with it.

Three hours later Brice Evans placed an overseas call to Greenwich, Connecticut. In the room Olivia and Sidney Hughes, the Whiplin chargé, occupied opposite ends of the sofa. The two men were well dressed, as though they'd been interrupted in the middle of dinner, which they had been. Brice paced the area before the marble fireplace in his Savoy suite, chain-smoking. The tips of his fingers were stained yellow with nicotine.

He was her first logical choice since she left James. Brice Evans, the man who had charted James's career for nearly two years now. Olivia would circumvent the authorities and give the film to Brice for his opinion. If he decided to bring Scotland Yard into it, she would agree. Either way she knew his best interests lay in James's best interests and she trusted his judgment.

She had tracked him down through his answering service at the Savoy and within ten minutes was talking to him at his dinner table across town. Immediately, she filled him in and sought his advice. Brice told her to be in the lobby in fifteen minutes, apologized to his hosts, and raced his Alfa to the Savoy. He watched the whole tape, start to finish, downed a glass of milk with three jiggers of vodka in it, and phoned Sidney Hughes. A branch of the same answering service located him at a private dinner party at Meridiana on Fulham Road. Sidney arrived twenty-five minutes later with an avocado stain on the silk lapel of his tuxedo. His subsequent viewing of the first five minutes of the tape cleansed him of his inebriated veneer. He drank milk without vodka to aid his parched throat.

"I wanted you to see that in case Smythe thinks I've finally flipped. When the call comes through, I'd like for you to have a word with him to substantiate what I've told and shown you," Brice said to Hughes. He leaned an elbow on the fireplace and smoothed his hair.

Sidney moved toward Olivia. "How did you come by this?"

"She witnessed the attack and got a look at the nutter who filmed it," Brice interjected.

"Not a very good look," she indicated.

Brice lit another cigarette and waited for his overseas call to come through. He resumed pacing. "These shitty phone systems in this country." He thought of something and stood still. "You understand, word of this is never to leave this room. You know what could happen if it did." He searched Sidney's face contemplatively.

"You have my word," he told him.

Silent chaos hung in the air. Brice was back leaning on the mantelpiece, picking a fingernail and smoking when the phone rang. "About time." He hurried to it.

"Overseas-to-America caller. You're through." The operator's voice was replaced with the gravelly sound of Benjamen Smythe. It was 5:30 P.M. in Connecticut.

"Hello, Evans. What the hell can I do for you? He's behaving, I hope . . ."

When Smythe finally slammed down the receiver after thirty-two minutes of almost constant invective, his mood had altered considerably. "That stupid cocksucking maniac!" Smythe shouted across his elegant Greenwich, Connecticut, office. He had uttered the same words before in reaction to other McLaren escapades. For the first time the words actually fit. A red-haired secretary with a figure like an Eighth Avenue blowup doll stepped into the office. "Out," he said immediately. She withdrew in a flash.

Smythe had been tempted, very nearly for one delicious moment, to call the whole thing quits. McLaren was one responsibility he could do without. "So what?" was his first reaction. When news came of Pam's kidnapping, he knew he had to act. The sordid business of kidnapping had ironically brought out the Catholic in him. It was his business to rescue her. He knew he couldn't involve the police. Involving them in the kidnapping would mean involving them in McLaren's scandal. The link was too obvious. He would have to bail them both out through some alternative means. It was this or risk the worldwide humiliation and condemnation that word of McLaren's party tricks would bring. If the tapes fell into the hands of a competitor or even some fly-by-night opportunist, McLaren was finished and a hefty chunk of the Whiplin profits would sink with him. "Stupid cocksucking maniac."

As usual, there was no point in consulting anyone. Smythe knew exactly how he would resolve the crisis. Discussions with his right-hand man, Whitney, would serve no purpose. He didn't want to put Whitney in the position of knowing what was happening. It was his responsibility to take the appropriate measures, no matter what the legal ramifications. His whole empire was at stake. Everything that meant anything to him was suddenly in jeopardy. With this in mind, he went to the wall safe and removed the leather billfold with the coded number. He dialed it and set up an appointment. For what he required, the fee would be double what it normally was, Martin told him. Smythe said he didn't care and to meet him at the regular spot. Then he hung up and left the office for the day.

He was standing beside his Porsche when Martin appeared. The station wagon pulled up parallel, then reversed and parked beside him. They left their cars and ambled through the little park on the corner of Mercer Street and Hibben Road. This time of the year the three-acre lot doubled as a softball ground for a town league. High wire mesh backstops loomed up behind the patch of earth known as "home plate." The grass was well trodden and sparse in spots, like an aging head of hair. It was Thursday, the league's night off.

Martin was a tall blond-haired man with thin, almost anemic features. To Smythe he was "Martin." To someone else he was whatever name suited him at the time. His words were well spoken and invariably of more than one syllable. He had a certain collegiate air; Smythe could envision him teaching English literature at a small college. Martin owned a condominium somewhere in Spain and had a house on East 39th Street in New York that he leased. He wore Brooks Brothers loafers, was six-feet-one, and had a moustache. On this occasion he smelled strongly of Pimms and was dressed in tennis whites.

They had been talking for a quarter of an hour. The soft earth of the park absorbed their footsteps. "I'll meet your fee on one condition."

"That being . . .?" Martin asked.

"That being that this business is taken care of by next week."

"Next Friday?"

"Yes, at the absolute latest." They walked some more, then turned back to the cars. "You'll notify me at the exact moment it's done. You can always reach me through my answering service. If I'm not available, leave your number and I'll call you," Smythe said. "You can pick up your deposit tomorrow morning."

"Marvelous," Martin said. Coming from him, the elegant word sounded normal. "Can I have anything more to go on? An old address? A name?"

"No, not this time. Try the leads I've given you. They should turn up something. Keep in mind the time element. Once that's past, the deal's void and you forfeit your remaining fifty percent. I still want him taken care of, however. Eventually."

"Anything you say, Benjamen. I'll leave tomorrow night."

The men stopped at their cars and shook hands. "I'm counting on you," Smythe said.

"Consider it done."

"Thank you, Martin. Until tomorrow."

When Smythe got home, it had begun to rain. He left the car idling in the garage adjacent the kennels while he weighed the consequences of what he had just initiated. However indirectly, he was soon to be responsible for the death of a human being. *But surely even the Church holds no compassion for such a man as this*, he thought. A kidnapper, blackmailer, extortionist. The devil incarnate. He switched off the engine and pocketed the keys. He noted that his wife was home, so he took a detour around the kennels by the tennis courts. Melba was taking in laundry from a clothesline in between the hedge of pines.

Decisions came easily to him. The reflex that preceded them was second nature. A snap of the fingers and judgments were determined. This instance had posed no exception, though in hindsight it worried him that maybe he should have consulted someone before sliding into the abyss of commitment. He knew his mind. The consultation would have served only to assuage his innate misgivings on the subject of murder. Perhaps in some small way the church could have helped? Certainly they would assist him after the fact. There was always Father McNeil at the local church. Christ! Smythe virtually kept the church going with his yearly donations. But was shitting on his own doorstep such a good idea? These options preyed on him. Maybe he should have spoken to Father McNeil. But decisions of any complexity had to be made abruptly. To seek counsel through the tortured channels of the church would have taken days. Maybe weeks. Smythe had only one week.

He stood behind Melba and watched her rescue the wash from the rain. She hadn't noticed him when he said, "How very provident of you, Melba."

She twirled around and almost dropped a pillowcase. "Oh, hello, Mr. Benjamen," she said quickly. "You're early today."

"Yes, I am." He stood perfectly still. "I see Mrs. Smythe is home."

"Yes, sir, she got home early from shopping. Said there was nothing in the stores she didn't already have."

He smiled but his thoughts were far away. "How observant of her." He noticed Melba had temporarily sacrificed her chore to chat with him. She held the plastic clothes hamper so it crushed against the thickness of her hip. She smiled awkwardly through the light rain. "Oh, sorry, Melba. I won't keep you. Carry on."

"Yes, sir, Mr. Benjamen." She yanked at the clothes, expertly plucking the clothespins off and grabbing the wash in one motion. The clothespins made a bulge in her apron.

When she had finished, she turned to Smythe. He hadn't moved. The lapels and collar of his blazer were turned up around his neck. His hands were in his pockets and his head was set at an oblique angle to the ground. He saw she was watching him and smiled. As she moved away, he called to her. "Melba."

She backtracked, clutching the hamper of folded laundry before her. "Yes, Mr. Benjamen?"

His vacant stare moved up until it found her. His mouth began to move as though speech was imminent. He closed it again. Finally, he said warmly, "Nothing, Melba. Thank you."

She excused herself to go to the house and left him standing in the rain.

London

She came back to him that night and saw he was still on the floor where she had left him. Olivia got closer and saw he was awake.

She cuddled beside him and cradled his head on her lap. She stroked his hair and rid his face of the tears with her soft hands. "I've got to go on, you know," he said. His voice cracked through the lingering sadness in his throat. "I thought about it and giving it up, and I couldn't."

"I know, James."

"I tried to imagine life without it, but I need what it does for me." He edged around so he rested on his back on his elbows. "I know half of them hate me. Shit! Probably more than half of them. But the ones that don't . . . what they give me means too much to pack it in." He bowed his head and raised it again. "As long as I'm able to be the best, I'm going to kick the shit out of a lot of people trying. Fuck Chekow. If he's my opponent, I'll wipe him up. So what if I still have to drop Wimbledon this year for Pam's sake? The way I do it, they'll all know I threw the fucking match." He glanced up and half-smiled. "I'll get the entire world press wondering what's going on." His words were not one hundred percent convincing.

"You won't have to, James," Olivia said softly. After all the trauma of the night's events, what she had to say seemed so unimportant.

"You know that for a fact?" he asked cynically.

"James, be nice." She pointed a finger. That she would come up with such a comment at this moment made him laugh.

"Okay, I'll be nice, for Christ's sake. My whole career's about to cave in and sailorgirl's worried about my nickel-and-dime sarcasm. You're priceless, baby." He slapped her thigh. "Now tell me how you know I won't have to worry. I've been worrying all my life."

"I showed Brice the tape."

His face went sour. "What?" He sat up and gazed at the video machine. "Did you really take it?"

"Of course I did, when you were asleep," she said confidently.

"Why? What good will that accomplish? Now Brice is going to call the cops and they'll see it and then my parents and then Smythe." He shook his head. "I don't believe it."

"Will you listen?"

"I simply can't believe it. It's over my head," he said incredulously.

"James. Listen to me for one goddamned minute. Nobody else will see it. Brice and Sidney are the only ones."

He interrupted. "Sidney Hughes? I can't stand it."

She carried on through his mumbling. "They saw it, and no one else. Brice needs Sidney there to confirm his report to Mr. Smythe in America. He called him and told him about you and Pammy. Smythe told Brice he would handle it his way without involving anybody."

"In other words, when my contract comes up they don't renew it. Big shit. I'll get by, but I still don't believe you gave them the tape. Where is it now?"

"Brice destroyed it. I watched him."

James hesitated and then said, "There's probably a hundred more of them just waiting to hit Fleet Street." He sat up straight. "I don't like it," he said, beginning to feel the despair again and the panic.

She countered with her sixteen-year-old implicit faith in things. "No, James, Mr. Smythe promised he would work it out before next week. I'm sure he will. Brice believed him."

"Brice doesn't know what the hell's going on. That guy meant what he said. This is probably the mafia or maybe the KGB, not some shoeshine that Smythe's capable of hushing up. This makes the coke bust look like a church function."

She listened. Most of what he said simply spilled out illogically. He was talking off the top of his head. Yet Olivia sensed a certain therapeutic value to his behavior and she suspected that beneath his words there lurked a sense of real relief; he was no longer going it alone. Brice and Smythe were there to share the burden. And, of course, Olivia.

"I did my best," she said. He was silent. "I really believe Smythe will catch that man, but it won't do any good unless you try." She watched James as he lit up a joint. "Will you?"

"Will I what?" He suddenly grasped his head. "A hangover at midnight."

"Will you try to win Wimbledon if Smythe can rescue Pam?"

He went over and picked up a racquet from the closet. He gripped it and hit it sideways against the bed. "I'd like to see that Russian bastard try and stop me." He chucked the racquet into the closet. From a foil packet near the bed he took four sleeping pills and swallowed them. "Come on, then, mate," he said, mocking her English accent. "If I'm going to beat Chekow, I need my sleep."

James fell asleep holding her.

He was up at dawn, the result of a persistent alarm call. He went through the motions, stood up, took a leak, then slumped back down next to Olivia. After half an hour the switchboard operator obeyed his previous instructions and rang him again. He dragged his limbs into the bathroom and stood under an icy shower. He dried off haphazardly; those parts of him requiring a degree of effort to reach remained wet.

He trudged back into the bedroom, fought off an urge to faint, and stepped into a track suit. His wet feet fought their way into a pair of cotton socks. He got into them by using all the strength in his forearms and stretching his legs out simultaneously, nearly displacing a finger in the process. He slipped into his running shoes.

On his way out he kissed Olivia and surrendered the dry warmth of the hotel suite for the early damp of Hyde Park. He jogged two miles, paused to stretch his limbs, then jogged four more. Each grueling mile had a restorative effect and cleared his mind. By the end of the hour-long workout he felt fine.

He stopped at a news agent near the start of High Street Kensington and bought a copy of the *Times* and a quart of orange juice. He drank and read the paper on a bench in Hyde Park. The news offered nothing special: some Wimbledon coverage, and the usual world turmoil.

It was a warm morning and generally misty at this early hour. Had he been anywhere but England, James could have accurately predicted the weather for the day. A young woman pranced by in shorts and a track top. She waggled her finely shaped derrier and sat down on the grass ten yards from him. She pretended to be sunning herself. As James watched she began releasing the zipper of her track top with the effect that a plump set of bosoms threatened to jump out. She lowered the zipper so it just barely contained her valuable assets. He waited for it and it finally came — a little later than most, but it came. She withdrew her arms coquettishly and slowly turned to face him. She acted as if she had just seen him for the first time and smiled widely. He winked at her. *Next week, honey, next week,* he thought. He worked the newspaper into a tight fold and slid it under his arm like a baton. He nodded her way and thought of Olivia as he walked to his hotel.

He ate a leisurely breakfast with Olivia at a café in Kensington. He kissed her good-bye and caught a cab to Queen's Club, where he'd arranged to meet his coach, Hal Jimson. As tomorrow marked his semifinals appearance against Simonson, he wanted to be as limber as possible. The request to practice had startled Hal somewhat. His coach had noticed the transformation even over the telephone. James's attitude was no longer myopic, nor his voice terse and somber. This was not the same James who had been more concerned with giving his girl friend the brush than winning Wimbledon. Something had happened to reinstill in him the will to retain his championship crown.

James arrived early to find his parents there. Hal told him before they began that Simonson — his opponent tomorrow — had been practicing approach shots all morning. "A bit late in the game to be learning," James replied.

He played nonstop for an hour, then, having raised a sweat, signaled to Hal that they had done enough. They picked up their gear and made for the locker room. "I take it this little lady must be very special. You haven't seemed so keen in months," Hal said.

"I suppose in a way she's responsible," James agreed.

"I'm glad to see things are working out. Have you heard anything from Janie?"

"No, my parents have. I think she's doing all right."

"A nice girl, Janie. I just never thought you two were suited."

"Many thanks for the advice, Hal. I could have used it a little earlier."

Hal slapped him playfully on the shoulder. "If I told you everything about life, you'd learn nothing. Ignorance is bliss sometimes, James, and so is discretion."

James smiled. "My coach the sage."

They were at the entrance to the locker room when his parents came strolling in his direction. James quickly brought up the point he'd been meaning to ask. "Hal, tell me something, will you?"

He read James's serious expression. "Name it."

"What did the lesbian thing do to Billie Jean King?" he asked. "What I mean is, would it have ruined her if she'd been at her prime?"

"Oh, the viewing public are a ferocious lot. I can't say for sure, but from a sponsor's point of view she would have been finished for a while at least." Hal worked his jaw to one side, as he often did when he was confused. "James, don't tell me you're getting bored with girls?"

James winced at the loud delivery. "You shouldn't worry so much at your age Hal; otherwise, you might have a heart attack. I'm trying to work something out, that's all," he said.

"If you go gay on me I'll have a stroke."

His parents were fifty feet and closing. James waved to them. "One more thing, Hal — supposing I meet Chekow next week. Do you think I'm ready?"

"What? James, that's not for me to say. You've beaten him five out of the last seven times. By your own admission the matches you dropped were because of a cold." He smiled hello to the parents of his pupil.

"Do the bookies think so, too, along with the rest of the public?"

"Most of them, sure. James, if you play your game, there's no way Chekow can beat you." Hal excused himself after the customary hellos to the McLarens. He went in to shower.

"James, all's forgiven about last night. Olivia called us before nine to tell us how tired you were," his mother said.

"I'm glad to see you're watching your health," his father added.

"We had time to change our plans and see that Dustin Hoffman film we missed when it came through New York."

So sailorgirl had gotten him off the hook by calling them, he thought. At the time their concern had been the furthest thing from his mind. She told them he was tired. What more fitting excuse was there? It occurred to him how savvy she was for her age.

Most sixteen-year-olds were too consumed with trying to get drunk or laid to think of anything else.

"You looked nice and loose," his dad observed. "After you knock out Simonson, you'll be all set for another final. The title's yours already. I can smell it."

His mother looped a hand through his perspiring arm. "We think it's going to be you and Chekow. Mr. Harley was telling us an interesting thing about Russian players at Wimbledon. He said they'll never win because of the weakness of the Soviet tennis system. He's been following it very closely and has even written a piece on it for the Sunday *Times*."

James bobbed his head affably and wondered who the hell Mr. Harley was. Probably some nut whom they met in the elevator of the Gloucester. "That's encouraging news," he said.

They were dressed in tennis gear, so he asked, "How was your tennis game?"

"Oh, it's okay, you know. My serve's been giving me trouble lately. It might be my wrist," his father said.

James often wondered if his father took tennis more seriously than he did. From the start his dad had invested in the best equipment for himself and his son. Lately he'd taken to wearing an array of joint supports and braces. Like his wife, he was always the first to try out any new trendy clothes or equipment. He'd once entered a friendly father-son tournament wearing rubber-soled sandals. The grit from the clay surface provoked a score of blisters and he had to bow out after the first set.

"You should use those wrist weights I got for you," James said.

His father pointed at him. "You've got a point, you've got a point." Then he remembered something. He gave his wife a tender shove on the shoulder. "Tell James about the coincidence." At first his wife was left in the dark by this statement. A few appropriate words from James senior and she, too, recalled the "amazing coincidence."

"Oh, of course. Listen to this, James. We were shopping around Victoria on our way from Buckingham Palace, and who do you think we bumped into?"

He hated these games so he said dispassionately, "The Queen."

"No, silly, we met Chekow and that coach of his, the handsome one." Had they been perceptive, which they weren't, they would have seen the dramatic change of their son's expression.

"Oh?"

"Yes, and they took us back to the hotel for coffee. Wasn't that nice? He's such a nice boy."

He felt the anger ripple inside him. His parents knew Chekow and Viktor from the endless post-tournament dinners and parties that surrounded the professional circuit like leeches. He scorned these forums for tennis groupies and greedy journalists. For a moment he debated shattering their illusion about the Russians, the same people who stole Pam and who were willing to blackmail James into throwing the match. He held back. There was no need to involve his parents.

His father's sneeze released him from the seriousness of his plight. "Son, why don't you go over and say hello to the boy? He's in there now changing."

"Chekow? In there?" James asked quickly.

"Yes, we saw him go in a couple of minutes ago. Tell him how much we appreciated the coffee."

James nodded and started away impetuously. He marched through the locker room doors and discovered Chekow lacing up his shoes. As he stalked him, he wondered how deeply the Russian was involved. How much of the torment had he been directly responsible for? What part did he play in the more nefarious aspects of the matter? The tape? The kidnapping? Before last night his feelings had been totally down the line with Chekow. Neither one way nor the other. In a world full of exhibitionists, James thought the Russian a reserved, quiet sort of fellow. Likable in his way. Now he knew differently. He hurried over to face him.

James took Chekow by his shirt collar and yanked him back. The shirt tore. The Russian fell backward over the bench and landed face up on the tile floor. "Don't ever approach my parents again, do you understand? You filthy commie fuck."

"What? Why, James? What you want?" Chekow began in his own limited English. The attack was so totally unwarranted. It confused him. Had he done something?

"I think you heard me, you piece of shit. Leave my parents alone. Don't get near them, don't talk to them for any reason." James exhaled slowly while he wondered what to do next. Instinct prevailed, as it often did in the clutch. "I know what your game is, and I would kill you for it if I could get away with it." A group of three players was at the far end of the lockers. Craning heads tried to make sense of the struggle. James tugged on the shirt collar and ripped it some more. "I won't dignify you with a clenched fist," he said. A resonant crack split the air as he slapped Chekow.

James began to walk away when a force from behind took him and pinned his shoulders to the lockers with a crash. He leered up at Viktor. His wiry arms couldn't release themselves from the hold. "No touch Chekow. Him not know. Him free," Viktor commanded.

James ignored him. "That goes for you, too, you big Russian cunt. If you look at my parents again I'll kill you. Communist fuckhead!" James shouted. "Let me go or I swear I'll kill you!" He struggled to free himself from Viktor's hold, but the Russian continued to hold him as he reasserted Chekow's innocence.

"Him free of it!" Viktor yelled for the fifth time.

"Like hell! Nobody's free in your shitty fascist country!" James spat back. Aid arrived in the shape of a towel-clad Hal Jimson just as James's shoulders were growing numb. Hal patted the steel forearms of the Russian. Viktor released him and James slid down against the lockers.

Hal apologized profusely. He went over and examined Chekow, who was bleeding from the nose. When he returned to James, he found him changing directly into his street clothes. "James, now what in the name of hell was that?" James shook his head quickly. "Just as I congratulate you on settling down, you go and pull a stunt like that." Hal waited. "Huh?" He saw James was trembling.

"Worried about the publicity, are we?" James asked bitterly. He was upset with Hal for automatically siding with the Russians.

"Fuck the publicity," Hal snapped. "What's going on?"

"No comment," James replied tersely. "I'm not saying anything."

Hal seemed to sense that the matter went deeper than a locker room scuffle. He eased off. "Come on, son. You don't do something like that and walk away from it without an explanation. Not if you want me as a coach."

The threat was a real one. James looked at him levelly and said in a calm voice, "Hal, I know it looks like I'm in the wrong. I don't know what the others told you and I don't particularly care. I know I look guilty, but I'm not. I can only promise you that I'm not."

"James, if there's something on your chest, let if off. That's partly why I'm here."

"It goes further than that." James slipped into a pair of loafers. "I'm through talking for now." He slammed the locker shut.

"Look, can we talk tonight? I'd like to know what's going on between you and Chekow before it goes any further."

"Sorry, Hal. It's not the right time."

"Well, when is the right time, James?"

James felt Hal was pressing him too much. He considered firing him on the spot. "I don't know." He started for the exit door. "If you stick around long enough you can read it in my memoirs. I'll dedicate that chapter to you." He breezed out of the room mumbling this last line just low enough so that his coach couldn't hear it.

Among the contributing factors to James's devastating victory in the semifinals was the anger still brewing inside him from being manipulated. By focusing his wrath on Simonson and channeling his negative energy into positive power against his opponent, James picked apart the player like well-boiled chicken meat from a bone. His assault was overwhelming and his shots mercilessly accurate. The combination wiped up Simonson and left him on the base line clutching his jockstrap and wondering why he had ever taken up the game.

James directed a similar scorn toward the public and the linesmen. He made no effort to taper his flow of abuse of the officials and came perilously close to incurring the type of penalty that had cost him five thousand dollars the previous year. He even slammed a ball after a double fault in the direction of the Royal tournament head, the Duke of York. The fact that other members of the Royal Family happened to be sitting around him did not seem to matter to James. The press flocked from the stadium at that precise moment to relay this news to Fleet Street.

He escaped from the match with a six-one, six-three, six-two win, five hundred pounds in fines, and a public warning. When he had finally overcome his anger he joined his parents and Olivia for a quiet dinner at Alexander's in Chelsea. Hal Jimson showed up with his wife, Betty, ostensibly to wish the family luck. Hal spent his entire time at his table across the room monitoring James for signs of stress. James had still not volunteered any explanation concerning the locker room brawl. But Hal was convinced that wear and tear and the media exposure were behind James's erratic behavior.

For twenty-five pounds a day, Martin had hired a former pugilist acquaintance to stake out the Ebury Street Hotel. He had learned through the tournament office that this was where the young Russian player and his coach were staying. By affecting a self-important American accent, he had persuaded the tournament chief, Sir David Dwyer's secretary, to give up the classified information. Jimmy Koper was now installed in a beat-up Bedford shuttle van one block from the Victoria Arms. In between listless bites of a dozen fish-spread sandwiches and cups of stale coffee, he kept note of all traffic through the hotel. So far, no one matching the description of the Russian had entered the building.

His instructions were simple, so simple that anyone with half a punch-drunk mind like Jimmy Koper could follow them. If anyone resembling the Russian appeared, he was to telephone Martin from the phone box on his side of the street. Martin was equipped for the week with the air-call message-beeper pack

favored by doctors. A call put through to Martin
would be intercepted by an intermediate operator.
She would flip a switch on the table beside her dough-
nut and seconds later a wedge of plastic no bigger
than a wallet would sound off in Martin's left pocket.
It was on his third day in England when the air
call sounded. Martin was doing his thrice-daily round
of all inner London grass courts where Chekow might
be practicing, on the off chance that the Russian
blackmailer might frequent the same places. When
the beeper sounded, Martin was drinking a lager
at the pool at Hurlingham. He reacted smoothly
to the incongruous sound and excused himself from
the thirty-year-old divorcée he'd been entertaining.
He rang the call box.

"Martin, is that you?" Jimmy Koper asked.

"Yes. What is it?"

"I think he's in here. I saw that lad and his coach
go in. The other chap came out of a café across
the street and followed them. He looks like our man."

"Thank you, Jimmy. I'm on my way."

Jimmy was happy to have pleased his employer.
Rarely in his life as a mediocre middleweight, and
as an even less-adept burglar, had he received the
praise he craved. He was happy this summer afternoon that he had done something right. Martin was
the type of man he liked to please — straightforward,
no bullshit. A job well done meant a comparable
reward and a word of sincere praise from the American with the moustache. A job fouled up meant
a straight salary, not a single disparaging remark,
and no possibility of ever working again for Martin.

He knew this from experience. He sat back down in the van and nibbled on a crust of bread and waited.

Martin sped across town in his rented Ford Escort. He knew London well — and, indeed, most of Europe — since the majority of his contracts took him to this side of the Atlantic. His functions ranged from making threatening words to a recalcitrant bill payer, to murdering a Mafia stoolie. He made no bones about which of his services was required. Only the fees varied. It was all business to him.

When he had left the States he had very little to go on besides a vague description of the Russian and a list of probable connections in the case. Once in London he had set up the most obvious stakeout and proceeded to cruise the list of "could be" locales, such as the All England Club when Chekow was playing, Queen's Club, Hurlingham. Martin was fifty thousand dollars richer than he was a week ago. If he failed to complete the contract by the required time, he was out of pocket maybe three thousand dollars in expenses of the fifty-thousand-dollar down payment. No big deal. The money was no longer the issue. He had long since reached a certain status both financially and professionally where all that mattered was his reputation. Like a master craftsman, he had his pride.

In his sport shirt and khaki trousers Joseph could have been mistaken for a tourist. His loose clothing concealed the automatic taped to a space on his calf where he had shaved the hairs. He knew what he was doing constituted an unnecessary risk. He could have phoned Viktor and delivered his final words in this way, but the impact was so much less potent. He preferred to deliver the message in person, appreciating the inherent risks but shrugging them off. Life was one big risk anyhow. Any time was borrowed time.

Their door was not locked and he elbowed past it into the room. Viktor was hanging up a shirt. Joseph saw that the great figure of the coach had dropped some weight. The flesh of Viktor's face had withered. The loose folds of skin about that granite jaw hung pendulously. "Hello, comrade," Joseph said.

Viktor moved slowly and took in Joseph. His muscles flexed automatically, a result of the sudden rush of adrenaline. Each time Viktor met him, the rangy assassin appeared substantially more affluent. The smart loafers, the Lacoste shirt. It was all a product of Joseph's having perfected his act. Yet all the cosmetic changes in the world could not disguise the hollow face of death. Viktor felt sweat break out on his back at the base of his spine. "Get out."

"Please, Viktor. I know how you feel about me and those I represent, but please, grant me a moment."

"I don't want the boy to see you. Get out and go back under your rock."

This comment angered Joseph. "Don't talk to me like that, Viktor. I won't put up with it!" Joseph debated going for the gun. A struggle with Popotov or McLaren was one thing, but Viktor's powerful and fit form was intimidating. He hated feeling threatened. "I'm here on a mission of peace. What I have to say will please you, I assure you."

Viktor hung up the shirt and faced him squarely. "Anything you have to say sickens me. When I see you it makes me want to puke." He stepped forward.

"I won't warn you again," Joseph said. He took a hesitant step backward, yielding his ground. He realized that if Viktor came any closer, it would be difficult to reach the automatic. Suddenly, Viktor relented. He crossed his bristly forearms.

"Very good, Viktor. I will leave you in a minute." Nervous perspiration was sponged up in Joseph's shirt. He took the liberty of closing the door with his foot. "I spoke to my superiors today. They would like to congratulate you on a great semifinals victory yesterday. Truly excellent. I came by this afternoon merely to inform you that the go-ahead has been established with McLaren." Joseph gulped nervously. "McLaren will not win the final. He has given his word."

Viktor narrowed his eyes and spat, "This was already agreed. It doesn't explain why you are here wasting my time."

"If you consider this a waste of time, that's your problem. I don't. I thought it necessary, knowing you as I do, to warn you of the penalty for betrayal. The KGB does what it does for very specific reasons, all of which benefit the state in the end."

"You tell me nothing new," Viktor said dryly.

"Maybe not. But often it is provident to repeat oneself for greater clarity. Just make sure nothing gets in the way of a Chekow victory with the Crimea. Perhaps he prefers his other racquets to ours. I'm here to promise you that the pressure's off. There's no need to fall back on any other racquet for false security. Chekow will win." He allowed a dramatic pause. "Further, there has been some controversy lately in Moscow over the death of Onegin and his trainer fellow. We all know very well that Chekow is guilty of their murders and you of assisting in the coverup. Our branch in Moscow intelligence is busy setting the record straight with the investigating authorities."

"You bore me, you son-of-a-bitch, with your empty threats."

"Do I?" Joseph asked angrily. "Would I bore you if I recommended to my people that the boy's family and any of your relations are repatriated to Siberia as a precaution for the next five years? Or until Chekow's usefulness has expired?"

Viktor said nothing. The muscles of his jaws contracted.

"Your tongue seems suddenly to have lost its power. Is it something I said?"

Joseph was smiling indulgently when Viktor crossed the distance between them in two bounding strides. He caught Joseph as he was going for the gun. A giant paw lifted him by the shirtfront and pinned him between the door and the doorframe. "No more. I've listened to all I'm going to listen to," Viktor said powerfully in a hushed voice. "I don't know who you are or who you represent, but I know this. One day you'll slip and drop your guard. I promise you on your whoring mother's grave." He accented the threat by slamming the door shut with Joseph in between, then snarled once and tossed the assassin backward into the hall.

From that point on Viktor was a marked man and he knew it. One did not wrangle with members of the KGB or whatever branch Joseph represented and live for long. Viktor went to the window and stared pensively at the trees that ran in a strip behind the building. He was not so old that a confrontation with Joseph was unwinnable. Viktor would meet the challenge, and though he might not win, the son-of-a-bitch would know he'd been in a fight. He would surprise him, he decided. For Chekow's sake, if not his own, he would surprise Joseph.

Joseph made his way rather less confidently back to the street. His once pristine shirt was soiled and stretched into a little ball at the chest. His regal bearing had been substituted by the quick graceless gait of a man infused with hatred. He could feel the sharp sensation of the gun against his calf. His pants leg chafed against it as he walked. Only the prospects of his future fortunes prevented him from flushing the gun and opening fire on the pathetic throngs of tourists. One wrong look and he would have snapped.

His thoughts and hatred focused on the emaciated captive in the rented flat on Cheyne Walk. He'd been too charitable with the stupid bitch. Her presence constituted a risk. No, he resolved, the time had come to end that nuisance. By killing her he could vent the hate he felt for Viktor and the rest of them. His heart beat rapidly with anticipation.

With his mind rife with images of her brutal and glorious death, Joseph failed to note the tail. Martin throttled the Bedford van and maintained a gentle tag on Joseph's taxi. They turned down Cheyne Walk. Martin parked in a space outside the Kings Head and Eight Bells pub and watched as the Russian left the taxi and marched out of sight into a white building. The edifice was large and rectangular. Probably a block of flats, Martin thought, and not a private house.

Martin hurriedly got out of the van and crossed the half block facing Cheyne Walk in time to meet the departing taxi as it swung left onto the embankment back toward Chelsea. He hailed the cab and it stopped; he slid inside. "Don't go anywhere. I just want to ask a question," Martin said. He erased the look of bewilderment from the Cockney driver's face with two twenty-pound notes. "I'm wondering if that was a friend of mine back there. That fellow you just dropped off."

"I couldn't tell you, mate. He didn't say much." The crisp bills were already folded into the driver's pocket.

"Damn," Martin said. He looked nonplussed. "I've got to meet some gentlemen from the Russian Embassy and I'm not sure of the number." He pointed to the row of houses.

"Russian Embassy?"

"Yes, a member of the Soviet Foreign Office. Lives over here. I'm with the American Embassy myself."

"Come to think of it, that one might have been Russian. He sounded foreign." The driver chewed on this, then added, "Yes, he's your man. He was Russian. I seen a movie once and the —"

Martin cut him off. He had his confirmation. "Thank you." He promptly stepped out of the taxi and crossed back to the white building.

Normally, as a precaution against having witnesses, he would retreat and come back at night with the .357 Magnum he kept in his mews house in Lennox Gardens. He had twenty-four years to go on the lease on this lovely Georgian house, which served as his European headquarters. His decision to go ahead and get it the hell over with reflected his changing attitude toward his profession. A part of him disliked the violence. He would do the job well — but he would do it swiftly and without ceremony to get it over with.

He jimmied the cheap lock with a screwdriver and took the stairs one by one. Martin gathered from the nameplates on the intercom that the house was divided into four flats. Three of these intercom buttons were marked with weathered and well-worn names. The fourth button, flat four, was marked by a crudely scrawled name in Gothic lettering. BROWNE, it read. This was his man. He pulled the .38 snub-nosed revolver from his inside coat pocket.

Joseph approached Pam in his bathrobe. With a fat kitchen knife he severed the leather bonds. "Am I free?" Pam asked feebly through chapped lips. The Russian tensed at this non sequitur inquiry. In his haste he had already branded her dead. That she spoke startled him. He lashed at her with one of the straps and raised a welt on her face under her eye. It occurred to him he couldn't remember the last time he'd given her her ration of Perrier and rice.

He thought of something. "Are you hungry?"

Pam craned her head and looked at him passively. Her face was drawn and bruised. "Thirsty," she said weakly.

"Do you think you'd be thirsty in hell?" he asked. The sadistic glint was back in his eyes.

"What?"

"That's where you're going, Janie. I have no choice but to . . ." Joseph realized he was torturing her. He decided to end it and be rid of her.

His first punch lifted Pam off the bed; she slammed back into the wall. Blood leaked from a burst lip. Joseph hit her again, this time in the temple. Her body spilled backward off of the bed. He kicked her and then punched her again and all the time he was beating Viktor and the sensation thrilled him.

Martin strode into the bedroom. He hesitated; inadvertently, the barrel of the .38 dipped toward the floor. The extent of the carnage was startling. There was almost as much blood on the sheets and walls as the time he had shot the arms dealer in Marrakesh and accidentally struck an artery. "Jesus!" He hoisted the .38. Only then did the Russian notice him. Martin pointed the gun. "You bastard."

Joseph sprang toward him; it was as if the idea of death was too much for him and by fighting back he could postpone it. His hollow face strained grotesquely as he charged, clawing the air in great wild sweeps. The American waited an indulgent second, then shot Joseph six times in the chest and stomach. Joseph crashed onto the carpet, twitching as the blood pooled beneath him.

Martin flipped him over. A cursory frisk uncovered the hidden automatic. He ripped it clear of the tape on Joseph's left leg and lobbed it into the next room. The guttural wet breathing from the punctured body meant death was not far away. Martin had fired all six bullets and wished now he had come more fully prepared. A bullet to the skull would rid the man of the loitering vestiges of life. Unlike many, Martin killed for money alone. He drew no satisfaction from it and saw pain and suffering as one of the nasty by-products of his profession. He saw the body twinge and then relax. The coup de grace had been delivered by nature.

He got up stiffly and walked to the girl. Her sinewy and bloodied frame lay motionless upon the bed. If he knew her name, he would have spoken it. He cleared the blood from under her nose with the sheet, then left the room and came back with a bucket of warm water and a towel. He cleansed her thoroughly. When he was finished, the water in the bucket was thick with the color of blood. Martin felt for her; her heartbeat was faint. Her breathing was steady. This was a good sign. He lay her out squarely upon a fresh blanket and examined her more closely. Bits of her cheek were torn and her nose was broken, though it still functioned as an air passage. Some of her teeth were snapped. Her lips were parched and torn. Parts of her face were already beginning to swell. Martin turned and looked savagely at the body of the Russian.

Placing a clean damp towel over her face, he left her momentarily to fulfill his final leg in the contract. Within fifteen minutes he had turned the flat upside down. For his efforts he was rewarded with a bundle of cassettes wrapped in cellophane and submerged in the tank of the toilet. A further two dozen tapes were in a Harrods bag under a desk. The Russian had been in the process of reproducing the tape tenfold. Martin cut off the threat of further blackmail by killing the goose that laid the fraudulent golden eggs. The goose lay toes up on the bedroom rug. Martin took these tapes with him.

He guessed she was in a coma. To leave her behind for the authorities to find would mean certain death. Although there was some risk involved, he would take her as far as St. Steven's Hospital and deposit her in the Emergency Ward. Then he'd come back and put things in order. He took her in his arms in the blanket and cradled her to the door. Her eyes opened. "Am I free now?" she asked.

The childlike enthusiasm depressed him. "Yes, my dear, you're free."

"Forever?"

"That's right, honey, forever," he concurred.

"Thank you, whoever you are. I was so alone and afraid."

"Anytime, beautiful. I'm one of your biggest admirers."

She stared at the handsome moustachioed man. A fellow countryman. She had attracted him, she thought happily. She still had it in her. She smiled through her injuries and sank back into the blackness. She died in his car three blocks from St. Steven's.

Joseph heard the door slam and waited. A short eternity later, he opened his eyes. The odds were, he decided, that he was not dead. Perhaps he was on his way. That was a possibility. He had a funny thought: *I've booked the ticket but have yet to board the plane.* He'd been hurt before — shrapnel, buck-shot, the odd slug from a field rifle. But never quite so badly. Having been there before, he was able, with a certain degree of accuracy, to pinpoint his injuries and assess their seriousness.

He'd taken four bullets from the revolver. Thank God it was of a comparatively small caliber. The first shot entered two fingers above his rib cage, splintering the bone on that side. The second ripped through the abdomen and sliced the stomach wall before passing clean through him. Another bullet pierced him low on the hip. It miraculously bypassed the network of ball-and-socket bone and, notwith-standing some minor internal bleeding, it did very little damage. The fourth shot, the one that would eventually kill him, bore a path through his left kid-ney, rendering it useless. To relieve himself would be to rid himself of the very life-sustaining force in his body, his thick black assassin's blood. Already his bladder was filling up with a bloody urine solution.

What had spared him had been the hasty handling of the attack by his aggressor. If Martin had checked, he would have seen that two of the bullets didn't fire. They discharged in their customary fashion, but the dampness of the powder resulted in only an audio reaction. The lead bullets had stayed in their casings due to a lack of sufficient force. It all filtered down to Martin's insistence to kill the man on impulse. The weapon he chose was one that had rested on the damp floor of his garage in Lennox Gardens for a year. He carried it in the boot of his rented cars while in London to ensure against emergencies.

Joseph stood up and found he could maneuver his way about the room with sharp, though endurable pain. It surprised him that the American had departed so swiftly. He still retained any documents of note on him: his wallet, his passports. Then he put it all together as he remembered the girl. The American had taken the girl with the intention of saving her before returning to him. In a perverse way the girl had saved him, he thought.

He stumbled along the couch and found his automatic where the American had thrown it. His hand shook as he depressed the clip. It was fully loaded. From the chest in the kitchen he extracted a vial of morphine and a syringe and plugged his left forearm full of the drug. He slumped into a chair and waited for the pain to subside. In fact, the pain didn't subside, but he could now function with it. He filled a shopping bag with morphine vials and threw in the used syringe and a couple of kitchen towels.

He changed shirts and slipped into a red cashmere jersey to absorb and mask the blood. Before the morphine injection he'd been wondering who had set him up. Popotov? The elders? He couldn't be sure. Since the morphine he'd given up caring. All Joseph knew was that McLaren, through existing, had led to his own assassination. And for this he would exact a sweet and complete revenge. He would rendezvous at the finals tomorrow and put a bullet in McLaren and then it would be all right; he could ensure Chekow's victory. He laughed but it hurt so he stopped. His plans made perfect sense in his drug-torn mind. He descended the stairs in a slow, hobbling walk.

Martin stopped the van at a phone box on Fulham Road past the ABC Cinema. He left the body of the girl on the front seat. Since she was dead, there was little point in making a visit to the hospital. Reclined, with her head against the blanket, she might have been sleeping. He dialed Smythe collect.

"Yes, Martin, what's the news?"

"It's done," Martin replied somberly.

"And disposed of?" Smythe asked.

He pretended he hadn't heard. "What?"

"And disposed of?"

"Yes, certainly."

"And what of the tapes?"

"I've got them and will erase them tonight. I found four of them."

"Only four?" he queried.

"It seems he was planning to make more. I found quite a few blank tapes as well," Martin said. Two bobbies strolled by from the direction of the cinema. They gazed at the car parked illegally, then at Martin. He waved anxiously. They grasped the connection and moved on.

"Lucky us," Smythe said.

"Yes, almost. There was some problem regarding the prisoner." He had to repeat this sentence due to a web of static on the line.

"I was worried about this. The Soviets can't be fucking trusted. How is she, Martin?" he asked uneasily.

"I'm afraid she isn't. Our man eliminated her before I arrived."

The phone went dead as Smythe considered the revelation. The quiet was finally broken. "What a damned pity. I liked her. Where is she now?" Smythe asked.

"With me. She died en route to the hospital."

Smythe said, "We were so close. Fucking Russians . . ." More quiet. "What do you propose to do?"

"Bring her back to the original place and leave her. I'll let the coppers over here figure it out." It was a simple solution, and one of the few available to them. They both seemed to realize this.

"Okay, providing they can't figure anything, those are my sentiments also," Smythe said. "They can't, can they?"

"No. There's no link. I've made sure of that. I'll double-check, of course," Martin said. He cleared a patch of steamed glass in the booth and took a look at her. He felt vaguely sad.

"That's fine. Notify the authorities yourself, anonymously, as though you've heard a disturbance," Smythe instructed. "I can't bear the thought of that child in there all alone." He let his Catholic upbringing show. "I shall pray for her."

"Right. See you next week, Benjamen."

"Yes," Benjamen said. His one word echoed along the line. He hung up.

Martin drove slowly through the rain back to the flat on Cheyne Walk. He located a parking spot a few feet from the door to the building and parallel parked. A pair of elderly women went by accompanied by a nurse carrying a large golfing umbrella. Martin bristled when the women hesitated beside his car. He checked the rearview mirror and then looked at Pam's lifeless body propped up in the seat to his left. She looked dead — or asleep — depending on one's perspective, he thought.

There was a sharp rap of knuckles on his window. He felt for the gear shift and with his free hand rolled down the window.

A tired old face, overly made-up, smiled at him and said, "Dear, your lights are on."

Martin thanked her, rolled up the window and switched the engine off. He thumbed the light switch and sat in the sudden quiet. Light rain drummed on the top of the car and spattered ankle-high on the pavement. A car went by, its tires sizzling on the tarmac.

Martin was swept by an abrupt feeling of exhaustion. He massaged the muscles in his neck as he reviewed the events of the past week: he'd met with Whiplin President Ben Smythe, accepted the contract, set up a surveillance in London, located the victim and her kidnapper and eliminated the latter without ceremony. For this he would receive a further fifty thousand U.S. dollars which would bring his total payment for the job to a neat one hundred thousand.

He contemplated an early retirement. But then he thought why retire from something you do so well? Didn't most professionals, regardless of vocation, retire when their stars began to fade and not before?

Carefully, he checked the street for pedestrians.

Seeing none, he leaned over and boosted Pam onto his shoulder. He edged out of the car, closed the door quietly, walked swiftly across the pavement, and disappeared into the apartment building. He jogged up the stairs supporting her body.

He laid Pam on the bed and drew the blankets up, tucking them around her chin. Feeling somewhat sentimental, he brushed Pam's long hair away from her bruised forehead. She looked at peace with the world. Now all Martin had to do was dispose of the Russian's body, dump it somewhere, and be on a plane back to the States to collect his fifty thousand . . .

Something bothered him. He had a sudden sense of something being out of place as he hustled from the bedroom into the adjoining room and the prostrate body of the dead Russian.

Only the Russian wasn't there! Joseph was missing. Martin began an immediate search of the flat, moving quickly but cautiously, crouching slightly in the event that by some miracle the Russian was alive and waiting to ambush him. *But I shot him six times with the revolver! Who could live through that?*

Martin hurriedly ripped the .38 from his overcoat pocket. He flicked the cylinder release and broke the barrel. The empty cartridges fell into his open hand. He sorted through the spent shell casings and then Martin realized his mistake. Two of the cartridges were intact and had failed to fire. He strained to determine the reason. The only explanation was that the bullets were bad — this sometimes happened — and they were bad because they were old and had been loaded in the gun for nearly a year. The gun had been stored in London. The damp English air had spoiled the ammunition.

Martin felt fleetingly demoralized. Professionals didn't make mistakes like that . . . unless their stars were fading. Fuck it. He would worry about that later. He stood up, jammed the empty gun in his coat and crossed the room. He knelt beside a thin smear of blood on the carpet. He guessed four of the slugs had hit the man.

Joseph was wounded and had fled the apartment leaking blood.

Martin had been gone maybe ten minutes during which time he'd talked to Smythe in America and attempted to drive the girl to a hospital. Joseph had a ten-minute head start, but Joseph was in pain and bleeding and it was raining outside.

Martin left the flat at a sprint. He nearly slipped on the stairs, caught the bannister, leapt the last seven steps to the carpeted landing, and slammed though the door. A fat man with an umbrella, walking a terrier, hustled to get out of Martin's way and tumbled onto his ass on the sidewalk. The little terrier yelped; Martin ignored it.

Joseph was wounded and was attempting to escape from the scene of the crime and the mustachioed American hit man. He needed a taxi; therefore he would move north toward King's Road where he stood the best chance of hailing one. Martin took off down Cheyne Walk and turned right, rounding the first bend in the street traveling north. He ran gracefully in long measured strides, assessing the side streets, searching the distance. His eyes spotted a faint red splotch on the pavement. He backed up, stooped down and touched the blood with his fingertips. He surveyed the pavement ahead and counted two similar patches on the concrete further ahead.

The rain was light but consistent. Joseph was not far off, otherwise the blood trail would have dissolved. The thought rallied the American as he jogged on, reading the blood trail.

Fifty yards up the street the trail stopped abruptly. Martin turned to his right and peered down a small cobblestone mews which ran into an adjacent street.

A gust of summer wind whipped the rain into his eyes, momentarily blinding him. He rubbed his eyes with his fists. His heart hammered. At the end of the block a lanky, short-haired man in a Burberry coat was limping along the cobblestones into the next street.

Joseph!

Martin raced down the mews, his long arms and legs pumping, a sudden rage powering him on over the uneven surface of the road.

Joseph reacted to the sound and turned, white-faced. He seemed to notice Martin but continued walking out of the mews, backwards now, as he drew an automatic from his coat in a long langorous movement. He leveled the weapon, tottered slightly, found his footing and fired three times.

The gunfire echoed down the tiny street. One bullet ricocheted off a cobblestone at Martin's foot with a singing sound. Martin dodged the gunfire and continued running. "Stop you bastard!" A puddle appeared in a depression in the road; Martin took it in stride, vaulting it like a hurdler, completing the action successfully, feeling the satisfaction of an athlete. Again Joseph fired; again the shots missed. The Russian stood planted at the intersection in the Chelsea Street aiming the automatic through the rain.

He's out of bullets, Martin thought as he sprinted the last forty yards, tasting his victory, his muscles tingling with anticipation. "I've got you," he shouted just as he tripped and went bandy-legged. Somersaulting across a slick stretch of stone, he landed on his shoulder in a pile of plastic trash cans.

He paused to fill his lungs with the damp fetid air. With a furious swipe of his hand he removed a collection of vegetable scrapings from his face.

A car braked, its tires keening in the rain. A door opened and shut and an engine roared.

Extracting himself from the garbage which had cushioned his fall, Martin stood, stunned, and waited for his vision to clear. He glimpsed the tail end of a taxi disappearing from view.

The son of a bitch had caught a cab.

Cursing, Martin trotted off after it, willing his exhausted legs to move. He turned into the connecting street. The taxi was two blocks ahead with its right-hand signal flashing. There was still a chance of catching it, or possibly trailing it and hailing a cab in the interim to follow it.

Having found his breath again, he upped his pace. The road sloped into a slight incline gradually increasing its gradient as it neared the high street. Martin kicked his legs out and bit back the overwhelming fatigue. His muscles burned and he could no longer draw a full breath. But so much was at stake here — not the least of which was his reputation and the fifty-thousand, which as a matter of pride, unless he killed Joseph, he couldn't accept.

He breasted the hill in wide exaggerated strides and turned into the high street: The King's Road. The taxi's lights were a pair of red dots on the horizon. The black cab signaled, turned once more and disappeared out of sight. No other taxis were in sight.

Martin leaned uncertainly against a nearby building, threw up and decided to reconsider his retirement.

Press conferences as a general rule bothered James. In his experience they were poorly organized, long-winded affairs which gave the press a chance to grill you publicly. But they did serve one purpose: They precipitated publicity — which was something he didn't need. As the number one ranked tennis player in the world, he didn't have to invite the attention of the media; lately he'd spent a good deal of his time avoiding it.

But as Brice Evans had said there was definitely "shit in the water." James's often precarious standing in the eyes of the public had worsened recently. Since his arrival in England he had struck a journalist, taken up with a sixteen-year-old after "heartlessly dumping his devoted girlfriend," and managed to insult every official in every match he'd played thus far. The world media had predictably leapt on these transgressions, using them to paint a truly disgraceful portrait of a spoiled and truculent tennis champion. What was worse, the always fickle public had believed the charges and accepted them at face value, rallying behind McLaren's opponents like never before.

James had noticed a definite increase in the boisterousness of the crowds at his early matches. He had always been a controversial figure in tennis, but he'd often had the feeling the public appreciated his antics. What harassment he'd known had been of a lighter kind, intended to enliven the match. This new reaction from the spectators was more vociferous and more passionate; they seemed to actually hate him. He had even noticed a change in the attitudes of some of the other players; they seemed colder lately.

"Why are people so fucking impressionable? Why do they believe this crap the media tells them?" James demanded of Brice Evans.

Brice was uncharacteristically taciturn, prompting James to shout, "Christ, not you too!"

"James, the climate is shifting. Now, I know it's not all your fault, but it reads badly, particularly from the pens of British journalists."

"They're not journalists, they're vultures. Journalists report the news objectively. These sons of bitches try to manufacture it by provoking me."

"You know that and I know that. The fact is that eventually this anti-McLaren sentiment is going to start influencing sponsors and any potential companies that would like to do business with you."

As much as it hurt to admit it, James had to agree. If the other players, people he had known for years, could be swayed by the poison pens of the news media, he could imagine the effect on potential sponsors.

Brice Evans had proposed a press conference to make apologies and clear the air, and James agreed. But before Evans could schedule the conference, James's situation had darkened still further. He had attacked his Russian rival in the locker room at Queen's Club, then he'd been threatened with the "Wimbledon Dossier" by the Russian blackmailer.

Either incident, if leaked to the press, could ruin him. If it got out that he had attacked Chekow, unprovoked, the world would rally behind his young Russian opponent. James's popularity would wane in light of this ultimate show of bad sportsmanship, and his sponsors might back out; certainly any new sponsors would be scared away. News of the "Wimbledon Dossier" was potentially even more serious. If word of his videotaped bacchanal got as far as the media, James would not only lose his lucrative endorsement contracts, but he would become the laughingstock of the sports world.

He didn't know if he could live with that.

Nevertheless he agreed to hold a press conference — on his own terms. He said to Evans, "I'll meet the press halfway. If I make it a straightforward question-and-answer thing, they'll do their best to get a reaction and they'll bring up Olivia's name and who knows, maybe that photographer I punched when I arrived in this Godforsaken country, maybe he'll be there . . ." James had a sudden vivid image of a wounded bear tied to a stake amidst a pack of starving dogs. He continued, "Plus there's the danger they'll have heard about the thing with Chekow

. . . or the tapes." He still found it hard to admit that the "Wimbledon Dossier" existed. "Therefore, I'll call them together and issue a statement."

"That's meeting them halfway?" Brice asked.

"I haven't finished. The danger here is that I may ostracize myself from the public and lose endorsement money. Therefore, I want you to prepare a statement saying how much Wimbledon means to me and how I'm under a lot of pressure, but I'm doing my best to handle it well."

"James, you're not the first controversial figure to try and soft-soap the media. They can smell this sort of thing a mile away. Anyway this doesn't answer any questions. There's no way they'll know about the tapes, that I'm sure of, at least I think I'm sure of; if the blackmailer released that information, he'd lose his advantage. But what if some hotshot journalist has found out about your fight with Chekow and asks you about that?" Brice drew a quick breath. "For the first time in history a Russian and an American are squaring off in the men's finals at Wimbledon. Reagan, Gorbachev, and a million others will be watching this match . . . How would it look if you ignored the issue of having picked a fight with that Russian player? If someone's found out about it, they'll demand some answers at this conference, and not just some public relations declaration . . ."

James interrupted. "You know, you talk a hell of a lot. Did anyone ever tell you that?"

"James . . ."

"Let me do this thing my way. For the moment I'll ignore everything. I want you to draft one page of grade A American apple pie. Don't overdo it, I don't want anyone crying in the audience," James almost smiled, "but make it heartfelt, the sort of thing you'd hear in church on Veteran's Day . . ."

"What?"

"Quiet. Say how much it means for me as an American to win Wimbledon for my country, and how honored I'd be to win it for the second time. Then make an allusion, only an allusion, to the tension behind the scenes at the tournament. Then say how people often appear to be in the wrong when not all the facts are in. Make it sound that there's a possibility that I'm being maligned, but that I'm satisfied that the public will find the wisdom to exonerate me, ultimately."

Brice said, "You left out Mother Theresa or any reference to the Statue of Liberty."

"Fuck you, Brice. Just do what I say for once." James was smiling.

Brice finished jotting down his employer's instructions on the back of an envelope. "For once, I will."

James arrived at the news conference which was in a private room at his hotel at exactly the scheduled time. The large room was completely filled with members of the press as well as from the the world's television networks. As James mounted the podium and extracted a plain single sheet of paper from his pocket, he could hear the newspeople beginning to form questions. Brice Evans was seated beside the podium next to a representative of the hotel. James looked blankly at Evans, then stared out at the full house. He could feel the tension in the very fabric of the air.

He quickly surveyed the room. As expected, the little fat photographer he had punched at Heathrow was in the front row wearing a bemused look. He had two black eyes. James sensed an opportunity here. Clearing his throat, he nodded pleasantly at the fat man and said, "How're you feeling today?"

"Okay," the man said hoarsely, startled by the question.

"Well I should hope so at those prices."

The crowd laughed.

A BBC reporter stood up and asked a question about James's bad manners on the court. A correspondent for an American newspaper stood up beside the BBC man and shouted out a question about why James was holding the conference.

James held up his hand. "Hang on." He flattened the single typed document — Brice Evans's masterpiece of propaganda — onto the podium desk. His eyes moving from the crowd to the paper, he read, "Being the world champion at anything ain't all it's cracked up to be . . ."

When he finished the statement, the crowd of story-hungry newsmen was momentarily quiet. Some of them wore pious expressions; others looked somber but reverent.

By God, I think they bought it, James thought.

A lanky figure in the extreme corner of the room, leaning against the threshold to the outside hall, was the first to move. The man turned slowly and walked through the door. James noticed him and watched him go. A feeling like nausea rose in him. He crumpled his speech in his hand and left the room by a back exit. After the crowd had dispersed, James returned to the conference room. He had already dismissed the sighting as his imagination; the Russian wouldn't come here and risk being exposed. How could he have known about the conference? Brice had only scheduled it an hour ago. Then why had James returned to make sure? He glanced about the room. By the front door where he had spotted the lanky man in the overcoat was a piece of red tape stuck to the doorframe. Curiously, James advanced. As he drew closer he realized that it wasn't red tape at all. James reached out and touched the mark with an almost morbid fascination. He looked down at the blood on his hand and wondered what it meant.

Miraculously, Joseph had survived the second onslaught.

He managed to extricate himself from the flat on Cheyne Walk, limping away to freedom before the American hit man returned.

Why had the American left like that? To save the girl, Joseph decided.

Then why would he return? To finish the job and dispose of Joseph's body.

Joseph had outsmarted him and nearly escaped when somehow the American had trailed him in the rain down the narrow cobblestone mews. The American's murderous intent was clear and it took all the presence of mind Joseph could summon to draw his weapon and fire. The American had finally gone down near the end of the mews and Joseph had been lucky enough to spot an approaching taxi. He hailed it, got in, and drove away.

Now his one and only priority was to exact his revenge by killing McLaren who, in a roundabout way, had caused it all. Joseph leaned back into the soft vinyl seat of the taxi. He searched his wounds with his fingers, probing his perforated skin to gauge the condition of his injury. To his relief the bleeding seemed to have stopped. *If I can stop the bleeding and continue taking the morphine and antibiotics, I might not die,* he thought.

Joseph felt reborn.

A voice came over the radio from the front of the cab. At this very moment, the BBC announcer said, most of the world's press was collecting in the conference room of the Royal Garden Hotel in Knightsbridge for a press conference with James McLaren. Joseph stiffened. He had asked the driver to take him to a run-down hotel in Putney, toward the outer precincts of London. At this very moment they were passing through Knightsbridge.

He looked out his window. To his left loomed the vast stone edifice of the Royal Garden Hotel. His mind swirling slightly from the morphine, Joseph thought *I'll attend the conference using my phony press credentials, get closer to McLaren, and finish him there.*

"Stop the taxi. Turn back and take me to the Royal Garden Hotel."

"But you said ..."

"Shut up and turn this fucking thing around before I ..."

The cabbie braced himself and faced Joseph,

simultaneously slowing the cab. "Before you what, mate?"

"Just do it."

The driver hesitated, trying to decide how to deal with the Russian's preemptory tone. Finally he braked, and swung the cab around.

Joseph slipped the automatic back into his raincoat. As the cab pulled into the hotel's entrance, he paid the driver, apologized for his harsh words, and got out. On the marble steps of the hotel he paused and realized how careless he was being, nearly drawing his weapon on the stupid, though harmless, taxi driver.

The pain had begun again in his side. Carefully, he mounted the steps and strode across the hotel foyer in the direction of a cardboard sign bearing the single word, "PRESS."

On his way down the carpeted corridor, he realized that the morphine had begun to affect his mind. He was not by nature an impetuous man. His was a calculated life, given over to rational thinking and deliberate action. Only a consummate planner could have pulled off the video coup in Monte Carlo, after all.

He pushed past a crowd of security men and flashed his press card. Immediately an employee from the hotel ushered him inside the conference room. Joseph stood by the back of the room against the door. McLaren was front and center delivering his ridiculous statement to the world. Joseph methodically scouted the room, estimating the size of the crowd, the number of security men, the distance to the exits.

The surge of misdirected energy that had brought him here extemporaneously, diminished. He wanted another dose of morphine to ease his mounting discomfort. A sharp pain spread out from below his kidneys and he nearly toppled over. Extending a hand, he steadied his tall frame against the door. McLaren came back into view as Joseph focused on the podium. All his life he had been waiting for this. All his life he had wanted to do something truly extraordinary for himself and his country. Tomorrow he could complete his dream in the stadium at Wimbledon as the insolent American took the court.

Why risk blowing it by acting rashly without the proper preparation? he thought.

Joseph took a parting glance at McLaren. For a moment he could have sworn that their eyes met. He left the room, listening to his heart beating in his head, concentrating on his triumph tomorrow, ignoring the icy, splintery pain.

Chapter Eleven

They spent a quiet evening, just the two of them, at a South Kensington wine bar. James ate pasta, as he always did the day before a match, and nursed a bottle of Perrier. Olivia ate fish and drank a glass of white wine. They were leaving when he recognized Sheila and a few of the Super Six in the entrance way. He stopped walking and gripped Olivia more tightly at the elbow. "What is it, James?"

He ignored her and continued walking. She saw them now, too. They met up at the door. He saw their eyes volleying between him and the blond creature at his arm. There was a hungry, almost offensive intensity to their stares, he thought; like they were high on drugs and had no inhibitions. With the exception of Julia Collins, who had scratched her way into the finals of the mixed doubles, the girls were out of the tournament. James read their dazed expressions and remembered Pammy and felt repulsed.

"Hello, James, good luck tomorrow," Sheila said. Despite her sincerity, he chose to take the remark as an insult.

He ignored it. "How's Pam?"

This took some of the wind out of their tight denim sails. They conferred silently with glances at one another. "Oh, I'm sure she's all right," Sheila began solemnly. "She's probably upset that she missed the tourney. She wasn't feeling that well lately."

"Oh, wasn't she?" James asked bitterly. "Why ever not?"

Cheryl stepped in to rescue Sheila. "How should we know?"

"Yeah, we're not married to her," Tony Lovett interjected. James sniggered at the remark. "She's just one of our more mixed-up friends."

"Sometimes she goes a little spare, James," Julia said. You should know that, if anybody." James frowned at their casual disloyalty to the ingenue they had corrupted.

"She's finding it difficult to enjoy life on tour at present, but we'll bring her around. Or kill ourselves trying." Cheryl laughed. The others were giggling.

The tension was thick. James imagined which of the group had been the first to seduce Pammy. Cheryl's last flippant remark had hurt him, for Pam's sake, for he knew the truth.

"We'll keep trying if it takes a lifetime," Tony added. Their laughter was husky and crass. The rest of the restaurant was staring at them. The sound of gossip spreading became apparent as the diners recognized James.

James took Olivia tightly by the hand and led her past the band of women. He paused abruptly. "If you were men," he said to all four of them, "I wouldn't hesitate to cram those teeth down your homely throats." He began to push on, then stopped again. He smiled cynically. "Of course, you're not far from being men anyway, are you?" His grin receded as he steered Olivia between them onto the street.

"James, should you have said that?"

"I'm not letting them in on any secrets." The air was heavy and warm in the aftermath of the early evening thunderstorm. They moved down High Street Kensington in the ethereal darkness. Suddenly, from a side street two other members of the Super Six emerged on their way to meet their pals.

"Oh, hello, James, good luck tomorrow," Marge said.

He looked at her and thought of saying something to betray the anger he felt. His expression remained stoic. "Sure," he said and moved on. The mixed-up bitches couldn't help what they were, he thought. Neither could Pammy. They had just made her realize it.

Brice met them in the lobby and joined them in the elevator. James was feeling understandably reserved on the eve of the final. "What are you so happy about?" he said to Brice.

His agent could barely contain himself. "James, I spoke with Smythe an hour ago. It's off — the contract. The blackmail. It's all been squashed."

"Says who?" James asked impatiently. He reached out and caught Brice around the forearm.

"Says Smythe. He's handled it."

Olivia hugged him. "Oh, James, isn't that wonderful?"

He shook Brice's arm vigorously. "Thank Christ." He shook his head slowly. "Whatever I said about Smythe, I take it back."

"All of it?" Brice joked.

"Most of it." James's levity ebbed. "What about Pam? Is she okay?" They stepped off the elevator. James faced Brice squarely.

Brice relayed the truth as he knew it. He spoke the lie Smythe had imparted to him. "Apparently, she's pretty shaken up, but in one piece. She's in the hospital at the moment."

James unlocked the door to his suite and let them in. "Why? Is she hurt?"

"I don't know James. Smythe didn't say."

James flipped on the lights and closed the door. "Then which hospital? Did he say that?"

"No."

"Did it occur to you to ask? I want to call her and say hello."

The diminutive agent sat down in the closest chair and crossed his legs. "James, Smythe promised everything was okay. He said he apologized for being purposely vague, but he said he was scared the police might get involved and stir up trouble before Wimbledon."

James reserved comment on Smythe's words as interpreted by Brice. Frankly, he could see Smythe's point. If the KGB were involved, or the Mafia, this could turn into a major scandal and he'd already caused enough problems without complicating the situation. He lifted the phone and dialed room service. Cupping the receiver, he mumbled to Brice, "I don't suppose you know how he took care of the Russian?" Brice shook his head. James said, "Hear no evil, see no evil." He winked at Olivia. "Right, baby?"

"Right, tough guy." She smiled.

Room service got on the line. "Bring a bottle of Laurent Perrier '69 to room 43-B. And some apricot juice, a quart of it. Thanks." He replaced the phone and said to them, "Don't worry, I'm only having one drink. But I think we deserve a celebration now that Smythe's put things right."

Olivia scampered to the bed and sat crossed-legged upon it.

"Why is it I always find myself agreeing with you and your schemes? What kind of personal manager am I?" Brice asked.

"The only kind," James told him.

The goods were delivered. James mixed the Bellinis and distributed them. "To Smythe . . . that son-of-a-bitch."

"May he prosper along with his products," Brice said.

"And may he recover from my next percentage demands." Brice stayed with them for an hour. They drank and laughed and exchanged some of the recent Wimbledon-related anecdotes circulating in the press. According to something Brice read, some guy in tennis whites was selling McLaren autographs for a pound outside the stadium. Brice wondered if he was entitled to his fifteen percent.

When his manager had departed, James killed the lights and began to undress Olivia. He slid the little-girl panties from her beautiful body and felt her there as he suckled her breasts. Her tiny nipples responded to his touch. The soft folds of flesh between her legs needed very little coaxing. They were already hot with desire and required only his caress to spread the fever throughout her. He walked her to the bed and moved with her onto the silk sheets.

The phone rang. He rolled over in his sleep and caught it. The sharp staccato pipping of a pay telephone preceded the caller's voice. James checked his watch: 6 A.M. He'd been asleep for eight hours. Finally, the pipping stopped as a coin was deposited. A voice said, "You're dead." The brief two-word exchange was enough to send a cold finger of fear down James's spine. He recognized the Russian accent and thought, *He's still out there*. The line went dead.

"Who was that, James?" Olivia asked.

A moment passed. She was already asleep when he replied, "Destiny." He stretched on his stomach and thought of his appearance at center court.

Things at the Chekow camp at the Ebury Street Hotel were no better. Viktor and Chekow had spent most of the preceding night listening to war stories and eating Royal Sevruga caviar at the Russian Embassy. Stantolen, the Russian ambassador, had succumbed to the extraordinary pre-Wimbledon influence of the media and invited the men to dine with him. Viktor decided it was best if they went. It was important to have friends in high places if one desired to get ahead in the Soviet system. Should Chekow ever bow out of competitive tennis, Viktor knew an acquaintance like Stantolen could help the boy. In the back of his mind he wondered if the ambassador might have influence with the Intelligence forces in Russia.

Later that night they added one steak each to stomachs littered with whole-wheat toast, raw onion, and sturgeon eggs straight off the boat from the Caspian Sea. Viktor allowed Chekow a large brandy to help him sleep and returned to his own room with a dozen beers and a bottle of vodka. The bottle of vodka would help him sleep. Unlike some of the other interested parties, Viktor had no way of knowing that the complexion of the match had changed.

Chekow came to him that evening. His bed lamp was on and threw a cone of light across the bed toward the door. Viktor was drinking a beer. Chekow entered the room and stood awkwardly like a kid on the threshold.

"I want out, you know," Chekow said flatly. "After tomorrow, regardless of who wins, I want out."

"Really, son?"

"Yes. This doesn't mean I won't try. I've still got pride in what I do. I'd like to be thought of as a champion when I step down. Unless he offers no competition, I'll play my best." There was a compact formality in the voice that Viktor had never heard before. In the light Chekow seemed older and more mature. The shadows highlighted the fine bones of his face: His face had changed in the past few months, Viktor thought. It seemed more mature.

"Why?"

"I can't tell you. Suddenly it's changed, all of it. I'm winning for all the wrong reasons."

Viktor took a long pull from the bottle of beer. "And what reasons are those?"

"I don't know exactly, but they are not my own."

"Have I told you this?"

"Some of it. I overheard some of your conversation with that man yesterday. The one who came here and you almost fought."

"Then you know something about the Crimea racquet?"

"Enough. I can understand why you want me to use it. I don't know why he does, and I don't care to know." Viktor set down the bottle of beer and cleared two empty bottles from the bed. Chekow continued. "I can suspect. I've seen the Crimea in the stores. It speaks for itself. That's one of my reasons for quitting."

"That's a sound reason, Aysop."

Chekow loitered awkwardly in the light. Viktor had very little to say to him. The truth thrown back in the coach's face had demoralized him. The boy turned to leave. Viktor's words brought him back. "Would it help if I told you I'm not satisfied with what that man said?"

"How so?"

"It makes no sense. Even Stantolen tonight had

no idea whatever of the Crimea. If the racquet was a state-sponsored product, Stantolen would surely have known."

"I know, Viktor. I too noticed that."

Viktor's copious jaw shifted. "Nor have I ever received one word about it from the Athletic Federation or the government representatives."

Chekow stopped fidgeting from side to side and sat on the edge of a chair. "Then who is he? Who does he work for?"

"I don't know really. I suspect a branch of the Intelligence agencies. He knows too much to be anything else. He is a professional. My opinion is he's not working alone."

"Does that mean we must do what he says?" Chekow asked.

"I've made inquiries. I made them tonight through Stantolen's secretary. We will know shortly, but not before tomorrow's match." Viktor eyed him. "Will this affect you tomorrow, knowing the threats he put to us?"

"Like I said, I'll play my game unless McLaren tries to throw the match. I know him well enough, though, and I doubt he will." Chekow paused. "One other thing, Viktor: I'd like to switch from the Crimea. The racquet is not for me. I'm not natural with it yet, and I don't like this. There is too much at stake tomorrow."

Viktor ran his tongue over his lips. The muscles of his face went taut. "There are risks involved. There was some mention of that time with Onegin and Igor. I can't promise that his authority is not genuine. Something can still be made of this."

"I know. I've always known this and it hasn't affected me. I am ready to take responsibility for my actions."

"I believe you." Viktor's penetrating eyes beheld the young man. "You heard him. You understand the personal risks involved?"

"Yes."

"We can always escape the scandal; of this I'm certain. I'm not without my own influences in our country. Should these prove assailable, then there is the other alternative, the common one."

"Defection?"

Viktor nodded.

"What of my family?"

Viktor grew evasive. "Yes, your family."

"But will they be affected?"

It was apparent the full force of the threats — both the likelihood of physical injury and the possibility of his family's exile to Siberia — had not overtly upset the boy. Perhaps these were the terrible veiled issues that Chekow did not comprehend. Viktor decided to exercise the total extent of his influence. He could appropriate the funds from his Swiss account and "persuade" certain government officials that Siberia was not the right setting for the Chekow family. He was confident that well-greased palms at this level could appreciate his view. There lingered the question of a personal attack on the boy. "This man you overheard has vowed to vindicate himself should we renege on the Crimea. He's killed one man already, Vladimir. Do you remember him?"

"Was he the plump fellow in St. Tropez who watched us practice?"

"Yes."

"He killed him. Why?"

"I suppose he got in the way. Up until that point he was involved in marketing the Crimea." Viktor's decision was made no less difficult by this disclosure. He examined Chekow. "So you see, his threats are not without substance."

"Are you trying to deter me?"

"Do you think I would?" Viktor asked.

"No." Chekow recalled his early days in Leningrad. Although poor and often threadbare, his father had never lost his indefatigable and deep-rooted sense of pride. And things had never hurt him as a boy and he had felt safe against his father's bosom. Sitting there in that room, so shameless in its Western opulence, his father's touching faith returned to Chekow and it moved him. "I'll play him tomorrow, Viktor, but my way," he said firmly.

It happened that someone had seen the incident between James and Chekow at Queen's Club and had sold the story to the *Daily Mail*. The news percolated across the sea. Every media source was quoting this paper. Obscure broadcasters from as far away as Guam Television featured it as their major story for the night. Tass, the Soviet news agency, behaved with its characteristic bias and reported the "jealous and drunken assault" against their star player. McLaren's singular display of anger, in the form of a slap, mushroomed via the press into something resembling a prizefight. Circulation of the dailies in England, up already due to the perennial interest in Wimbledon, doubled. Everybody loved a rivalry, especially when it encompassed the two most aggressive countries in the world in the most competitive of contests.

James's tendency to redirect the blame at times of crisis found a distinct lack of scapegoats. He had attacked Chekow — seemingly unprovoked — and there had been witnesses. It was that simple. Without divulging the whole story, James would appear to be the bad guy. Those who knew the truth thought differently.

He arrived at the All England Club alone in a limo. This was the way he wanted it. No Hal, no Brice, no Olivia. Just him alone without any possible distractions to disrupt his concentration. The limousine plowed through the crowded street outside the grounds and James watched bemusedly through the tinted glass while he smoked a last reefer. The dope burned his throat and tickled his lungs, but the overall effect was soothing. It was for this reason that he chose to hire his own car rather than accept the escort offered by the club. The All England Club drivers had an inclination toward gossiping.

Inside, the grounds were crowded with concessions selling cheap champagne and strawberries and cream, anxious television crews, and fourteen thousand exceedingly fortunate ticket holders. Outside, the street hummed with the blare of ticket touts selling what few coupons they retained for fifty times their worth, and seventeen thousand relatively unfortunate ticketless beings.

James survived the throng of pressmen stationed outside the club entrance. The sounds of shutters clicking and journalists cackling stayed with him even

in the changing room. As expected, ninety-nine percent of their questions dealt with his "fight" with
Chekow. Only once did he hear an allusion to his
split with Janie. This was old news. The public had
had that installment last week along with the photos
of James and Olivia cruising arm in arm through
Chelsea.

I've got the press out of the way, he thought. *The
rest is business as usual. This is just another match.*
He knew his opponent and what he had to do to
win. He was convinced Chekow would be feeling
uneasy now that the threat of the tape had been
rendered void, that was if Chekow even knew the
tapes had existed. Of course James would crush
Chekow anyway, on general principle.

Sidney Hughes, his chargé, whom James had managed thus far to avoid, was ordered to reserve Alexander's Restaurant on King's Road. A victory celebration was planned with vintage champagne and
filet steak flown over from a caterer in Dallas. All
of James's close associates in England, including
those fellow players he could tolerate, were invited.
And of course so was Pam, as a sort of wounded
guest of honor. Sidney was still working on locating
her. Sidney's obvious question to all this dealt with
the possibility of Chekow's not losing. James
breathed some deprecating comment and quoted a
Dylan Thomas line about life eternal. Win or lose,
James insisted the party be scheduled for Saturday
night. In effect, he already had one victory under
his belt, and that in itself called for a celebration.

He went through his pre-game ritual at his locker
in the dressing room. He laid his tennis clothes on

the bench in the exact sequence in which he would don them, starting with his jockey shorts and finishing with his pair of Reebok sneakers. It was a sun-filled day, though a breeze had come down from the north and with it the promise of rain later in the weekend. What mattered was that the weather stay clear for the next three hours. He slipped into his Davis Cup warm-up jacket.

It was a credit to Smythe that his word alone could instill in James a sense of relief. Some quality in Smythe, some brash yet stalwart quality, elicited a sense of confidence in others. He may have been self-centered and artless, but he did things effectively, his actions born of a rare inner strength. His word was gold. James had his word that the threat had been averted. Consequently, he was only slighty concerned by the early morning call from the man with the Russian accent. Could this have been simply a cruel hoax? he wondered.

The All England Club trainer and a few of his mates were busy traipsing about the lockers in their shirtsleeves trying to look indispensable. In previous years James had asked them for a quick massage while he discussed strategy with Hal or business with Brice. Today he had asked to be left alone. The message was spread among the locker room staff and the herd of minor officials who patronized the Wimbledon locker room before a match. The only noise in the room today emanated from the far end of the lockers. James could hear the broken Russian-English dialogue of Chekow and Viktor as they finished dressing. "Stupid commies," he said with distaste. When the referee finally came in to notify him it was almost time, James nodded and shut the last of his belongings into the steel cabinet. He sat for a moment psyching himself, a stack of Whiplin racquets on his lap. He could hear the Russians gather their gear and start outside. As the reigning champion, he had an image to maintain. He waited for a grueling fifteen minutes, then followed them onto center court.

The chattering of the crowd rose dramatically as he strode out from the green promenade onto the well-worn but hallowed turf. An observant grounds crew had thrown a tarpaulin over the court at the beginning of yesterday's thundershower. The little rainwater that escaped under the tarp had since dried up. The grass was firm but pliable. The breeze blew back the curls of his hair. Unlike many players, he didn't mind the wind. It would force him to play down the slice in his approach shots, but it would also cool him and keep him alert.

The sound of the crowd continued for some time after he had taken the court. He'd long since learned to ignore them through concentration. He phased out the spectators, the noise, the television cameras, and the lights. The threatening phone call no longer mattered. The idea that he could have thrown the match seemed like madness to him now when all he could think about was all he'd ever thought about since the age of ten: winning Wimbledon.

During the warm-up James did his usual stunt of cross cutting the ball so severely that Chekow would hit each shot straight into the net. McLaren supporters leaped on the early opportunity to hurl abuse at the Russian. Fans of Chekow — anyone against McLaren — started in with their snide remarks toward the American. "Two minutes, gentlemen!" the umpire exclaimed from his elevated chair. "One minute!" Finally, he uttered the enticing phrase that five hundred million television-watching denizens of the globe were waiting to hear. "Commence play, gentlemen!" A roar went up.

James shed the warm-up suit. He toweled the grip of his racquet and took the court. As they crossed the net toward their respective sides, Chekow looked at him. "I promise I knew nothing about it," he muttered. "Good luck to you."

James frowned. He was still wondering about the Russian's declaration as he stepped into the first serve.

Joseph sat in perhaps the second-best seat in the house smiling through a tennis hat, sunglasses, and the overpowering influence of morphine. He turned uneasily and checked the condition of his fellow linesman. In his white shirt and pants and green jacket there was little to distinguish him from the rest of the linesmen. He uncrossed his legs, emulating the form of the nearest to his left.

How he came to be there mirrored the true extent of his guile and the effect of the pain-killer on him. He arrived early after leaving his bed-and-breakfast room in Putney. As a precaution against the horde of tennis people en route to Wimbledon on this final day, he had moved to Putney because of its proximity to Wimbledon. A ten-minute taxi trip up Putney High Street and he was there.

He had spent the night in the euphoric though

restless slumber inherent of morphine addicts. Each time the pain threatened, Joseph fixed another hit. As his condition worsened, he increased the dosage and frequency of injections. Morphine residue had begun to form in the syringe and within the needle itself. Twice he'd had to submerge the needle under a hot tap to unclog it. The effect of the morphine was such that by now he had lost practically every trace of his former self except one: his almost maniacal determination. He had to get McLaren.

It was this overwhelming obsession that drove him on and kept him from taking too much of the life-sustaining drug. His years in the KGB had taught him the effect of too large a dose. His veins would relax to such an extent that his blood would puddle, his blood pressure would plummet, and he would die within minutes of cardiac arrest. What was left of his mind warned him of this reality. He had two missions left in life: He had to kill McLaren, and he had to regulate the dosages of morphine. The former thought motivated him. The latter one kept him alive.

His strategy alone spelled the depth of his drug-induced decline. He would provoke the final irony by murdering McLaren while posing as an official. One well-aimed shot between the eyes. Joseph would then escape — somehow — in the ensuing panic to bask in the spoils of his ill-gotten gains. He had no conception that his plan could fail.

False credentials purporting him to be a representative of the Soviet Sporting Federation got him past the two guards at the Wimbledon gate. He explained to the trainer upon entering the changing rooms his intentions to make an informal search of the area. "Sure, mate, help yourself," the little black-haired man told him. The search was deliberately more intricate than the Russian implied. The same trainer followed him once around the lockers and the shower facilities, then got bored and left him alone to determine the security of the windows.

Joseph opportunized on the fellow's waning interest. The moment the trainer turned a corner, Joseph pushed through the doors into the building's east wing, where a distance of twenty-five feet separated the players' quarters from those of the officials.

On the other side of the opaque glass door was Bert Gregory. The willowy former Davis Cup Player sat reading the day's form in *Sporting Life*.

Joseph opened the door and stepped casually inside. Gregory put down his paper, smiled, and stood up in his underwear. The Russian realized he'd been lucky as he appraised the linesman. Their heights were similar. Their builds varied by maybe ten pounds at most. "You'll do," Joseph said.

"Pardon me?' Gregory asked.

"No, pardon me."

Flame spurted from the barrel of the automatic and a little concussive sound echoed in the room. Gregory's inert form continued to twitch for a full two minutes. Joseph bent over painfully and clasped the man under his arms and dragged him behind the row of large wooden floor lockers. He had to pause and gather his breath. The taste of his own blood from his wounds sickened him and evoked images of his ravaged kidney failing to do its job. He grasped the locker bolt and frailly pushed it aside.

Over a period of ten minutes, working in spurts, he stowed the body in the wooden locker. After placing a pile of dusty rags over the face, he replaced the door and slid the bolt.

The uniform fit tightly in the shoulders but was otherwise okay. The inseam of the leg was exact. He collected his new clothes and threw them into Bert's open locker, then slammed it shut. To prevent his blood from seeping through the white shirt, he used a piece of rag to cover the bandage on his chest. Each time he breathed, the splintered rib bones touched his diaphragm, instigating a fresh blood flow in that area. The simple act of breathing unleashed a terrible slicing pain about his chest and stomach. He breathed shallowly from the tops of his lungs. He left the room two full minutes before the next officials arrived. The copy of *Sporting Life* was still folded on the chair.

By arriving at the absolute last minute prior to the commencement of the match, Joseph took his position with a minimum of commotion. He slid straight into the vacant chair behind the base line nearest the scoreboard. An irate figure in a suit gestured at his watch from across the court. Joseph threw up a hand ambiguously and the man quieted. Meanwhile, a young woman and a fat man near the umpire seemed confused by his presence. Their awed expressions indicated they expected Bert Gregory. Where was he? They glanced at each other, then at the man in the suit. For a moment Joseph thought they would ruin it and that he would have to act immediately, although McLaren was at the opposite end of the court. As they moved to put their questions to the referee, the confident voice of the umpire brought them back to their chairs. "Commence play, gentlemen!"

Joseph suddenly wanted another hit. It had been two hours since his last one and the pain, combined with the anxiety of being found out and the effect of porting the dead official, made his nerves pop. A kind of rage swept through him that he was hurt at all and needed the morphine. His entire life had been structured to need no one, nothing — then why did he need the fucking morphine? Why had he let himself get shot? His head seemed clearer due to the pain. He could hear his breathing: tight, hoarse sounds similar to those of a scuba tank regulator underwater. He could feel the weight of the automatic in the green blazer pocket. Under different circumstances he'd have wondered if its outline showed against the cloth. He suddenly felt like laughing, but he looked across at McLaren and felt the hate again and his mind clouded.

To Joseph's surprise as play commenced, McLaren took the court nearest to him and was only feet away from where he sat with the automatic in his pocket. Joseph readied himself mentally to draw the gun.

His thoughts switched to the morphine — he had to have it — and he presently watched James serve two straight aces. The serves were followed by a brilliant passing winner and an overhead smash, and before Joseph knew it, McLaren was on his way to the far court. He cursed himself and felt the pain swell in his chest. He would have to endure a further two games before they switched sides again and McLaren was beside him and within range.

James assumed a position on top of the base line, his muscular form poised in anticipation of Chekow's service. He assessed the service on impact and bounded back a full yard and to his right. The ball dropped a yard in altitude and spat toward a portion of grass in the extreme corner of the service court. James permitted it to bounce high off the court and slammed into it during the instant if hovered at its pinnacle. It shot back across the net near to the base line. The point of impact was dubious. They waited for the call. Joseph stiffened in the chair. The acute pain was clouding his reactions. To his horror he realized it was up to him to call the shot. "Out!" he hollered belatedly. The pain in his chest nearly cut off his air supply. Had he panicked, he would have lost his breath altogether, but he didn't, and the feeling retreated.

James went into the song and dance that made him the biggest draw since Elvis. "What?" he screamed indignantly. "You idiot! It was in!" As the crowd began to react, loving the drama, James charged the umpire. "What was that?"

"You heard him correctly, Mr. McLaren. The shot was out. Play on, Mr. McLaren."

James poised his arms akimbo. "Did you see where it landed? Were you bothering to watch?"

"Yes, Mr. McLaren. The point goes to Mr. Chekow, fifteen love. Play on, please." James vented his wrath on a tennis ball at his feet, kicking it in the direction of the stands. It lobbed into the backstop and bounced back. James nearly tripped on it. One of the ball boys retrieved it and, in doing so, slipped and fell. The crowd was loving it. James's actions prompted the umpire to repeat himself. "Play on, Mr. McLaren, please." He addressed the fourteen thousand voyeurs. "May we have quiet, please, ladies and gentlemen?"

Grudgingly, James returned to the base line. A disparaging remark about the umpire having the mind of a gnat luckily went unheard. Chekow waited until James had taken position, eyeing James obliquely as he bounced the ball. He threw it up and in front of him, and sent a near perfect serve blistering within the chalk of the service box. James batted back a near perfect return that maneuvered Chekow to his backhand in the deep end near the alley. A weak slicing return landed mid-court. James rushed it and sent it buzzing off of the actual base line itself. A plume of chalk went up in testament. He shrugged scornfully at the linesman in the sunglasses and turned away. The single word, "Out!" brought him fuming to the net.

"What the hell is your problem? I saw it and it was in. Give me a break." Noise from the stands rose a couple of octaves.

The umpire intervened to keep the peace. "The point was good. Fifteen all. Play on. Quiet, please."

James voiced his silent contempt for the linesman in question. An open look of derision was glued to his face for all to see. Predictable chants from his more loyal and vociferous fans were directed at the linesman. "Quiet, please," the umpire interjected. "Fifteen all. McLaren leads one game to love. Quiet, please." The noise makers relented for no other reason than that they wanted play to resume so something else could go wrong.

Suddenly, Viktor made terrible sense of it. The lean figure of the official. The pallid countenance behind the sunglasses. The strangely inept calls, each of which had carried the accent of a familiar inflection. *Oh, my God!* he thought. *Joseph.* He rose in his private box and excused himself from the Soviet Foreign Secretary, who had arrived from Moscow that morning. He hurried through the aisles, between the rows of spectators, moving sideways nimbly, his hard stare on the tall man in the traditional green-and-white uniform of the Wimbledon official. The same man was seated only yards behind Chekow, and Viktor wondered then whether Joseph had noticed that Chekow was not using the Crimea racquet.

Chekow threw his weight behind a third service. McLaren stepped into it and sent it spiraling wildly off the racquet wood. He cursed the man who had put him off his game. Pointing at Joseph, he yelled, "You suck, buddy! You really suck!"

"Mr. McLaren, public warning," the umpire called with an air of finality.

"What? Why the hell should I get penalized for that guy's incompetence? Jesus! I don't believe it." He moved closer to the umpire. "You characters are really out to screw me, aren't you? There's a plot here — I swear there is. It's fucking obvious."

"Play on, Mr. McLaren. The score stands at thirty-fifteen. Quiet, please."

James stood glowering at the umpire. He cupped his hand to his mouth and said under his breath all the things he would have liked to say out loud. Yet he knew that with one more public warning he'd forfeit the match. This understanding forced him to shut up and play on.

The television people were reveling in the drama. Telling close-up shots focused on James's parents and Olivia for their reactions. Viewers around the world were treated to close-ups of the Russian assassin. NBC, the major American sports network, was speculating what its share of that Saturday morning in America would be. One of those contributing to NBC's Neilson ratings — which would allow the network to increase its next year's advertising rates — was not so pleased. "Goddamned cocksucking maniac!" Smythe kicked the Off switch to his television set and left his roomful of guests to walk the dogs in the fields. McLaren made him sick. "So goddamned ungrateful!" he shouted to the heavens.

Joseph was weakening. The sharp pain of the splintered bone had faded into a heavy numbness inside his chest. He appreciated the slackening pain, yet he was suspicious of it. He knew he was fading. The controversy over his calls accelerated his expiration. He hadn't anticipated the flurry of attention coming his way. His raspy breathing sounded more resonantly in his head. Effort was expended to keep his eyelids raised and his deportment correct. He thought incongruously of the time as a boy in Russia when he'd fallen asleep while riding his bicycle. He sat up and forced his eyes open.

He saw the next shot distinctly and judged it. Twice he had made negative judgments only to earn the ridicule of his quarry. Logically, therefore, he would reverse his opinion. This way, at least, he was obliged to say nothing. The stitching pain would not arise if he said nothing. It made a very real sense to him. He watched the ball slide past and sat there placidly.

But there seemed to be no pleasing them. The discordant chorus of the spectators was far worse this time. Chekow, the young Russian whom he ostensibly controlled, was now the one making noises. "The ball was out!" the umpire called over the crowd.

Joseph saw McLaren saunter in seeming slow motion to the umpire's chair. He could hear pieces of the ensuing argument over the sound of his breathing. He felt comfortably cool, though when he felt his forehead he was dripping wet. He cleared the cavities of his eyes and could see again. Sweat traced a line from his forehead into his mouth. He tasted the salt, then the blood, as he hiccoughed. Depression enveloped him like a shroud. When the well-dressed man with the clipboard accosted him and suggested politely he vacate his seat, Joseph had to agree with him. The exposure was too much for him and there was a danger McLaren could be scared off. He resolved to wait in a less vulnerable spot outside the stadium to bag his prey. He walked stiffly, flat-footed, behind the referee to the locker rooms. The man was being overly apologetic and Joseph watched a spot at the back of his head, thinking, *I could kill you, too.*

Death brushed by a seated McLaren and came

within a foot of him. James regarded the retreating linesman with a mixture of curiosity and contempt. "Good riddance," he said flatly, and Joseph simply turned and smiled.

The referee's courtesy extended as far as the locker rooms. He said something and patted Joseph's back fraternally, then hurried back to the match. Joseph went at once to the trainers' room, where he'd left the vials of morphine. There was a distant chance someone would have discovered the body and removed it along with his clothes, he thought illogically. If so, he could always settle for a handful of benzedrine tablets or Quaaludes — anything to free him from the stifling bonds of his malaise.

Viktor arrived, breathless, moments after Joseph had been escorted off the court. The Russian coach had chosen to wait on the sidelines within striking distance of the assassin in case he made a move for either boy. If he could, Viktor would avoid telegraphing the scandal to the world's population over the television camera. He would wait and if possible deal with Joseph once he had left the stadium. He saw him disappear and followed.

Viktor crept down the hallway hugging the wall. The soles of his athletic shoes folded and unfolded silently over the concrete. Once and for all he would end it. It no longer mattered to Viktor who Joseph was, what he represented, or what the repercussions would be. What mattered was that he extinguish the constant deadly threat to the two tennis players and save face for his Russia — whether Russia wanted it or not.

Adrenaline surged through him, allowing him to

function regularly and without fear. He knew what Joseph had done to Vladimir, knew what he was capable of when cornered. That he had tried to pose as a linesman indicated to Viktor the crazy extent of the man's resolve. He came to the end of the corridor that led to the trainers' and officials' quarters. He perceived the green-and-white movements of Joseph behind the wall of translucent glass surrounding the trainers' office. The door was open. He breathed deeply and thought of Russia and walked inside.

Joseph was seated on his desk. His white shirt was open and the bandage was pulled to one side. A blood-red hole in the rib cage was surrounded by a circle of decay the size of a plate. The flesh was mottled and bluish-green. Colorless liquid seeped from the pricked opening in the skin. Viktor felt suddenly sick; than the hatred returned. "It looks like somebody got to you first," Viktor said, moving slowly closer to the assassin.

Joseph looked up calmly and grinned through the pain. "Hello, Viktor. Are you enjoying the match? I guess I'm not the Renaissance man I thought I was. My talents do not lie in officiating tennis," he said hoarsely. Blood in his lungs gave his words a wet sound.

"You pathetic son-of-a-bitch. You were there in case we reneged on the deal. You wanted to be ready to enforce your threats if it came to that."

"To be honest, there were other things on my mind, Viktor. In fact, I failed to notice if you even did 'renege.'" Joseph glanced at the door, then at Viktor. "It must be obvious to you that I am not a well man. Before you do what you came here to do, allow me a few moments' peace. Find me something to dull the pain." He signaled to the open box of first-aid equipment. "Find me a syringe. I broke mine."

"You're the great barterer," Viktor said cynically. He swung the door closed behind him and stepped forward. "I'll see you get the dope to keep you alive for the authorities, but for a price. First there are some questions I need answered."

"Whatever you say, just name them."

"Was the State in any way responsible for you and what you represent? Was that the truth when you implicated the government? Were they involved?"

"Yes, Viktor, of course they were," Joseph said, lying. "It was their project from the start."

Joseph had misjudged Viktor's naïveté. The big coach frowned and batted him hard in the mouth. His head rang and his vision fogged out. It cleared again as he steadied himself on the desk. "You lie. Tell me the truth or I'll twist the truth out of your lying throat," Viktor demanded.

"Okay, Viktor, okay, I lied. Shit, man, where is your compassion?" Joseph spread his arms to either side of the desk for balance. "I'll tell you what you want, but please, just find me something for the pain."

"Start talking." Viktor regarded Joseph scornfully. "Or you'll die where you're sitting."

"You knew I was lying, Viktor. The State had no affiliation with us or the Crimea. It was backed by a team of industrialists. They acted alone."

"Russian ones?" Viktor cut in.

"Yes, they were Russian." Joseph wiped the spittle

from his mouth with the back of his hand. His eyes were rolling back into his head. They focused. "Please, the medicine."

Viktor shrugged and casually began sorting through the open medicine chest. Joseph immediately crouched forward. His hands were pressed against the pockets of his coat, his fingers discerning the piece of steel. "Will this do?" Viktor asked gruffly. A packet of tranquilizers dangled from his huge hand.

"There must be something stronger than that. Please. I need a syringe."

"Keep talking," Viktor snapped.

"That's it. It was just a group of hungry businessmen looking to make a deal. They want to cash in on Chekow."

Viktor resumed his search of the medicine chest. "What was your connection?"

Joseph answered through a mist of pain. "What . . . ? Oh, my connection was to be the front man. I took the risks and got paid for it."

"Are we to suspect someone else once you've been eliminated?"

"I can't make any promises. I would think not. It's all falling apart," Joseph said truthfully.

"I see," Viktor said.

But he didn't. The automatic was leveled at his skull. It went off with a bang, and a mark appeared above the big man's ear below the hairline. Viktor sat down awkwardly — upending the medicine chest — looking confused, and died.

When the match had ended and the trainer returned with his indispensable crew to the office, he found them. The big man was comfortably seated against the wall. His face was pleasant and for some time they thought he might only be asleep. The thin fellow in the official's uniform was perched on his side in a fetal position. His blue face was horribly disfigured. It accurately depicted the crippling glove of pain that had finally killed him. His mouth was open and the thin teeth were caked with blood. Dark vacant eyes stared earthward as though delineating the direction his soul would take. A gun was on the floor next to an unopened syringe.

A pinstriped courier arrived at Chekow's hotel the following day to deliver the letter. Chekow took it and thanked him and retreated to the quiet of his bedroom. He tossed it among the pile of condolence telegrams and messages that had found him so soon after the incident. He awoke from his nap having dreamed about the same letter. Something about it stayed with him. His heart skipped as he regarded the ornate stamp in the sealing wax. He recognized it: Viktor's seal. Between the tears he read the letter and withdrew the twin plastic bankbooks of the Bank of Zurich. By all accounts he was now a rich man and need not go without ever again. He reread the final sentences of the letter four times:

As someone said, and don't expect me to know who, things are never so bad that they might not be worse. Stay fit, stay proud, but most of all stay as noble and caring and concerned as you always have been. For then you will never lose.

Salut,
Viktor

He fell asleep clutching the letter with his memories and his tears.

They met again at a ceremonial service at a little church on Zuma Beach in Malibu near where Pam had lived — the two rivals who had provoked the world into a plateau of anticipation such as they had rarely seen before or would rarely see again. James was there, with Olivia and a few others, looking painfully out of place in a suit. His nose was held in place by a band aid that testified to the left hook of a photographer who hit back. James was still James. The two-time Wimbledon champion — whose oyster was the world and whose penchant for folly threatened to evict him from the world that revered him — would never change.

Chekow stood in the back row, though he was the first to arrive. A priest emerged and confronted the capacity house and said the customary things that should have been said before the fact. When it was over, they filed out to the funereal cadence observed in churches, whatever the occasion.

Chekow was starting back to his car when a jabbering crowd strode by in front of him. He recognized them. He watched them pensively and was about to continue when a hand took his elbow. He was surprised to see James. Sunglasses had been put on over the bandage to shield his eyes from an adoring public. As it happened, no public was there today.

"Hello, James."

"The big cunt in the sky has got both of them now," he said in a whisper.

"Yes, James."

An economic smile danced upon James's lips. "Good luck to him." James squeezed the elbow fondly and made off after his friends and Olivia.

Chekow eased his lanky body into the Porsche and drove for his apartment in Santa Monica. He thought of how things used to be and cried all the way.

FREE!!
BOOKS BY MAIL
CATALOGUE

BOOKS BY MAIL will share with you our current bestselling books as well as hard to find specialty titles in areas that will match your interests. You will be updated on what's new in books at no cost to you. Just fill in the coupon below and discover the convenience of having books delivered to your home.

PLEASE ADD $1.00 TO COVER THE COST OF POSTAGE & HANDLING.

- -

BOOKS BY MAIL

320 Steelcase Road E.,
Markham, Ontario L3R 2M1

210 5th Ave., 7th Floor
New York, N.Y., 10010

Please send Books By Mail catalogue to:

Name _____

(please print)

Address _____

City _____

Prov./State _____ P.C./Zip _____

(BBM1)